PIONEER SPIRIT

Book Three: Wars and Rumors

Earle Jay Goodman

Also by Earle Jay Goodman

DISCREET – Book One: Childhood's End
DISCREET – Book Two: Growing Pains
DISCREET – Book Three: Round Up

PIONEER SPIRIT - Book One: Overland Trail
PIONEER SPIRIT - Book Two: Indian Affairs
PIONEER SPIRIT - Book Three: Wars and Rumors
PIONEER SPIRIT - Book Four: An Uneasy Peace
PIONEER SPIRIT - Book Five: White Indians
PIONEER SPIRIT - Book Six: Perilous Times
PIONEER SPIRIT – Book Seven: War Drums

To see photographs and maps of actual historical people and places during the time of Connal Lee's story, please visit:

https://goodmans-pioneer-spirit.blogspot.com

"...and the desert shall rejoice, and blossom as the rose."

Isaiah 35:1

PIONEER SPIRIT

Book Three: Wars and Rumors

Earle Jay Goodman

Dedication

Boca Raton, Florida
2018

I dedicate this book with love and gratitude to my wonderful parents and grandparents, on both sides of my family, who raised me on the stories of my great and great-great-grandparents, some of the earliest pioneers and settlers of America's Intermountain West in the mid-1800's;

and, to my friend and advisor since 1973, mentor, and de facto book editor, Edward P. Frey, Esq. – Thanks, Ed;

and, last but not least, to my first real love since 1979, then business partner, then domestic partner, and now married partner, James John Goodman. You are the light of my life. I love you, Jim.

---Earle Jay Goodman

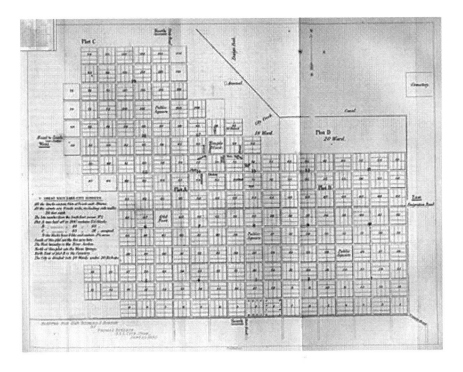

Map of Great Salt Lake City
in the time of Pioneer Spirit.
The original City stretched
from 8th North to 9th South,
and from 9th West to 8th East,
for a total of 135 Blocks.

Population in 1860 Census:
Great Salt Lake City – 8,236
Salt Lake County – 11,295
Territory of Utah – 40,273

Table of Contents

Chapter 1: Christmas

After hosting Connal Lee's family reunion to celebrate the arrival of Captain Reed and Lieutenant Anderson at Fort Hall, Connal Lee and his spouses packed up Short Rainbow's tipi. They rode south to Chief SoYo'Cant's winter camp, where they settled in for the duration of the winter.

After supper that evening, White Wolf pulled Bright Star in to sit beside him with his arm around her shoulder. She blushed a little but snuggled up to his side. Connal Lee let his instincts guide him. He crawled over on hands and knees and laid down beside Short Rainbow. He reached out and began caressing her pert breasts before leaning over and giving her a lingering kiss. Screaming Eagle quickly joined in. He reached over and pulled Connal Lee's doeskin shirt up and off his arms. Then he began undressing Short Rainbow while Connal Lee untied his leggings and removed his loincloth. Soon, clothes flew everywhere as they rushed to get naked, laughing at their enthusiasm and impatience.

No one had played with Bright Star during their short journey to Fort Hall and back. Gently, White Wolf helped her remove her leggings and beaded smock. He quickly slipped off his clothes and then sat against one of the beaded sling chair backs suspended from a tent pole. He reached out and pulled Bright Star to rest against him, snuggling her bare back against his naked torso. Her head fell back to rest on his shoulder. White Wolf wrapped his arms around her just below her tiny breasts, humming his pleasure and contentment to finally feel her smooth, lithe body in his arms. He leaned down and kissed her cheek, then her lips. Bright Star wrapped her arms over White Wolf's and snuggled back.

On the other side of the tipi, Connal Lee entered Short Rainbow. They began actively thrusting and withdrawing, sharing their bodies and joy with each other. Screaming Eagle scrounged around under the inner tipi lining until he found the small clay jar White Wolf had filled with a slick ointment. They used it when Screaming Eagle wanted to make love to White Wolf more intimately. With his left hand, he anointed his straining erection until slippery. With his right hand, he caressed and smoothed the oily mixture over and into Connal Lee's exposed rear end. With a fierce look of total concentration, Screaming Eagle positioned his hard cock. He timed it carefully until Connal Lee began withdrawing, then slowly shoved in. He heard Connal Lee moan loudly. Whenever Connal Lee pushed into Short Rainbow, he pulled away from his husband's swollen member, joyfully milking it. When he pulled out of Short Rainbow, he thrust himself back on Screaming Eagle's strong masculinity. Soon all three moaned in pleasure.

Bright Star had watched couples copulating before, but this felt different, much more intimate and arousing. Her eyes grew wider as she watched, wondering when she would finally experience love-making as a grown woman. She felt White Wolf's penis grow erect behind her back. She snuggled in closer with a little wriggle, increasing their contact. White Wolf didn't want to rush her or push her into anything she didn't find pleasurable, but he found it harder and harder not to be a more active participant. They avidly enjoyed the erotic show before them. Connal Lee began sweating from his athletic exertions. Short Rainbow smiled enchantingly. She reached up and grabbed Screaming Eagle's long braids, then pulled his face down beside Connal Lee's so she could take turns kissing her beloved husbands while they rutted over her.

Slowly, lightly, White Wolf allowed his right hand to drift down Bright Star's slender stomach until his fingers reached between her legs. He began softly tickling and teasing her, seeking out that special sensitive nub all women enjoyed. His left hand began stroking her nipples, massaging her breasts until she writhed in his arms from the loving attack on two fronts. Before she expected it, Bright Star shuddered through her first orgasm at a man's hands, moaning, "Oh, White Wolf. What you do to me! It makes me melt in happiness."

Connal Lee and his partners heard her. They glanced over, delighted at the blissful look on her face. They watched while White Wolf thrust his erection against Bright Star's lean back as he hugged her closer, tighter, and more sensuously. Finally, he reached his ecstatic conclusion. As he relaxed, he pulled Bright Star down to cuddle beside him on their sleeping furs. He spent several minutes kissing Bright Star's face, neck, eyes, and lips as they came down from their erotic highs.

The lusty trio pressed on to their athletic conclusions without an audience. The men collapsed over Short Rainbow until she gave them a hard shove. "I can't breathe, you great heavy beasts. Roll over!"

Screaming Eagle reluctantly withdrew from Connal Lee's slick warmth. He collapsed on his left side and stretched out beside Short Rainbow. Connal Lee had already gone soft, so he just rolled over to her right side. He leaned on his elbow so he could kiss Short Rainbow. His hand reached out and grabbed Screaming Eagle's bulging bicep and gave it a squeeze. "I love y'all, Short Rainbow. I love y'all Screaming Eagle."

They all cuddled up in a pile to sleep.

A week later, Connal Lee visited the fort leading two pack-horses loaded with trading furs. Even though below freezing, he found it a beautiful day for riding. The briskness made him feel vital and strong, breathing the crisp, clean air and soaking up the mild radiant heat from the sun rising on his right. Connal Lee invited Captain Reed to return with him to his adopted father's winter quarters. "I think it's time for you to meet the great Chief Arimo, John. You can stay with us in our family's snug tipi."

After Connal Lee introduced the captain to Chief SoYo'Cant that evening, they accepted the Chief's invitation to stay for supper in his tipi. Later that night, they returned to Short Rainbow's tipi. The captain spread his buffalo skin blankets alongside Connal Lee's distinctive red fox fur blanket. They all sat around the small hardwood fire that warmed the big tent, making small talk and enjoying the captain's company.

Later that night, Connal Lee pulled the captain into his happy family as they all made love together.

While they ate breakfast, Lieutenant Cooper approached the camp from the north, riding his stallion hard. Shoshone Warriors became alarmed and intercepted him before he reached their encampment. The Lieutenant reined in his steaming horse and raised his arm in the sign of peace and friend. "Peace."

The warriors returned the sign and greeted him, "Peace."

Thinking he now had permission to enter the encampment and impatient to deliver his report to Captain Reed, he kicked his stallion and started to ride around the guards. They stopped him, again, with raised hands. "No! Stop!"

The excited Lieutenant called out in a loud voice, thinking if he spoke loudly enough, it would force the men blocking his way to understand him. "I need to report to Captain Reed right away. Let me by. Where is Captain Reed?"

One of the warriors spoke enough English to catch his drift. He pointed his finger to the center of the camp. "Go Chief SoYo'Cant. Now. Go!"

The Lieutenant saw he would need permission from Chief Arimo before he could deliver his message, so he agreed. "Please lead the way. I go to Chief Arimo, now."

The English-speaking warrior turned his big palomino stallion around and trotted back to the large encampment. A few minutes later, they approached the chief's outdoor council chamber. The lieutenant leapt off his horse, faced the Chief, and gave him a crisp military salute. The chief rose to his feet and made the sign of peace. Lieutenant Cooper returned the peace sign. Chief SoYo'Cant pointed at him. "Who you?"

"I am First Lieutenant Brandon Cooper of the First Contingent of Mounted Riflemen, Company G, Sixth Infantry, presently stationed in Fort Hall under the orders of Captain Reed, sir."

He pulled a thin leather satchel off a long leather strap over his shoulder and held it towards the chief. "I come bearing emergency communiques from Major Sanderson, commander of Fort Laramie and of all the Overland Trail. May I please have your permission to deliver my messages, sir?"

"Welcome. I Chief Arimo. Go. Warrior Yo-ko-ap lead way." The chief pointed at the warrior who had led the Lieutenant into the camp. "Lead this young cavalry officer to Short Rainbow's tipi, Yo-ko-ap, right away. He has important business with Captain Reed."

The imperious warrior leapt onto his horse's back, then turned and beckoned to Lieutenant Cooper. "Come."

The Lieutenant nodded his thanks to the chief and rushed over to mount up and follow. Within moments they arrived at Short Rainbow's tipi, where they found everyone sitting around the cookfire finishing their breakfast. When the captain spotted his first lieutenant riding quickly towards them, he stood up in alarm. Yo-ko-ap called ahead, "Screaming Eagle! Chief SoYo'Cant ordered me to deliver this pale face to your friend Chief Fort Hall."

Screaming Eagle stood up as they approached the campfire. "Thank you, Yo-ko-ap."

Connal Lee stood up next to the captain and translated. The captain made the sign of peace to Yo-ko-ap with a polite nod. "Thank you."

Captain Reed watched his lieutenant dismount. White Wolf strode over to Lieutenant Cooper. "Here. I take horse."

The lieutenant nodded. "Thank you." Turning, he stood at attention before Captain Reed and saluted. He then jerked the leather satchel off his shoulder and held it out to the captain. "Captain Reed, sir. Late last night, a rush courier arrived from Fort Laramie. He handed me this dispatch containing a copy of an army intelligence report forwarded with orders from Major Sanderson."

"Thank you, Lieutenant. At ease. Please have some coffee while I read the dispatches."

The captain resumed his seat beside the fireplace. He unfastened the leather belts securing the thin message bag and removed several folded pieces of paper. He shook them out and began reading. It took him twenty minutes to study the long intelligence report and read the major's orders.

When he set the papers down on the satchel, Connal Lee leaned forward and stared at the captain, anxious to hear the news. The captain sat silently for several minutes, digesting everything he had read. Then he glanced around at Connal Lee and his family. "Would you please accompany me to visit Chief Arimo? I believe he should know about the events described in this report I just received from the Military Intelligence Division of Army Headquarters back in West Point."

Everyone stood up. Screaming Eagle led them directly to the Chief's outdoor council chamber. After they exchanged warm greetings, Connal Lee took charge. "Father SoYo'Cant, Captain Reed receive important message from United States of America government. He want you know what happen."

"Thank you, son. Please, everyone, take a seat while I send for Teniwaaten to translate for me."

Connal Lee waved his family to sit around the blazing fire. The captain understood and joined them. When Teniwaaten arrived, the Chief introduced him to Captain Reed. The captain stood up to shake hands. "Can you translate my message for Chief Arimo, please?"

"It's nice to make your acquaintance, Captain Reed. It would be my pleasure, sir."

"Would it be easier for me to read it out loud and then you translate, or would it be easier for you to read and translate it directly for yourself?"

"If the hand of the writer of the message is clear to my eyes, it will be faster if I read and translate. Please sit next to me so you can clarify it for me if I can't make out a word."

"Very well. Here is the report. Please let me know when I can be of help."

Teniwaaten sat down beside his chief and patted the ground on his other side. The captain sat down with his legs crossed, Indian style. "Teniwaaten, before you start, please let the Chief know that this is a report of the political situation back in the Federal Capital. It also contains a copy of the orders sent to Colonel Johnston's army. All the information refers to the Utah problem and how the president and congress are handling the crisis."

Teniwaaten began translating. An hour later, he finished the intelligence report. Everyone around the council fire waited respectfully for their revered chieftain to respond. The chief thought about what he had learned and finally turned to Teniwaaten. "Please ask Captain Reed for his evaluation of these developments. What does he think it means for us and our Mormon allies?"

Since the conversation began in Shoshone, Captain Reed had been thinking of nothing else. He looked Chief SoYo'Cant in the eye. "Well, sir. Most of the news is favorable, although it still leaves Salt Lake Valley highly vulnerable to invasion. I didn't like hearing about orders to bring the invading army back north along the Oregon Trail and then south through our lands here rather than going directly southwest on the Mormon Trail, which was their original path. Of course, it will delay them as they will have to travel north to the trail, then west, then back south, again, from Fort Hall. However, the approaching winter season might help us. It's so late in the year, the mountain passages are bound to be unpassable due to snow and below-freezing temperatures."

The Chief nodded his agreement. "I liked hearing about the Mormon's allies in the senate and how unpopular this war has become with Congress. I am glad Congress keeps delaying funding the president's requests for more money to pursue this unpopular war. It is good that the newspapers report how badly things are going with this military mission. The one item of greatest concern to me is the report of sending reinforcements to Colonel Johnston that would bring his force up to five-thousand armed men."

After listening to the translation, Captain Reed nodded his agreement. "Yes, sir. That would place Johnston in command of one-third of the entire armed forces of the United States, five full battalions. It will take some time for the men to meet up with Colonel Johnston, especially this time of year. Perhaps of more immediate concern was Johnston's promotion to Brevet Brigadier General. That will give him a lot of influence at central command and make him one of America's most powerful field officers. Only a handful of Major Generals now outrank him."

The chief scowled. "Yes. Very bad news about five battalions of men directed towards the Mormons and the rest of us who also live in these territories. Do you know this Albert Sidney Johnston, Captain Reed?"

"No, sir. I have never met him. However, I know him by reputation. I understand he is from Kentucky. He is a graduate of West Point. He owns an enormous plantation on the southeast coast of Texas, south of Houston. He has so many slaves he runs a school for their children on his plantation. He's a very progressive thinker and strategist. He has fought Cherokees and Mexicans in the Texian

17

Army. After he helped liberate Texas from Mexico, he served as Secretary of War for the Republic of Texas for several years. Then he fought in the Mexican-American war. He is very experienced in leading men and very aggressive in pursuing his military objectives. He's strictly a by-the-book man in following his orders."

Teniwaaten hesitated, then glanced over at the captain. "Captain Reed, what does 'by-the-book' mean?"

"Oh. It means adhering strictly to the exact wording of an order no matter what extenuating circumstances might arise."

"Ah, yes. I understand."

After Teniwaaten translated, the Chief looked Captain Reed in the eye. "I think Chief Brigham Young should know of these political maneuverings in the Federal Capital and of the planned increase in troops heading our way. What do you think, captain?"

"I concur, sir. I was thinking much the same thing. I can dispatch riders to deliver the intelligence to Governor Young immediately."

The chief shook his head no. "Federal soldiers riding to Great Salt Lake City are bound to be delayed if not stopped outright. What if we send Screaming Eagle's family with Connal Lee to translate. The Mormons still allow us, their allies, into their forts."

Captain Reed thought about it, then nodded his agreement. "That might be for the best. If they each took three horses so they could change mounts as needed, they could cover a lot of ground in a hurry. They wouldn't need to take much in the way of provisions. If they are willing to accept this mission, I believe it would be the best course of action."

The suggestion excited Connal Lee. His family listened most attentively as Teniwaaten translated for their chief. Chief SoYo'Cant leaned forward and peered into the faces of his nieces and nephews. "Will you accept my orders to ride south at all possible speed to deliver this information to Chief Brigham Young?"

They all nodded their heads eagerly. "Yes, Chief SoYo'Cant."

Connal Lee leapt to his feet. "Yes, Father SoYo'Cant. If White Wolf and I rode out immediately, we could return by nightfall with our family's army surplus tent for shelter during the night. Screaming Eagle, Short Rainbow, and Bright Star could organize the horses and supplies while we fetched the tent. We could leave at first light tomorrow morning."

The chief looked back at Captain Reed. They both nodded their heads, approving Connal Lee's plan. The captain stood up. "I will ride back to Fort Hall with you, Connal Lee. While you ride on to Zeff's homestead to pick up your tent, I will copy the report for my records so I can study it further. You can pick up the original on your way back here and take it along to Governor Young."

Everyone stood up. The Chief shook hands with Captain Reed. "Good. Thank you."

The captain pointed to Connal Lee and White Wolf. "Let's mount up and be on our way."

Everyone scattered to their duties. As the captain walked beside Connal Lee, he asked if he could borrow another horse so he could change horses midway. Connal Lee helped him cut out one of his large Crow victory horses, about the same size as Paragon, from the clan's general herd. As they saddled up, the captain recommended they ride at a trot the entire way.

Connal Lee and his family arose before dawn. They ate a hot breakfast, saddled their horses, and loaded their provisions. At six-thirty, they took off riding south, alternating every half hour between a trot and a cantor. They stopped for a short rest every four hours and ate a cold meal standing up. The temperatures never rose above fifty degrees but fortunately stayed above freezing that night. They moved their saddles and supplies to fresh horses and rode for another four hours. The horses made too much noise for conversation. By the end of the third four-hour segment of their journey, the horses and humans began lagging. They slept like logs after eating a satisfying supper of stew made from dried meats, vegetables, and herbs.

On Friday morning, the twenty-fifth of December, Short Rainbow and Bright Star prepared a hearty, hot breakfast before sunrise. The men saddled the horses and loaded up the tent and travel provisions. By dawn, they continued their exhausting, mile-eating pace. They rode up to the west gate of Great Salt Lake City around nine-thirty that morning. A small group of volunteer civilian guards challenged them. Connal Lee pulled ahead to greet them. "Peace. I am Connal Lee Swinton, the adopted son of Chief Arimo. Chief Arimo and Captain Reed, the commander of Fort Hall, ordered us to deliver important military intelligence to Governor Young at the best possible speed. Please let us through to the Beehive House."

The guards recognized the Shoshone family as allies and waved them through with calls of merry Christmas. Connal Lee and his family followed Screaming Eagle with all their horses directly to Beehive House. After they tied up their fifteen saddle horses and six packhorses, Connal Lee took charge. He marched up and knocked briskly on the door in the massive wall, decorated with a four-foot-wide pine wreath. An oversized bow of cotton cloth dyed bright red tied the branches into a circle. The same middle-aged women who had greeted them on their last visit recognized them. Clutching a heavy shawl around her shoulders, she pushed open the heavy gate. "Good morning, and Merry Christmas to you all. Please come in where it's warm." She led the way up the porch. "By the way, we didn't introduce ourselves when you were here last month. I'm Mary Ann Angell Young, Brigham's wife. I'm called either Mother Young or Sister Young. And you are?"

After they walked through the mansion's front door, Connal Lee introduced everyone, ending with himself. "We are a delegation sent by Captain Reed of Fort Hall and Chief Arimo of the Shoshone Nation with important intelligence for Governor Young."

"Please wait here a moment while I inform him of your arrival. He returned a few minutes ago from his church office next door and immediately sat down to consult with officers of the Nauvoo Legion." She pointed to a large oak hall tree with a narrow mirror in its middle panel. "You may leave your coats, capes, and weapons here in the entrance, then wait in the parlor, please. I will be right back."

"Thanks, Sister Young."

Connal Lee gazed around at the Christmas decorations with garlands of pine branches over the doors and windows, even over the hall tree. A fragrant pine tree stood in front of the parlor's window overlooking the street, decorated with chains of popped corn and dried red and purple berries. Garlands of dried flowers added a touch of color. Each window held a candle sitting on the sill in a simple brass candlestick.

Within minutes, Connal Lee watched a parade of six uniformed officers march out of Brigham Young's office. Mrs. Young ushered in the Shoshone delegation. They shook hands with Governor Young, introduced Bright Star, and exchanged Christmas wishes. Brigham Young invited them to take the recently vacated chairs already placed in a half-circle before his desk. "Now, what's this about bringing me important military intelligence?"

Connal Lee leaned forward and recapped the events of the past two and a half days, then stood up. He lifted the army dispatch bag off his shoulder and placed it on the desk. They watched as the Governor opened it and withdrew the packet of papers. He looked up at Connal Lee and then gazed around at his Shoshone family. "Thank you for bringing this to me so swiftly. Is there anything I can get you to eat or drink? This will take me a few minutes to read."

"No thanks, Governor. We ate breakfast this morning. We are here to await y'all's orders, suh."

Brigham Young nodded, put on his reading glasses, and focused on the report. When he finished, the Governor leaned back in his big leather desk chair. "I want to share this information with some of my key officers, Master Connal Lee." He looked at the small wall clock opposite his desk, amazed it wasn't even ten o'clock. "Please let me invite you and your delegation to return in two hours to join me for a Christmas luncheon at midday. We can discuss our plans, and I will prepare missives for you to return to our good ally, Chief Arimo, and to Captain Reed. If you will excuse me, I have a lot to do."

Connal Lee led his family out to the street. They decided to take advantage of the time to erect their tent. They set up camp beside the Jordan River, where the Chief had made camp on their last visit. They expected to at least be there overnight.

After a delicious meal of roasted goose served with roasted vegetables, the portly governor sat back in his chair at the head of the table. "Please give me a half-hour or so. I would like to write letters to Chief Arimo and Captain Reed for you to take back with you. You may rest here or walk outside as you please."

When Brigham Young stood up, they all did. Connal Lee looked at his family. White Wolf indicated for them to remain in the warm dining room. Connal Lee shook hands with the Governor. "We can be found here whenever y'all are ready for us, suh. Thanks very much for the kind hospitality and the delicious meal, Your Honor. Merry Christmas, suh."

The Governor nodded his agreement, then strode briskly out the door. After Connal Lee and his family resumed their chairs, two of Brigham Young's daughters brought them plates of gingerbread and sugar cookies with red and green icing. A young servant girl from the kitchen carried in a fresh pot of hot chocolate and a bowl of peppermint candies. They all adored the sweets. Brigham Young returned at two-thirty and handed Connal Lee the messenger packet. "Thank you for your services to my people. Please extend our thanks to the chief and the captain for keeping us abreast of important developments. I already expressed my gratitude in the letters in this pouch, but please reinforce our appreciation for their thoughtfulness and your kind services. Goodbye for now. Safe trails and a very merry Christmas to you all."

They shook hands and departed for their camp. An hour later, they had packed up and took off, heading north. They rode at a steady trot covering around eight miles an hour all the way back, changing horses when they sensed them tiring. They arrived at Short Rainbow's tipi late the afternoon of their second day. White Wolf suggested Screaming Eagle find them some fresh meat for supper. Their marathon trip left them all tired and hungry for a hot meal. The young family tended their weary horses. As soon as they finished, White Wolf pointed to the center of the encampment. "I think Connal Lee and I should go deliver Governor Young's letter to Uncle SoYo'Cant right away. Tomorrow morning, Connal Lee and I will ride to Fort Hall and deliver the governor's letter to Captain Reed."

That evening, Chief SoYo'Cant expressed his thanks for a speedy and successful mission.

Connal Lee and White Wolf joined Captain Reed for his midday meal at Fort Hall the following day. The captain also thanked them, congratulating them on the successful conclusion of their first diplomatic mission. "Well done, gentlemen. Well done, indeed."

Chapter 2: Fort Lemhi

Bitter cold weather sat hard over the territory that winter. The temperature never rose above freezing, day or night. Connal Lee and his family worked hard at hunting and tanning leather despite the icy season. They worked just as hard and enthusiastically at teaching Bright Star all the different ways to make love and enjoy sharing each other's healthy bodies. Fulfilling his daydream, White Wolf had the honor of taking Bright Star's virginity.

Shortly after the first of the new year of 1858, Short Rainbow and her husbands invited Bright Star to join their tipi. Bright Star had been hoping for this since she first traveled to Fort Hall with the young family to greet Connal Lee's cavalry brothers. Even though Bright Star didn't enjoy hunting and fighting like her four spouses, she contributed to the family in many other ways. She took tender loving care of her three husbands, which brought a lot of joy to their tipi and blankets. She found marriage to four warriors exciting enough. She felt no need to go hunting or looking for a fight. She found contentment in taking care of her spouses and the chores of tending the tipi and preparing food.

The first week of February came and went. Zeff and Sister Woman had always told Connal Lee he had been born the first week of February. But since they didn't keep track of the calendar back in the Ozarks, no one knew the exact day of his birth. He turned thirteen and became a teenager without any fanfare or celebration. One night Connal Lee surprised his spouses with a special treat when he used his Bowie knife to open a can of peaches after supper. Everyone enjoyed the sweet delicacy.

Connal Lee and Arimo attended Chief SoYo'Cant's council meetings in his tent most afternoons.

Towards the end of the month, a young Bannock warrior rode into camp and asked to speak to Chief SoYo'Cant. The guards escorted him to the chief's tipi. He introduced himself as Big Horn, the youngest son of the aging Chief Buffalo Horn of the Bannock tribe. He briefed the chief on trouble brewing north of his winter camp, just north of Fort Lemhi. He told of several groups of angry warriors from various tribes working themselves up with war dances every night.

"It all started when a couple of white trappers in the area kidnapped two young Bannock girls to use for their lustful purposes," Big Horn told Chief SoYo'Cant with a big frown. "A group of Shoshone warriors found the dead girls' corpses about a week later, badly abused and beaten to death. This inflamed the Bannock warriors with fierce indignation. They gathered together with bands of renegades roving the area around the great river where we fish for salmon in the spring. They held councils of war. When their large angry pack learned about General Johnston's army heading towards their sacred hunting grounds, they decided they could no longer share their ancestral lands with the white man. They danced the war dance every night around huge bonfires that lit up the sky. They decided to attack Fort Lemhi and drive the evil white man colony out of their land. When I heard their plans, I thought my Shoshone brothers should know what was happening up to the north in your ancestral lands. We all know how you welcomed the Mormons and even became a member of their religion."

The Chief sat silently for several minutes, scowling. "Thank you, Big Horn, for your warning. This is a serious development and affects us all. Please join my council this evening while we discuss what this means and what we should do."

Arimo leaned forward to catch Chief SoYo'Cant's attention. "Father, around three years ago, when I met my lovely Ute wife, Kimana, down south of Bad Waters Lake at their tribal sun dance, we fell in love. Her family didn't want her to marry outside their tribe, so I stole her away. We rode north to return to your camp. Her family sent three warriors to stop us. By the time we reached Fort Call, my horse was verging on collapse from exhaustion. We had been riding hard all night with only my one horse. We rode up to a small farmstead along the Bear River, where I met a young white settler named Andrew Hayes. He took compassion on us and agreed to exchange one of his rested horses for my foundering horse. He saved my life that day."

Chief SoYo'Cant nodded. "I remember, son. I met him and his Mormon wife a little later when I went to thank them."

"Well, Andrew saved my life. I vowed to myself I would save his life if the opportunity should arise. I'm concerned for his safety. His life might be in danger up at Fort Lemhi. With your permission, I will ride north and do what I can to protect my white friend."

"It's a three-day journey, Arimo. When will you leave."

"I think it best if I leave first thing tomorrow morning. I'm very uneasy with this turn of events. I don't want to see any harm come to my friend. Please excuse me now while I make my preparations."

"Safe journey, son."

That night Connal Lee lay awake after he and his spouses shared an exuberant lovemaking session, pondering what he had heard from Big Horn about possible warfare up at Fort Lemhi. When he woke up, he told his family he felt he should ride to Fort Hall and let Captain Reed know about a battle brewing in his territory. White Wolf considered it, then agreed. "I will accompany you, Connal Lee, but I won't stay. I will leave you in the protection of your captain. Let's put together some travel provisions and head out right away. I want to make it back before nightfall."

They rode their horses at a brisk pace all the way to the fort. Connal Lee pulled his usual big packhorse behind him, loaded with sleeping furs, travel provisions, and tanned skins to trade with Mr. Mackey.

As they drew closer to the Fort, they could see and hear the men of the garrison at work building new barracks, corrals, and horse barns north of the old fort. Connal Lee spotted one man standing down by the riverbank looking through some sort of telescope held on top of a wooden tripod. Later he learned about the surveyor's transit and compass. When the boys reached the big wooden doors of the fort, Connal Lee clasped hands with White Wolf. "Thank you, White Wolf. I appreciate the company. I will see y'all in a few days, depending on what Captain Reed says. Be safe. I love y'all."

Connal Lee tied up his pretty brown mare and big packhorse to the hitching post in front of the captain's log cabin office and knocked on the door. A moment later, he heard, "Come."

He walked in and found Captain Reed sitting behind a simple rough, unvarnished desk, taking care of paperwork. "Connal Lee! This is a surprise. What brings you here to see me this morning?"

26

"Well, suh, last night Ah attended Chief Arimo's council in his tent. In came this young Bannock warrior with the name of Big Horn. He informed Chief Arimo about a lot of unrest up north of Fort Lemhi, along the river where they fish for salmon in the spring." Connal Lee recounted the entire story. "Ah felt y'all should know, if ya didn't already, that some Bannocks have joined with other renegade packs and are preparing for war. They want to drive the white men out of Fort Lemhi and out of their lands."

"Well. This is a fine turn of events. Did Big Horn say how large the war party was?"

"He said around three hundred warriors. Most are there without their families, so there's no controlling them. Big Horn said they were dancing war dances every night, getting themselves all worked up for a fight."

"Hm. Well. Thank you for letting me know. Let me think a minute. I only have around a hundred armed men, which may not be enough to win a direct conflict even with our superior weaponry." The captain leaned back in his chair. Connal Lee jumped when the captain suddenly shouted, "Ned! Two cups of coffee, if you please."

The teenager shouted down from the second floor. "Here Ah comes, suh."

A minute later, Connal Lee heard footsteps running down the stairs. The door opened, and Ned walked in carrying two tin mugs of steaming hot coffee. Connal Lee and Ned nodded at each other. Ned handed a mug of coffee to the captain, then gave the other to Connal Lee.

"Thank you, Ned. That will be all."

"Yessuh."

"So, tell me, Connal Lee. Have you ever visited Fort Lemhi?"

"No, Ah haven't. Chief SoYo'Cant and his son, Arimo, said it's easy to find. Arimo said it's a three-day trip riding the horses hard. The chief said it's located around a hundred ninety miles northwest of here, nearly to the Salmon River."

Captain Reed walked over to a large printed map tacked on the log wall of his office. "Would you like to join me for a hard trip north, Connal Lee? I think I would like to go check things out for myself. I wouldn't want to commit my men to any action which would leave the trail unprotected. My orders are to protect travelers on the Overland Trail first and foremost. However, any attack against whites is a matter to be taken seriously."

Connal Lee nodded his head, silently agreeing to accompany the captain. Captain Reed walked out of his office. He opened the door to the two-story log cabin barracks next door and leaned in. "Lieutenant Cooper. A moment, if you please."

He returned with the lieutenant who used to command the fort. "Lieutenant Cooper, I have just received disturbing intelligence of a possible renegade Indian attack on Fort Lemhi, up north of here. I'm going to go do some reconnoitering of my own. I will be gone six or seven days surveying the lay of the land. You will be in charge while I am gone. Connal Lee and I leave in an hour."

"Sir, yes, sir!"

The captain shouted again for Ned. Ned scurried down the stairs and entered the office. "Yessuh?"

"Ned, prepare my saddlebags with a change of clothing. Saddle up Paragon and two packhorses. I'm going to need enough provisions for two men. We'll be camping in the wilderness for a week. Don't forget my new buffalo hide sleeping furs, either, or I will probably freeze to death at night." He looked at Connal Lee and winked. Connal Lee chuckled. "I'll also need a two-man pup tent. Come, Connal Lee, let's find a hot meal and hit the trail."

Connal Lee scooted ahead so he could sell his hides and free up his packhorse. While he traded his furs, Mr. Mackey pointed over at two shelves hung on the wall. "Connal Lee, I'm surprised you haven't been in to borrow a book now that we have a little lending library here in the post."

Connal Lee spun around, spotted the books, and jogged over to inspect them. "Wow, Mister Mackey. Look at all the books! And here Ah am, all in a rush with no time to look at them. Oh, well. As soon as Ah return from Fort Lemhi, Ah'll be back. Y'all can count on it!"

Mister Mackey chuckled. "I'm somehow not surprised."

After Connal Lee pocketed some silver coins, he gazed longingly at the bookshelves. With an impatient shake of his head, he rushed out to eat with the captain in the barrack's crowded little mess.

An hour later, they exited Fort Hall and took off traveling north past the bustling construction site. They pushed their horses to maintain a steady trot. They stopped to say hello to Zeff and Sister Woman within the hour. They sat on their horses talking. Connal Lee told them of the war brewing a couple of days north of them. "Ah am riding to Fort Lemhi with the captain on a scouting mission and will be back as soon as we can."

They said goodbye and nudged their horses back into a businesslike trot, waving as they rode up out of the shallow riverbed canyon.

As the sun lowered over the rolling hills to the west, Connal Lee spotted a bevy of grouse scrounging for food around a tree where the snow had blown away, leaving the ground exposed. He held up his hand for the captain to stop. He pulled out his rifle, loaded buckshot, and shot three grouse for their supper. The captain pointed off to a stand of small leafless trees. "Let's see if there might not be water over there, Connal Lee. We may as well pitch camp while we still have light to see by."

Connal Lee and the captain rode up to the trees, where they found a small meandering creek running with fresh water. They unsaddled their horses and warmed them down. The captain rubbed wool rags over Paragon's strong muscles. Connal Lee used soft chamois skins on his dark brown mare. They put their saddle blankets back on the horses so they wouldn't take a chill. After unloading the packhorses, Connal Lee gathered deadfall to build a fire. The captain raised his little two-man army tent, in which he spread their sleeping furs. He paused to admire Connal Lee's luxurious red fox fur blanket, running his hands over the soft multi-hued skins sewn together in stripes. Connal Lee stacked the wood for a fire. The captain lit the fire with his small portable flint and tinder box.

An hour later, after supper, they relaxed and chatted amiably until the hour grew late. A bright half-moon rose in the sky, lighting the snow-covered landscape around them. They caught each other yawning and chuckled. "Guess it's time to go to bed. What do y'all think, Captain Reed?"

"Yes. Let's go."

Before he entered the tent, Connal Lee quickly stripped off his clothes, then dove into the furs. The captain looked askance. "You aren't going to wear any bedclothes, Connal Lee?"

"No, suh. My Shoshone family taught me that shared body warmth under the furs is the best way to stay warm at night. Join me. Y'all will see."

The captain hesitated to follow suit. He shrugged, then gave in to Connal Lee's suggestion. He had been sleeping cold every night since he led his men out of Fort Laramie some weeks past. He yearned to be warm again at night while he slept. Naked, he crawled in between the sleeping furs. Connal Lee rolled over and pulled him into a gentle embrace. "Well, Connal Lee. This is kind of intimate, isn't it?"

"Yes, but at least we will be warm."

They both relaxed as they warmed up. "You know, Connal Lee, if we're going to be so familiar, I think you should start calling me by my name. Except in front of my men at the Fort, of course. Would you please be my friend and call me John?"

Connal Lee pulled the captain in closer. "Ah would be honored to be your friend and call you John. Thanks so much, suh."

At daybreak, they made a pot of coffee and ate stale rolls from the mess hall. Connal Lee wondered if Mother Baines had baked them. They rode hard again all that day. Their route didn't bring them close to any water their second night out, nor did they come across any game for their supper. After they set up their little camp, the captain pulled out a folded map of the region and made a note about the lack of water the second night out from Fort Hall. Connal Lee leaned over to study the page filled with lines, names, and hand-written comments. "What are y'all doing, Captain?"

"When I travel, I always update my maps with whatever land-marks, observations, or helpful notes will make it easier for me or my men to travel this way again. Have you never seen a map be-fore?"

"Just the one on the wall of your office in the fort. Ah couldn't make heads nor tails of it. What do y'all need maps for, anyway?"

"Well, consider for a moment. Suppose you lead your men on horseback into territory you have never traveled before. You have four heavy supply wagons and two heavy cannons with you. Wouldn't it be more efficient for you to know in advance where to find the best trails, where to find fords or bridges to cross the streams and rivers? If you didn't know, you would waste time re-exploring the land, turning around to back track, or making diversions to find other crossings or sources of water. It's much safer and more efficient to obtain maps of the region you will travel through. Now, do you understand?"

"But how do maps tell you all that, Captain?"

"Hm, I see I will have to give you a crash course in map making and map reading. The army has an entire four-month course in maps as part of their officer training program. Now look here in the lower right corner. We call this fancy design of a starburst within a circle a compass rose. It always indicates North on a map so you can align your compass with it and find your way. Do you know how to use a compass?"

"Yes, suh. But Ah don't own one. Ah used my Paw's back in the Ozarks, and Ah borrowed Captain Hanover's when Ah went out hunting away from the handcart company. But, Ah lost it when Ah was wounded by those Crow warriors. Please show me how it works with a map."

The captain pulled out his compass and placed it beside the map's compass rose. He turned the map until its alignment matched the north-seeking needle of his travel compass. "You see, Connal Lee, with the map facing in the correct direction, you can see where, if you followed the path directly west of here, you would run into a small mountain range. See these lines and symbols here? They indicate mountains that could pose barriers to our travel if we were heading west. And look here. These squiggly lines show the path of a river or creek due north of us. We will have to cross it before continuing to Fort Lemhi."

Connal Lee listened attentively for nearly an hour as full dark descended. With insufficient light to read by, the captain neatly folded up his map and tucked it away. "Let's stop and have something to eat. Aren't you hungry?"

31

"Why, now that you mention it, Ah'm starving!"

After they brewed a pot of coffee, Connal Lee introduced the captain to pemmican. Connal Lee had developed a taste for it, but the captain found it strange. They chewed on spicy venison jerky, which took work to soften up. They ate square hardtack crackers made of plain flour and water from the captain's travel supplies. Connal Lee found them bland and unsatisfying. They finished their cold supper with a tin mug of black coffee before retiring to their blankets in the little tent.

Connal Lee felt a bit frisky that evening. He missed his brother husbands and wives and their frolicking under the blankets. When the captain pulled Connal Lee into his arms for warmth, Connal Lee couldn't help himself. He attained an erection that demanded release. He turned over, pulled the captain to lay on top of him, then rhythmically rubbed his erection along the captain's hairy belly. It didn't take long before the captain responded by growing erect as well. He thrust back with increasing enthusiasm. "What are we doing, Connal Lee?"

"What do y'all think, John? Ah've learned a lot about lovemaking with my brother husbands and my lovely wives. Ah miss them so much tonight. Please let me show y'all how nice it can be, even though we are both men."

"I know what men can do together, Connal Lee. I've been on patrol with all-male troops many times over the years. I prefer women, but sometimes a man will do after lights out."

Connal Lee didn't want to talk anymore. He pulled the captain's face down to his and gave him a lingering, open-mouthed kiss. They snuggled up, arms around each other, kissing and licking each other's lips and faces, squirming in pleasure for a good half hour. Connal Lee surprised the captain when he turned around and burrowed under the buffalo hide until his lips found the captain's leaking manhood. He took his time and lavished his passionate affection on the captain's large erection until saliva dripped down and soaked his balls. The captain took hold of Connal Lee's erection and slowly pulled his foreskin up and down. Half an hour later, they both thrilled to an ecstatic release. When Connal Lee turned around to lay beside the captain, he leaned over and gave his new lover a kiss.

The captain hadn't expected to taste his own seed but avidly returned the kiss anyway.

The next day they crossed the shallow meandering Lemhi River several times. Each time, Captain Reed and Connal Lee checked the map for accuracy. The third time they stopped, Connal Lee looked closer at the map. "Oh! Ah see now. If Ah were an eagle flying up high looking down at the land, Ah would see the lay of the land like looking at a map."

"Well, that's an interesting way to put it. But you are correct, Connal Lee. Let's take a bite to eat, then push on."

Late in the afternoon, they rode past neat log corrals and what appeared to be fields and gardens covered by a foot of snow. They approached the open gates of a modest-sized fieldstone and adobe fort and passed two newly dug graves piled high with frozen clods of dirt. The graves would remain like that until the spring thaw melted the frozen soil and filled in the holes. As they entered the small fort, Captain Reed became alarmed at the silence surrounding them.

They rode into an empty village square. A door opened in a log cabin to their right. A mature woman stepped out, clutching a shawl over her shoulders. The captain rode over to her. "Good afternoon, ma'am. I am Captain John Reed of Company G, Sixth Infantry, Commander of Fort Hall, at your service. What is going on here? Where are all the people? Where are your horses and cattle?"

"It's nice to meet you, Captain. I'm Sister Phyllis Gladstone. Please come in out of the cold."

The captain and Connal Lee dismounted and walked into a small log cabin crowded with women and children huddling along the four walls. "Well, Missus Gladstone, now can you please tell me where the men are?"

"Yes, Captain. Early this morning, a young Injun brave by the name of Arimo, the son of the Shoshone Chief Arimo, rode into the fort asking about his friend, our Brother Andrew Hayes. The Elders told him about the attack on the fort yesterday morning when a pack of renegade Injuns made off with all our livestock. The Elders told him Andrew had been away from the Fort guarding our cattle the night before they attacked. They told him Andrew was missing and

esumed dead since they hadn't found his body. Arimo took off all
in a panic and rode out in search of his friend. Apparently, he found
Elder Hayes shivering on the ground a couple miles north of here,
wounded with a shot to his shoulder and with bloody head wounds.
Young Arimo reported that Andrew had been struck on the head,
knocked unconscious, and left for dead. Arimo said he covered
Brother Andrew with some furs, then rushed back to us here in the
fort. Arimo told the Elders he had found Andrew Hayes alive but
wounded and unconscious.

"Bishop Chandler asked how he could possibly be sure? How
would he even know what Elder Hayes looked like? All in a rush,
in broken English, Arimo told how Andrew Hayes had saved his life
a few years back by exchanging a fresh horse for Arimo's exhausted
one. He was trying to escape some Ute warriors chasing him and
his new wife. Arimo convinced the Elders he really did know
Brother Andrew by sight. Arimo left here, leading the Elders out to
where he found Andrew. They all rushed off to rescue him. Since
all but three of our horses were stolen during the attack and raid, the
Elders had to walk out to rescue him. They should be returning
shortly."

The captain turned to Connal Lee. "Well, shall we ride out and
meet Arimo and his rescue party?"

Connal Lee nodded. Without another word, they walked outside, leapt on their horses, and spurred them out the fort's gate.
About a mile away, they encountered a group of men carrying a
stretcher. The missionaries had jury-rigged it using two young pine
tree trunks bound together with the men's shirts. The stretcher carried a bandaged man swaddled in buffalo fur blankets. Eight men
carried the improvised litter, four to a side. The other men surrounded them on guard duty. Arimo had taken position at the front
of the stretcher by Andrew's bloody head.

They stopped for introductions. Connal Lee jumped off his
mare and strode over to pull Arimo into a warm embrace. In Shoshone, he asked, "How are you doing, Arimo? How is your friend?"

Arimo glanced down at Andrew Hayes and shook his head. "He
is seriously wounded, Connal Lee. He's suffering half-frozen from

34

lying outside in the cold without a coat, hat, or blanket, with serious wounds. I'm very worried about him."

"Come, we'll accompany you back to Fort Lemhi. Let's get him indoors and warmed up."

The solemn group of Mormon missionaries carried their wounded brother into the fort. When they arrived, the ladies had a hot meal prepared of freshly baked brown bread and a big pot of venison stew. Their gardens and fields had flourished the past summer, leaving them well supplied with food. Some of the Sisters washed Andrew Hayes and rebandaged his wounds. A lead ball had lodged solidly in his shoulder, flattened against the bone. They didn't want to make the injury worse, so they left it in his shoulder, where it remained for years.

While they ate, the captain asked Arimo if he wanted to ride back with them to Fort Hall. Arimo declined. "I want find horse I trade Andrew Hayes for fresh horse. I ride his horse still. I want return my horse."

Captain Reed grimaced. "Well, now, Arimo. That could be extremely dangerous."

"They no hurt Shoshone. They want kill white man. I safe."

The captain led Connal Lee into the big log cabin meeting house that served the Fort as chapel, schoolhouse, and town hall. They marched up the center aisle to the front. Connal Lee stood slightly behind the captain. Captain Reed turned and gazed out at the Elders sitting on plain split log benches, clustered close to a big fire blazing in a fieldstone fireplace. "Now, gentlemen, what can we do to be of assistance? Is there anything the cavalry can do for you?"

A middle-aged man stood up and introduced himself as Bishop Chandler. "Thank you, Captain. Yesterday morning, renegade Bannocks, led by clan Chief Shoo-woo-koo, attacked us. Hudson Bay Company fur traders called him Chief Le Grand Coquin or The Big Rogue because he's a giant of a man. They were joined by a bunch of wild Sheepeater Shoshones from up around the Yellowstone Valley. They killed two men and wounded five of us. They stole around three-hundred head of cattle, all our oxen, and over thirty horses. Now, we are all hunkered down inside the Fort's stout walls. Since the war party stole all our livestock, we are stuck here until help arrives. As soon as we picked ourselves up from the attack, I dispatched Elder Barnard and Elder Watts on the only two sound horses left in the mission. They slipped out after dark last night to inform President Young of our troubles. We'll sit here and tend our wounded while we wait for a rescue. Brigham Young is bound to send some of the Nauvoo Legion to help us depart the area safely. Our mission these past three years has been to teach and convert the Shoshone, to make them friends and peaceful neighbors. Chief Big Rogue welcomed us with open arms three years ago. Well, we have converted and baptized over a hundred local Bannocks and Shoshone. Three of our younger missionaries even took Shoshone wives. We've been teaching them English, the gospel, and how to farm using Mormon irrigation. We thought we were all friends, living together in peace and prosperity. But all that changed two days ago. Fortunately, our crops flourished this past summer, so we are well provisioned to last until help arrives. We do appreciate your concern, though, Captain Reed."

"Well, since you are secured here behind your stout walls with plenty to eat, we will leave and send our reports about this unfortunate incident. The army will not be happy to hear about bands of renegade natives roaming the land attacking whites."

Connal Lee and the captain rode south until sunset. Connal Lee spotted a covey of pheasants and shot two for their supper. After they ate, they undressed and climbed into their fur blankets. For the first time all day, Connal Lee felt warm. That night he leisurely kissed and licked John's erection. When he tasted John's natural slickness oozing out of his manhood, Connal Lee notched up their lovemaking to the next level and sat down on John's straining shaft. He let out a happy sigh and a long deep moan until he bottomed out. Connal Lee sensuously leaned over and kissed and licked John's face. He found John's musky natural perfume very erotic, an aphrodisiac that spurred him on. After bouncing up and down for a while, Connal Lee grabbed John's broad shoulders and flipped them over, so the larger man ended up on top.

The captain had experience making love to women but not to men. The most he had ever done on patrol was some mutual masturbation and occasionally getting serviced orally by an obliging private. However, he instinctively knew what to do. He began thrusting and withdrawing in the old, familiar dance. Connal Lee moaned louder and louder until he reached his peak. They both climaxed simultaneously, straining in the joy and ecstasy of their release. After John shrank and withdrew from Connal Lee, the young teen collapsed over John's muscled, hairy chest. They had both broken out in a sweat from their exertions. "Ah love y'all, John Reed. That was really great!"

Captain Reed pulled back to look at Connal Lee's face, lit only by the remains of their little campfire. "You know what, Connal Lee? I never expected to say such a thing, but I believe I might love you too. I'm glad you came into my life and accompanied me on this scouting trip." He leaned over and rested a tender kiss on Connal Lee's lips. "I love you, too."

Chapter 3: Winter Quarters

They reached Fort Hall late on the third afternoon of their return trip. They passed through an empty construction site. The workmen had gathered around their cookfires in the tent city to the west of the fort.

Ned saw them riding into the fort from the second-floor window of the captain's small two-story log cabin. He yanked on his coat, hat, and gloves and clambered down the stairs. As the captain dismounted, Ned rushed over and took Paragon's reins. He held out his hand to take the reins of Connal Lee's mare, too. "Let me take care o' the horses, suhs. Y'all can go on in an' warm yerselves up. The stove is all stoked up, awaitin' y'all's return. I'll bring supper up t' the bedroom, suh, if'n y'all would like."

"Thank you, Ned. That would be most satisfactory. We are both frozen through from a long day in the saddle." The captain waved at Connal Lee. "Come on, Little Brother, let's go get warmed up."

Connal Lee grabbed his sleeping furs and saddlebags off his packhorse and followed the captain up the split log steps to the small upper room of the log cabin. When they opened the door, blessedly warm air welcomed them. A wax candle burned inside a brass and glass travel lamp, giving the room a soft glow. They pulled off hats, scarves, gloves, and greatcoats. They tossed their blankets and saddlebags into an open space in the far corner of the crowded little room. The bed took up most of the floor space. They smiled at the warmth from the stove. The captain unbuttoned his collar and sat down at a small table with a sigh. He invited Connal Lee to have a seat with a gesture towards the other chair. "Ah. That's better."

Connal Lee rubbed his hands together to warm them up.

Ned had laid out tin coffee mugs and a tin sugar and creamer set. A coffee pot sat on the heat stove. The captain stood up and poured them both coffee. They spooned in sugar and cream, lifted the mugs in their cold hands, and wrapped their fingers around the heat to warm them up. They both leaned back and contentedly sipped the strong coffee, glad to be out of the brutal winter weather.

Ned showed up with their supper on a simple wooden tray. Warmed up and ready to eat, they dug in like starving men, grinning at each other in their rush. Riding in the bitter cold had given them both healthy appetites. While they ate, Ned unpacked the captain's saddlebags. He placed one of the captain's buffalo hide blankets over the top of the bed's blankets, then turned down the covers. Connal Lee watched the simple nightly ritual, puzzled and curious about all the fussing. Ned reached under the bed and pulled out a white enameled tin bedpan. He lifted the lid to make sure it had not been used, then placed it on a shelf of the rustic washstand beside the bed. The washstand held a water pitcher in a large washbasin on its top. Ned walked over to the little table, grinning broadly. "More coffee, suh? Shall I clear away the tray, suh?"

"Yes. Thank you, Ned. Well done. That will be all for the night." Ned carried the tray out and closed the door behind him. Connal Lee and John Reed lounged around in their stockings, chatting about their mission. The captain invited Connal Lee to join him in bed. Connal Lee stripped off his clothes and left them on the wooden chair. The captain did the same. Connal Lee walked over and ran his hand over the sheets. "John? What is this?"

"What? Oh, you mean the sheets?"

"Sheets?"

"Sheets are how civilized white men sleep, Connal Lee. They keep the mattress and blankets from getting dirty. Plus, they are smooth and comfortable against the skin. They keep scratchy wool blankets from touching your body." He lifted the top sheet and blankets. "Here. Slide on in. You'll see what I mean."

Connal Lee slid his naked body between the two cool sheets. "Oh. This is real nice, John. So smooth. So soft. Y'all live such a fancy life, Captain Reed. Such, uh, luxuries. I never even knew such things existed."

The captain chuckled, but in a kindly way. "There are many nice things out there in civilization, Connal Lee. I hope maybe I can show you more of them as time goes on. I'm going to blow out the candle and go to bed now. Are you all settled in?"

Connal Lee nodded yes and held up the sheet and blankets for his handsome new lover to join him. He hugged the captain to warm up beneath the clean, cool sheets. "Things don't matter very much to me, John. Only people and pulling my own weight in putting food on the table concern me. Ah like family and food, but not luxury stuff."

The captain nodded and gave Connal Lee a light kiss on his forehead. After they warmed up, they spent a delightful evening soiling the clean sheets with their ardent frolicking.

The morning after their arrival dawned bright and freezing cold. The captain and Connal Lee ate breakfast with the Baines in their tiny one-room cabin. Lorna served delicious freshly baked bread still hot from the oven.

Connal Lee stood up and hugged Lorna, Gilbert, and the captain. "Well, it's time for me to get back to my wonderful family. Ah'm going to head out now. Ah need to report to Chief SoYo'Cant about what happened to his son and his Mormon friends up at Fort Lemhi."

While saddling his horses, he remembered the new lending library. With a surge of excitement at finding something new to read, he left his mare tied up to the hitching post and jogged into the general store. Mr. Mackey had been stirring up the banked coals in the potbelly stove when Connal Lee burst through the doors. He stood up and chuckled. "Good morning, Connal Lee. I wondered when you would be back for a book."

All distracted, Connal Lee walked straight towards the shelves at eye level on the wall, waving his hand at Mr. Mackey. "Good morning. How are y'all doing this morning, Mister Mackey?"

Connal Lee focused his attention on reading the spines of the used books on the rough shelf, ignoring the trader. He pulled out a beat-up leather book and held it up. "What's this book about, Mister Mackey, do y'all know? *Poor Jack?*"

"Well, now. Let me see. I think I read it years ago before coming out west to the frontier. As I recall, it's about a sailor's young son who struggles to survive on London's waterfronts without any help from his father. He eventually grows up to be a pilot on the river and makes his fortune."

"Oh! That sounds like a good story, like something Charles Dickens might write. Ah've never heard of Frederick Marry – uh – Marryat, but could Ah borrow it please?"

"Certainly, young man. Just step over here and sign my ledger that you are borrowing it and promise to return it or purchase it when you are done."

Connal Lee grinned with delight as he carefully dipped the pen in the inkwell and signed his name. Mr. Mackey blotted the ink. "I hope you enjoy it. You know, Connal Lee, I just got in a leverless Baby Dragoon pocket pistol. Let me show you while you're here."

He reached onto a shelf behind him and picked up a polished oak box. He set the box down on his big trading table and lifted the lid. "See, Connal Lee. It's a smaller version of Colt's big forty-four caliber Dragoon Revolver like the good captain carries. The Dragoon Revolver is big. It's fifteen inches long and weighs nearly five pounds. This Baby Dragoon is much lighter at only one and a half pounds, though it carries quite the kick. It's basically a small pistol that shoots rifle loads. This lovely little baby holds five thirty-one caliber bullets in the rotating cylinder. Believe it or not, you can shoot five rounds per minute with this beauty."

"Wow, that's a lot of firepower!"

"Yes, it is. Mister Colt developed them some years back for the civilian market. These cost ten dollars new back in Connecticut, but I can let you have this used one for only fifteen dollars here on the frontier."

"Gee, that's a awful lotta money, Mister Mackey."

"Yes, but they are hard to come by this far west. This is the first one I've seen in about six years." Mr. Mackey picked up the pistol by its barrel and held it out to Connal Lee. "With a four-inch barrel, it's made to carry in a coat pocket, although you can also wear it in a holster. And see, it comes with a brass Colt powder flask, bullet mold, bullets, balls, and percussion caps. I can throw in a holster with a flask attachment for two bucks."

"Ah don't know, Mister Mackey. Ah've always used a shotgun. Ah've never even fired a pistol before."

Captain Reed walked in and clapped Connal Lee on the back. "So, are you considering buying a pistol now, Connal Lee? The

Baby Dragoon is a good weapon, although it can't hold a candle to my trusty revolver."

He pulled out his pistol and laid it down next to the Baby Dragoon. Connal Lee glanced at the captain. "May Ah pick it up, Captain?"

"Certainly."

"Oh, this is a lot heavier. Ah'm starting to like the Baby Dragoon more and more. If Ah bought it, would y'all show me how to load and fire it?"

"It would be my pleasure, Little Brother. Mister Mackey, sorry to interrupt, but I need another ream of writing paper if you please."

Mr. Mackey handed him a package wrapped in brown paper and tied with twine. "Here you go, Captain. I'll charge it to the army's account."

"Thank you. And Connal Lee, I think a pistol is a good idea out here on the wild frontier. I think you should buy it."

"Oh. All right. Thanks, Captain Reed. Ah believe maybe Ah will."

The captain holstered his big Dragoon Revolver and waved goodbye as he strode out the door. Mr. Mackey picked up the Baby Dragoon. "Here, Connal Lee, let me show you how to load this sweet little baby. Tap out the barrel wedge, then pull the barrel off the frame. Got it? Then pull the cylinder off the arbor, so it comes out of the frame. See?" He glanced up. Connal Lee nodded yes. "Fill each chamber with gunpowder, then push in the lead ball using the cylinder arbor on the frame. Understand? Your percussion caps go into each nipple, then reassemble the pistol. Pull the hammer back to rest on the safety pin, and you are ready to fire. Got it?"

"Is it safe to carry loaded, Mister Mackey?"

"If you lock the hammer to rest on the safety pin, yes. If you aren't in dangerous territory, it's best to carry it unloaded just like with a shotgun. Just be careful, like with any loaded weapon. But you know that."

"Yep. Ah got it, Mister Mackey. Ah'll practice stripping and loading it back at our camp."

Connal Lee forked over seventeen dollars in coins. Mr. Mackey handed him the box and a nicely tooled cow leather holster on a matching tooled belt. The holster came with a pouch to hold a powder flask and a sheath to carry a knife. He transferred his Bowie knife to the new holster, then buckled it over his knife belt. He picked up the box with his new pistol with a big smile. "Gee, thanks, Mister Mackey. This is great! A new book and a new pistol both on the same day. Thanks. So long now."

"Thank you, Connal Lee. Have a safe trip back to Chief Arimo's winter headquarters. Please extend the chief my regards."

Young Arimo, the chief's son and namesake, arrived back in the winter camp a few days later. He attended his father in White Dove's tipi that evening after the tribal council meeting. He reported to his father how the missionaries expected the Mormon Church to send a rescue party to Fort Lemhi. He said the Mormon Elders decided to close the Salmon Mission and abandon Fort Lemhi. The missionaries traded their stores of wheat, corn, beans, and hay with the peaceful Shoshone Mormon converts. Their Shoshone converts had recovered some of the stolen horses and cattle, but only a token few. "The Mormon missionaries weren't comfortable having me around, so I left to return here. I wish I could have done more. In the spring, I think I will ride down to Fort Farmington and check up on my friend, Andrew Hayes. I hope he has a full recovery. At least I was able to keep my promise. When Andrew exchanged my exhausted horse for a fresh horse, he saved my life. I swore to myself I would save his life in the future if I could. Well, I helped save him. I kept my word."

After Arimo made his report, things returned to normal in the camp. Around the middle of March, Connal Lee and White Wolf braved a freezing cold breeze to take their furs to Fort Hall. When they arrived, they noticed the Fort seemed very quiet. They couldn't hear any construction coming from the new barracks or barns north of the fort. In a rush to get out of the cold, the boys carried armfuls of tanned pelts into the trading post and plopped them down on the big table for Mr. Mackey to evaluate.

Mr. Mackey held up his hand to stop them. "I'm sorry to be the one to tell you, Connal Lee, but the damn influenza epidemic reached the fort a couple of days ago. Nearly all the garrison are in bed sick as dogs. We've already had one death. Dear Missus Baines is nursing them out in their cold tents, but it's a huge job. She told me to tell you the minute you arrived that you must leave immediately and not return for at least ten days to reduce your chances of catching the flu."

Connal Lee heard White Wolf take a startled breath. White Wolf grabbed him by the arm and yanked him towards the door. In Shoshone, he nearly shouted, "We must leave now. Don't touch anything. Let's go straight to the horses and out the gates immediately. Go!"

Connal Lee stood frozen for a second. "But the trading... a new book to read... the captain."

Mr. Mackey picked up a ledger and his usual stump of a wooden pencil. "Go on, Connal Lee. I'll keep a record of the credit owed you for these furs. Stay away, like Missus Baines ordered. Your friend, Captain Reed, is fine. I'm sure he would tell you to protect yourself from exposure. This year the epidemic is as bad as the worldwide epidemic of forty-seven and forty-eight, which I remember only too well. You don't want to catch the flu and take it back to your Shoshone friends, now, do you?"

Connal Lee turned on his heel and scampered out the door. He found White Wolf already on his great stallion, spurring him to a run out the gate. Connal Lee followed closely behind, a sense of panic welling up in his chest at the thought of spreading another deadly disease among his adopted clan.

They arrived in camp, breathless from the ride, and stopped at Short Rainbow's tipi. White Wolf explained the problem and asked Short Rainbow and Bright Star to rub down their horses. He wanted to report the outbreak of influenza to Chief SoYo'Cant immediately. Connal Lee followed him to White Dove's tipi, where the Chief held his council meetings. The chief welcomed Connal Lee, Screaming Eagle, and White Wolf. He invited them to sit with a gesture of his hand. White Wolf remained standing. "Uncle SoYo'Cant, weeks ago trader Mackey told us of an influenza epidemic spreading across the entire world. He said it is very lethal, and people who have been sick with the flu are catching it again. Today, when we arrived at Fort Hall, he warned us that many of the cavalry in the Fort had taken to their sickbeds with the new influenza. They have even had one death."

The Chief and everyone in the council sat up straighter, alarmed at this news. The Chief looked over at one of his young nephews sitting around the edge of the great tipi. "Little Bumble Bee, run like the wind and bring Firewalker, Burning Fire, and Short Rainbow to me here."

The slender preteen boy jumped to his feet, pulled a fur over his shoulders like a cape, and ran out of the tipi. While they waited for their medicine man and shamans to arrive, Chief SoYo'Cant reflected on the last time a worldwide epidemic struck his people. He turned sad eyes to Connal Lee. "Many snows ago, around ten winters now, we caught the white man influenza. Everyone came down with it. Many of our elderly did not survive. The Newe lost much wisdom and experience, leaving the tribe weaker than before. I remember it well. We must assure that we are not exposed to this new influenza."

Connal Lee and White Wolf nodded their agreement. They heard a stir at the entrance to the tipi. Burning Fire entered and stood aside for Firewalker and Short Rainbow. The Chief nodded at them and gestured for them to take a seat around the fire. Short Rainbow skipped over and sat between Connal Lee and White Wolf. "White Wolf, please repeat your news from the Fort for Firewalker and Burning Fire."

After White Wolf finished his report, the Chief asked for advice. Everyone voiced an opinion made up primarily of fearful complaints. After several minutes, Teniwaaten spoke up. "The English have a word that has no translation into our language. The word is *quarantine*. It means to put up barriers so healthy people do not come in contact with the sick. They lock away the sick in their homes with signs on the door warning people to stay away."

The elderly medicine man, Firewalker, stood up. "We must educate and order everyone to avoid contact with anyone outside our encampment for two weeks. Once the sickness enters the camp, it will spread like before. Our only chance is to not let it get started. If we don't get close to strangers or touch items belonging to strangers, we might survive without catching the influenza."

Chief SoYo'Cant ordered his council to spread the word. He wanted every single person in the clan to know of this new prohibition: No travel to Fort Hall for two weeks. No interaction with strangers under any circumstances for at least two weeks. Stay in the winter camp and stay safe.

Most everyone in the camp remembered the tragic epidemic of the winter of 1847 and 1848 and the lesser waves of flu since then. They took the chief's orders very seriously.

The quarantine seemed to have worked. The chief's clan had a winter free of influenza for the first time in many years. Captain Reed, unfortunately, had to write fourteen condolence letters to the families of the men under his command who succumbed to the flu.

Eventually, the fort was free of influenza.

That spring, Connal Lee reached the height of five foot seven inches tall. Short Rainbow and White Wolf made him new clothes to fit his growing, muscular body. Connal Lee loved how the fringes of his new leggings swished as he walked. He walked with a bit of a peacock strut to his step when he wore them. He grew into the army overcoat he had purchased in Fort Laramie. Connal Lee practiced loading and firing his new pistol, then taught his family how to handle it. He and Screaming Eagle practiced every day until they became expert shots with the Colt Baby Dragoon.

On the last day of March, a Major in the Nauvoo Legion approached the winter camp from the south leading two spare saddle horses, a packhorse, and a spare packhorse in a train behind him. He arrived just as the sun began setting around 6:30. Some hunters returning to the camp greeted him and escorted him to meet with their chief. The Major wore a pale blue frock coat with a tall up-standing collar. A sash over his shoulder held a sword at his left hip. He had a matching belt with a pistol holster, powder flask, knives, and a leather ammunition pouch. Polished brass buttons glittered in the setting sun. His black felt hat sported a tall crown with the left side of the brim pinned up with a fancy feathered military cockade.

Connal Lee and Screaming Eagle spotted him as they returned from hunting. Connal Lee nudged his brown mare into a gallop, dragging his packhorse behind him. The packhorse carried a beautiful spotted Bobcat whose fur would fetch a high price with Mr. Mackey. Screaming Eagle hurried to catch up.

When the visitor reached the edge of the camp, he dismounted to walk his horses through the maze of tipis and campfires. Connal Lee, curious as ever, handed his reins to Screaming Eagle, then rushed over with his hand extended. "Good evening, suh. Ah'm Connal Lee Swinton, the adopted son of Chief Arimo. Welcome to Chief Arimo's winter camp."

The Major stopped, came to attention, and held out his hand for a handshake. "A pleasure to meet you, young man. I am Major Robert Miller Harris of the Nauvoo Legion, Third Regiment of Infantry, at your service. Yesterday, Governor Young, the Commander in Chief of the Territorial Militias, ordered me to ride with all dispatch to deliver an official communique to our ally, Chief Arimo. I bring an invitation to visit Great Salt Lake City to be on hand for an important political event scheduled to take place on April the twelfth. Would you please escort me to Chief Arimo?"

While the Major introduced himself, Connal Lee enjoyed looking him over. The Major appeared to be around forty but still very trim and athletic. He had a proud military bearing which reminded Connal Lee of Captain Reed. His clean-shaven face showed a day or two's stubble, exposing prominent cheekbones and a slightly cleft chin. He had a narrow, proud nose and expressive eyebrows. He had oiled his black hair and combed it back off his forehead, exposing a slight widow's peak in the center. He wore his hair cut even with his strong jawline and tucked back behind his ears. Connal Lee found the Major very attractive, despite appearing older than Connal Lee's father back in the Ozarks.

"Certainly, Captain. It would be my pleasure to introduce you to Chief Arimo." Connal Lee waved over a couple of the Chief's nephews who had gathered around, curious about a stranger in the camp. He gestured towards the captain's five horses. "Please take our guest's horses over to Short Rainbow's tipi, unsaddle them, rub them down, and see they get some water. Thank you, boys."

He looked at the captain and shifted to English. "These youngsters will take your horses over by my family tipi and take good care of them while we meet with our chief. Please follow me, and Ah will introduce y'all to my adopted father, the great Chief Arimo."

"Thank you, young man. Most obliging of you."

They approached the sizeable outdoor lodge where they found the chief ending a meeting with his councilors. Connal Lee made introductions. The chief sent for Teniwaaten and then invited the major to take a seat close to the warm fire. The temperature had only risen into the fifties. Rain had fallen earlier, but now the setting sun shared a mild, welcome warmth.

Before he sat down, the major handed Connal Lee a leather packet. "Please give this letter to the great chief, Mister Swinton." He then sat down Indian-style beside the roaring fire. "Thank you."

Connal Lee opened the leather envelope and handed the chief a fancy white paper envelope closed with a red wax seal. The chief broke the seal and shook out a nine page handwritten letter. He glanced at the writing and handed the letter back to Connal Lee. Anxiously Connal Lee began reading, thinking he would translate for the chief. But with such formal language, he decided he better wait for Teniwaaten. Before long, Teniwaaten approached the fire and warmly greeted his uncle, the chief. He sat down next to Chief SoYo'Cant and indicated for Connal Lee to sit beside him. Connal Lee felt delighted to sit close so he could read along with Teniwaaten. While Teniwaaten translated, Connal Lee followed the fancy copperplate script in English.

"On this the twenty-ninth day of March, in the year of our Lord eighteen hundred and fifty-eight, I, Brigham Young, Governor of the Territory of Utah and President of the Church of Jesus Christ of Latter-day Saints, do hereby send my warmest greetings and salutations to the Honorable Chief Arimo and our valued allies, the great Shoshone Nation.

"By these presents, I do formally invite and entreat you, along with whatever delegates, counselors, and guards you deem fit to have accompany you, to attend me at the Governor's Mansion, the Beehive House in Great Salt Lake City, on the upcoming eleventh day of April, eighteen hundred and fifty-eight, for the purpose of witnessing the arrival of the new governor of this great territory, Alfred Cumming, duly appointed by President Buchanan, who will arrive the following day."

The lengthy letter described how Brigham Young had sent a rush message to the Church's friend, Colonel Kane, pleading with him to intercede on the Mormons' behalf with President Buchanan. After meeting with Buchanan, Colonel Kane had traveled to Great Salt Lake City and met with Brigham Young. The colonel had then traveled to Camp Scott and met with Governor Cumming. Eventually, he convinced the new Governor he would be peacefully welcomed to the Territory of Utah if he entered without an army.

Teniwaaten finished translating the long letter. "And so, my dear ally and friend, we look forward to welcoming you to Great Salt Lake City in the very near future. Yours, most respectfully, signed Brigham Young, Governor of the Territory of Utah."

Connal Lee turned to Major Harris. "We don't keep a calendar here in camp. How many days until the eleventh of April would y'all happen to know?"

"Yes, Mister Swinton. It is eleven days from today."

"Oh, good. That gives us enough time to travel with our tipis. It wouldn't be another rush diplomatic journey like the last time we traveled to Great Salt Lake City."

Connal glanced over at his family. They all nodded their heads enthusiastically, hoping the chief would invite them to accompany him again. They watched the chief anxiously, waiting for him to respond.

Through Teniwaaten, Chief SoYo'Cant announced his decision. "Good Major Harris, you have the gratitude of the Shoshone people for bringing us this invitation. I regret to say I myself am not well enough to travel at this time. It is nothing serious. Just another white man cold, I believe. But a six-day journey in inclement spring weather would not be advisable for me." The Chief had noticed Connal Lee's excited look of anticipation, supported by his spouses. "In my place, I will dispatch my adopted son, Connal Lee Swinton, with his family and my first son, Arimo, and his wife. They will travel to Great Salt Lake City as the official delegation of the Shoshone Nation. They will represent us when Chief Brigham Young greets the new governor, and they can witness the peaceful transfer of power for me."

Connal Lee and his family looked at each other with big smiles, excited to have another diplomatic mission. Major Harris nodded his head. "Thank you, sir. That would be most satisfactory."

The conference broke up. Connal Lee waved for the major to accompany him. As Connal Lee and his spouses walked north to Short Rainbow's tipi, they made plans and divided up the chores of preparing to be gone for three weeks or more. Along the way, Connal Lee turned to Major Harris. "Would you like to accompany us, sir? We will leave in the morning and should arrive in six days, seven if weather delays us any."

"Thank you, young man. But I think it is my duty to return posthaste and make my report to Governor Young. Would you like me to deliver a message from the chief? I will reach the governor the day after tomorrow if I leave at first light."

"Ah don't know, captain. Let me go ask my adopted father what his wishes are. Will y'all please join us for supper in our tipi?"

"Thank you, young man. Very hospitable of you."

"Ah'll be right back. See y'all at the tipi."

Half an hour later, Connal Lee returned to his family's campfire. He found everyone sitting around the hot blaze, getting acquainted and discussing travel plans. Short Rainbow and Bright Star bustled about cooking a simple supper. Before Connal Lee had a chance to sit down, Arimo strolled up, leading his slender Ute wife by the hand. His wife held the hand of a younger girl. Arimo called ahead. "Hello, White Wolf, my brother. Good evening, lovely Short Rainbow and beautiful Bright Star. How are you tonight, Screaming Eagle? Hello, Connal Lee,"

Everyone stood up to welcome their cousin and adopted brother with big smiles on their faces. After Arimo hugged White Wolf, he indicated the young girl with him. "This is my dear cousin on my mother's side who will be joining us to help my lovely Kimana care for her tipi. Her name is Koko."

Koko hugged everyone as Arimo introduced them. Connal Lee whispered in Shoshone as he returned her gentle embrace, "It is so very nice to meet you, Koko. I look forward to getting to know you on the journey."

Connal Lee stepped over beside Major Harris and gestured towards Arimo. "Major Harris, may Ah present Arimo, Chief Arimo's first son and namesake. He was raised with White Wolf like brothers since they are the same age. This is his Ute wife, the lovely Kimana. Kimana means Butterfly in English. And this is my adopted cousin, Koko. Koko means Night in English."

The Major stepped up and shook hands with Arimo. "Very nice to meet you, Mister Arimo."

Kimana and Koko stood with their heads lowered shyly, so he didn't try to shake their hands. He only smiled and nodded his head. "It's my pleasure to meet you, too, Missus Kimana and Miss Koko. Mister Arimo is a fortunate man."

Short Rainbow invited everyone to have a seat, but Arimo shook his head no. "Sorry, Short Rainbow, but we have far too much to do to prepare to leave in the morning. I just wanted to coordinate our travel plans. Shall we meet two hours after dawn on the south side of the camp so we can travel together? White Wolf, is that good with you and your family?"

"Yes, Arimo. We will be ready to travel by then. Sleep well tonight, my brother."

"Good night to all of you." As they walked away towards Kimana's tipi, Kimana and Koko shyly waved their goodbyes.

Short Rainbow sat down and resumed cooking. She invited everyone to join her around the cookfire with a broad gesture. As he sat down, Connal Lee spoke in English for the benefit of the major. "Ah am requested to go see Teniwaaten first thing in the morning before we depart. He will have a letter from the Chief for y'all to take to the governor, Major Harris."

"Very well. Thank you, young man. Much obliged."

"Please let the governor know we will be traveling with our tipis, so he need not be concerned about providing accommodations or provisions during our delegation's visit."

"Oh, that's actually very good to hear. What with all the commotion in the northern parts of the Territory, that will certainly be for the best."

"What do y'all mean, Major? What commotion?"

Everyone leaned forward to hear the news. All eyes turned to the major. "Well, you see, it all started back on the twenty-fifth of February when Colonel Thomas Leiper Kane arrived in Great Salt Lake City."

"Excuse me, again, Major. But did y'all say Colonel Kane arrived in Great Salt Lake City on February the twenty-fifth? That's the exact same day those Bannock Indians joined with a bunch of renegade packs and attacked Fort Lemhi up by the Salmon River. The very next day, Captain Reed and Ah rode into the fort to check out rumors of Indians wanting to drive the white man out of their hunting grounds. What an amazing coincidence!"

"Yes, Mister Swinton. Colonel Kane arrived on February the twenty-fifth. I was there and saw him, myself. He was traveling in disguise as Doctor Osborn. He had taken the name of his slave for his incognito. He wanted to see for himself if the Mormons remained hospitable to strangers. He had heard all kinds of foul rumors back east. After he was made welcome, he revealed his true identity. He told us he had departed Washington on December the twenty-eighth. He said he took a steamer to Panama, crossed the Isthmus on the new overland railroad, then took another steamer north to San Pedro Bay close to Los Angeles. He then traveled by covered wagon and ox teams to San Bernardino, then up the Southern Mormon Trail to Great Salt Lake City. He met with Governor Young and other church and territorial officials while he rested and recovered his health. He has been poorly most of his life, suffering from respiratory ailments. But that has never deterred him. Some say he suffers from bilious fever. He's a small man, only five foot six inches tall and a hundred-thirty pounds. But he's an industrious man, intelligent, determined, and focused on the job at hand. He finally talked Brigham Young into agreeing to receive Governor Cumming, provided he arrived without an army escort.

"On the twelfth of this month of March, I accompanied Colonel Kane and General William Kimball of the Nauvoo Legion, along with other guards, to visit Camp Scott. When we drew near, Colonel Kane left us behind to await word of his negotiations. He entered the camp alone. The soldiers challenged him and shot at him, then arrested him as a spy. This treatment infuriated him so much that he challenged General Johnston to a duel! Governor Cumming interceded and demanded an explanation from the army."

"Wow, Major Harris. Ah'm sorry to keep interrupting your story, but that was around the time Fort Hall was laid low by the influenza epidemic that has swept around the world. We didn't know anything about what was happening in Great Salt Lake City, then."

Major Harris glanced at Connal Lee and his family sitting around the fire. "I hope you were spared. From what I've read, this winter's influenza has been very serious. Well, getting back to Camp Scott. Colonel Kane reported to us later that the new Governor is a corpulent man weighing upwards of four hundred pounds. He's also a man who enjoys his liquor. Jovial and loquacious, he's very friendly. He brings experience in government, having served as Mayor of Augusta. He also served in the military during the Mexican-American War as a non-combatant and was Superintendent of Indian Affairs in upper Missouri.

"On the seventeenth, Kane reported to General Kimball, waiting with us in our camp, that he had not yet gained Governor Cumming's confidence. He went on to say he had unintentionally alienated the entire army in the meantime. General Kimball left me in charge of the guards waiting for Colonel Kane while he rode to report to Brigham Young the following day.

"That Sunday, at a regularly scheduled sacrament meeting in the tabernacle, Brigham Young convened a special conference. He announced, got adopted by the congregation, and initiated the contingency plans that had been in the works for some time. He ordered all Saints north of Provo to pack up all their belongings and relocate south of Provo. Five hundred families departed almost immediately. He ordered all grain to be cached or ground into flour and transported with them, along with all other foodstuffs.

"President Young organized the exodus south by ward. He ordered them to first move food and provisions south, then return for their families and personal goods. Everyone is taking all their belongings and tools of their trades, driving their herds before them, even as we speak. Within a week, wagon trains began passing in front of the Governor's Mansion to turn south onto State Road. State Road runs south directly to Provo and beyond to Los Angeles in southern California. We now have four to eight hundred wagons a day passing through the city to where it looks like one endless wagon train, going in both directions!

"Brigham Young wants the territory emptied of humanity so there can be no chance of direct conflict with the army if and when they invade. He assigned a thousand stout men and boys to stay behind to protect property from vandalism by man or beast. He ordered them to water the crops and gardens and maintain the fences in good order. He ordered them to fill all the abandoned buildings with straw, prepared to be put to the torch if the army invaded in a belligerent manner. Brigham Young is determined the army will conquer and occupy nothing more than a barren desert if they dare to attack."

Bright Star served everyone drinking horns of red tea. The Major nodded his thanks before he took a sip. "Just a couple of days ago, General Kimball returned from meeting with Colonel Kane again. He brought word that Cumming had overridden General Johnston's objections and agreed to enter the territory without the army. Colonel Kane and Governor Cumming are due to arrive on the twelfth, which is why you were invited to attend the welcoming ceremony."

When Major Harris stopped speaking to take a drink of hot herb tea, Connal Lee looked around at his family, then turned to the Major. "We were in Great Salt Lake City back in November for the chief's annual fur trading expedition. The governor invited us to attend a council of war. We met with leaders of the Nauvoo Legion, the Mormon Church, and officials of Great Salt Lake City. During that council of war, the governor explained their plans to execute a scorched earth policy to deny any help to the army. He said all the Mormons supported the plan. So, they are really doing it? What an amazing turn of events!"

"Yes, young man. Around ten thousand devout Mormons are mobilizing north of Salt Lake Valley, and another twenty thousand from Great Salt Lake City are heading south away from possible trouble, as we speak."

Short Rainbow and Bright Star danced around the men serving them generous portions of rainbow trout along with gourd bowls of venison stew made with dried vegetables and herbs. The group around the warm fire grew quiet as everyone focused on eating. The moment they finished, they all stood up. The men strode out to the general herds to pick out their livestock for riding and for pulling travois.

Short Rainbow and Bright Star began sorting through what food and clothing they would take and what they would leave behind in the camp. Even though the Spring weather had been pleasant lately, Short Rainbow packed their big army tent in case it rained. They would not have time to raise their tipis each night and pack them up each morning.

Late that evening, they sat in the warm tipi, relaxing. Major Harris removed his winter frock coat and lounged comfortably in his shirt sleeves. Connal Lee couldn't help but notice the prominent bulge of his tight uniform pants to the right of his crotch. He found himself intrigued about what might be hiding beneath the Major's skin-tight trousers. Connal Lee raised his eyes from the Major's crotch and looked him in the face. "So where did y'all come from originally, Major Harris?"

"Well, young man, I was born in Ohio, where I lived until I attended West Point. I graduated from West Point in thirty-five. For the next couple of years, my work with the army took me all across our great nation. I met and married my first wife, Thelma, in Chicago in thirty-seven. One assignment sent me to Saint Louis in thirty-eight, where friends introduced Thelma and me to two Mormon Elders. My oldest boy was born shortly after we settled in Saint Louis. After we were baptized, I mustered out of the army, and we joined the Saints in Nauvoo. We arrived just after trouble had begun with the surrounding neighbors. That's when Joseph Smith founded the Nauvoo Legion to protect the city. He called me to join the legion as a First Lieutenant. I met and married my second wife, Mary Ellen, in Nauvoo. Both wives bore sons while we lived in the beautiful City of Nauvoo.

"Later, I was sent as an officer of the Mormon Battalion and fought in the Mexican-American War. When the war ended, I made my way to Great Salt Lake City, anxious to be reunited with my family. Brigham Young asked me to be an officer of the Territory's Deseret Militia, which became the Utah Territorial Militia. When Brigham Young called up the Nauvoo Legion last year, they transferred me to the command of Lieutenant General Daniel Wells, who commands me to this day."

The Major yawned. Connal Lee yawned, too. "Hah! Yawns are catching, aren't they? Well, good night, suh. We have an early start in the morning. Sleep well."

The rest of Connal Lee's family bid the Major goodnight when he left for his little tent beside the tipi. Everyone undressed for bed. Connal Lee dived under his family's sleeping furs and snuggled up to Bright Star for the night.

When he woke up, Connal Lee found Major Harris packed and ready to leave at the first hint of dawn. Connal Lee strode briskly over to Teniwaaten's simple tipi. Teniwaaten gave him three flat leather pouches. He explained that the smallest held the Chief's letter. The larger two contained bone breastplates, similar to what the Chief wore. Each breastplate had two horizontal rows of four-inch wide ivory-colored beads, with round black horn beads trimming the outer edges and center row. Connal Lee couldn't wait to show his family. He had never owned nor worn any jewelry before. The chief gave them to Connal Lee and Arimo as badges of honor, announcing to the world their status as sons of a chief.

The moment Connal Lee handed Major Harris the chief's letter to Brigham Young, he mounted up and rode off at a trot. He didn't wait for breakfast or even a cup of coffee. Two hours later, Short Rainbow and Bright Star had the tipi mounted on four travoises. Their cooking equipment, food, and clothing filled two more travoises. In addition, they each led a packhorse loaded up with sleeping furs, weapons, and ammunition. They met up with Arimo, Kimana, and Koko just outside the sprawling camp. The Shoshone delegation headed south at a slow horse's walk to make the 164-mile journey. They stopped twice during the day to transfer saddles and travois to spare horses so they could maintain a good pace.

Chapter 4: Exodus

Towards the end of the fifth day of travel, the Shoshone delegation wearily approached the small farming community of Box Elder. Their mayor and bishop, Lorenzo Snow, had been called by Brigham Young to lead other families to the area to expand the settlement. Years later, when they incorporated as a city, they would change the name to Brigham City. Connal Lee only saw smoke from one fireplace a mile or so away towards the center of the spread-out farming community. White Wolf decided they didn't have time to pass through. The river ran wide and deep through the broad valley, so they would have to skirt around it. He recommended they stop beside the raging Bear River and set up their camp. Connal Lee took off into the trees and scrub brush to hunt for their supper. Snow-capped granite mountains rose tall to the east of the flat, fertile river plain.

The young Shoshone families halted their train of horses. Screaming Eagle, proudly wearing his tall war bonnet, stood up in his saddle, ready to dismount. A lead bullet knocked him off his great war stallion with a shocking loud bang. He toppled clumsily to the ground, clutching a bleeding wound in his left bicep. The rest of the group immediately dropped to the ground seeking cover. They all peered around anxiously, trying to find the source of the attack. Arimo fumbled for his bow while keeping low.

Connal Lee heard the loud report of an antique flintlock musket. Alarmed for his family, he returned as quickly and stealthily as he could. When he drew near the river, he jumped off his mare and tied her to a big box elder tree. Walking silently, as Zeff had taught him years ago, he snuck closer to where he had left his family. His anxiety level rose along with his heartbeat. Slowly he turned his head, searching for any movement. He grew more concerned for his loved ones. He heard a horse neigh closeby at the same moment he smelled the burnt ammonia stink of discharged gunpowder. Instantly he turned towards the sound and crouched down. He moved silently from tree to tree, searching for a man and a horse. He spotted a small man wearing a ragged homespun shirt kneeling on one knee, frantically trying to load an ancient musket.

Connal Lee stood up, took careful aim, and shouted at the top of his voice, "Drop that rifle! Don't turn around!" With as much venom and menace as he could manage, he lowered his voice threateningly. "Don't even breathe! Ah would as soon shoot ya as look at y'all."

The heavy long rifle dropped to the rocky soil.

"Put yer hands up. Now!"

He watched the man's shaking hands reach up to the heavens. When the man started to turn his head, Connal Lee shouted, "Ah said don't turn around."

The man froze. Connal Lee snuck up behind him. As he drew closer, he smelled where the settler had peed his pants in fear. Connal Lee drew his pistol and used it like a hammer to deliver a harsh blow to the side of the man's skull. The blow knocked him out cold. The farmer fell forward onto his face. Connal Lee ran to his packhorse and grabbed a thin leather rope from the packsaddle. He jogged back and expertly tied the man's hands securely behind him. He rolled the stranger over onto his back. It surprised him to find an older teen, not yet a man, shorter and thinner than himself. Based on the farmer's scraggly beard, he was clearly older than Connal Lee. He wore rough clothing, ragged and worn but clean.

Connal Lee picked him up under his armpits and dragged him over to the packhorse without any concern for the teenager's comfort. With a great grunt, he heaved the boy up onto his stomach across the packsaddle. Connal Lee tied him securely to the horse. He went back to where he found the settler, picked up the old flintlock musket, and fetched the farmer's horse. The teen had been riding a worn-out leather saddle on an old swayed back broodmare. He tied the decrepit horse behind his packhorse, leapt onto his lovely brown mare, and trotted back to his family.

Connal Lee's breath caught in his throat at the scene before him. Screaming Eagle lay rigid with pain on the ground. His war bonnet had fallen aside. White Wolf knelt beside him, holding a chamois cloth to a bleeding wound. Short Rainbow and Bright Start hastily sorted through their storage bags, looking for the herbs and bandages White Wolf required. Bright Star began crying quietly as she helped. Connal Lee rode up to them. Fear choked him up to where he couldn't talk. Finally, he blurted out, "Screaming Eagle isn't dead, is he? Please tell me he's alive."

Connal Lee felt tremendous relief when he heard Screaming Eagle grunt out, "No, I'm not dead. Not yet, but I feel like I will be soon. Ouch! Be careful, there, White Wolf. That hurts!"

"Oh, shut up. It's your own damn fault, Screaming Eagle. You just make too tempting and magnificent a target standing up on your stallion wearing your war bonnet."

Connal Lee jumped off his saddle and secured the horses to a small cottonwood by the brown river. Still furious at the farmer for wounding Screaming Eagle, he smacked the teen as he walked by on his way to the fire. When he reached Screaming Eagle, he crashed to his knees and examined him intently. He picked up Screaming Eagle's head and cradled it on his lap while White Wolf worked quickly to clean the wound. "How is he, White Wolf? Tell me the truth. How is he, really?"

"He took a clean shot through his left bicep. The lead ball didn't hit his bones or sever any major blood vessels. He wasn't wearing any clothing over his arms, so he won't have foreign matter inside the wound to cause festering later on. Once I clean the wound and stop the bleeding, he will be fine. Although he's going to be in pain for several days while his arm heals. Go start a fire, Connal Lee, so Short Rainbow can brew willow bark tea for the pain. I'll also need sage tea to clean the area before I close up and bandage the wounds. Then, take Bright Star and raise the army tent."

Without saying a word, Connal Lee jumped to his feet and began searching for deadfall. He soon had a hot fire burning. He put water to boiling in their new tin coffee pot. Short Rainbow skipped over and started brewing the willow tea. Connal Lee jogged to the packhorse carrying the big army tent. Bright Star joined him with tears still running down her face. Kimana and Koko rushed to lend them a hand. Connal Lee positioned the tent to the west of the fire. Working as a team, they raised the tent in short order.

Short Rainbow selected a fine steel needle from the cardboard packet of sewing needles Connal Lee had purchased at Fort Hall. She walked to the horses and plucked several long hairs from their tails. She dampened several goat skin chamois in the running water, rinsed off the horse hairs, and carried the suturing implements over to White Wolf. "Thank you, Short Rainbow. Would you please assist by wiping up the blood so I can see what I'm doing?"

"Certainly. That's what I'm here for."

Ten minutes later, both bullet holes had been cauterized with a great deal of complaining, squirming, and yelling. When Screaming Eagle calmed down, White Wolf carefully sewed shut both holes and then wrapped the wounds with clean bandages to staunch any bleeding.

Connal Lee heard the stranger moaning. He untied the barely conscious young man and pushed his limp body off the packhorse. It collapsed to the ground with an audible plop. The skinny boy lay there stunned, whimpering in fear. Connal Lee checked that his captive couldn't escape and turned to help his family set up camp and tend to Screaming Eagle.

Two hours later, they relaxed around the campfire. Screaming Eagle leaned back wearily against a box elder's hefty trunk. About the time they finished eating, the young settler called out weakly with his voice trembling in fear. "Could I have some water, please?"

Angry again, Connal Lee rose to his feet and stomped over beside the prisoner. He jerked the boy up to a sitting position on the ground and put his fists on his hips. "What's y'all's name, stranger, and why did y'all attack us without provocation?"

The boy looked up fearfully. "I'm-I'm J-Jeff M-Morgan. I th-thought we were b-being attacked b-by w-wild Injuns. Who-Who're you?"

"We're a delegation of the Shoshone Nation riding to Great Salt Lake City at the invitation of Governor Brigham Young. Y'all just shot Chief Arimo's nephew and apprentice War Chief, a personal friend of Brigham Young, ya asshole."

The boy cringed. "I didn't know. I-I'm sorry. I was t-told to protect our p-property from l-looters and invaders. You l-looked like wild Injuns coming to l-loot our abandoned farms. I was only doing my d-duty." The teen broke down in tears as he struggled to pull his hands loose.

Still angry, Connal Lee stomped over to where his saddle and belongings sat on dry ground next to the tethered horses. He carried the old canvas water bag over and held it up so Jeff could take a sip of water. When the young farm boy settled down, Connal Lee untied his arms, pulled them in front of the boy's scrawny stomach, and retied them securely. Seething, Connal Lee ignored Jeff tearfully begging to be untied. Connal Lee went back and sat down next to the fire.

"What are we going to do with Jeff, White Wolf. He's just going to slow us down."

"Maybe you should find out who else is left in the area to guard the empty farmsteads. Ask Jeff who is in charge here and where he can be found. Then, I think you should take him to his chief and deliver him, still tied up. Tell his chief what happened and that we will make a full report of the sneak attack to Chief Brigham Young."

With a sigh, Connal Lee rose wearily to his feet. He interrogated Jeff, then told him what they were going to do. As soon as Jeff understood he would be taken to his grandfather at their family farm, he became cooperative, grateful these savages didn't kill him in revenge for shooting their war chief. Half an hour ride later, as dusk settled over the river bottomlands, Connal Lee and Jeff approached a poor, simple log cabin, the source of the smoke they had seen when they first arrived. Now sitting up on his swayed back mare, Jeff called ahead, "Grandpa! Grandpa! Come quick. I need you."

A grizzled old man opened the cabin door and peered out. "Jeff? What in tarnation's going on out there? Who is this stranger?" When the old man saw Jeff's hands tied in front of him, holding onto the saddle horn, his horse's reins held in another boy's hands, he became alarmed. "Who're you? Why do you have my Jeff all tied up?"

Connal Lee hopped down off his mare. He pulled his pistol out of its holster but didn't aim it at the gray-haired man. "Peace. We come in peace. My name is Connal Lee Swinton. Ah am the adopted son of Chief Arimo of the Shoshone Nation. Ah am part of a delegation traveling to Great Salt Lake City at the invitation of Governor Brigham Young."

The old man looked astonished. Connal Lee stepped over and pulled Jeff to the ground with his left arm. "Your grandson here attacked us without provocation. He shot Screaming Eagle in the arm. Screaming Eagle is Chief Arimo's nephew and apprentice War Chief. Chief Arimo will not be happy about this attack by his fellow Mormons. The Chief is a Mormon, too, just in case y'all haven't heard."

Connal Lee untied Jeff's hands and gave him a hard shove in the back. Jeff staggered towards his grandfather, who clutched him in a hug. "I'm sorry, Grandpa. I thought we were under attack by renegade Injuns come to ransack our town. When I spotted a fierce warrior on a war stallion wearing a big war bonnet, I acted out of instinct." Sobbing silently, Jeff hugged his grandfather. "I'm sorry, Grandpa. I'm sorry. I made a mistake. I don't never want to let you down, Grandpa. You know I don't."

The old man patted the shaken boy on the back while he inspected Connal Lee from top to bottom. He saw a clear-eyed young man dressed in fancy beaded doeskin clothing. He took in Connal Lee's fine horse, weaponry, and confident stance. "Quiet now, Jeff. Yer safe, now. Go inside and change yer pants, then come back out and join us."

Jeff ducked into the tiny log cabin. The gray-bearded old man stepped over to Connal Lee with his right arm extended for a handshake. "My name is Jedediah Jason Morgan, Mister Swinton, was it? Please relax and join us for a spell while I get to the bottom of this. I would invite you in, but all the furniture has already gone south as we are evacuating the area."

"Ah've heard about the exodus south, Mister Morgan, but this is the first I've seen of it."

"Please come have a seat on the front step so we can work this out."

"My family and fellow delegates are furious about your grandson attacking us without provocation. Believe you me, we're going to make a full report to Governor Brigham Young as soon as we arrive in Great Salt Lake City."

"I don't blame you, young man. Now, please sit down and rest a spell."

Jeff returned, smelling much better, his head bowed in shame at having disappointed his grandfather. Connal Lee retrieved the old musket and handed it to Jedediah Morgan. "Thank you, young sir. I was afraid Jeff lost it. I carried this here flintlock to the Mexican-American War with the rest of the Mormon Battalion. We walked nearly two thousand miles from Council Bluffs, Iowa to San Diego, California. Then it came with me when I drove a wagon and team from Los Angeles up to Great Salt Lake City, another nearly seven hundred miles. It's saved my life more than once. Thank you for returning it to me."

"I'm sorry, Grandpa. I just reacted. I didn't think. I was alarmed at seeing Injuns with war bonnets and just reacted."

"Let's all sit down now. Let's let calmer heads prevail. I'm sure this is something we can all work out, somehow."

Jeff glanced at Connal Lee. "I'm sorry, Mister Swinton. How can I make it up to your Mister Eagle? I'm so, so sorry."

Connal Lee took sympathy on the Mormon farm boy. He stood up and plopped his hat back on his head. "Tell you what, Jeff. We're going to rest a day for Screaming Eagle to start mending before we continue on our diplomatic mission to Great Salt Lake City. Ah invite y'all to come join us at noon and share dinner with us. We can discuss it then. Ah'm too tired right now to even think about it." He shook hands with Jedediah and Jeff. "Goodbye. If y'all are serious about apologizing, come visit our camp. So long now."

The next day just before noon, Connal Lee and his family, sitting around the fireplace, heard horses approaching. Everyone stood up except Screaming Eagle. Screaming Eagle sat, once again, leaning against a box elder maple's gnarly trunk, shaded from the sun. Connal Lee walked forward to meet the visitors. He pointed to where they had tethered their horses. "Peace. Please leave your horses over there and come meet my family."

Jedediah Morgan raised his hand in the peace sign. "Peace, Mister Swinton. Peace, everyone. Thank you."

Jeff raised his hand, too. "Peace."

When the poorly dressed Mormon settlers walked up to the cookfire, Connal Lee made introductions. Short Rainbow indicated with a sweep of her hand for the guests to join them around the fire. Before he sat down, Jeff glanced over at Screaming Eagle. "Mister Eagle, I apologize most sincerely for shooting you yesterday. I know now I made a big mistake. I wish I could say it was an accident, but it wasn't. I shot without thinking, and for that, I ask your forgiveness."

Jeff gazed pleadingly at Screaming Eagle, watching his face to see how we would respond. "Huh! Good words. No good hurt. I no can fight. Wounded." Screaming Eagle gave the cowering teenager a stern scowl. "You know English word compensate?"

Jeff nodded yes with a frown, concerned about where this might be going.

"How you compensate for wound, for hurt?"

"I don't know, Mister Eagle. What would you accept in compensation?"

Connal Lee interrupted. "Our apprentice War Chief is named Screaming Eagle. Eagle is not his last name."

"Oh. All right. I understand." Jeff looked down at the ground, conscious of all the eyes on him. "What can I do for you, Screaming Eagle, so you will forgive me?"

White Wolf spoke up. "Do you have fine horse to give Screaming Eagle?"

Jeff looked at the strong horses in the camp's small herd. He looked at his swayed-back old broodmare. Silently, he shook his head no.

Short Rainbow looked up from cooking. "You have fine clothing to make amends?"

Jeff looked at how clean and neat all the Shoshone were dressed in finely beaded doeskin and shook his head.

Short Rainbow frowned. "Food, dry for travel?"

"I'm sorry, Missus Rainbow, but all our food went south for safekeeping."

White Wolf stood up. "Then, to make amends must come with us. Screaming Eagle need someone tend him. He can't take care of self. You agree?"

"But...but...my grandpa needs me! Bishop Snow called us to protect Box Elder from the army. If General Johnston invades, Grandpa isn't young enough or strong enough to ride in a hurry to all the farmsteads and burn all the houses and barns." He turned pleading eyes to Jedediah. "Please, Grandpa, what am I going to do? I can't leave you alone. I promised Bishop Snow."

Jedediah Morgan nodded silently at his grandson, waiting to see what the Shoshone had in mind.

Screaming Eagle frowned fiercely. "You nothing offer? Why me let go? Shoshone way eye for eye, hurt for hurt if no compensate. No horse? No clothes? No food? Then, eye for eye!"

Now quivering nervously, Jeff looked imploringly at his grandfather. "What do you mean, Screaming Eagle? Eye for eye?"

Connal Lee looked up from where he sat beside the fire. "While crossing the great plains, I read Captain Hanover's Bible and the Book of Mormon. I read where the Hebrew law calls for an eye for an eye and a hand for a hand. You must take a gunshot wound to your arm if you can't do anything else to earn Screaming Eagles' forgiveness."

"But...Mister Swinton, sir, Christ came to earth and taught us to leave the old law and turn the other cheek."

Screaming Eagle shouted angrily, "I no Christian. What? I turn right arm, let you shoot? No!"

Jedediah stood up and placed his arm protectively around the quivering young farmer's narrow shoulders. "Have courage, Jeff, my boy. Stand up straight and strong. You made a mistake, and now you have to pay the price."

Jedediah had already decided he trusted these young people. Rather than defend his grandson, he decided to wait and see what the Indians wanted for their justice. He could always intervene if he objected to their decision. Jeff looked up pleadingly into his grandfather's warm, sympathetic eyes. "I can't, Grandpa. I'm scared."

He tucked his face into the old man's shoulders. Connal Lee stood up, all business. "Well, let's get this over with. We don't have all day. Short Rainbow, y'all are the best shot in the family. Since Screaming Eagle can't hold his shotgun, please take care of it."

Short Rainbow rose gracefully to her feet and skipped lightly over to the packs beside the horses. She pulled out her shotgun, loaded a single lead ball, then smiled up at Connal Lee.

Connal Lee walked over and grabbed Jeff by his right arm. "Come on. It will only take a second. Be brave. If y'all are not brave, Screaming Eagle will think y'all are a coward and not worthy of his forgiveness. The Shoshone value bravery very highly. So, tell me, are y'all brave? Did y'all make a stupid mistake and have to pay the consequences? Yes. Yes. And yes. Come!"

Connal Lee jerked Jeff out of his grandfather's embrace and spun him around to face Short Rainbow standing beside the packs thirty feet away. Without any hesitation, Short Rainbow aimed and fired.

Blam!

The bullet passed harmlessly between Jeff's left arm and skinny torso. He felt the breeze of its passing.

Jeff fell to his knees. He thought his heart had stopped. He feared he had been killed, only he didn't feel any pain. He muttered under his breath fearfully, waiting for another shot from the double-barrel shotgun, "Please, Lord, don't let them kill me. Please. Please."

Connal Lee pulled Jeff to his feet. He spun Jeff around and looked him square in the eye, then gripped Jeff's shoulders. He felt Jeff quivering with nerves, nearly going into shock from fright. "Y'all showed yourself to be a brave man, Jeff. Y'all stood up and took your punishment like a man. By this, y'all proved yourself worthy of Screaming Eagle's leniency. Now, come join my family around our fire. It's time to eat dinner and Ah'm hungry!"

Jeff turned and hugged his grandfather, then burst into tears, overflowing with strong emotions. Fear. Nerves. Relief. Embarrassment. Disbelief the ordeal was over so fast. Jedediah patted Jeff on the back. "There, there, boy. You did good. Real good. You can stop crying now. Come, let's go sit down like Mister Swinton invited us and join them in breaking bread. There, there. Stop crying, Jeff. It's all over. Come on."

Jeff stood up tall, wiped his cheeks with his hands, then pulled his shoulders back. Putting on a brave face, he walked over to stand before Screaming Eagle and bowed his head contritely. Screaming Eagle nodded. "Brave. Good. You earn forgive. I no anger now. Sit. Eat."

"Oh, thank you, Screaming Eagle. I'm so sorry I caused you pain with my stupidity."

"Done. Finish. Sit. Eat."

Jeff nodded his head with a weak smile. "Thank you, Screaming Eagle. Thank you."

Jeff walked back to the fireplace and sat down Indian-style next to his elderly grandfather. He glanced around at all the bright eyes watching him from around the fire, then looked down bashfully at the fire. Short Rainbow served him a fillet of trout on a piece of white birch tree bark.

"Thank you, Missus Rainbow."

After they finished eating, White Wolf and Short Rainbow changed Screaming Eagle's dressing. While they worked, Connal Lee glanced over at the Morgans. "So, Mister Morgan. How did y'all end up here on the frontier doing guard duty for the Mormon Church?"

All eyes turned to the old man. He coughed self-consciously into his fist, then looked up at Connal Lee. "Well, Brother Swinton – may I call you Brother Swinton?"

Connal Lee nodded his head yes. "That's what Captain Hanover and everyone in the handcart company called me as we crossed the great plains. Ah know that's how Mormons address each other. Shall we call y'all Brother Morgan?"

"Yes, please. Anyway, I was born in seventeen ninety-four in Herefordshire, England. When I was growing up, times were tough. I couldn't find work, so I enlisted for a seven-year term in the British Army as a fusilier when I turned sixteen. They assigned me to work with the army's engineers building bridges. When I received my discharge at the age of twenty-three, I went to work as a civilian doing carpentry. Because of the skills I learned in the army and my experience in building bridges, I ended up working with a group of civilian engineers building railway bridges. I got married as soon as I was discharged and returned home. My oldest son, Jeff's father,

67

was born to us in eighteen twenty. We named him after me, but we called him Jay Jay. We didn't want to call him Junior.

"About the time I turned forty-six, I met Brigham Young. At that time, he was the senior Apostle of the Church's Twelve Apostles. The apostles were in England doing missionary work. They converted four thousand saints during their mission. Brigham Young taught me himself. I was thrilled at the message of a modern-day prophet speaking the Lord's words to us again, like back in Biblical times. He baptized me in, oh, let me think, yep, it was in forty-one. Brigham Young was ready to return to Nauvoo, so my family and I traveled to the United States of America with him.

"When we settled in Nauvoo, we loved it. Such a lovely city. Such a beautiful temple. The farmlands surrounding Nauvoo were rich and fertile. We thrived. Jay Jay's son, Jeff, was born in forty-two in Nauvoo. My lovely wife and I had four more children there. The Church asked me to join the Mormon Battalion in August of, when was it? Yep, in forty-six. At fifty-two years old, I was one of the most senior men in the Battalion. They issued me that model eighteen-sixteen flintlock musket I still have on my saddle over there. We marched on foot around two-thousand miles, opening up the southern route to California. We eventually ended up in San Diego. While I was away doing military service, the prophet was assassinated. Twenty thousand saints fled Nauvoo ahead of armed mobs. My wife and our nine children, three of whom were married, took our five grandchildren in one small covered wagon. They escaped Nauvoo during the great exodus of Mormons traveling here. They followed Brigham Young, without my help, to Great Salt Lake Valley with the second wave of settlers.

Connal Lee, always curious, interrupted. "What was the Mormon Battalion all about, Brother Morgan?"

"Well, you see, the United States went to war with Mexico over who would govern Mexico's northern territories. Those territories were down in what is now Texas, you know, and the Territory of New Mexico to the west of Texas. The Mormon Church offered to raise a regiment of volunteers. We formed the first religious regiment ever. All other regiments were raised in cities, counties, or states. In the end, Mexico ceded their northern territories to the

United States. President Polk took control of Mexico's northern territories and routes to the west coast, which was his goal.

"I mustered out in July of forty-seven. To earn a stake for my trip home, I went to work as a civilian building Fort Moore in Los Angeles. That's where I learned adobe construction. When they stopped work on the fort, I went to Sacramento with other veterans and worked for a while at Sutter's Mill. I was working there when they discovered gold. I'll never forget that date. It changed the west forever. It was the twenty-fourth of January back in forty-eight. The discovery of gold started the California gold rush that brought so many people across the continent to California. That's when the overland trails became major roadways. A year later, I helped transport seventeen thousand in gold, donated by the veterans of the Mormon Battalion, to Brigham Young in Great Salt Lake City.

"What a thrill to be reunited with my family and to renew the special friendship I had with Brigham Young. He was by then confirmed as the Church's second president and our modern-day prophet. He asked me to help build bridges and dams in Salt Lake Valley for the Department of Public Works. Three years later, because of my experience building with adobe, President Young asked me to work with the Church's architect, name of Truman O. Angell, to construct a big adobe tabernacle on Temple Square. It can seat two-thousand five hundred Saints under one roof at one time. Can you believe it?"

Short Rainbow and White Wolf finished rebandaging Screaming Eagle, then quietly approached the fire and took their seats.

"The following year, Brigham Young called me and all my family to accompany Lorenzo Snow to further develop the little settlement founded by William Davis back in the early fifties. Brother Davis named the area Box Elder Canyon after the maple trees flourishing in the area. Lorenzo Snow assembled his entire family of nine wives and eighteen children into a great wagon train with all of their belongings. My family joined the train along with nineteen other large families. Lorenzo Snow is one of the Church's Twelve Apostles, in addition to serving as our Bishop and Mayor.

"The flatlands along the Bear River, between the Wasatch Mountains and the Great Salt Lake, are rich and fertile with lots of water available for irrigation. My beloved wife of thirty-eight years passed away in eighteen fifty-five after a lingering illness. Our children were all grown, married, and on their own. I was getting old and starting to feel my age, so I sold my farm to my third son and his two wives. Jeff's parents invited me to move in with them. That was three years ago. Now, all my family has moved with the Box Elder Ward down south of Provo for their safety. We miss them, don't we, Jeff?"

Jeff nodded his head, sadly, homesick for his parents, especially after the traumatic last two days. He yearned for a comforting hug from his mama.

Connal Lee stood up. "Well, Brother Morgan, Ah've got to ride out and hunt down something for our supper. Is there anything we can do for y'all now that we are friends?"

Jedediah stood up. Jeff scrambled up quickly to join him. "As a matter of fact, Brother Swinton, I wrote my friend Brigham Young a letter. I took full responsibility for Jeff's mistake. I believe I was overzealous in instructing Jeff on his duty, perhaps with too many examples from my military experience. I apologized and asked Brigham Young to please forgive Jeff and me for our mistakes in judgment. Would you kindly carry this letter to our beloved prophet when you go on to Great Salt Lake City?"

Connal Lee stepped over and accepted the letter, written on a folded piece of brown wrapping paper. "It will be my pleasure to take y'all's letter to Governor Young, Brother Morgan. Well, Ah'm off. A pleasure to meet y'all, suh. Jeff, Ah wish ya lots of luck. Ah certainly hope y'all don't have to torch this settlement. Please be more careful before ya start shooting at people. It could land y'all in a heap of trouble otherwise. We'll look y'all up on our return trip if y'all are still living here. Ah don't know when that will be, though. So long, now."

Still embarrassed, Jeff silently nodded his head. As Connal Lee walked off to saddle his horses, Jeff waved goodbye.

The Shoshone delegation prepared to depart the lush Bear River valley the following day. White Wolf and Short Rainbow helped Screaming Eagle wash up. They changed the bandage on his arm. White Wolf made a simple sling to take the weight off the wounded bicep. Short Rainbow tied the wounded arm to Screaming Eagle's ribs so riding wouldn't bounce it around as much. "Now, if the pain of riding becomes too great, let us know. We can make you a comfortable nest on top of one of the travois. Traveling by travois won't jostle your arm nearly as much as riding a horse."

"What? Ride the travois like a papoose? I'm no baby!"

"No need to be brave with us, bearing pain unnecessarily. We're all family. If your arm hurts worse, it means the bouncing has reopened the wounds. All we want is for you to heal. The quicker the better. Do you understand, you great grumpy bear? If the wounds begin bleeding again, it will take you longer to heal."

Screaming Eagle gave a quick nod in answer, vowing to himself he would never be humiliated by riding on a travois.

Two and a half hours later, the train of travois walked closer to Willow Creek Fort, a simple adobe and fieldstone wall. The lovely farming valley appeared deserted. Massive granite cliffs reared out of the mountains to the east like stone walls. Several miles to the west, the Great Salt Lake could barely be seen as a thin line of reflective water on the flat horizon. They had nearly passed the little fort when they saw two burly young men approaching at a gallop, shotguns in hand. Connal Lee shouted out for everyone to halt. "Stay here, if you please. Ah'll handle this."

Connal Lee rode towards the guards at a businesslike trot. As he grew closer, he called ahead, "Hello, my friends. We come in peace. We are a Shoshone Delegation invited to attend Governor Brigham Young in Great Salt Lake City."

The three drew together and chatted briefly, still on horseback. "With y'all's permission, we will continue riding south. We're just passing through on our way to the Beehive House to meet with our friend, Governor Brigham Young. Good luck to y'all. Ah hope there's no need to burn the settlement here. It looks like a very pleasant place to live. So long, now. And good luck!"

Not wishing to have any unpleasant confrontations with guards left to protect other settlements along the corridor, they traveled further west off the beaten trail. They avoided Bingham's Fort, Mound Fort, and Fort Buenaventura. They stopped for the day only some twelve miles south of Willow Creek Fort. Screaming Eagle needed rest. The clouds blowing overhead looked like they might bring rain, so they erected the tent just to be safe. Connal Lee rode out hunting.

Screaming Eagle had become exhausted after riding for only four hours and needed help dismounting. Short Rainbow scolded him at great length for not speaking up and riding on a travois. They all worked together to get him settled comfortably on his sleeping furs in the tent. White Wolf changed his dressing, carefully inspecting it for the first signs of infection. The four women bustled about setting up camp and building a cookfire. Connal Lee returned with several fat grouse for their supper.

Their slightly worn pathway led them close to the Fort of Farmington after two more partial days of travel. Arimo helped them unsaddle the horses and lower the travoises to the ground, then announced he wanted to go see if his friend Andrew had made it home safely from Fort Lemhi. Connal Lee decided he better accompany Arimo to translate. He didn't want to see any harm come to his adopted brother because of any misunderstanding. White Wolf rode off hunting for their supper while the young women set up camp.

Connal Lee and Arimo rode past abandoned farms, searching for someone who could give them directions to Andrew Hayes' home. As they drew near the simple Fort, two men rode out to challenge them. Connal Lee introduced themselves and explained their mission. The guards relaxed. When Connal Lee inquired as to the location of Andrew Hayes' farmstead, the older of the guards nodded his head. "Yep. I know where Andy an' Ely make their farm. Andrew still isn't back from Fort Lemhi, but 'is first wife, Ely, is there a waitin' fer 'im. She got word he's wounded. The rest of 'is family left with the others o' the ward, headin' south below Provo with most o' their belongin's."

"Thanks. That's what we wanted to know. Good luck protecting y'all's settlement. We hope y'all don't have to burn it down. We'll be off, back to our camp. Tomorrow we will move on to Great Salt Lake City. So long, now."

After he returned to camp, they had to wake Screaming Eagle up from a nap to eat his supper. Short Rainbow kept reaching out and placing her slender hand across his broad forehead, checking for the first hint of fever. White Wolf changed the dressing. He examined the wound and sniffed the dressing, relieved he found no signs of infection or inflammation. The sutured wounds were closing up and scabbing over nicely. Exhausted, they all took to their beds early.

The next day dawned bright and clear. The Shoshone delegation loaded up their camp and departed around seven. The temperature gradually warmed up from a chilly forty degrees during the night. They followed the well-worn path leading south.

They soon spotted a great train of white-topped wagons moving towards them, small in the distance. A caravan of covered wagons, freight wagons, farm wagons, and two carriages approached. When they drew close, Connal Lee pulled his brown mare to the side of the roadway and waited for the lead wagon. A simply dressed man pulled on the reins of the first wagon until the ox team stopped. Connal Lee saw a man in his forties with dark hair brushed back in a wave. The stranger wore a trimmed beard, but his mustache had been shaved off. The driver stood up in his seat. Connal Lee rode closer. "Good morning, suh. Ah'm Connal Lee Swinton, the adopted son of Chief Arimo." Connal Lee pointed at his family with their train of travoises. "The Chief sent my adopted family and me as a delegation representing the Shoshone Nation at the invitation of Governor Brigham Young."

"Good morning, Mister Swinton. I am Lorenzo Snow, one of the Apostles of the Mormon Church and the Bishop of Box Elder Ward. How do you do? I'm traveling back to my home and hotel in Box Elder to salvage all the hotel's furniture that we can."

"Box Elder Fort? We visited there just a few days ago and met Jedediah and Jeff Morgan, the guards y'all left behind. All is well up there. Is there anything we should know about the road between here and Great Salt Lake City?"

"Well, young man, the road will grow increasingly crowded, going in both directions, especially as you near Beehive House on the corner of Brigham Street and State Road. Everyone is turning onto State Road to take the cleared road directly down and around the point of the mountain heading towards Provo. Brigham Young and all his family are still in residence. Although he has begun moving furniture, musical instruments, stoves, and lots of provisions south in great wagon trains. He has his sons and employees ferrying back and forth between the Brigham Young Estate and Provo, salvaging everything possible. I met with him briefly yesterday, only long enough to pray together, then I returned back to my work. You might want to take only your riding horses when you visit the Governor, as the roadways will be crowded with wagons, carriages, and herds of livestock."

"My thanks, suh. Best of luck to y'all on the way back north. Please tell the Morgans we sent our best wishes. So long, now."

The Shoshone travois train passed alongside the twenty-seven wagons of Lorenzo Snow's family wagon train. Connal Lee waved his leather cowboy hat goodbye as they rode past.

Screaming Eagle began hurting and needed a rest. They were ahead of schedule and could spare the time, so they pitched camp early. The next day Connal Lee and his family stopped for a brief cold midday meal shortly before they reached Fort Bountiful. They knew they only had another couple of miles before they arrived at Great Salt Lake City.

By now, they all knew the way to Chief SoYo'Cant's favorite campsite outside the west gate of the city walls. They pitched their tents, tethered their livestock beside a feeder creek of the large Jordan River, and freshened up. Late that afternoon, they helped Screaming Eagle onto his big horse. He proudly donned his war bonnet and led the delegation towards Beehive House. The traffic on Brigham Street grew as heavy as Lorenzo Snow had warned. They rode in single file until they neared Beehive House. Screaming Eagle saw the hitching posts close to Beehive House packed with horses, buggies, and carriages. They hitched their horses in front of Temple Square, then walked the two long blocks east to Beehive House. With all the traffic on the avenue, as well as all the men milling around the Governor's Mansion, they had to wend their way through the crowd to reach the open gate.

As soon as they entered, Connal Lee spotted the dashing Major Harris waving at them from the covered porch of Beehive House. Connal Lee's eyes opened wide in awe at the major's gorgeous dress uniform. A dark blue jacket stopped at the waist with tails in the back. The jacket had a single row of polished brass buttons down the center. Fringed epaulets embroidered with acorns accentuated the major's broad shoulders, which in turn emphasized his slender waist. The jacket's high upstanding collar, topped with a white shirt collar, accented the major's long neck and proud bearing. Tight white britches, with the major's manhood dressing left, were tucked into highly polished black knee-high riding boots. A brilliant red sash with tasseled ends held his sword's polished brass sheath from his right shoulder and then wrapped his trim waist.

The major strode towards the delegation with his hand held out and a welcome smile on his even open face. "Let me be the first to welcome you, Mister Swinton, and fellow Shoshone delegates." Major Harris shook hands all around, then smiled at Connal Lee. He gestured back towards the street with a big sweep of his right hand. He had to speak up to be heard over all the commotion. "Please follow me a short distance to the Social Hall. It's just across State Road and down half a block. It will be quieter there, easier to talk."

"Lead on, Major Harris. We will follow y'all."

When they reached the intersection, two broad ditches of clear running water flowing down each side of the broad street amazed Connal Lee. They had to walk across six-foot-long footbridges to reach the dirt road, then cross another bridge to the raised footpath on the far side. Major Harris explained they had diverted the water from City Creek to the north to water newly transplanted trees. "We want to have tree-lined avenues like in the great cities of the world."

As they walked across the extra-wide street, Connal Lee watched the constant traffic of big freight wagons, covered wagons, and carriages heading south, overflowing with foodstuffs and personal belongings. A train of empty wagons traveled in the opposite direction, returning to pick up more salvage and cached foods. "Bishop Lorenzo Snow was right, Major Harris. This traffic looks like one long wagon train, doesn't it?"

They arrived at the spacious two-story adobe hall only to find it full of men, most in uniforms, clustered in groups. A low din of conversation saturated the building. "Sorry, Mister Swinton, but I thought it would be quieter here. When I hitched my horse behind the hall this morning, it was certainly nice and quiet. I guess others had the same idea."

Connal Lee sized up the situation in a glance. "Major Harris, suh, if Ah might suggest. Let's pick up our horses and return to our camp on the Jordan River unless we have some business to attend to here in the city. It's peaceful and quiet out there."

"No. We have no business we can't discuss at your camp. Excellent idea. Where did you leave your mounts?"

"We hitched them up in front of Temple Square."

"I'll fetch my horse and meet you there."

Five minutes later, Major Harris arrived riding his big prancing stallion. Connal Lee thought he looked very dashing wearing his feathered hat at a jaunty angle. Today the major wore a brass acorn leaf major's insignia on the front of the hat's crown. The major waited while everyone mounted up, then pulled his horse up beside Connal Lee's sprightly mare. "Mister Swinton, I think I want to change into my regular uniform and keep my dress uniform spotless for tomorrow's formal festivities. My home is not far away. I'm going to go change. Then I'll meet you beside the Jordan River. I'll only be about fifteen or twenty minutes behind you."

"All right, Major. We're the only camp with two tipis on the Jordan River. We should not be hard to find."

When they arrived at their camp, the two Shoshone families removed their horses' bridles and saddles. The four men tethered the horses with the others down beside the wide river where they could find grass and water. The four girls had stayed behind to light their cookfire and prepare a hot supper. Soon the major rode up on his prancing stallion wearing the same everyday uniform he had worn when he visited Chief SoYo'Cant's winter camp. Connal Lee strode over to lend the Major a hand taking care of his horse. They led the handsome stallion down by the river and tethered him to the rest of the horses.

By the time they returned to the fireplace, they could smell the sizzling of venison steaks and wild onions frying. Connal Lee's stomach growled. "Major, please take a seat and join us for supper. We've been traveling all day and have worked up quite the appetite."

The major nodded and sank down to sit Indian-style next to Connal Lee. "Thank you, Mister Swinton. It's very nice of you to invite me. I find myself hungry too, now that you mention it."

They watched while White Wolf carefully changed Screaming Eagle's bandages. The major nudged Connal Lee with his elbow. "What happened to Screaming Eagle, Mister Swinton?"

"Well, suh, when we rode close to Box Elder Fort, an excited young Mormon guard mistook us for renegade Indians and shot Screaming Eagle right off his horse. Ah captured the young man and tied him up. After we set up camp and attended to Screaming Eagle, Ah took the scrawny teenager named Jeff back to his grandfather, Brother Jedediah Morgan, at their farmstead. Bishop Lorenzo Snow had assigned them to stay behind and protect the community and burn it should Johnston's army arrive. The next day, the two Morgans showed up at our camp so Jeff could apologize to Screaming Eagle. Screaming Eagle demanded compensation. Since the boy had nothing to offer, Screaming Eagle applied Shoshone law and demanded an eye for an eye. Ah grabbed the boy out of his grandfather's arms and stood him up facing Short Rainbow. Short Rainbow is the best shot among us. She aimed at the boy and fired one shot. It passed harmlessly between Jeff's ribs and left arm. Even though he nearly passed out from fright, he didn't cower or call out. Screaming Eagle felt satisfied Jeff paid the price of his error in attacking us unprovoked and learned his lesson. We invited them to eat with us. We talked a while and became friends before we left."

Major Harris gave Connal Lee a stern look, then shook his head, amazed. "So, listen, Mister Swinton."

Connal Lee held up his palm. "Major Harris, please call me Connal Lee. Mister Swinton is my old man, not me. There's no need for formalities among friends and allies, now, is there?"

"Very well, Connal Lee. Thank you. Please call me Robert, except in front of my men when I am on duty. Now, as I was about to say, I would like to tell you and your delegation something in the strictest confidence. Please don't reveal what I'm about to tell you to anyone until after you hear about it from other people. Can you all agree to keep my secret?"

Connal Lee translated for the others to make sure they understood. They all nodded their heads or said yes. "Yes, Major Robert. We all agree to secrecy. So what is it? Ah'm dying of curiosity, now."

"Well, my friends, the officers and strategic brains of the Legion came up with a subterfuge that has Governor Young's blessing."

"Sorry to interrupt again, Major Robert, suh, but what's sutterfooj?"

"What? Oh, the word is subterfuge, Connal Lee. It means playing a trick, like creating an illusion. It means deceiving the enemy to help achieve our ends."

Connal Lee nodded silently, then looked anxiously at the Major, waiting for him to explain.

"We made the plan weeks ago, timed for when the new Governor, Alfred Cumming, was scheduled to leave Camp Scott and come to Great Salt Lake City. This took place back a week ago, on the fifth of April. Our good General William Kimball took a large honor escort of militia officers and men. They met the new Governor after he came through the Federal military lines. The Governor was traveling in a fancy carriage drawn by six decrepit donkeys with Colonel Kane as his guide. Two black servants accompanied them. One drove the carriage. The other drove the luggage wagon. The Nauvoo Legion rendered Governor Cumming full military honors, including presenting arms with four flourishes and a nineteen-gun salute. They had to use rifles as they had no cannons. They changed the Governor's starved donkeys for fresh horses.

"When they reached Echo Canyon some ways east of Great Salt Lake City, General Kimball persuaded the Governor to be a gentleman, since technically there still exists a state of war between the Federal government and the Territory of Utah. He convinced the governor to pass through the twelve-mile-long canyon at night, so he couldn't make notes on our fortifications to share with General Johnston. He agreed. The governor's escort told him we had stationed fifteen-hundred armed militiamen on top of the great cliffs overlooking the canyon, secure in dug-outs, camps, and rifle blinds. The closer they took the governor to the narrows, the more bonfires and campfires he saw burning atop the fortifications. With only a hundred fifty militiamen, our men had built three-hundred fifty campfires on the hillsides, with most of them burning along the high cliff top."

Kimana interrupted the Major when she served him a thin venison steak. Short Rainbow danced by handing out gourd bowls of a savory kidney and vegetable stew. After he finished eating, the Major looked around at his hosts and allies. "The carriage and attending parade reached a checkpoint at the first bend of Echo Canyon before the narrows. The governor and his escort were stopped by sharply yelled demands and the clanking of arms. Our pickets demanded the countersign to prove they were authorized to pass. Once cleared, the guards obeyed the shouted orders of their sergeant and presented their arms as a salute to the governor. Governor Cumming stepped out of his great carriage and addressed the militiamen. Standing outside his carriage, he looked up and saw what appeared to be cannons lit by campfires. Little did he know they were trunks of cedar trees painted black and placed over the top of the fortifications."

Connal Lee shook his head, delighted at the trick. The Major accepted a tin mug of black coffee, blew on it, then took a sip. "The armed men came to attention and saluted the governor when he passed. After he moved out of sight, they ducked around in the dark to rush ahead to salute the governor again, further along. At the second checkpoint, they heard a bugle sound the call to arms. The men staged a mock effort at taking the governor prisoner. But at the last minute, officers arrived just in time to save Cumming. After General Kimball supplied the password, the men saluted the governor when he stepped out of his carriage. The governor made another short speech. When Cumming got in his carriage, the men dispersed into the dark of night. They jogged ahead to intercept him at the third checkpoint, where the same men heard the same speech for the third time. The caravan exited Echo Canyon around eleven that evening and camped at Weber Station. We hoped to convince the new governor that we had the narrow passage into Great Salt Lake

City so heavily armed we could cause General Johnston's army serious damage if they were to try to push their way through. You see?"

Everyone nodded their heads. Connal Lee grinned. "Good trick, Major Robert. Ah bet it gave the new governor a right scare."

"Well, we certainly hope so. They are traveling towards us now, using the same route to Great Salt Lake City that Brigham Young traveled when he led the Saints into the valley. I was given the enviable assignment of arranging a warm welcome for the governor, showing him that we have additional fortifications before they enter the City. They will be passing at dusk tonight through Fort Wells at the mouth of Little Emigration Canyon. Fort Wells is the grandiose name of two hills commanding the mouth of Little Emigration Canyon, where we built two artillery batteries. The batteries have the trail in their crossfire. Yesterday I ordered a small detachment of militia to go man the batteries. I sent a messenger ahead to advise General Kimball of our subterfuge since I made my plans just two days ago. I asked the general to inform Governor cumming that we have a full regiment of a thousand militiamen stationed on both sides of the canyon walls to defend the city as a last resort. My problem is, we don't have that many men available. Most of our soldiers are relocating their families and possessions south. I selected a hundred of my young unmarried men, who were not busy protecting their families, to go put on a bit of theater. The past couple of days, my men have laid fifty fires of all different sizes along the steep canyon roadway. We plan to greet the governor's carriage when he enters the valley with our fires blazing. Armed soldiers will stand up and escort the carriage until it pulls ahead. Then our men will duck down and run ahead, behind the fires, so they don't show up and reappear down the road – just like we did back at Echo Canyon."

Connal Lee's face lit up, delighted at the idea of playacting to fool the new governor again. "Yes, suh. What a great idea!"

"Now, yesterday, when I was making plans to meet you today, I had an inspiration. How would you and your delegation like to join us on the fire watch so the governor sees we have native Indian allies fighting at our side? Would you like to join my cast of thespians and help me deceive the new governor? It should actually be a bit of a lark."

"Excuse me for interrupting again, Major Robert, suh. But what's a thesbian?"

The Major smiled. "A *thespian* is someone who takes to the stage to entertain an audience. You know, actors and performers."

"Oh. Now Ah understand, Major."

Connal Lee explained what the word meant to his family.

"You realize, of course, the new governor will send reports to the army. The army is, after all, under his nominal command as Territorial Governor. We hope he makes General Johnston fear the canyons leading into Great Salt Lake Valley from Echo Canyon all the way to the city limits. Are you interested in joining my subterfuge?"

"Oh, yes, Major Robert. Excuse me while Ah explain to those of my family who don't understand English so well."

Connal Lee explained the plans. They all liked the idea. White Wolf ordered Screaming Eagle to stay behind to protect Bright Star, Kimana, and Koko, who didn't want to join them. Screaming Eagle objected strenuously. Finally, he acknowledged it would be too exhausting for him to walk and jog a couple of miles in the dark with his fresh wounds. Connal Lee asked him to lend them his war bonnet to add to the deceit. "Oh, Major Robert. Ah like this game of subterfuge. Now, what would y'all like us to do?"

"Well, let's put on our thinking caps and work out how to integrate you into my plans. We'll need to leave right after eating supper to be in place before dark. We have more than a ten-mile trip due west up the canyon. My new phase of the plan is to meet the governor's carriage close to the city after they pass the fortifications at the top of Little Emigration Canyon. It will be full dark by the time they get here."

The major invited Arimo, Short Rainbow, and White Wolf to put plenty of feathers in their hair to help make them more recognizable as Indians. With great smiles of anticipation on their faces, they saddled their horses and followed the major through the city and up to Little Emigration Canyon. When they reached the first of the unlit fires closest to the city, they hobbled the horses and continued on foot. The major chose the less steep south side of the canyon since his guests didn't know the terrain. He led them in a small parade walking east. He greeted his men already in position with torches burning, ready to light the fires when night descended, and the governor arrived. They strolled along for over an hour, occasionally stumbling over unseen obstructions until they finally reached the first unlit bonfire at the far eastern end. "Sit down and rest, now. We need to wait until we see the carriage lanterns on the governor's fancy carriage and six. We'll hear the honor guards' horses in plenty of time to take our positions. Remember, each time you change places, hold your weapons differently, change your weapons, and pass the war bonnet around. We want the governor to think we are a mass of infantry guarding the city. Are you ready?"

Everyone nodded eagerly. "Ready."

"Excellent. The governor should be arriving soon."

At the first sign of the approaching parade, the soldiers on both sides of the canyon lit their bonfires, signaling for all the campfires to be set ablaze. After the soldiers on the canyon's west end lit their fires, they jogged over to cluster around the first fires on the east end. When the great carriage lumbered into view, everyone stood up and watched the governor and his honor guard pass by below. They held their rifles across their chests in Port Arms position to salute the governor. Then they milled around the fires so the governor could identify them all as armed militiamen. The Shoshone danced in and out, rushing forward to get a better view, then shaking their bows or rifles overhead threateningly. A couple of the youngest men waved merrily at the carriage as it passed by. As soon as the carriage cleared the first fires, everyone ducked down and hurried to the next fire so they could repeat the play-acting. Connal Lee couldn't stop chuckling.

When the guards reached the last bonfire, they watched as the carriage started down into the valley, heading to the hot springs where the mayor and other local officials waited to greet the new governor. "Thank you, my friends. You did an excellent job. Any time you want to take roles in acting, just ask me for a recommendation. You were wonderful. Perfect improvisation, shaking your feathered war bows in the air, Arimo and White Wolf. Just right! Now, it's getting late. Let's mount up, and I will escort you back to your camp."

When they approached the two tipis, Connal Lee invited the major to spend the night with them. "Thank you, Connal Lee. Normally I would, but my home is not that far away. Besides, I should probably be there if my commanders try to find me. They will probably want a full report tonight of how our theatrical event played out. Besides, I'm sure I'll receive a summons to attend General Kimball first thing in the morning, now that he has returned to Legion headquarters with Governor Cumming. With your permission, I will return tomorrow two hours past high noon. Please dress in your finest ceremonial clothing. We will all be attending a small but formal reception in the home of Elder Staines, one of our territorial delegates. He will be hosting the new governor and Colonel Kane in his gracious home three blocks west of Beehive House. Good night everyone. Thank you all, once again, for your help tonight."

After traveling all day and then scampering around the rocky side of a canyon for three hours, everyone fell into their blankets, exhausted.

Chapter 5: Diplomacy

After they woke up, Connal Lee and his family joined Arimo and his family taking leisurely baths in a side eddy of the surging Jordan River. Their camp stood a few miles west of Temple Square beside the broad river. The tree and grass-lined river ran brown, but the water washed them clean, anyway.

After they ate a light noon meal, they saddled their horses for the trip to the city. When ready, they began dressing for the formal reception to meet the new governor. They groomed each other's hair very elaborately but differently from when they attended the council of war back in November. Short Rainbow got creative with Connal Lee's hair, pulling it into a short ponytail. She tied the ponytail with three thin leather ribbons, yellow, brown, and blue. Eagle feathers died to match danged from the ends of the ribbons. Each feather had two ceremonial notches, representing the two Crow enemies Connal Lee had killed in service to the tribe.

White Wolf carried over a bundle wrapped in soft doeskin and handed it to Connal Lee with a big grin. "We decided our spokesman needed more than used army clothing to represent the great Shoshone Nation in this delegation."

Connal Lee lifted up a new jacket. "Oh, thank you. It's the most beautiful jacket I've ever seen!"

The pale tanned doeskin, so soft it felt like velvet, sported a single row of buttons down the front. Short Rainbow had imitated cavalry epaulettes with beads. The jacket had a high collar, nearly touching Connal Lee's chin, solidly beaded with three bold stripes. Connal Lee's eyes grew large when he saw the britches cut after the pattern of his used army pants and dyed a pale blue. Triple lines of beading ran up the outer sides of the legs, similar to the yellow stripe on cavalry uniform pants.

They all helped Connal Lee into his new ceremonial uniform. He stood up proud, wishing he could see how he looked. Screaming Eagle tied a narrow headband of three rows of beads around his forehead and gave him a big hug. "Good. Now look proper delegate. Good."

"Thanks, everyone. Now Ah feel like one of y'all in every way. But, tell me, do the three colors signify something special?"

Short Rainbow smiled. "Yes. The brown represents the land and our Shoshone people's beautiful skin. The yellow represents white man's hair, the color of straw, for you and your Mormon friends. The blue represents the cavalry and your army family. See. You bring us all together in harmony."

"Oh. Ah love the symbolism. Thanks so much. How Ah love y'all, each and every one!" He walked around and shared a warm hug and kiss on the cheek with his entire family.

Arimo and Kimana joined them, also dressed in their ceremonial finest. Koko and Bright Star had decided to remain behind to guard the tipis and horses since they were neither great warriors nor diplomats. White Wolf held up his hand. "Wait a minute. One more thing." He pulled the hair bone breastplates out of the leather gift packages and ceremoniously tied them around Connal Lee and Arimo's necks. "These show the world that you are sons of the great Chief SoYo'Cant and future leaders of our Shoshone nation."

They sat down to relax around the fireplace while waiting for Major Harris to arrive. Connal Lee fingered the beading on his pant legs. "So, tell me, Short Rainbow. How did y'all manage to sew me up this beautiful suit of clothes without me ever knowing?"

Connal Lee noticed Short Rainbow exchange a glance with White Wolf. They both smiled at each other. "Well, husband, it is very hard to keep anything secret from you. You are always snooping around, asking about every little thing. We had to watch for when you left hunting, then work as fast as we could. At the first sign of your returning, we scurried to tuck the new clothing out of sight. We wanted to surprise you."

"Well, you sure managed to surprise me. And such a wonderful surprise. Ah love the way these new clothes fit and feel. Ah only wish Ah could see what Ah look like. Ah'm not a vain person, but Ah'm delighted to have nice clothes for important occasions like y'all have. Thanks again, everyone."

Screaming Eagle knew he couldn't wear his war bonnet inside their host's home for the reception, so he reluctantly left it behind.

Around two o'clock that afternoon, Major Harris galloped into the camp. Connal Lee's breath caught in his throat when he saw the dashing major arrive in his fancy dress uniform with tight white britches and cocky plumed hat. When the Major pulled on the reins of his great stallion, it reared dramatically and spun around before coming to a stop. It wanted to run and pulled at the bridle, tossing its head. With a firm hand, the major settled his mount. He smiled when he looked over the delegation in their finery. "Impressive. Most impressive, everyone. I'm so glad Brigham Young invited you to meet Governor Cumming. I dare say you will be quite the most popular guests at the reception. Are you ready? Then let's mount up and be on our way."

The major led the delegation at an easy trot back through the gateless opening in the city wall and then along Brigham Street. He stopped four long city blocks short of Beehive House in front of a lovely British cottage surrounded by English-style gardens. The adobe mansion sat on two and a half acres in a parklike setting. The owner, William Staines, hadn't followed the plan of the rest of the city. He had built the fancy three-story adobe bungalow one hundred thirty feet back from the avenue near the center of five combined city lots. A sizeable cold frame greenhouse stood on the home's west side for starting seeds and cuttings early in the spring. He had planted an orchard of prize specimen fruit trees in front of the house.

Mr. Staines, the foremost horticulturist in Utah, owned a thriving three-hundred-acre farm in Fort Bountiful, where he cultivated fruit tree seedlings and raised vegetables, fruits, and nuts. He also raised flowers for their seeds. When Mr. Staines first arrived, he served for a time as superintendent of the gardens and orchards on the Brigham Young estate. He became the first librarian of the new Territorial Library. He worked as an elected member of the territorial legislative assembly. He owned several businesses and shops, including the popular Globe restaurant in the growing metropolis.

Horses and buggies crowded the avenue in front of the home. A large fancy carriage drawn by six strong horses stood along the driveway to the carriage house. Connal Lee saw two young black men dressed in gray uniforms unharnessing the matching black draft horses. Major Harris invited everyone to dismount. They tied up their horses to the simple hitching posts along the broad avenue. "Please follow me. Let me introduce you to everyone inside."

They entered the wrought iron gate in the fence surrounding the property. As they walked through the gardens heading towards the front door, the lovely clusters of spring flowers amazed Connal Lee. He did not recognize most of them. The delegation walked through the subtle perfume of blooming apple trees. Connal Lee found himself taking deep breaths. He had never smelled such a lovely fragrance.

Before they climbed the steps to the tall double front doors flanked by four columns, a man opened the door on the right. He stood tall, a big man with piercing pale blue eyes and a long bushy beard that completely hid his bowtie. Major Harris introduced everyone to the doorman one at a time. "And this is Porter Rockwell, Deputy Marshall of Great Salt Lake City and personal bodyguard to the President of the Mormon Church, Brigham Young. He also served as a bodyguard to our beloved Prophet, Joseph Smith, back in Nauvoo."

Mr. Porter nodded and smiled at the delegation. "It's a pleasure to meet our friends and valued allies. You are expected. Please come in. You will find tables just inside for your hats, gloves, and weapons."

"Thank you, Brother Rockwell."

They left their hats and gloves on the varnished tables in the grand foyer. Connal Lee removed his holster and left his pistol and knife on the table. Major Harris retained his dress sword. They walked in and joined the growing crowd of dignitaries in the spacious parlor, well lit by three tall bay windows facing south. Major Harris spotted the rotund Governor Cumming standing beside a massive fireplace faux finished to look like polished marble, talking quite jovially with Brigham Young. Connal Lee observed a short bearded man in an army uniform standing beside the two heavyset, well-dressed gentlemen. He also noticed a shorter man with a twisted torso and small humpback. Major Harris led the way through the milling crowd of dignitaries towards Brigham Young.

Brigham Young saw him approaching. "Major Harris, please come and meet the territory's new governor. Governor Cumming, it is my pleasure to introduce one of the finest officers in the Nauvoo Legion, Major Robert Harris. Major Harris, this is my designated and duly authorized replacement, his excellency, Governor Alfred Cumming."

"How do you do, sir? On behalf of the officers and men of the Nauvoo Legion, please permit me to welcome you to the Territory of Utah."

"Thank you, Major. A pleasure to meet you, sir."

Brigham Young turned to the Shoshone delegation with a welcoming smile. "Governor Cumming, may I present Chief Arimo's delegation from our longtime friends and allies, the great Shoshone Nation. This dapper young man is Mister Connal Lee Swinton, the adopted son of Chief Arimo. Since he is a native-born English speaker, he acts as spokesman for the delegation. Although his adopted Shoshone family understand and speak English quite well on their own."

The heavy-weight governor stepped up to shake hands. "A delight to meet such an accomplished young man."

Connal Lee gave a short bow as he shook hands with the enormous man. "On the contrary, suh, the honor is all mine. We've been hearing about y'all, accompanied by a huge army, for some months now. It's a pleasure to welcome y'all here peacefully on behalf of the great Chief SoYo'Cant, whom the Mormons call Chief Arimo. Ah am at y'all's service, suh, as are all the Shoshone delegates here with me."

"Well, now. Do my ears hear the gentle speech of a fellow southerner? I, myself, was privileged to be born in the great state of Georgia."

"Perhaps, suh. Ah come from the back hills of the Missouri Ozarks. Since Ah learned to read and write while crossing the plains with a Mormon handcart company, my school teacher, Missus Lorna Baines, worked very hard to rid me of my hillbilly accent. It appears as though a touch of a southern accent still lingers on, though, despite her earnest efforts."

"Perhaps we will have time to talk later, young man. You interest me."

Brigham Young gestured at Screaming Eagle with his right hand. "Your excellency, may I present Screaming Eagle of the Shoshone delegation. He is Chief Arimo's nephew and apprentice War Chief, a formidable and honorable warrior."

Screaming Eagle stepped forward with his hand held out. The governor looked up at the tall, muscular man wearing elaborate native clothing as they shook hands. "A pleasure to meet you, Screaming Eagle."

As he had practiced for this occasion with Teniwaaten, Screaming Eagle ducked his head respectfully. "I am at your service, your honor, as are all my family with me here today."

The Governor looked surprised at hearing such proper English and seeing such refined manners from a savage warrior. When he had served as Superintendent of Indian Affairs for upper Missouri, he had found the decimated Otoe-Missouria tribe reduced to poverty and starvation, struggling just to survive. The once great tribes had lost their warriors in battles over the years. Smallpox had killed off so many of their people that the two tribes merged on the poor reservation onto which the government forced them to live. The Governor stopped his reflections with a sad shake of his head and returned to the present. He noticed the doeskin sling. "What happened to your arm, Screaming Eagle?"

Connal Lee put a hand on Screaming Eagle's shoulder. "Well, suh, when we entered Box Elder, a farming community some miles north of here, a teenage Mormon guard mistook Screaming Eagle for a renegade come to ransack their abandoned settlement. Everyone but the young guard and his grandfather had evacuated south of Provo. He shot Screaming Eagle off his horse. After he apologized, we all departed friends."

The Governor shook his head, amazed at the story.

That reminded Connal Lee of Jedediah's letter. He withdrew the letter from an inside jacket pocket and held it out to Brigham Young. "Governor Young, suh, Ah was asked to deliver this to y'all. It's from Jedediah Morgan up north in Box Elder."

"Why, thank you, young man." Brigham Young opened the letter, gave it a quick glance, then slid it into a pocket to read later. He stepped over to stand beside Governor Cumming. "May I present White Wolf, another of Chief Arimo's nephews. He's a shaman and a medicine man. White Wolf, this is the new governor of the Territory of Utah, the honorable Alfred Cumming."

White Wolf took two steps forward with his hand outstretched. "How do you do, Governor. Like Connal Lee said, we are all here at your service, sir."

"And this is the delightful Short Rainbow, Governor. She's a niece of Chief Arimo and a shaman, as well."

"How do you do, Governor Cumming?"

"So lovely. I am totally enchanted to meet you, my dear. Thank you for joining us."

"And this is Arimo, Chief Arimo's first son and namesake. Arimo, may I present Governor Alfred Cumming."

"Nice to meet, sir. Thank you for receive Shoshone delegation."

"It is nice to meet you too, Mister Arimo. Welcome."

Connal Lee realized Brigham Young hadn't met Arimo's wife, so he stepped forward. "Your honors, may Ah have the privilege of introducing Arimo's Ute wife, the lovely Kimana. Kimana means butterfly in English. Kimana, this is the governor, Alfred Cumming, and the former governor, Brigham Young."

With a glorious smile, she delicately shook hands. "Nice meet. Nice meet."

Brigham Young turned to the bearded military officer standing in their circle. "Ladies and gentlemen of the Shoshone Delegation, may I introduce my dear friend, Colonel Tomas Kane. It is through his good offices that Governor Cumming agreed to enter Great Salt Lake City and assume his duties as governor without bringing General Johnston's army. Colonel Kane, may I present the official delegation of Chief Arimo and the great Shoshone Nation."

Colonel Kane shook hands all around, calling each delegate by name after hearing them introduced to Governor Cumming. Even Connal Lee stood taller than the colonel.

Brigham Young pointed to the elegantly dressed hunchback standing beside Colonel Kane. "And this is our host for this auspicious meeting, Elder William Staines, who built this lovely cottage and planted the surrounding gardens. Our gracious host serves as our Territorial Librarian and is a member of the territorial legislature, in addition to his many services to his Church."

The short gentleman shook hands with everyone. His hands felt large and rough from manual labor. Connal Lee figured the stout man had grown up crippled and deformed. He didn't appear to have a neck. He had adult-sized arms and legs with a stunted and barrel-shaped torso. His lungs seemed too bulky for his body, which gave him a pigeon-breasted look. In a crisp British accent that reminded Connal Lee of Mother Baines, Mr. Staines bid everyone welcome to his home with a warm smile.

When Connal Lee heard the word librarian, his attention focused on their host. "Excuse me, suh, but y'all are a librarian? Ah didn't even know y'all had a library here in Great Salt Lake City. Ah'm always looking for new novels and books to read."

"Yes, young Master Swinton, it is indeed my privilege to be the Territorial Librarian. If you are going to be in town for a couple of days, it would be my pleasure to take you to Council House and show you our fine library. We now have over three thousand books, including a complete law library."

Connal Lee's eyes grew round in awe. "Three thousand books! Ah had no idea so many books even existed. Ah would so enjoy visiting your library. Thanks so much, Elder Staines. Ah can't wait. Ah only own two novels myself. They were gifts from Captain Reed and Lieutenant Anderson of the cavalry on the Overland Trail. But Ah've read six whole novels all told. Ah enjoy reading novels a lot more than reading the Bible or the Book of Mormon, don't y'all, suh?"

Everyone chuckled and nodded. "Well, young man, our Territorial Library is overflowing with all the great books of literature and biographies of important people throughout history, plus many various and sundry reference books. I dare say we can find a book or two for you to borrow."

"Oh, that would be great. Thanks so much, suh. It's a dream come true. Ah wish Ah had known about the library on my last visits to Great Salt Lake City."

A young kitchen maid, passing around a silver tray of cookies, interrupted them. Connal Lee's eyes lit up. Mr. Staines gestured to the cookies. "These nuts came from my own tree farm north of here in Bountiful. We enjoyed a most abundant crop last fall."

Connal Lee picked up a chocolate cookie topped with roasted walnuts and a sugar cookie topped with roasted almonds. "Um, delicious, Elder Staines. Really great."

Governor Cumming helped himself to three of each kind of cookie. The young maiden handed him the entire tray with a small curtsey. The governor nodded his thanks and bit off half a cookie in one gulp. After swallowing his first bite of chocolate cookie, he smiled. "You are right, young Master Swinton. These are indeed delicious."

While Connal Lee made conversation with the Governor, Major Harris invited the rest of the Shoshone delegation to join him in refreshments. He led them towards the tables along a side wall. Everyone wanted to meet the exotically dressed Shoshone guests as they crossed the room. Major Harris made introductions right and left. The distinguished-looking Mayor Abraham Smoot pulled White Wolf aside for a lengthy conversation. One of the Mayor's black slaves from Kentucky looked on, alert for trouble from the savage warrior. Four young officers of the Nauvoo Legion surrounded Short Rainbow and Kimana, enchanted with their beauty and graceful, athletic poise. Short Rainbow soon had the gentlemen laughing with her stories. Kimana hardly spoke any English, so she just watched, smiling when Short Rainbow smiled and laughing when Short Rainbow laughed.

After Major Harris and the Shoshone delegation walked away, Governor Cumming turned to Brigham Young. He smiled and gestured towards one of two tall upholstered Spanish-style chairs in front of the enormous fireplace. "Won't you please have a seat and join me for a moment, President Young? We haven't yet had an opportunity to get acquainted."

Mr. Staines looked around at the governor's entourage. "Let me send over some more chairs so we can all sit down."

Moments later, three of Mr. Staines' gardeners carried in enough chairs to seat everyone. The laborers placed the chairs in a circle before the massive fireplace and silently left the way they came.

Brigham Young pulled a pocket watch out of his black silk vest and checked the time with a frown. "Well, only for a few moments, sir. With thirty thousand of the faithful on the move, I am swamped with questions and pleas for help from all sides."

"Yes, President Young. Colonel Kane informed me you had ordered all the Mormons living north of Provo to evacuate south. But I am here now, graciously and peacefully received. I find everything in good order, despite all the rumors and vile lies so rampant back in Washington. Certainly, you do not need to continue the evacuation. Please call your people back to their homes, sir. I can vouch for their safety. There is no need for them to be dislocated, losing their prime planting season and upsetting their wives and children."

"I am sorry, Governor Cumming, but so long as the army sits poised with orders to invade, my people will give up their homes and move away from danger. Can you guarantee that General Johnston will stand down? That the army will lay down their arms and come peacefully into the territory? No, sir. You cannot. Our reconnaissance informed us that General Johnston's character is such that he would only obey orders from his superiors received through the proper chain of command. So far, he has orders to subdue the territory to federal law in order to place you and your federal judges in positions of power. We will not see our daughters corrupted by crude soldiers. We will not see our young men brutalized by unfeeling beasts, whatever uniform they wear or government they represent. Now, if you will excuse me, around a fifth of the members of our various wards need assistance in making the move south. They are so poor they lack not only wheels and livestock but sometimes even such basics as shoes and food. I must meet with the administrators of the Bishops' tithing warehouses to see that all our people are equipped to move to safety."

Brigham Young started to rise to his feet. Governor Cumming held up his hand. "Excuse me, President Young, but did you say your people are poor and lacking shoes and food? That's hard to believe when I see so many gracious homes and gardens here in Great Salt Lake City. I thought all you Mormons were thriving here in the Territory of Utah."

"Well, sir, it's important that you understand the people you will be governing, so please permit me to take a moment to share a little of our history. From our arrival in forty-seven until the winter of fifty-four and fifty-five, our crops and herds flourished. But that winter, we received next to no snowfall and no rain that spring. We entered into a serious drought that continues to this day. The drought drove locusts and great flying grasshoppers down out of the mountains into the valleys, making matters worse. When the clouds of locusts departed, nothing green remained. They consumed two-thirds to nine-tenths of the newly sowed fields and gardens through-out the entire territory. Our people turned out to drive them off with no success. Then, with such dry conditions, forest fires swept the Great Basin late that summer. We experienced a harsh winter that year. Between freezing temperatures and lack of hay and grains, many of our northern communities lost seven out of eight of their cows and other livestock, leaving them impoverished and hungry."

Brigham Young leaned back in his chair. "We Mormons fast one day a month and give the food we would have eaten to the Bish-ops to distribute among the poor. During that time, we fasted much more often. We had to feed our brethren, somehow. While things have improved somewhat since then, we still live in a condition of drought compared to when we first arrived. Huge flying grasshop-pers attack our spring plantings. Some areas can barely support our small outposts. We have sadly had to abandon other farmlands. Now, please excuse me. I may not be governor any longer, but as the President of the Church, I still have responsibilities to my peo-ple."

Brigham Young stood up. While shaking hands, he noticed a well-dressed gentleman enter the room accompanied by three strong men carrying crates. Brigham Young raised his hand to catch their attention, then turned to Governor Cumming. "Your honor, may I introduce you to my former territorial secretary, the honorable William Hooper, esquire. Brother Hooper, this is his excellency, Alfred Cumming, the new Governor."

"It's an honor to meet you, sir. Governor Cumming, it gives me great pleasure to formally deliver the Executive Seal of the Territory of Utah into your safekeeping. Sir, I have also taken the liberty of delivering such other public property, documents, and secretarial supplies as you might need in the execution of your duties."

Mister Hooper handed the seal to the governor with a slight bow. They shook hands. When Mr. Staines saw the crates of supplies, he gestured for the porters to follow him. "With your permission, Governor, we will place these supplies in your temporary office in my library. Please follow me, brethren."

Brigham Young finished shaking hands and took his leave of the dignitaries. When he headed towards the door, several other high-ranking officials of the Mormon Church and the Nauvoo Legion joined him. As he passed through the front door, his hulking bodyguard fell in close behind him. The remaining guests picked up their conversations in louder voices.

Shortly after Brigham Young departed, Major Harris managed to convey the delegation to the refreshment tables. Mr. Staines' first wife, Elizabeth, stood behind the first table serving beverages. When they approached, she smiled a warm welcome. White Wolf thought she looked very proud and elegant in her fancy European clothing and elaborate hairstyle. "Now, what can I get for you this lovely afternoon? We have ginger tea, mint tea, spicy Brigham tea, fresh-pressed apple cider, wine or unfermented grape juice, beer, sarsaparilla, and coffee. At the next table, my sister wife Lillias is offering miniature donuts, little cakes, a variety of cheeses, and bowls of nuts from our farm up in Davis County. She also has some delicious deviled eggs she made herself just this morning."

Elizabeth served them beverages in various teacups, coffee cups, water glasses, and small wine glasses. After Major Harris took a glass of apple cider, he moseyed over and joined the group around the fireplace.

Seated across from the rotund new governor, Connal Lee listened to Mr. Staines. "You are welcome to the use of my home,

Governor, for you and your wife, who I understand awaits you in primitive circumstances back at Camp Scott. Within the week, my wives and all our household and garden staff will depart south for safety. My men have already taken all our wagons, carts, and carriages and transported our food, seeds, tools, and valuables south. They will be back to load up all the furniture tomorrow except what you and your servants will need to remain here as our guests."

"But why do you continue with this foolish exodus south, Mister Staines? There is clearly no longer any need."

"Governor Cumming, sir, you heard the beloved leader of our Church. Until the threat of armed soldiers is removed, we will follow the instructions of President Young, our latter-day prophet. I will gladly burn this house, chop down all my fruit trees, and put my gardens and fields to the torch before I will leave them for any marauding Federal troops to enjoy. If they come, they will only conquer and occupy a barren desert."

The Governor shook his head sadly while munching yet another cookie. Connal Lee gazed around the spacious parlor. He smiled when he saw his family surrounded by several guests, fully engaged in conversation. He turned back to the group around the new governor in time to witness Colonel Kane giving Alfred Cumming an 'I told you so' look before they nodded at each other.

Major Harris noticed the sun's low angle shining in the bay windows and turned to Connal Lee. "Well, young Master Connal Lee, I was charged with the enviable task of being your official host and guide during the Shoshone delegation's diplomatic visit. I wondered if I might invite you and your Shoshone relatives to join me tomorrow morning on a tour of Great Salt Lake City. From what I have been told, I don't believe you have seen much beyond the Beehive House and the shops and Post Office on Main Street. Is that right?"

Connal Lee nodded yes with a look of keen anticipation on his eager face.

"Then please permit me to invite your fine delegation to be my guests tomorrow morning. I can escort you around so you can get better acquainted with all that our fine city has to offer. Would you like that?"

"Oh, yes, suh. Ah would really enjoy seeing more of this big city. Ah would appreciate it, suh."

The major leaned forward to make an appointment, but before he could speak, Governor Cumming interrupted. "My good Major Harris, sir. After all the glowing reports I have heard about your fine city, I would dearly love to join you on your excursion. I would sincerely like to know more about the people and territory for whom I am now responsible. Might there be room for one more in your party, sir?"

The major and Connal Lee looked at each other in surprise. They both nodded. Major Harris turned to the governor. "We would be pleased to have you join us, your honor." He looked at the corpulent man overflowing his chair, obviously a pampered, self-indulgent gentleman. Trying to be discreet, he tactfully inquired, "Did you bring a ride, Governor, or would you prefer your fine carriage?"

Governor Cumming chuckled. "Will we be going off the beaten path to where I would need to be on horseback, sir?"

"Not necessarily, Governor. I actually had in mind showing the Shoshone delegation our public works and fine public buildings. There is more to Great Salt Lake City than the shops and trading stores on Main Street. Now that you mention it, though, we won't be going off-road. You could certainly ride in comfort in your carriage, sir."

Major Harris turned back to Connal Lee. "How many of your delegation do you think would like to accompany us, Mister Swinton?"

Connal Lee frowned as he thought about it. "Well, suh, Ah believe Ah am the only one who would be interested in taking you up on your tour. The others don't really care how white folk live in crowded cities."

Governor Cumming lifted up his forefinger, which grabbed everyone's attention. "In that case, Major Harris, may I offer my carriage for the excursion? Mister Staines, might you like to join us tomorrow? I would welcome your insights and history of the area as we explore your lovely city."

"Why, yes, sir. It would be my pleasure to join you. Thank you for inviting me, Governor."

Major Harris nodded as he changed his plans to suit the new circumstances. "In that case, gentlemen, may I recommend we reconvene here at nine o'clock tomorrow morning? We can tour the city and end up at my little cottage north of the city, where I had anticipated entertaining Connal Lee and his fellow delegates. I dare say we can see most all there is to see by midday and then break for a luncheon."

"Why, thank you, Major. Are you sure my inviting myself along won't put you out?"

"Not at all, sir. It would be my pleasure to welcome you to my humble abode. After my second wife passed through the veil, I was introduced to a widowed Swedish convert who needed a position. She agreed to keep my city home in return for room and board. I was fortunate because she's an excellent cook, an absolute magician in the kitchen. Tomorrow, she will be preparing marinated cutthroat trout caught fresh in the morning over in the Jordan River. She said she would serve the trout with dill new potatoes. I asked her specifically to prepare trout because I heard that trout and salmon are favorite foods of the Shoshone people, our guests. For dessert, she volunteered to prepare her specialty, almond caramel cake, which will satisfy even the most jaded palate."

"Excellent. Let's all meet here in the morning for the grand tour. I am looking forward to it, Major. Thank you, sir."

Connal Lee nodded his head. "Ah can't wait either, suh. Ah appreciate y'all thinking of us, Major."

They all stood up. After handshakes, Major Harris rounded up his Shoshone guests. He nearly had to drag them away from the men intrigued by their native visitors. The Mormons in the valley regularly saw Indians of the local Ute and Piute tribes who came to the city to trade. The local clans lived much poorer and more primitively than their Northern Shoshone cousins. In the summer, they barely wore loincloths, which embarrassed the Mormon women. In the winter, they covered themselves with untanned rabbit skins which stank. The natives trading on Main Street with their poor blankets, dirty unkempt hair, scrawny donkeys, and emaciated horses invited neither admiration nor conversation. Besides, none of them spoke English.

Major Harris courteously escorted his guests back to their camp. They arrived about six o'clock. Bright Star and Koko had supper sizzling over a hot cookfire. The delegation unsaddled their horses and tethered them with the rest of their horses. When they returned to the camp, Connal Lee pointed towards Short Rainbow's tipi. "Please wait a minute, Major Robert, while Ah change out of my new ceremonial clothes."

"Of course, Connal Lee. Take your time."

Connal Lee returned almost immediately with his red fox fur blanket. "Here, suh. Please sit on this. It will help keep y'all's fine uniform clean."

"Why, thank you, Connal Lee. Very thoughtful of you."

The Major sat down Indian style. He enjoyed watching the graceful way the Indian maidens moved through their chores, unhurried and totally at ease. Unconsciously, his fingers stroked the soft fox fur blanket beneath him.

Connal Lee walked over a few moments later and dropped to sit on his blanket beside the major. He smiled when he smelled trout sizzling in a cast iron fry pan. "Are y'all hungry, Major?"

"Smelling delicious food cooking over a hardwood fire has certainly stoked my appetite. I guess I didn't partake of enough refreshments at Elder Staines' mansion."

"He surely does have a fine home, doesn't he, Major?"

"Yes, Connal Lee. One of the finest in the territory. Despite his physical appearance, he's a cultured and learned gentleman of great refinement and taste. Why rumor has it, he has over nine hundred volumes in his personal library, the largest private library in the entire territory."

"Wow! Mother Baines never told me there were so many books. Books are rare in the Ozarks and on the Overland Trail. We only have something like three dozen books in the lending library up in Fort Hall. Mother Baines told me that a great world of fine literature awaits me, but Ah had no idea." He looked away from the fire and studied the major's chiseled profile. "So, while my wonderful family prepares supper, please tell us about y'all, suh. Did y'all tell the Governor that y'all's two wives passed away?"

"Yes, Connal Lee. While living in Nauvoo, I had the good fortune to meet and fall in love with Mary Ellen, a lovely daughter of Zion. My first wife, Thelma Louise, bore my first and third sons. My middle son is from Mary Ellen. They traveled to Great Salt Lake City in the third wave of pioneers after spending the first winter on the trail at Winter Quarters on the Mississippi River in Omaha. The men of the company built eight hundred cabins and sod houses for the winter. Even trading with the Omaha Tribe, they had a simple and sparse diet during that long hard winter. Many of the Saints came down with blackleg, which the doctors called scurvy when it affected humans. Sadly, my dear first wife, Thelma Louise, contracted consumption in the harsh winter clime. Her breathing became increasingly difficult as she wasted away. She died in the spring, leaving Mary Ellen to carry on alone caring for my three boys. When they arrived in Great Salt Lake City, Brigham Young recommended they go south and join the new settlement around Fort Utah, south of Provo. He told them the area had rich soil with abundant water for farming. They took their small covered wagon and livestock down and homesteaded in the Provo Second Ward."

Connal Lee perked up when he heard the major mention the Provo Second Ward. "Why, Ah've been there, Robert. Bishop Hanover captained the Mormon handcart company we joined to come across the plains. He used to be the Bishop of the Second Ward. What a small world, isn't it, Major?"

The major smiled and nodded. "Yes, it is. I've had the privilege of meeting Bishop Hanover, Connal Lee. He's also a fellow officer in the Nauvoo Legion, although now retired. I rejoined Mary Ellen and my three sons in Provo after mustering out of the Mormon Battalion down in California. My oldest son is twenty years old now. A fine young man. He married two sisters a couple of years ago. My second son is nineteen and just got married last year. They run my five hundred-acre ranch for me while I'm here in the city tending to my duties in the militia.

"My youngest son doesn't enjoy farming like his older brothers. It leaves him bored and dissatisfied. He lives with me, spending his days reading and studying. He's determined to follow in my footsteps and attend West Point back in New York State. I don't want to discourage him from what he feels is his true calling in life, but with the drought and all, we don't have the wherewithal to send him back east. Each cadet must pay their own travel expenses. Only time will tell. Edward left last week with most of my furniture to live with his brothers until it's safe for us to return. Too bad. I think he would have enjoyed meeting you."

Short Rainbow interrupted by serving supper. After eating, Connal Lee accompanied the major down to the river for his big stallion. "See you in the morning at Elder Staines' home, Connal Lee. Thank you, again, for supper."

The delegation awoke to find half an inch of snow covering the land. Their breaths steamed in the cold air. By the time Short Rainbow and Kimana had the cookfire roaring, a drizzle of rain began falling that soon washed away the snow. The clouds blew to the east an hour after sunrise, and the sun warmed the land.

Connal Lee started to pull on his regular clothing, but White Wolf recommended he wear his ceremonial Shoshone clothes as a delegate from Chief SoYo'Cant. Connal Lee wore everything but the headband and breastplate. Bright Star combed his hair straight down and back with a clean part in the middle. He plopped his big leather hat on his head and took off at an easy cantor towards Great Salt Lake City.

Chapter 6: Civilization

When Connal Lee arrived at the Staines' mansion, the governor's luxurious carriage stood harnessed along the street in front of the hitching posts. Connal Lee recognized Major Harris' lively stallion tied up behind the coach. He dismounted and tied his pretty mare beside the major's big horse. He saw mud from the road on his mare's hoofs and splattered over her rear legs. Wind blew rainclouds overhead, blocking out the sun intermittently. Connal Lee looked up, hoping rain wouldn't spoil their tour.

Connal Lee strolled through the lovely garden, once again enjoying the perfume of apple blossoms on the young trees growing in the front and side yards. He knocked briskly on the varnished oak doors. Mr. Staines' first wife, Elizabeth, pulled the doors open with a big smile. "Good morning, Brother Swinton. Please come in. The Governor is expecting you."

"Why, thank you, Sister Staines. And a lovely good morning to y'all, too."

Connal Lee entered the large parlor. The portly Governor called out jovially, "Well, now. We appear to all be here at last. Shall we be off on the grand tour? Good morning, young Master Swinton. It's good to see you again this morning."

Connal Lee shook hands all around. "Good morning, your honor, suh. Good morning Elder Staines. Major Harris, suh. It's good to see y'all this fine morning."

Major Harris led the way to the entrance hall. "Shall we, Governor? Let's be off."

The governor's two black servants, dressed again in simple gray uniforms, helped the rotund governor board his fine coach. Connal Lee watched the carriage dip and sway as it adjusted to the Governor's heavy bulk. Great leather straps attached to steel springs suspended the enclosed body of the coach to cushion passengers from bumps in the road. The drivers held the doors open for the major, Elder Staines, and Connal Lee. After everyone settled into the comfortable tufted leather seats, the servants climbed up to the driver seat perched in front of the carriage. Connal Lee examined the upholstered interior walls with great interest, amazed at the luxury and fine craftsmanship. Elder Staines lowered a leather curtain over the window beside him, so the sun didn't shine directly in his eyes.

Major Harris took on the role of tour guide. "First stop, Gentlemen, will be the tabernacle on Temple Square. We'll start close to Elder Staines' home and then make our way further afield as we go."

They had barely settled onto their bench seats when the coach came to a stop alongside the south wall of Temple Square. The servants opened the doors and lent their hands to help the passengers step down. They approached the huge tabernacle looming overhead. Connal Lee glanced up at an enormous triangular pediment above the second-story windows. The pyramidal gable contained a bas-relief sculpture of a rising sun with sun rays radiating up and out in a fan pattern. Two great chimneys rose above the steeply angled roof. The Major led them at a slow walk, out of consideration for the governor, towards the left door. They entered a spacious hall with a barrel roof overhead. The floor pitched down at a gentle angle, leaving each row of bench seats slightly above the row below so everyone had an unobstructed view of the podium. The pulpit stood upon a raised stage. The round bandshell shape of the back of the stage improved the acoustics.

The Major closed the door once they had all entered the hall. "Our tabernacle can seat two-thousand five-hundred Saints all at the same time. More, with standing room."

"Wow, Major. It's so big. Ah've never seen a building so big before. Hey! What's that?"

They all heard a dulcet musical tone from one of the gold-painted pipes along the curved back wall of the stage. A cluster of pipes of all different lengths made of metal and wood, square and round, loomed over a large oak console. The console held two short ivory and ebony keyboards with a pedal keyboard to be played by the feet. "Ah. Perfect timing. It appears Brother Ridges is tuning the organ, getting it ready for Sunday's presentation of the governor to the people of Great Salt Lake City."

"What's an organ, Major Harris?"

"You've never seen an organ before, Connal Lee?"

"No, suh. This is my first time ever being in a church. What is an organ?"

"Well, young man, a pipe organ is a musical instrument favored to accompany a choir and congregational singing. We have an excellent tabernacle choir here in Zion. You will hear it Sunday if you stay for the presentation of the governor. Brother Ridges crafted the organ in Australia. After he and his family joined the Mormon Church, he immigrated here to Zion. He transported the organ on the six-month journey by sailing ship and overland wagons to end up here. Some of the crates holding the pipes were as big as the wagons carrying them. Excuse me for a moment. Have a seat while I go ask Brother Ridges if he could give us a short recital so you can hear the fine instrument he built."

The major strode up the aisle a few moments later and sat down next to Connal Lee.

A plainly dressed man sat down at the organ console. Unseen by his audience, he pulled and released the Calcant stop on the console two times, which rang a little bell to alert his assistants. His apprentices also served as his bellows treaders. The young men began stepping up and down on foot levers to build up air pressure to sound the pipes. The organist launched into his recital with the bright, dramatic opening of Bach's Toccata and Fugue in D Minor. Loud trumpets startled Connal Lee. Connal Lee slowly rose to his feet without being consciously aware of it as the performance continued. He leaned forward, resting his hands on the pew before him, straining to hear every musical note and nuance. He stood captivated, surrounded, and engulfed by sound. Ten minutes later, the music ended with ponderous chords supported by throbbing bass notes. The last echo died away gradually in the cavernous room. Connal Lee sat down, stunned and bewildered by the experience.

When his tour mates stood up, Connal Lee blinked and gazed around. "Major Harris, suh. Ah cannot express my gratitude for bringing me here this morning. Ah've never heard anything like that music before. The only music Ah've ever heard was people singing on the Overland Trail with maybe a flute or violin or banjo to accompany them. This is totally different. It... it... transported me to a place Ah've never been before. Ah almost feel like Ah just left a sweat lodge, kind of all spiritual and quiet like in my soul."

The governor and Elder Staines looked at each with raised eyebrows, smiling at Connal Lee's innocence and youthful wonder. Major Harris put his arm over Connal Lee's shoulders as he faced the organ. "Our thanks, Brother Ridges. That was beautiful. Just beautiful. Thank you for letting us hear your fine instrument and your magnificent playing. So long, now."

Connal Lee walked outside, his thoughts still dwelling on the magic of the pipe organ's music. He didn't pay attention to their tour guide's next lecture. "This empty field used to hold our third Bowery, a great shaded outdoor space built to accommodate up to eight thousand Saints for the Church's semiannual general conferences. We dismantled it in preparation for the advance of Johnston's army. As with many of the public buildings we will see today, the Department of Public Works has men removing all the doors and windows and caching them in safety until after Johnston departs. Wood and glass are so expensive they must be protected. It's easy and cheap enough to make dobies to build our structures. But it's difficult to replace window frames and glass window panes. Of course, they will help Brother Ridges transport the tabernacle's pipe organ south to Provo. I understand packing it for transportation will begin immediately after Sunday's presentation of the governor to the Saints."

Governor Cumming gazed up at the tabernacle. It appeared constructed of dressed stone. "What are dobies, Major? I'm not familiar with the word."

The Major grinned. "That's what we call adobe bricks, sir, simple sun and air-dried clay, straw and dung building blocks. Without ready sources of wood, cement, or stone, it is nearly the only building material we have to work with. We are fortunate that so many of us traveled the southwest with the Mormon Brigade during the Mexican-American War, where we learned how to make dobies and build with them. We brought the technique back here to Zion, where it has served us well."

"Oh. I see. But it looks like stone building blocks."

"Almost all our public buildings are adobe structures with the bricks smoothed over with a simple clay plaster for a more pleasant appearance. Most of our local clay is naturally gray. I agree. When the waterproof plaster dries, it looks like natural quarried stone. Attractive, isn't it? We enjoy the services of several excellent architects who work miracles with our lowly clay and straw bricks. You'll see as we continue the tour."

Major Harris pointed to the simple Endowment House, the only other structure still standing on Temple Square. He explained they used the Endowment House to perform sacred Church functions. Connal Lee remembered sitting in the building with Chief SoYo'Cant for the War Council back in November. The small group returned to the coach. The major looked around as they exited the south gate of the fifteen-foot tall wall surrounding Temple Square. "Gentlemen, let's walk to our next destination across the street on the corner of Main Street."

They wended their way through the heavy traffic of covered wagons and men on horseback. When they reached the other side, the Major held up his hand to stop them and pointed back at the buildings across the broad street. "That is the Bishop's Tithing Office and Warehouse diagonally across the intersection. Beside it are the corrals, barns, and offices of the Nauvoo Legion, where I work. The big building further along with all the attic dormers is Brigham Young's Lion House, built to house several of his forty-seven wives and many children. The two small buildings to its right are the Church offices. Next is the Beehive House, which President Young used as his Governor's Mansion until yesterday. Now, if you would please turn around, gentlemen, we are standing in front of the first public building erected in the city, the Council House. We began work on it less than two years after the Saints first arrived in the valley. We built it of local red sandstone and finished it in eighteen-fifty. Please follow me around the corner to the entrance on Main Street. Let's go inside, shall we?"

Major Harris held open the gate in the seven-foot-tall white picket fence enclosing the entire lot. As Connal Lee walked through the gate, he looked up at the two-story edifice and noticed the tops of four chimneys. The simple square cube of a building held a widow's walk on its rooftop. A glass-sided lantern cupola admitted natural light to illuminate the open interior stairwell. Constructed of local sandstone blocks, its earthy color had a distinctive pale pink cast.

Elder Staines resumed the tour. "This is one of my favorite places in the city, gentlemen. Until we completed the Endowment House in fifty-five, I had the privilege of conducting endowment ceremonies in the top floor here in the Council House. For the past three years, I've been doing endowments on Temple Square."

Connal Lee tilted his head as he gazed down into Elder Staines' eyes. "Excuse me, please, suh. But what does endowment mean?"

"Well, young man, the word endowment means a gift or inheritance. The word has special meaning for the faithful, though, because we learn more about God's plan for us here on earth during the endowment ceremony. We learn what he requires for us to return to our Heavenly Father's presence after this life. We learn how to grow closer to our Lord and Savior. It's a very spiritual experience that adds a lot of meaning to the lives of the Saints. Tell me, Master Swinton, have you been baptized?"

"Nope, sorry, suh. My adopted father, Chief Arimo, is a member of the Mormon church. My foster parents, Lorna and Gilbert Baines, are Mormons and follow the Church's teachings and beliefs. When Ah was traveling the trail with Bishop Hanover, Ah read the Bible and the Book of Mormon. Ah discussed their teachings at length with my foster parents and Bishop Hanover. But Ah never felt any desire to be baptized. Not that Ah don't respect y'all's church and its teachings, Ah just don't believe in all that."

"I see. Well, perhaps as you grow up, you will come to embrace the truth of the restored gospel and be baptized. Once you are a member, I can tell you more about the endowments. For now, let's move on, shall we?"

Elder Staines pointed to a suite of rooms being remodeled. "Governor Cumming, sir, when we complete the renovations in just another week or so, these will become your offices. Since the former governor never used them, we used them for other purposes. Upstairs we have various meeting rooms used by the territorial legislature and other public programs. We even have a classroom used by the University of Deseret. Major Harris, I believe your son attends classes here. Isn't that right?"

"Correct, sir. During all the unrest, they canceled nearly all the classes. But whenever they held classes, he attended. Of course, he could always be found close by, anyway, studying law, history, and politics right here in the Territorial Library six days a week."

Elder Staines swung open two heavy double doors off the hall surrounding the broad square central stairwell. Inside stood rows and rows of varnished oak bookshelves. Study tables sat beneath three tall windows on the north side of the whitewashed room. Connal Lee stopped up short with a gasp. "Oh! Oooh, just look at all the books!" Connal Lee looked at Elder Staines with eyes open wide in delight. "Just look!"

While the older gentlemen discussed the uses of the public building, Connal Lee wandered around overwhelmed. From time to time, his hand reached out to pet the fine leather bindings as though petting living creatures. He heard his name called a second time before he snapped out of his spell. He glanced around and found Major Harris smiling at him. "We're leaving Connal Lee. Are you joining us for the remainder of the tour?"

Connal Lee looked down at the floor, then nodded his head. Reluctantly, he allowed himself to be led out of the library. Elder Staines whispered in his ear, "Young Master Swinton, I will be happy to bring you back when we don't have the governor waiting on us. Will that be satisfactory to you?"

"Oh, yes, suh, Elder Staines. Ah would very much appreciate spending more time here exploring. It's like a dream come true. Only Ah never even knew it was my dream until Ah saw this room. So many books. So many stories. So much information and knowledge. Ah'm speechless. Words just fail me. Yessirree, Ah'm absolutely speechless."

Major Harris looked amused as he took Connal Lee's elbow and guided him back to the waiting carriage. "That's funny, Connal Lee. I hadn't noticed that you were speechless."

The men chuckled on their way out to Main Street. Connal Lee kept looking back, yearningly, over his shoulder.

They rode slowly down Main Street for an hour. All kinds of abandoned and boarded-up stores and workshops lined the broad street. When Brigham Young declared martial law last summer, their owners either fled west to California, returned back east to the States, or evacuated south below Provo. Four miles south of Temple Square, they approached the Post Office and the Globe Restaurant and Bakery, the only two places still open. Only at the Globe Saloon, as everyone called it, could gentiles buy food and beverages.

The coach drove them back north, then stopped a block west of Main Street and two blocks south of Temple Square. Major Harris invited everyone to disembark and tour the County Courthouse. Before they walked under the impressive columned porch, Connal Lee glanced up and saw a domed tower rising above a mansard roof. Three chimneys rose into the sky on each side of the flat roof. They entered a grand two-story block of a building with soaring ceilings and enormous windows. Each spacious room sported a fireplace. The Major explained how they had a Probate Judge and three Selectmen comprising the County board. The Courthouse held offices for the Supreme Court judges, tax collector, and County Treasurer. "Gentlemen, let's move on. There's still plenty to see."

An hour later, they had either visited or passed by all the significant buildings like the Assayer's Office and the Social Hall, where they held concerts and plays for up to three-hundred fifty people at a time. They rode past The Deseret News Building. Major Harris explained they attempted to publish a newspaper once a week – provided they had paper. "Paper is hard to come by on the frontier. We've tried to manufacture paper, but it hasn't been successful yet. They usually end up printing every other week to conserve on paper."

Just before noon, they stopped at the entrance to Little Emigration Canyon. They all stepped out of the carriage to take in the view of the route Governor Cumming had traveled two nights earlier. Connal Lee caught the major's eye. They both nodded and shared a discreet grin as they remembered playacting around the bonfires when they greeted the new governor.

109

Connal Lee noticed Governor Cumming standing by himself, staring east into the distance. He stepped closer to the rotund gentleman. Governor Cumming glanced over at him with a shrug and a sad smile and placed a heavy hand on Connal Lee's shoulder. "I was just thinking that a few days ago, I departed Camp Scott and my tent accommodations to come here. My wife and I have been freezing cold literally for months, stuck in the camp with almost nothing to eat and no transportation out. The temperatures seldom reached freezing during the day and plunged well below freezing every night. The constant winds whistling across the empty plains added to the cold. It's the camp's high elevation, you see. The troops and my servants had trouble finding firewood as the camp had cleaned out all the ready wood for miles around over the months of being stranded there. Towards the end, the troops harnessed themselves to wagons so they could haul back wood for the huge camp. It's a sad thing to see men reduced to beasts of burden. Now I have arrived here to comfortable, warm temperatures. Above freezing at night. Plenty of fine foods and beverages. What a difference. I hope my sweet wife can join me soon. Poor, long-suffering Lizzie, always willing to attend me in my duties and travels. Lizzie made us a home in Camp Scott with five combined tents. One had a chimney and served as our kitchen. We have a large double wall tent which she divided into a parlor and bed chamber with a tiny heat stove. She always remained cheerful and protested she was quite comfortable. But I hate to think of her still suffering a week's journey east of here. Well, let's go back and join the others, shall we, Master Swinton?"

They rode back to Temple Square from the canyon and then turned north onto East Temple. After a short ride up the gentle incline of the foothills, the Major pointed out a sizeable barnlike building on their right surrounded by thick adobe walls. "That's the Legion's arsenal where we cache our arms and ammunition stored safely away from people and buildings." A short distance further, they arrived at a modest adobe house on Center Street. The major had situated his simple home so the covered front porch overlooked the valley, spread below them in an orderly grid. Young box elder maples and cottonwood trees lined the sides of his half-acre plot,

110

leaving the view unobstructed. After the carriage pulled up and parked on the wide street in front of the major's home, the servants opened the doors and helped the men step down to the gentle hillside. The heavy governor grunted when he stepped down. "Oh, excellent. Dinner at last. I'm positively famished."

Major Harris gestured towards his whitewashed home. "Welcome, gentlemen. This is my home when I'm not on my farm south of Provo. Please come in and refresh yourselves."

He proudly led the way up the hillside and stepped up onto a full-width covered porch. "Please come in, Governor."

The party walked through a door centered between two multipaned windows. They entered a narrow hallway that extended the length of the modest home. The major led the way into a plain parlor on their right. The parlor held a simple plank table and six spindle chairs with needlepoint seat cushions. "Please have a seat, everyone. Sorry that all my furniture and rugs have been shipped south for the duration. Now, who would like to have a cocktail before dinner? Elder Staines? Governor? I am fortunate to have a jug of Valley Tan Remedy from Brigham Young's own distillery."

The Governor's eyes lit up. "What is this Valley Tan, sir? I've never heard of it."

"Well, sir, Valley Tan is a local spirit made from a blend of wheat whiskey and oat whiskey. Some swear it's brewed from fire and brimstone. It's so strong, it's not recommended to drink it square. Best to add a generous splash of creek water."

"You have me intrigued now, sir. I would like to try your local whiskey if I may."

Major Harris pulled out four tiny glass tumblers from a rustic board cabinet built into the corner of the dining room parlor. He poured a generous amount of the honey-colored beverage into one glass, then added a splash of water from a clay pitcher. He looked at Elder Staines, who nodded and held his hand up with his forefinger nearly touching his thumb, indicating a small amount. The Major understood he would drink only to be sociable with the governor, who clearly relished his alcoholic beverages. He poured a small drink and then topped off the glass with creek water. He looked at Connal Lee, shook his head, and filled the next glass with water.

Then he prepared another light drink for himself. He really didn't care for anything stronger than wine. The four men clinked their glasses and took sips.

"Excellent, Major. I'm puzzled, though. Why such a strange name. What did you call it, Valley Tan?"

The Major chuckled. "Yes, sir. When the Saints first arrived, they established a tannery as one of their very first enterprises. They began brewing alcohol to tan leather. They also used the alcohol as medicine to clean wounds and deaden the senses for surgeries. It also served to preserve foods. Some men like drinking whiskey, so it quickly became a popular beverage, as well."

The Governor chuckled. "Tan leather. Ha! Well, it is pretty strong, isn't it? I'm surprised it didn't singe the hair right off the hides."

A tall young woman walked into the parlor. The men stood up. Connal Lee looked surprised at her hair, even paler than his, so blond it appeared nearly white. She wore her hair braided and wound into a bun on top of her head, held in place with a crocheted hairnet. She wore a simple gray dress of homespun fabric with a long white apron made of flour sacks. "Gentlemen, may I present Sister Ingrid Ohlsson, my housekeeper and cook. She lives in the back bedroom with her two young sons, aged four and six. Where are your boys today, Ingrid?"

"They are playing out back, sir. I ordered them to stay out of the way while you are entertaining. May I serve a little tidbit to tide you over until dinner is served? I need another fifteen minutes for the trout. I didn't dare start them before I knew when you would be here."

"Certainly, Sister Ingrid. Please bring extra for his excellency, the governor, as he complained he is starving plumb to death. We must not have his untimely demise on our conscience!"

Everyone chuckled as Ingrid scurried back to the kitchen. Within moments she returned carrying two white plates. One held six thin pancakes wrapped around a dab of crème fraiche topped with jam made from sour berries. The second plate had two crepes. She handed the governor the larger serving and Elder Staines the smaller serving. She then retrieved four forks out of the parlor's

112

cabinet and placed them on the table. She noted Connal Lee's bright eyes looking at the governor's plate and decided she better give him extra helpings, too. Since she had two younger brothers at home, she understood the appetites of growing teenage boys. She quickly returned with six pancakes for Connal Lee and two for the major.

After taking two large bites, the Governor felt inspired to wax effusive. "Oh, thank you, my good Major Harris, sir. Delicious appetizers. Just delicious! I haven't enjoyed anything this fine all winter long. What do you call these excellent hors d'oeuvres?"

Mrs. Ohlsson walked in with napkins. "In my country of Sweden, we call them plättar, but I believe the French call them crêpes."

"Just delicious. Thank you, Missus Ohlsson."

Connal Lee cleaned his plate in short order. Major Harris stood up. "Connal Lee, I believe we have time enough to tend to our horses. Would you like to accompany me?"

"Yes, suh, Major. Good idea."

They walked down to the street to their horses tied to the back of the carriage. They loosened the cinches on their saddles and removed the bits from their horses' mouths. "Good. So, are you still hungry, Connal Lee?"

Connal Lee nodded his head yes with a big smile.

"Well, let's go into dinner then, shall we?"

During casual conversation around the table, Connal Lee complimented the Major on his lovely home. The Major nodded with a smile. "I built this small city home for when I have duty with the Legion, which I can't manage from my farm. I have three bedrooms. My own at the front of the house, my son's tiny but adequate bedroom in the middle, and Ingrid's small bedroom in the back across from the kitchen and pantry. A covered walk leads from the back door to the outhouse and root cellar. Behind my home, I have a small lean-to barn and corral for my stallion and a milk cow. The Legion provides corrals and hay at the headquarters beside the Tithing Office, but I prefer to keep him close by."

The Governor ate five large fillets of trout by himself. When Ingrid saw his appetite, she left the heavy clay bowl of dill potatoes with a big wooden spoon beside his plate. She smiled and curtsied before returning to the kitchen to put the finishing touches on her almond cake.

Connal Lee and the Governor finished eating at the same time. They both set down their tin forks. Connal Lee glanced up and found the Governor looking at him as he wiped his lips with a linen napkin. Connal Lee smiled and nodded. "So, tell me, your honor, how did y'all find the journey here from Camp Scott? Ah've never been to Fort Bridger and the area."

The Governor chuckled. "Well, young man, it didn't start out so well. We left on the fifth. Colonel Kane accompanied me as my aide-de-camp."

"Excuse me, suh. What's an aide-de-camp?"

"Oh, that's fancy military talk for a personal assistant, a special helper, you know. He was really traveling along as my friend and guide. He not only kept me company but helped out as he could. We had my two drivers, Jim and Petty. Jim drove the carriage and served me. Petty served as the camp cook and drove the wagon with our luggage and provisions. He attended to Colonel Kane. The mules were sad creatures, nearly starved and frozen after a rough winter in Camp Scott. On the first night out, Petty's wagon overturned on a hillside and became mired in a snowbank. We slept rough that night without our tent or blankets. The next day, Jim and Petty took the mules from the carriage and went back to salvage the overturned wagon.

"I waited for them, lounging on a pile of carriage cushions on the hillside. Later that morning, Colonel Kane abruptly stood up and drew his pistol. Startled, I looked around and watched a healthy-looking young man wearing a splendid hat riding toward us on an elegant horse. He stopped and waved for the colonel to draw closer. When he saw the colonel carrying his pistol, the soldier rested his hand on his holster, although he didn't appear at all threatened by the colonel's gun. They talked briefly after introductions. I heard most of the conversation. The colonel asked if the soldier were alone. He replied no that his men surrounded him. The Colonel asked if he were in charge. When he shook his head no, Kane announced he would wait to speak with the soldier's commanding officer. The soldier said to please remain where we were, then saluted and rode away at a gallop.

"It didn't take long before I heard horses coming over the hill, approaching at a trot. Kane called out an invitation to advance closer. I stood up from my cushions and found a band of horsemen quite resplendent in their fine uniforms. Colonel Kane introduced me as the new governor. The young officer we first met dismounted and introduced us to his officers, including General William Kimball of the Nauvoo Legion. He also introduced me to Orrin Porter Rockwell, whose reputation preceded him as a notorious lawman and bodyguard to Brigham Young."

Ingrid interrupted with her caramel almond cake and a pot of coffee. The governor ended up eating a fourth of the cake by himself. As he stirred the third teaspoon of molasses sugar into his cup of coffee, he resumed his tale. "Well, young man, as it turned out, the men of the Legion saluted me as the new governor. General Kimball took us under their protection and assigned me a body guard, to my pleasant surprise. They changed our sorry mules with military efficiency for some healthy draft horses for the coach and fresh mules for the commissary wagon. General Kimball led us to the Yellow River, where we found a camp already set up. The general introduced Mister David Candland as the steward of the mess, traveling for his health. Kimball also introduced Colonel Kane and me to Mister Palmer, David Candland's cook. They had a magnificent meal prepared for us, including some very welcome bourbon and a respectable wine. We enjoyed a delightful repast in the wilderness that evening.

"Late the following day, we reached Echo Canyon on our way to Weber Station just as the sun was setting. Fires blazed along the high canyon ridges. The men of the Nauvoo Legion saluted us as we passed. Their defenses appeared most impressive."

Connal Lee coughed into his hand. He caught Major Harris' eye. The Major winked. Connal Lee grinned discreetly.

"We made the rest of the trip in good order. I am quite contented with the fine reception the city and Brigham Young extended me. My thanks to you gentlemen, as well."

Elder Staines smiled. "We're just glad you made it here all in one piece. And without an armed force backing you up. You know you need only ask, and if it is within our power to do so, we will help you in any way we can."

"Thank you, Mister Staines. Thank you, Major. You two, Connal Lee."

"Ah'm at y'all's service, suh."

The four men helped themselves to second cups of coffee loaded up with brown sugar and thick cream. Connal Lee turned to William Staines. "Ah'm sure y'all are a busy man, Elder Staines, but Ah was just wondering when Ah might arrange a visit to the magnificent Territorial Library? Ah'm so excited to explore the Library's books and novels."

Elder Staines pulled a large silver pocket watch from his vest pocket and checked the time. He looked over at the Governor. "Sir, if you could spare a moment, we could drop Connal Lee off at the Council House. I could introduce him to my dear friend, Elder John Lyon, my assistant at the Territorial Library. Connal Lee could explore the library at his leisure while we continue on to my home."

"Certainly, sir. I'm always glad to be of assistance to a young man who wants to improve himself."

The Major observed everyone had finished their desserts and coffees. "Shall we be off, then, gentlemen? After we drop Connal Lee off at the Library, I believe I will take my leave of you and stop in at the Legion headquarters."

When they exited the Major's cottage, Connal Lee saw Ingrid talking with the two Negro servants standing by the governor's carriage and six. She had obviously taken them plates of food while they waited. Connal Lee liked her for being so considerate. She picked up two empty plates and two forks from the governor's men and headed toward the house. When Connal Lee passed her, he tipped his hat to her. "Many thanks, Ma'am. Y'all's dinner was delicious. Really fine. Ah'm glad my friend, Major Harris, has someone to watch after his home and cook such good food for him. He deserves it."

"Why, thank you, young man." Ingrid then nodded to the governor behind Connal Lee. "Goodbye, Governor Cumming. A pleasure meeting you, sir."

Connal Lee spent a thrilling afternoon in the library. After exploring on his own for an hour or so, John Lyon offered his assistance. They chatted about what Connal Lee had read and what he liked in a story. John Lyon recommended two new novels by Charles Dickens, *David Copperfield* and *Hard Times*. He also suggested the new book by Herman Melville, *Moby Dick*. "It's a hard read, young man, but it will open up entirely new worlds to you. Oh, we have another new novel so pertinent to our times with the abolitionist movement spreading across our great nation. It's called *Uncle Tom's Cabin* by Harriet Beecher Stowe."

Connal Lee carried the books cradled in his arms as they wandered the stacks. "Gee, Elder Lyon, suh, these books hardly look read at all. They look like they are brand spanking new! Are y'all sure it will be all right for me to take them with me back to Fort Hall?"

"Yes, Brother Swinton. All we ask is that you protect them and return them when things are peaceful once again in the territory. We're encouraging everyone to check out all the books they can to keep the books in case we end up burning Council House. Now, since you are a self-educated young man, I think I should recommend a couple of other important books to expand your knowledge of science and history. Follow me over to the anthropology section. Since you are involved with native American people, this is a book written by George Catlin, one of the first white men to study the culture and life of Indians before white men arrived on our shores."

"Oh! Ah never knew there was a book about Indian tribes. Ah can't wait to read it. My family will also be interested to hear about other tribes and clans. Thanks very much, suh."

As the closing hour drew near, John Lyon wrapped Connal Lee's books in brown paper and tied them up with butchers' string. Connal Lee proudly signed his name next to the ledger where they kept track of books checked out and returned to the library. "Good night, Elder Lyon. I really appreciate y'all's help this afternoon. Y'all have a good night, now, ya hear?"

Connal Lee barely made it back to camp by nightfall. Short Rainbow served him some cold leftover supper along with quite a few barbed words about making his family worry when he didn't return until so late. "Sorry, Short Rainbow. But Ah'm a grown man, now. Ah can take care of myself. Y'all don't need to worry about me."

White Wolf sat down beside Connal Lee and gave him a one-armed hug. "We always worry about you, Connal Lee, when you are out of sight. You are an important part of our family. We love you, so we worry about you when you are not with us, safe and sound."

"Well... thanks. Ah love y'all too. Sorry. Ah'll let y'all know if Ah'm going to change plans and be later than expected in the future. But, just wait until Ah show y'all the great books Ah borrowed from Elder Staines' Territorial Library. We're going to have plenty to read when we get home."

Major Harris approached the Shoshone camp shortly after sunrise the following morning. Connal Lee stood up to greet him. "Good morning, Robert, suh. Please come join us for some coffee." Connal Lee walked with the major to tether his stallion to their small herd down by the river. "Are y'all hungry this morning, Major? Would y'all like to join us for breakfast?"

"Thank you, Connal Lee. I had a buttered roll this morning on my way out the door, but I could use some coffee now that you mention it."

The major greeted all the delegation while Connal Lee poured him a tin travel mug of black coffee. He sat down beside the major and handed him the hot cup by its handle. "So, what do y'all have planned for us today, Major?"

"Well, Connal Lee, that's why I rode out to see you. A couple of things happened after I dropped you off at the library. First, Governor Cumming asked me to invite your delegation to join him for supper at the Staines' mansion Saturday evening at six o'clock. He said until then, he would be too busy inspecting the books and records of the territory and writing his reports to his interim government still camped out next to Johnston's army. The governor said

118

he also had to write President Buchanan and the Secretary of War to advise them of his peaceful entry into the territory. He seemed anxious to hear your story, Connal Lee, of how you came to be adopted into the Shoshone nation and learned their language.

"After I got home and unsaddled my horse, I received a visit from the Legion's Orderly of the Day inviting me to wait on General Kimball at the Legion offices. I immediately walked down the hill and reported in. The general relieved me of all duties besides being your official host until you return north. He also asked me to invite you to attend sacrament meeting in the tabernacle this coming Sunday morning when President Young will introduce Governor Cumming. General Kimball said you may attend or not as you wish, but you would be welcome to be there to receive the new governor to the territory as part of the official delegation. I need to let him know your answer so he can reserve seats for you. They expect a huge turnout."

The major blew on his coffee and took a sip. He looked at the delegation sitting around the campfire eating broiled trout and smoked salmon for their breakfasts. Bright Star handed the major a simple wooden platter with both kinds of fish.

"Thank you, Bright Star. I returned home from meeting with the General and found that my two youngest sons had arrived early with our family white top and farm wagon. They are empty, so we can load up more belongings to take south. I woke up this morning and thought I might invite you to join me on a trip down to my family farm south of Provo, west of Payson. Unless there is something else you would like to do. I mean, besides camping out in the library!" The Major winked at Connal Lee, who sat vigorously nodding his head at the idea of returning to the Territorial Library. "I thought if you wanted to come, we could pay a social call on Captain Hanover on the way. I would like to see for myself how the Saints are managing the move south. My boys told me last night that they invited several refugee families to camp out along the creeks crossing our fields, so they have a safe place to live in the interim. It will be a slow journey on the way down there if you would like to go. But if we left fairly soon, we could make it to Captain Hanover's farmstead around supper time, spend the night, then go on to my family property Friday morning. If we depart Saturday morning, we can make it back to the governor's supper in the evening."

The major looked at Connal Lee for an answer. Connal Lee met his gaze, then glanced around at his family. "Ah wouldn't mind seeing more of the exodus and seeing Captain Hanover again. Would y'all like to join me?"

Arimo shrugged. "We don't know your Mormon friends. We will stay here. We can hunt and fish while we await your return. I thought I would take a ride out to Antelope Island this afternoon and explore it while hunting."

"Well, what do y'all say, White Wolf? Shall we take our tent and leave Arimo to guard our tipi and horses while we go on an excursion?" His family all nodded their acceptance. Connal Lee stood up. "Well, Major, since we won't be traveling with the tipi, we can be ready to leave in about half an hour."

Major Harris stood up and brushed off his pale blue pants. "Excellent. I will rush home and help my boys finish loading up the wagons. We will leave as soon as you arrive. Do you remember the way to my home north of Temple Square?"

Connal Lee smiled and nodded his head yes. "We'll be there within the hour, Major."

Connal Lee and his family made it to the modest adobe house before the sun poked up above the snowcapped Wasatch Mountains. They carried their sleeping furs tied on behind their saddles. They wore all their weapons and led heavily laden packhorses with their tent and cooking provisions. White Wolf and Short Rainbow always traveled with their medicine bags, which required two more big packhorses loaded to capacity.

The major's jacket hung off a tree branch beside the wagons. He had rolled up his shirt sleeves to help his sons load the wagons. When the Shoshone delegation came to a halt behind his wagons on the street, the major stopped working and wiped the sweat from his forehead with his shirtsleeve. "Boys, come meet my friends, the official delegation representing Chief Arimo and the Shoshone Nation. They came to welcome the new governor to the territory." One by one, the major introduced Connal Lee and his family, telling his sons a little about each person.

Major Harris put his arm over his youngest son's shoulders and pulled him into a hug. "This is my youngest son, who I told you wants to go to West Point. He's the brains in the family. His name is Samuel Edward, named after his mother's father. My middle son, that tall young man standing by the tailgate, is James Mitchell, also named after his maternal grandfather."

Edward and Jim shook everyone's hands.

With the introductions completed, the Major took charge. "Edward, did you pick up the crates of books you told Elder Lyon you would help salvage from the library? Good. Well, all right, boys. Let's fasten down the freight and get rolling. It's a beautiful day to be on the road."

Ingrid rushed out of the Major's home carrying a cutting board piled high with cinnamon rolls. The rolls looked like knots of dough sprinkled over with powdered sugar. She offered everyone a sweet roll. "Here's something for the road, boys. Have a safe trip."

With so much traffic on State Road, they moved at an extra slow pace. As they rode south along the valley, the Major pointed out the different grist mills and lumber mills on the creeks and rivers flowing out of the mountains draining down to the Great Salt Lake. Once they rounded the granite cliffs at the south end of the valley, they could move faster. As they drew closer to Provo, the traffic slowed down again as the road became more congested. Major Harris waved their troop to head off cross country, turning south off the main roadway. "Before the exodus, less than three-thousand Saints lived in Utah County. Now close to fourteen-thousand souls and all their livestock live around Provo, straining resources to the maximum. We're running late, so let's not get mired down in all that congestion."

They arrived at Captain Hanover's farmhouse after eight hours on the road, weary from the journey. Screaming Eagle barely managed to dismount. He stood clinging to his saddle for stability. White Wolf saw and rushed over to prop him up. Connal Lee and Short Rainbow spread sleeping furs so he could immediately sit down and rest.

Captain Hanover invited them to join his family for supper. The captain had invited dozens of displaced Mormon families to camp on his property. His three wives worked at feeding the new arrivals from their kitchens until they set up their own cooking facilities. The captain's daughters served supper to the visiting delegation at a great board table improvised over sawhorses. His sons had set up the table under the trees between the farmhouse and their kitchen garden along the river.

During the leisurely meal, Captain Hanover told of an impoverished family his second wife had invited to stay in their home across the creek. "The poor Sister an' 'er growin' children only owned one change o' mismatched ol' clothes provided by the bishops tithing warehouse. Her husband passed away just weeks after they arrived in the valley some four years ago, leavin' 'er with five little children an' no man t' provide fer 'em. When 'e died, 'er youngest was a babe in arms who had been born on the trail. The bishop o' the fourteenth Ward loaned 'er a little shack behind 'is house t' live in. It had once been a chicken coop that 'e later closed up t' make a tool shed. Since they only had one pair o' shoes each, they walked barefoot all the way down here, carryin' their shoes tied around their necks t' preserve 'em. She explained how ever Saturday evenin' after her children went t' sleep, she mended an' washed their only clothes so they would have somethin' clean t' wear fer Sunday school the next mornin'. She took in washin' an' sewin' t' help support 'er little children. Since she couldn't leave them untended, it limited what she could do t' make a livin'. It was a right sad sight t' see 'em walkin' on their dusty bare feet as they approached Hobble Creek. She carried everythin' they owned in a potato sack tied over her shoulders with her baby held in her arms. She had sold all their belongin's when she first arrived t' help support 'er children. Her oldest had just turned fourteen before they evacuated south from Great Salt Lake City. Nice lookin' lad. Although poor in worldly possessions, she obeyed Brigham Young's advice t' leave the meager comfort of 'er little home an' move south. What an act o' faith!"

The temperature made it up to the mid-sixties that afternoon, which everyone found very comfortable. However, they knew the cloudless night would allow temperatures to plummet nearly to freezing, so Short Rainbow and Bright Star took the time to pitch their tent. Connal Lee meandered down Hobble Creek, running between the captain's two farmhouses. A variety of tents, including a few big Sibley tents shaped like tipis, except with only one center pole, lined the creek. Some families lived out of their wagons until they could improvise some shelter. Others had built simple wicki-ups covered with blankets to sleep under.

Connal Lee and Captain Hanover stayed up late, reliving their experiences on the Overland Trail. Major Harris listened in, glad to learn more about his young friend's life.

The following day while they drank coffee around their camp-fire, Captain Hanover's wives and children carried baskets of freshly baked rolls to all the camps lining the river. An hour after daybreak, Connal Lee's company said their goodbyes. Major Harris led his boys and the Shoshone delegation southeast to skirt around the edge of Provo Bay. Two hours later, they crossed a simple stone and wood bridge over Beer Creek and entered his family farm and ranch. The major's five-hundred-acre property stretched from the creek on the east to West Mountain on the west, then north to Utah Lake.

The major happily led their short parade up the path from the bridge towards a small compound. His buildings nestled between the juncture of Beer Creek, a thirty-foot wide river, and Spring Creek, a ten-foot-wide creek. Green spring grasses and wild hay covered the land. Various trees and sagebrush grew along the creek beds, mostly cottonwoods with a few chokecherries and a few gray mountain mahoganies. They rode past a small earthen dam that diverted water into a series of irrigation canals and ditches, meticulously dug and maintained over the past ten years to water their kitchen garden, fields, and pastures.

The boys drove their wagons to the big barn behind a log cabin home. The log cabin had obviously been added onto over the years. The major waved at the Shoshone to follow him into the compound. "This is my country home when my duties with the Legion permit me to be out of the city. My darling wife, Mary Ellen, and my three boys built it in the spring of forty-eight before I got here. The board house on the left is Junior's, and the one on the right is Jim's. We added their homes when they got married. They cut the trees and hauled them to the new sawmill southeast of here over by Payson.

With a supply of cut boards, they built these fine homes themselves. Shortly after Junior got married, my dear wife Mary Ellen took sick. A couple of days later, she passed through the veil. We think maybe it was a burst appendix, but we didn't have a doctor in Payson at the time to tell us for certain. The Elders came and gave her a health blessing, but she didn't survive, anyway. I guess it was God's will. We miss her still. Well, come on in. My daughters-in-law keep the place cleaned and aired out for when I come to stay or for Edward to use when the university lets out for the summer."

Everyone dismounted. "You are welcome to sleep in the cabin or erect your tent here in the front yard. We have a large corral with fresh running water behind the barn for the horses. I have an outhouse behind my farmhouse, or you can use the creeks, whichever you prefer. Please, make yourselves at home."

Working as a well-practiced team, the Shoshone family unpacked their saddlebags, corralled the horses, and pitched the tent. Connal Lee wandered off looking for Major Harris. He found the major a short walk south of the compound, standing with his hat held in his hands, gazing down at the ground. When he drew closer, the major looked up. "Hello, Connal Lee."

"Robert."

Connal Lee looked down at a simple granite block sitting in the grass with words carved on top: *Mary Ellen Mitchell Harris – Beloved Wife and Mother – 1813 to 1850.* Connal Lee placed his hand on the major's shoulder and stood with him for a moment in silence. He turned and walked away with a sigh, leaving his older friend to his memories. As he strolled back to the farm compound, he admired the majestic mountains far away to the east of the flat farmlands. They stood blued and hazed in the distance. The top third of the mountains were still snowcapped, clearly visible in the bright sunlight. The low hills to the west were green with early spring growth. Connal Lee walked on, thinking about how all that pleasant green will turn golden brown in the first hot days of summer.

Junior's wives hosted a grand supper to welcome their father and his guests. They didn't have a dining table large enough to seat twelve adults and two babies, so the major's sons hauled their three small dining tables outside. They put them together in front of the original log cabin to make one long table. As the sun began setting behind the gentle green hills to their west, they sat down to eat. The Major's three daughters-in-law scurried around serving a beef barley soup, then a big pot roast with plenty of root vegetables roasted to perfection. A chocolate cake topped with sour cherry preserves capped off the festive meal.

Connal Lee and White Wolf lit the campfire. Short Rainbow and Bright Star brought out fur blankets for everyone to sit on around the bonfire. Junior's two young children romped about, too wound up to sit and rest with the grown-ups. Jim's young wife, Evelyn, stood up. "I'm sorry. Suddenly I don't feel... I think I'm going to be sick!"

Evelyn lifted the front of her long skirt and apron and took off running for the outhouse behind her farmhouse. Jim leapt up and jogged after her. A few moments later, he rushed back to the fireplace in a panic. "Christina! May! I need help. Evelyn was throwing up when she suddenly went into an odd spasm and collapsed. I think she passed out. I don't know what's wrong with her. Help me get her into bed."

The two sisters jumped to their feet and dashed after Jim. Before they turned around the corner of the unpainted house, White Wolf and Short Rainbow gave each other a nod, stood up, and followed quickly. They arrived at the two-hole privy behind the farmhouse in time to see Jim picking Evelyn up by her armpits. Christina and May were bent over, lifting Evelyn's legs. White Wolf sized up the situation in a glance and took charge. He looked at Jim's panicked face. "No carry on back. What if vomit? Carry on side."

White Wolf gently grasped Evelyn's shoulders and tipped her over to her side. Short Rainbow shouldered Christina and May aside so she could pick up Evelyn's legs. White Wolf ordered Jim, "Hold head. Easy. Easy. Now, walk." He glanced over at Christina and May. "Lead way."

Christina ran ahead and held open the back door of the farmhouse. By the time they reached the door, the entire party sitting around the fireplace had joined them to find out what was going on. Junior's little children ran for their mothers, grabbing onto their long skirts, crying in fear at seeing Aunt Evelyn limp and unconscious.

Major Harris invited May to take the children home. "There's enough excitement here without them bawling their heads off on top of everything."

White Wolf followed Christina through the kitchen into the front bedroom. After she turned down the quilts, they gently laid Evelyn down on her side. They no sooner had her on the homemade mattress when she began dry retching. Christina reached under the bed, pulled out an enameled tin bedpan, and handed it to Jim. "Here. Hold this under her chin in case she throws up some more. Oh, what could be the matter with her? What's wrong? Why is she twitching and sweating so much?"

White Wolf stood up. "Please. Quiet. No talk."

Short Rainbow began unfastening Evelyn's simple cotton blouse and skirt, now covered with vomit. When she recognized blood in the vomit, she silently pointed it out to White Wolf. He frowned and placed his ear over Evelyn's breast to hear her heartbeat. "Heart slow. Breath fast. No good!"

He stood up and examined the young woman as Short Rainbow stripped off her undergarments. He noticed her flushed skin, damp with sweat. Tears leaked out of her closed eyes.

"Food poison. Bad, bad food poison."

White Wolf pointed at Christina. "Please. Water to clean and cool." He stood up and spoke in a fast rattle of Shoshone. "Bright Star, please boil some fresh water. Short Rainbow, please see what you can do to clean up Evelyn and make her comfortable. I need to identify the source of the food poisoning to determine what remedies might give her relief."

White Wolf looked at Jim standing beside his wife, wringing his hands. "Please, Jim. Show where Evelyn cook. Show where store food." Jim returned a blank look. "Quick. Now!"

Jim shook himself out of his panic attack and nodded his understanding. "Follow me, White Wolf."

Jim led White Wolf into their simple kitchen. Major Harris and Connal Lee followed, curious about White Wolf's interest in Evelyn's kitchen. Bright Star stayed to assist Short Rainbow in cleaning up the patient. White Wolf examined the used pots and pans, then the wood cutting boards and knives. Shaking his head, he glanced around the room. His eyes fell on a wooden pail filled with discards from preparing supper. He bent down to look more closely. Jim touched his shoulder. "That's just the slops for the pigs, White Wolf. What are you..."

White Wolf held up his hand to stop the distraction. He lifted the pail onto the plain bench cook table and inspected the potato peels, eggshells, trimmed fat from meat, and chicken bones. Then found what appeared to be small wild onions. Gingerly he picked one up by the green grass-like leaves sprouting from the top of the bulb. The bottom half of the bulb had been bitten off. He smelled the bulb, then shook his head. He knew what had happened.

White Wolf stood up with a determined look on his face. "Connal Lee, please inform the Major's family that I believe Evelyn harvested what she thought were wild onions, only they were not. I don't know the English word for these plants, but there are two kinds. The bulbs with purple flowers are edible. Those with white flowers are very poisonous. I'm afraid Evelyn must have picked some of the poisonous variety. A couple of years back, I met a wise shaman of the Nez Perce traveling with their traders. We were up around Chief SoYo'Cant's favorite summer camp that the white man named Teton Peaks in Yellowstone Valley. Both kinds of this false onion grow there. He showed me how the Nez Perce prepare a mash from the bulbs of the purple blossoms and bake it into a kind of sweet bread. He told me the only remedy for the poison of the white blossom bulbs was a mild tea made from the leaves of a night-blooming plant he called dreaming visions. I don't know the name in English. Its fragrant flowers only bloom at night. He told me a tea made from their leaves can be used for breathing problems and nerve diseases. With a larger dose, one sees visions of things not of this world. With an even larger dose, death comes quickly. Now, please excuse me while I search for some of its dried leaves in my medicine bags. Even if it helps, the only thing for food poisoning is time for the body to rid itself of the poison and heal. Recovery is not a fast process, at best, I'm afraid."

Connal Lee translated as best he could to the worried family around him. "White Wolf and Short Rainbow are both smart and well trained in all kinds of healing, Robert. Y'all's daughter-in-law

127

couldn't be in better hands. White Wolf is going to brew a tea that might help, although he said in the end, it's the body itself that does the healing. He said it's a slow process to heal from food poisoning."

Half an hour later, White Wolf carried a tin mug of jimsonweed tea to Evelyn's bedside. Because of the bitter fumes from the tea, White Wolf had mixed in generous amounts of mint tea and honey, hoping to make it more palatable. With Short Rainbow's assistance, they turned Evelyn onto her back. White Wolf carefully lifted her head. Even though she remained unconscious, he held the cup up to her mouth. He tipped out a couple of drops on her closed lips, trying to entice her to take a sip. She licked her lips, swallowed a little, then coughed. Her eyes fluttered open briefly. "Here, drink little more. Good. Good. More. Good."

After a few sips, Evelyn's eyes closed. White Wolf nodded and patted her on the shoulder. "Sleep. Rest. Heal."

White Wolf turned to Jim, who stood frowning beside the bed and spoke to him in English. "She live. Heal slow. Patience, now. Short Rainbow stay with Evelyn all night. No worry. You sleep. Understand? Evelyn live. No danger. Understand?"

"Thank you, White Wolf. I don't know what we would have done without you and Short Rainbow. It surely is a blessing that Papa brought you to visit. Otherwise, who knows what might have happened. We don't have a doctor in these parts, not even in Payson. Thank you, my friends. Thank you so very much."

White Wolf patted Jim on the back and gestured for him to lie down beside his sleeping wife. "You rest, now. No good worry. Sleep."

White Wolf herded everyone out, leaving only Jim and Short Rainbow to attend the sick young woman. Bright Star took White Wolf's hand. "Come, husband. You are tired. I can see it. Come to bed and let me massage your neck and shoulders. You need to relax now, too. You have finished your good services for the night. We will see what the new day brings us."

Connal Lee said good night to everyone and followed White Wolf and Bright Star out to their tent. Screaming Eagle saw them coming around the side of the farmhouse and joined them. He had felt useless and a bit claustrophobic standing in the bedroom, so he had gone outside for a breath of fresh air. Before they entered the army tent, Major Harris walked up and shook White Wolf's hand. "Thank you, White Wolf. I will never forget your kind assistance this night. Thank you, my friend."

Bright and early in the morning, White Wolf and Connal Lee visited the sick room. Evelyn appeared to be sleeping. She still twitched occasionally, like in the throes of bad dreams. White Wolf found her breathing a little slower and her heart beating faster. He shared the good news with all the worried faces around the bed. "Recommend broth until stomach normal. One two day. When sit up, soft food until strong. Understand?"

White Wolf shared some further instructions with Connal Lee and asked him to translate. "I give more tea. Only little. You give more at night. Only little. Little is medicine. Lot is poison. Understand?"

Connal Lee turned to Jim. "White Wolf asked me to warn y'all. These bulbs with white blooms that look like wild onions are poisonous to all living things. He recommends that when Evelyn is up and around, y'all have her show y'all where she found the bulbs. He said to kill them all or at least fence them off. If cattle or horses eat them, they will get sick and die. Look at what just half of one little bulb did to Evelyn."

"Thank you for the warning, White Wolf. And thank you for helping my poor sick wife. God bless and God speed. You will always be welcome in our home. Please come back when you can stay longer. Safe travels, my friends."

Connal Lee took off for Junior's home. He told Christina and May about White Wolf's directions for Evelyn's future care and feeding so they could help Jim take care of his wife during her recovery.

The Shoshone family knew they needed to leave before too much later to make it back to the governor's supper that evening. They would be able to travel a lot faster without the wagons, but they would still have a long day on the road. Junior and his two wives sent the Major and the Shoshone delegation off with a hot breakfast of omelets and warm, freshly baked brown bread.

To avoid the congestion around Provo on State Road, they traveled cross country once again. That afternoon, when they drew close to Great Salt Lake City's downtown district, Major Harris recommended they part ways, dress for the formal supper, then meet at the Staines mansion. Connal Lee looked at White Wolf, who nodded his head. "We know the way, Major. We will meet you there. Thanks."

When the delegation arrived at their camp, Connal Lee looked at the sun nearly touching the distant mountains to their west. He estimated they had less than an hour to wash off the dust of the road in the Jordan River, get dressed in their ceremonial finest, and ride to the governor's supper. Short Rainbow suggested they wear their hair loose so it could dry as they traveled. They each tied on beaded headbands, foregoing any other ornaments in dressing their hair. Connal Lee thought his spouses' relaxed, loose hairstyle made them appear much less fierce and warlike, softer, gentler, and more approachable. He liked the idea of presenting this peaceful face to the Mormons and the new governor.

An officer of the Nauvoo Legion acted as the doorman on the governor's behalf, turning away any uninvited guests. Governor Cumming needed a guard at the door. The new governor had heard about people wanting to leave the Territory who were not given passes for one reason or another. He made a public announcement that anyone seeking his protection could come to him at any time. Since then, he had petitioners knocking on his door from dawn to dusk.

When Screaming Eagle led the delegation through the gardens and up the steps, the officer threw open the door. He smiled, made a curt little bow, and gestured for everyone to enter. "Be welcome on behalf of Governor Cumming and his host, Elder Staines. Kindly leave your hats, gloves, and weapons on the hall table. One of the housemaids will show you through to the dining room."

Connal Lee entered the mansion and smiled at the doorman. "Thanks very much, suh. And a pleasant evening to y'all."

A young girl wearing a white bag hat covering all her hair curtsied to the Shoshone family. "Please follow me."

She led them through the parlor where they had met the governor earlier in the week. She opened double doors into a large room on the side of the house behind the parlor. Late afternoon sun lit the room through three tall windows edged with fabric draperies. A great mahogany table and fourteen matching dining chairs dominated the room. Governor Cumming saw them ushered in and stood up. "Welcome, Master Swinton and fellow Shoshone delegates. Master Swinton, your chair is here beside me. Major Harris, perhaps you could help the others find their names on the place cards."

Connal Lee strode to the head of the table. After the Governor resumed his seat, Elder Staines held Connal Lee's chair and helped him sit down. All the dishes, silverware, and glasses sitting on a spotless white tablecloth on the table intimidated Connal Lee. "Good evening, Governor. How are y'all doing this evening, Elder Staines?" Connal Lee looked across the table and nodded. "Nice to see y'all again, Colonel Kane."

He leaned forward and looked down the long table. His family sat interspersed with the other guests, Mormon, Shoshone, Mormon, Shoshone, in such a way it had to be deliberate. He grinned when he saw Short Rainbow and Bright Star sitting on the needlepoint chair seats with their legs crossed under them as if they were sitting on the ground. He spotted Elder Staines' wives, Elizabeth and Lillias, on each side of Screaming Eagle. He nodded and smiled. They all three smiled back.

The governor harrumphed a slight cough into his fist. Everyone quieted down and turned to look at him. "Ladies and gentlemen, friends and allies, it is my pleasure to welcome you all to my little dinner party in our kind host's gracious home. Thank you, Mister Staines and your lovely wives for making Colonel Kane and me feel so welcome. Now, if you will all please stand, I would like to propose a toast welcoming the Shoshone Delegation to the Territory of Utah."

Connal Lee and his Shoshone family imitated the others who rose to their feet, holding a slender wine glass in their right hands. The Governor grunted when he stood up. "To peaceful relations with our friends and allies, Chief Arimo and all the great Shoshone Nation."

Several men around the table seconded him, "Here, here!" They all raised their glasses and took a sip. Connal Lee noticed White Wolf spat the wine back into the delicate glass and gave him a questioning look. In Shoshone, White Wolf whispered, "The fruit juice has gone bad. It is not good to drink."

Connal Lee put his drink down untouched. Concerned that perhaps Elder Staines wasn't aware his fruit juice had turned, he quietly translated what White Wolf had said. Elder Staines chuckled. "Thank you, Master Swinton, but we intentionally fermented the grape juice to make wine. Don't your native Indian friends drink fermented fruit beverages?"

Puzzled, Connal Lee shook his head. He watched as others at the table sipped the pale wine, smiling as they made conversation with their neighbors.

"Young Master Swinton, I have been curious about your history since we first met at the welcoming reception. Your speech sounds like that of a gentleman of the South, but I believe you told me you were born in the back hills of Missouri. Do I remember correctly?"

"Yes, suh. That is correct."

"Well, please tell me how a hillbilly boy from the Ozarks grew up to be an impressive young man out here on the frontier. I'm dying to hear the story."

Connal Lee felt intimidated when conversation died down, and all eyes turned to him. He wondered if he should stand up and mumbled, "Where to start?"

Elder Staines, sitting beside him, heard. He clapped Connal Lee on his shoulder. "Why, start at the beginning, Master Swinton. That's where all stories start."

"Right, suh. Well, Governor, my story began back the first week of February in eighteen forty-five when Ah was born. My poor Mah died giving me birth. My Paw hated me for killing my mother. He was always mean to me and my older brother Zeff and his wife, Sister Woman. We lived in the mountains with no neighbors close by. My old man and Zeff kilned bricks for cash money. We didn't have any school or church to go to. Well, suh, two years ago, shortly after Ah turned twelve, our old Paw turned real mean. Zeff and Sister Woman took their baby boy and me, and we escaped

132

for our safety. We walked all the way north to Independence, Missouri."

While Connal Lee spoke, two kitchen maids began serving bowls of soup and fresh dinner rolls. Connal Lee nodded his thanks. Taking his time, he told of joining the handcart company and learning to read and speak proper English. He shared the story of Captain Reed becoming his big brother and how the Baines became his foster parents.

Connal Lee saw the kitchen maids clearing the empty bowls, so he stopped talking and quickly slurped up his lukewarm soup. Mr. Staines looked at Colonel Kane on the other side of the table. "We've crossed the Continental Divide more than once, haven't we, Colonel Kane?"

"Yes, sir. I've crossed the divide on the Overland Trail several times, now, going both ways, plus once down in Panama most recently."

Connal Lee set down his soup spoon. When he looked up, the Governor nodded. "Please do go on, Master Swinton. What happened then?"

Connal Lee shared the story of his hunting excursions, the Crow attack, his wounding, and being saved by his Shoshone family.

White Wolf leaned forward to get Connal Lee's attention. "Don't forget you rescue Screaming Eagle after capture by Crows. Very important."

"Yes, thanks, White Wolf. Screaming Eagle didn't return after tracking a small group that split off from the Crow war party we were following. Early the next morning, Ah tracked him to where the Crows held him captive. We killed the Crow warriors and freed Screaming Eagle. Screaming Eagle adopted me as his brother. Then we all adopted each other since we felt like family by that time. When we finally joined Chief Arimo, he was ready to lead his clan down here to Great Salt Lake City for their annual fur trading expedition. To thank me for saving Screaming Eagle's life, the great chief adopted me as his white Shoshone son in a beautiful ceremony that included smoking the peace pipe."

The kitchen maids carried in platters and set them down in the center of the table. The platters held whole roasted chickens, a spit-roasted piglet, and a large beef tenderloin. With a brief smattering of conversation, the men began carving the meats and passing them around to everyone. The young maids returned with bowls of creamed new potatoes and peas smothered in butter. They carried in platters of roasted root vegetables from last fall's harvest. The sight of the food made Connal Lee hungry, so he heaped his plate high and dug in with a will. The governor likewise focused on all the fine food before him.

After a few minutes, Connal Lee took a sip of water and sat back, quite contented. He smiled at the company around him. Connal Lee leaned forward and resumed his life history. He told about meeting Brigham Young with Chief Arimo and returning to Fort Hall to find his white family. "During our travels, the friendship with my Shoshone family grew into love. They asked me to share their tipi. For the Shoshone, this meant to join them in marriage. Ah was so happy. A lot happened after that. My foster brothers, Captain Reed and Lieutenant Anderson, arrived at Fort Hall. Late last February, Ah rode to Fort Lemhi with Captain Reed to check out rumors we heard of Indians preparing to attack the Mormon fort. We reached it the day after the attack. We couldn't do anything at that point, so the captain returned to his command at Fort Hall, and Ah returned to Chief Arimo's winter camp. We were there when Major Harris rode in with an invitation from Governor Young to join him as allies in welcoming your honor, suh. And that brings us to the present day, eating a delicious supper with y'all in Elder Staines' beautiful home."

Governor Cumming led the small dinner party in applause when Connal Lee finished his story. Connal Lee stood up, gave a slight bow to the governor, then resumed his seat. His cheeks blushed pink with embarrassment. The governor then turned a penetrating stare at Connal Lee. "Hm. Interesting story, Master Swinton. I confess I find myself rather amazed. You educated yourself while traveling across America, picking up older brothers, foster parents, and a goodly number of friends. You adopted a Shoshone family – and then you were adopted by Chief Arimo. As Chief Arimo's son, you were introduced to important men in the military, the territorial government, and leaders of the Mormon Church. You speak like an educated man, not like a hillbilly from the Ozark Mountains. Amazing, don't you think, Colonel Kane? Not many young men can make such claims, now, can they? I think I'm going to have to keep an eye on you, young man. Your career just might prove interesting as you grow up and take your place in the world."

Major Harris nodded and smiled at Connal Lee. "Yes, Governor Cumming. Connal Lee moves in interesting circles for a man of such tender years. As the official host of the Shoshone Delegation, I invited the delegates to travel with me these past few days to visit my farmstead down south of Provo. While there, my daughter-in-law came down with a severe case of food poisoning. White Wolf diagnosed the cause of the food poisoning and prepared an antidote in short order. He and Short Rainbow tended to her needs most diligently and solicitously. While visiting Chief Arimo in his winter camp, I saw for myself the high regard the chief has for Screaming Eagle, an accomplished and honorable warrior. The chief told me he is a leader who has successfully battled marauding Crow horse thieves. Yes, I believe our young friend married into an exceptional family. I agree, Governor. I think this young man is going places."

When Elizabeth Staines noted everyone had finished eating their desserts, she invited the guests to join her in the parlor for after-dinner beverages and conversation. Everyone made their way into the parlor, now lit by wax candles in glass lamps. Elizabeth entertained the company for the next half hour by playing Mozart Sonatas on her grand pianoforte, recently imported from Germany. Once she began playing, Connal Lee unselfconsciously walked over and stood in front of the lid propped open above the big brass piano harp. Intrigued by both the mechanics of the piano and the delightful music, he stood spellbound. He heard someone talking on a settee across the room and sent them a dirty look to be quiet so he could listen to the music. When Elizabeth stopped playing and stood up, Connal Lee clapped louder than anyone. After the applause died down, everyone stood up and began taking their leave.

Connal Lee walked up to Governor Cumming and held out his hand. "Many thanks, suh, for inviting us to this wonderful supper. So long, for now. We'll see y'all tomorrow morning at the tabernacle unless something unexpected comes up."

"My dear Master Swinton, it is I who thank you for providing us with such an interesting story to entertain our supper table. I wish you and your adopted and foster families all the best during these times of change. I can only hope for continued peace between the Shoshone nation and all our white settlers in the territory. Good night, young man. Until tomorrow morning."

On the way out, Connal Lee sought out Mr. Staines. "Our thanks to y'all for a delicious supper. Good night, suh."

"Good night, Brother Connal Lee. Until tomorrow, then."

Sunday dawned cool. Clouds passed overhead, blowing easterly. An occasional sprinkle reached the ground, but not enough to be inconvenient. With the temperature in the breezy fifties, Connal Lee pulled on his old army pants and coat. They didn't expect Major Harris until around eight-thirty, two hours after sunrise. He knew the sacrament meeting in the tabernacle would begin at nine o'clock. While waiting for breakfast, Connal Lee walked down and inspected their horses beside the Jordan River. He couldn't help but notice how the river ran higher than the day before. He figured rain or snow had fallen in the mountains during the night, and the water was just then reaching the lower valley.

After breakfast, Connal Lee changed into his ceremonial clothing. Screaming Eagle and White Wolf decided to accompany him, so they dressed up in their finest as well. Short Rainbow and Bright Star worked on the men's hair, wrapping furs and beads into fancy designs. Connal Lee wore his tri-colored headband with notched feathers dangling from leather ribbons. He proudly put on the breastplate designating him the son of Chief Arimo.

When Major Harris arrived, Connal Lee invited him to have some coffee. "Sorry, Connal Lee, but we need to hurry. They expect an overflow crowd coming to hear the new governor this morning. Let's get underway as soon as possible."

On the ride east to the gateless entrance in the city walls, Major Harris called out loud enough to be heard over their horses, "Elder Staines invited us to tie up our rides in front of his home and walk to the tabernacle. Most of the crowd will walk, but some will come from further away, creating a congestion on the streets."

When they arrived at the Staines mansion, they waved as the governor and Colonel Kane left in the carriage. Mr. Staines and his wives strolled out of the house and joined Connal Lee walking on foot. After exchanging smiles and greetings, Mr. Staines led the way with a wife on each arm. "I'm glad to see you made it early. We have boys saving you seats in the front row where everyone can see your delegation. But with the crowd gathering at the tabernacle since early this morning, they will have trouble keeping your seats too much longer. We better go claim your places right away."

A cold, damp drizzle began during their walk. Lillias Staines chuckled and opened a parasol that matched her light raincoat. "When the Saints meet, the heavens weep. It never fails. Every general conference, we expect rain, even though we live in the desert."

As soon as they arrived, young men ushered them into the cavernous hall. A murmur of conversation surrounded them. Connal Lee heard the pipe organ playing background music as people walked in. Mr. Staines escorted the delegation up onto the stage to exchange greetings with President Young and other church dignitaries. They shook hands with Governor Cumming and Colonel Kane. Brigham Young checked his large gold pocket watch and invited everyone to find their seats.

White Wolf and Screaming Eagle hadn't been in the tabernacle before. They gawked at the size of the building and the thousands of people crowding to enter. The doors and windows in the back of the tabernacle stood wide open so latecomers, forced to stand outside in the drizzle, could hear the proceedings.

Brigham Young walked up to the pulpit and gazed out at the congregation. Within moments, the throng quieted down with their hats and gloves held in their laps. The music grew louder, announcing the start of the meeting. When the music stopped, Brigham Young welcomed everyone. "I shall now ask my first counselor, Brother Heber C. Kimball, to open our meeting with prayer."

Connal Lee watched a well-dressed bald man step up to the podium. When he began the invocation, everyone bowed their heads to complete silence. Connal Lee couldn't help but notice the odor of damp wool and cotton worn by the congregation around him, wet from the drizzle. After the prayer, Brigham Young introduced the tabernacle choir. A brief organ introduction played while the choir stood up in front of their chairs surrounding the dignitaries on the stage. With a joyful loud voice, the choir conductor led them in singing, "Come, come, ye saints, no toil nor labor fear..." The four-part harmony of the choir, accompanied by the miraculous pipe organ, enchanted Connal Lee. After several minutes, the choir began a new stanza, singing very softly. "And should we die before our journey's through, happy day! All is well." Connal Lee noticed quite a few of the ladies pulled crochet-edged handkerchiefs out of their sleeves and wiped away their tears. The music grew louder and louder as the hymn drew to its triumphant climax. "All is well! All is well!"

The final chord gradually faded away.

Brigham Young announced they would now share the holy sacrament of the Lord's supper. Connal Lee had seen this during the handcart journey when his family sat in on the company's Sunday services. The congregation sat quietly as young men recited the blessings on the bread and wine. A bevy of young men walked past the sacrament table. Each boy picked up a plate of broken bread and an ornate silver cup of wine. As the boys walked up the aisles, they handed the plates and cups to the first person in the row. The Saints each ate a small piece of torn bread and took a sip of wine, then passed the plates and cups to the person sitting beside them. The deacons served the entire congregation of over three thousand in about ten minutes. Whispering, Connal Lee tried to explain to White Wolf and Screaming Eagle what this strange ritual meant to the Mormons.

When all the teenage deacons returned to their seats in front of the sacrament table, Brigham Young stood up. In a loud public speaking voice that carried clearly throughout the hall, he introduced Governor Cumming. "Let us all make him welcome and assist him in preserving law and order in the territory, protecting the God-inspired Constitution of the United States of America. Governor Cumming, would you like to say a few words, sir?"

The Governor stood up, shook hands with Brigham Young, and stepped up to the pulpit. For the next half hour, he spoke forcefully about the Constitution and the supremacy of Federal laws meant to give all citizens fair and equal justice under the law. He explained how he meant to execute his duties in upholding the law. He said if someone breaks the law, the perpetrator can expect to be judged by a trial of his peers. He swore he would not subject the citizens of the territory to a trial by the army or its hangers-on in the camp. Connal Lee noticed with surprise how quiet the large group of people had become as they listened to their new governor. Visitors watching Chief Arimo's tribal councils never sat this quietly. He only heard people coughing, such a familiar background sound no one paid attention to it. Once a little child began fussing in the very back of the hall. The young mother quickly picked up the boy and bustled him out the door.

Connal Lee thought the meeting would end when the governor finished his speech. But then the new governor opened up the floor to questions. "I would be glad to hear from any who might be inclined to address me or ask questions on topics of interest to the community."

For the next two hours, speaker after speaker complained of the wrongs done to the Mormons by governments back east. They spoke of state militias driving them out of their homes more than once. They declaimed the martyrdom of the Prophet Joseph Smith while under the protection of the Governor of Illinois. They bragged about the sacrifices of the Mormon Battalion to an ungrateful country. They lamented their hardships and losses crossing the plains. And last but not least, they denounced introducing Federal troops into their territory.

From time to time, the congregation raised their voices in complaints or in agreement with the forceful speakers, completely lacking the respectful silence shown when the governor had addressed them.

Finally, Brigham Young stood up and calmed down the audience. Once again, Governor Cumming reiterated he had no intention of stationing the army in immediate contact with any Mormon settlements. Connal Lee heard many people shouting out how they would rather destroy their homes and suffer death than be subjected to godless invaders. It took a few minutes, but Brigham Young calmed down the congregation a third time. He adjourned the raucous proceedings with a simple prayer spoken loudly enough for everyone to hear, even those standing outside. Triumphant chords of organ music accompanied the Saints as they walked out of the tabernacle, still voicing their grievances.

Elizabeth Staines touched Connal Lee on his arm. "Would you and your fellow delegates grace our table for Sunday dinner, Brother Swinton? It will just be a simple family meal. I'm afraid the governor will need a quiet afternoon after all this hustle and bustle."

"Why, thanks very much, Sister Staines. That is so very nice of y'all to think of us. We would be pleased to join y'all. Please lead the way. We will follow."

The governor seemed much less jovial and chatty than usual, while the kitchen maids served a lovely roasted chicken dinner. He and Colonel Kane rehashed many of the complaints of the Saints while they ate. The governor drank several glasses of wine during the course of the meal.

Finally, Governor Cumming excused himself. "If you don't mind, I would like to lie down for a short nap. This morning rather took it out of me, I'm afraid. Please excuse me, everyone."

They all stood up as the Governor left the table. Elizabeth Staines accompanied him to his guest bedroom next to the library he used as his office.

Connal Lee turned his attention to Mr. Staines, sitting across the table. "Elder Staines, suh. From what Elder Lyon told me when Ah checked out my books, Ah understood that y'all are trying to move all the books to safekeeping in case y'all have to burn the Council House. Then, Major Harris' son, Edward, told me he took three cases of books to his family farm for storage. If it would help, Ah could carry two cases on one of my big packhorses. Ah would hate to see any books burned. That would be such a waste!"

"Why, yes, Brother Swinton. That would be very nice of you. We appreciate all the help we can find. I will swing by and ask Elder Lyon to prepare two crates for when you leave. Do you know yet when you will depart the valley?"

Connal Lee looked at Major Harris sitting between White Wolf and Screaming Eagle. "Major Harris, suh, do y'all know if President Young has anything else he requires from our visit?"

"No, Connal Lee. I believe this morning's introduction of Governor Cumming to the Saints is the end of the planned diplomatic activities for your delegation. I know President Young and the other leaders of the Church and the Legion appreciate your delegation's attendance and services. Now we will all focus our attention on evacuating everyone to safety. On behalf of the Church and the Legion, please accept our sincere gratitude for your time and efforts, Connal Lee. You too, Screaming Eagle and White Wolf. Thank you all so much."

"Well, in that case, we will most likely leave in the morning." Connal Lee looked at White Wolf, who nodded his agreement.

Mr. Staines leaned forward. "Then I will drop by Elder Lyon's home and ask him to prepare two crates for early tomorrow morning."

"Oh, thanks for offering, suh. But Ah'm sure y'all are a busy man. Ah can drop by the library and tell him myself on the way back to our campground."

"Sorry, Brother Swinton, but the library is closed on the Sabbath day. No need to worry. I will be glad to make the arrangements. The responsibility for saving our library is very high on my list of priorities. Thank you for offering to help."

Lillias leaned forward and looked at her husband. "Honey, when you are ready to go visit father this afternoon, please let me know. I would like to accompany you."

Lillias Staines saw the look of surprise on Connal Lee's face when he realized Elder Lyon was her father. She chuckled behind a raised hand. "Brother Swinton, you didn't know that John Lyon is my father?"

"No, ma'am. It's such a small world, isn't it?"

Mr. Staines smiled. "My dear friend John Lyon came to consult with me on buying a variety of seedling fruit trees shortly after they arrived in the valley. A couple of days later, I happened to hear him recite some of his own poetry at a meeting of our dramatic society. We got to talking. John had published an entire book of poetry back

141

in Scotland before joining the Church and coming to Zion. He donated a copy to our Territorial Library. We soon became fast friends. He was a professional weaver back in the old world and brought the makings of a home loom with him. He soon became Brigham Young's personal weaver, turning out lots of lovely plaids for President Young's wives and daughters. He even taught President Young's daughters how to weave. Now he is a part-time unpaid assistant in the library on top of everything else he does. Sweet Lillias caught my eye around the time she turned eighteen. I proposed. President Young married us in the sacred endowment rooms on the second floor of Council House. We've been a happy family ever since."

"Well, suh, Ah'm very happy for the three of y'all. Elder Lyon certainly has accomplished a lot in his life, hasn't he?"

The Shoshone delegates stood up and took their leave after thanking the Staines for their hospitality. "Good luck down in Payson, Elder Staines. It's lovely country down there. Ah hope y'all's home here survives the army."

"Thank you, young man. You may pick up the books any time after eight o'clock tomorrow morning. Have a safe journey home. I'm sure we will see you again. Goodbye now."

Major Harris accompanied the delegation back to their camp. "Well, Ah guess we will return home in the morning, then, Major Harris, suh. Thanks so much for taking such good care of us during our visit." Connal Lee gave him a big hug. "Thanks again, Major. Ah appreciate y'all's friendship and hospitality. Please call on me if Ah can do anything for y'all. Please send us a note in care of general delivery at the Post Office in Fort Hall when y'all get word about Evelyn's recovery. So long, Major."

"Safe trails, Connal Lee. It was a pleasure getting better acquainted with you and your Shoshone family. My compliments to Chief Arimo. Goodbye for now!"

First thing the next morning, Connal Lee rode into the city with an empty packhorse and fastened the crates of books to the packsaddle. "Good luck, Elder Lyon. Ah sure hope everything works out for y'all and the library. The next time Ah come, maybe y'all can show me the book of poems y'all wrote. Ah don't have time to read any today. Ah'll return these books as soon as Ah hear it's safe to do so. Goodbye, suh."

By the time Connal Lee returned to the Jordan River, his family had packed up the tipis. He helped load up the packhorses before they headed back to the Portneuf River. Connal Lee spent the day in his saddle, reliving all his new experiences and everything he had learned during their visit to Great Salt Lake City. That evening he opened the first of the four novels checked out of the Territorial Library, excited to read a new story to his family before full dark descended.

Chapter 7: Messengers

By mutual agreement, the Shoshone delegation pushed hard on their journey back to Chief SoYo'Cant's winter camp on the Portneuf River. They started early each morning and ended their arduous rides late in the evening. Screaming Eagle struggled with the long hours, though he bore his fatigue stoically. They made it back in record time, arriving late on Friday the twenty-third of April. Too tired to raise their tipis, they fell into their blankets. Screaming Eagle woke up so weary that White Wolf recommended he spend the day at ease.

Sunday, shortly after high noon, Captain Reed rode down to the winter camp accompanied by two young privates. He asked the warriors who intercepted them outside the campsite to take them to Chief Arimo. The young warriors led the captain to the chief's open-air lodge. The chieftain stood up when he noticed Captain Reed striding towards him. The captain raised his arm. "Peace, Chief Arimo. It is good to see you again, sir."

Chief SoYo'Cant raised his arm in the peace sign. "Peace, Captain Reed. Welcome back my fire."

They shook hands.

"Thank you, sir." The captain looked around, hoping to see Teniwaaten. "Is your translator available? I came with important news to share with you."

In Shoshone, Chief SoYo'Cant ordered one of his nephews to go ask Teniwaaten to attend him. After the boy took off jogging, the captain asked if Connal Lee and his family could also join them. The Chief understood well enough. He nodded and then ordered one of his nieces to run to Short Rainbow's tipi and invite them to join him in the lodge. She skipped away, delighted to be of help to her important uncle.

The chief's niece delivered the invitation to Connal Lee's family to wait on the Chief. They immediately set aside their work and rushed to the council lodge. After they greeted their chief, Connal Lee stepped over and shook hands with the captain. "Captain Reed! How nice to see y'all, suh. What brings y'all by this afternoon?"

"Good afternoon, Connal Lee. Let's wait for Teniwaaten, so I only have to tell this once, if you don't mind. In the meantime, would you please guide my two privates and our horses over beside Short Rainbow's tipi? They need to erect their pup tents and lay in a cookfire." The captain turned to his men. "Private Johansson, Private McCabe, unsaddle the horses and give Paragon a good warming down, then take care of your own mounts. Pitch your tents and make camp. Prepare your own meals from your travel rations. Don't go out hunting for fresh game around the camp. We won't be leaving until first light tomorrow."

"Sir. Yes, sir!"

Connal Lee smiled and beckoned them with a wave of his hand. "Follow me. It's not far."

After showing the young Privates where to pitch their tent and tether the horses, Connal Lee hurried back to the lodge. He didn't want to miss a single word. He arrived when Teniwaaten walked up. They greeted each other. Connal Lee gave him a brief hug. The chief invited everyone to sit down around the cheerful fire. The young trees forming the half-round open lodge had begun sprouting leaves overhead. Connal Lee sat down beside the captain. The chief turned to Captain Reed. Through Teniwaaten, he asked why he had come to their encampment and how the Shoshone people could be of service to their friends in the cavalry.

"I received another express rider from Fort Laramie late last night, sir. Major Sanderson forwarded some important information regarding the Utah War to me. I felt strongly that you should hear about it as it affects all of us living out here on the frontier."

"Please continue, Captain Reed. What is this new information?"

The captain took his time and explained in detail. As he spoke, he consulted a long letter to make sure he had all the particulars correct. He recapped recent events that Connal Lee had experienced firsthand during their last journey south, such as booby-trapping the canyon trailways and the Mormons relocating south out of harm's way. "Army Intelligence also sent us word that President Buchanan dispatched a Peace Commission with a proclamation that includes pardons for the Mormon rebels, as he called them. The Peace Commissioners are expected in Camp Scott at the end of May with the official proclamation. Perhaps Connal Lee and his family might be our envoys and take a copy of the proclamation to Governor Young. This way, he will be prepared when the Peace Commission arrives in four or five weeks. Army intelligence included a page of the Daily National Intelligencer with the full text of the proclamation."

After Teniwaaten translated the wordy proclamation, Chief SoYo'Cant nodded his head. "I agree, Captain Reed. These are important matters that will greatly affect how the war proceeds. Chief Brigham Young deserves to know what you have just told me. Connal Lee and his family reported to me how Chief Brigham Young peacefully greeted the new governor and yielded his position as governor to him. As you said, Brigham Young also ordered all Mormons north of Provo to evacuate south. They have all closed up their homes and are moving south, driving their herds of cattle with them. I understand that the food they couldn't carry, they buried away in hiding for when they return. Everyone has gone except for a few stout fellows to water the crops, prepared to torch all the buildings if the federal army invades."

Connal Lee and the captain looked at each other. Connal Lee nodded his head. "Ah attended a council of war with Chief Arimo back in November when we were in Great Salt Lake City on a trading expedition. Ah told y'all about it, Captain, remember? Governor Brigham Young told us they would scorch the earth, meaning they would burn all their crops and homes rather than let the invaders get any value from their years of hard work. We saw for ourselves last week that they are actually evacuating, even now as we speak."

The Chief frowned. "Maybe Chief Brigham Young will call his people back to their homes while they still have time to plant their fields and gardens. I fear for my Mormon friends south of us. They will have too many people living in one place to live off the land, so they will have to eat their reserves and their cattle. They may have stored up food, but can they survive an entire year without their hay, fresh vegetables, and grains? I predict a lot of hunger this winter. It will be very bad for the Mormons. And if the army invades, they

146

will have to rebuild all their homes and buildings, too. Very, very bad."

The chief, the captain, and Connal Lee's family worked out the details. The new delegation would ride out at first light in the morning for another rush trip south like last Christmas. When the Chief's council broke up, Connal Lee invited the captain to be their guest in Short Rainbow's tipi.

"Thank you, Connal Lee. I was hoping you might invite me. I would enjoy spending the rest of the afternoon and evening with you and your family."

They all walked north to Short Rainbow's spacious tipi. Connal Lee complained they hadn't completely unpacked from returning from their last trip to Great Salt Lake City. "We were resting up yesterday from a hectic two weeks of traveling and attending meetings and receptions."

While they ate a midday meal, White Wolf observed Screaming Eagle slumping with fatigue. "You know, Screaming Eagle, we really pushed hard on our trip home. Perhaps too hard. Your body has not had a chance to rest and recover completely from your wounds. I'm thinking it might be a good thing if you stayed behind and rested this time. Bright Star could remain with you to tend you in your recovery. Other than a nervous teenage guard, we didn't encounter anyone to fight on our last visit to Great Salt Lake City. I think we could make this journey faster if the two of you stayed here and rested."

Screaming Eagle frowned and complained but finally yielded to White Wolf's logic. Bright Star sat down beside Screaming Eagle and gave him a big hug. "I will be glad to stay at home for a few days, Screaming Eagle. I'm not a warrior or a diplomat. I don't speak English well enough. This is where I belong."

Connal Lee told John all about their journey and adventures down in Great Salt Lake City. The captain chuckled when he heard about their deception when they welcomed the new governor in Little Emigration Canyon. The captain felt impressed to hear that Connal Lee and his family had met the new governor. Short Rainbow and Bright Star repacked their provisions for the road while they visited.

Connal Lee asked his wives to find his old cotton shirt and heavy army boots. "They don't fit me anymore, but Ah think they might fit Jeff Morgan. You know, Ah finally figured out why so many of the Mormons dress so poorly. It puzzled me at first. First, it costs a lot of money to ship fabric here from the States. Secondly, everyone is too busy to take the time to grow cotton, harvest it, card it, spindle it into thread, and weave fabric. That's why the youngsters only have hand-me-downs and makeshift clothing to wear."

White Wolf hugged Connal Lee. "How nice of you to think of Jeff Morgan, Connal Lee. I'm sure he can make good use of your old boots this coming winter. You are so generous, so unselfish. It's part of why we love you so much."

Connal Lee just shrugged and smiled.

As the sun began setting, the men went to the general herd outside the camp and cut out the horses they wanted to ride or use as pack animals. The captain erected his pup tent next to his privates' tents. He chatted briefly with the two young recruits as they cleaned up after eating their simple supper. The captain ordered them to take all their horses over beside a small feeder creek and tether them where they could find grass and water. When he finished inspecting his men, he walked out of the camp and helped Connal Lee with the horses.

They decided to travel in the same manner as for their Christmas diplomatic visit, with three saddle horses and two packhorses for each person. This meant they would need fifteen strong horses for the trip. They returned late to eat supper. Full dark descended around them as they finished eating. Short Rainbow invited everyone to retire to her tipi for the night.

They sat around the small, smokeless hardwood fire, talking. John Reed joined Connal Lee on his red fox fur blanket, sitting with his legs crossed like the Shoshone family. Connal Lee pointed at Short Rainbow. "Guess what, John? Short Rainbow is expecting a baby."

"How marvelous. Congratulations, my friends."

Short Rainbow stood up and tucked her hands above and below the gentle swell of her belly's barely noticeable bulge. With a big smile, she turned sideways so the captain could see. "Father is Connal Lee. I sure."

"What?"

"Connal Lee make baby with me. We all so happy."

Screaming Eagle and White Wolf pulled her back down so they could snuggle up together, delighted with the start of a new life in their family. Connal Lee beamed with joy. The captain put his arm over Connal Lee's shoulder and gave him a congratulatory squeeze.

After a leisurely evening where they all made love, everyone fell asleep in a pile. Connal Lee snuggled up to the captain's hairy chest and listened to his beating heart.

They got on the road early in the morning with a minimum of fuss, adept by now at organizing themselves efficiently for travel. John dressed and saw them off. "Good luck. Safe trails. I wish I were riding with you. Come see me when you are back. Goodbye, now!"

The diplomatic party alternated every half hour between a trot and a cantor for four hours, as they did on their express trip at Christmas. They rested a few minutes, ate a cold meal standing up, went to the toilet, changed horses, and set off for another four-hour stint of hard riding. They arrived at Box Elder Fort late that afternoon. Connal Lee confidently led the way to the Morgan farmstead. They all wearily dismounted, glad to stretch their legs. Connal Lee knocked on the door. Jedediah opened the door and peeked out. "Why, bless me if it ain't our friends from the Shoshone delegation come a calling. Welcome back to our little corner of paradise, me friends. How are ya, Brother Swinton? Good to see ya, White Wolf and Short Rainbow. Please come sit a spell. Ya all look plumb wore out."

"Thanks, Brother Morgan. We've been riding for nearly ten hours straight. We left Chief Arimo's winter camp on the Portneuf River at dawn this morning."

"Why, where on earth are ya going in such a all fire rush?"

"Captain Reed, the commander of Fort Hall, and Chief Arimo asked us to carry some important information to President Young. It's regarding actions President Buchanan has taken about the Utah War."

"Well, it's nearly supper time. Won't ya please stay and let me return yer hospitality from yer last visit? By the way, where is Screaming Eagle? He's all right, isn't he?"

"Oh, yes, suh. He was just tired from our rush trip back home. Since we're riding this express diplomatic message in such a hurry, White Wolf ordered him to stay behind and take it easy."

"Well, please come have a seat. Jeff should be home soon. He went hunting for something fer the pot. I'll cook us up some food, and ya all can take a rest break. How does that sound?"

Connal Lee instinctively looked to White Wolf for a decision. White Wolf nodded, then answered in Shoshone, "We only have another hour or two of travel left today anyway. I think we can afford to take a break early and rest up. We'll leave at first light in the morning to make up for it."

By the time they pitched their tent, Jeff had returned with two grouse and two rabbits hanging off his saddle horn. Rather bashfully, he walked up to Connal Lee. "Hello, Brother Swinton. It's good to see you again. Hi, Short Rainbow. How are you, White Wolf?" He glanced around the yard. "Where are Screaming Eagle and Bright Star? Screaming Eagle's not still mad at me, is he?"

"No, Screaming Eagle is not the type to carry a grudge, Jeff. Y'all don't need to worry about that. He and Bright Star stayed behind so Screaming Eagle could rest and finish healing. We moved around so much since he was wounded that he needs time to recover."

"Oh, I'm glad he's recovering and not mad at me. Bishop Snow told us that he met you on the trail to Great Salt Lake City. I'm glad you are back, again, for a visit. Now, let me go help Grandpa get supper ready. We can talk while we eat."

Connal Lee and White Wolf led their horses down by the creek where they diverted irrigation water onto the small farmstead. They tethered the small herd within reach of grass and water. Short Rainbow unloaded the packsaddles and saddlebags, then spread their sleeping furs inside the tent. Connal Lee and White Wolf returned carrying armfuls of deadfall to build their usual evening campfire.

A couple of hours later, they all relaxed around the fire as dusk settled around them. Connal Lee stood up and walked over to their packs beside the tent. He scrounged around inside a leather saddle-bag and pulled out some clothing and his old army boots. "Here, Jeff. Ah've outgrown these clothes, so Ah thought maybe y'all could make good use of them. If the boots don't fit, maybe one of y'all's friends or family can use them."

"Oh! What? For me? Really?" Jeff dashed around the fire and fell to his knees beside Connal Lee. "Wow, look, Grandpa. Boots!" He thrust his bare feet in the used boots, stood up, and took a few experimental steps. "And look! They fit me. Boy howdy, these're the first boots I've ever had. Thank you so much, Brother Swinton."

Jeff sat back down by the fire with a huge smile. Short Rainbow handed him the shirt she had mended when she first met Connal Lee. "Here. For you. Shirt bring luck. See bead on back?"

In Shoshone, she asked Connal Lee to tell the story of the bear attack and how she had repaired the shirt they had cut off his back. Connal Lee explained about the Crow arrow, the bear attack, and being saved by his wonderful Shoshone family. By the time he finished the story, full dark had fallen. A nearly full moon rose slowly above the steep mountains to their east. Exhausted from the demanding ride, they said goodnight and retired to the tent. Connal Lee snuggled up to White Wolf and Short Rainbow. "Boy, Ah sure miss Screaming Eagle, don't y'all? He has always been here with us, so strong and quiet and loving. Ah hope he's doing all right back in camp. Ah miss Bright Star's big smile, too. Ah can't wait until we are all back together, safe and sound. Well, good night, White Wolf. Good night, Short Rainbow. Ah love both of y'all."

Jeff and Jedediah woke up early, used to rising with the sun. They helped Connal Lee and his family pack up their tent and saddle their horses. With only a cup of black coffee for breakfast, they took off as soon as they had light enough to see the way. Jeff and Jedediah waved as they rode off at a cantor with a cloud of dust trailing behind them.

Around midday, they approached the walls of Great Salt Lake City. Unlike the past two times they visited, no civilian guards challenged them at the doorless bastions of the city gate. They encountered wagons moving in both directions, but Connal Lee noticed far lighter traffic than when they left nine days earlier. Many of the houses were now boarded up with rough sawn lumber, their windows and doors stored away awaiting the homeowners' return. Only a few homes had smoke rising from their chimneys. They didn't hear any dogs barking in the city. Such a familiar sound wherever humans lived, they noticed its absence. The city felt empty and abandoned.

They rode at a walk past the Staines mansion. When they passed the tabernacle, Connal Lee saw workmen had removed the large windows and boarded up the empty holes. Connal Lee wondered if the magical pipe organ had been moved south to safety. They passed a bustling crowd of wagons and men working outside the southern and western gates of the Tithing Office, loading wagons and carts as fast as they could. Smoke rose from the chimneys of Brigham Young's Lion House and Beehive House. Wagons stood in front of the Church offices between the two grand homes, loading crate after crate of Church books and records for removal to Provo. They tied up their posse of fifteen horses to the chain hitching posts in front of Beehive House. The heavy gate in the thick wall surrounding the Brigham Young Estate stood open, so they walked on through. Connal Lee knocked on the door. They waited several minutes. They could hear people moving around inside the house, so they knew someone was home. Finally, Mary Ann Young opened the door. She pushed a stray lock of hair off her face and tucked it back under a dust scarf. Her smile seemed a little weary. "Welcome, Brother Swinton and Shoshone delegates. I apologize for keeping you waiting. We're busy packing. We are all leaving the day after tomorrow. Now, how might I help you today?"

"Well, Sister Young, Captain Reed and Chief Arimo sent us with important news from Army Intelligence at West Point. They want President Young to know what has happened back in the Capital. May we see him, please?"

"Oh, I'm so sorry. Brigham is in Provo today, where they are moving the Church offices into the new Seminary Building. If he's not out inspecting the camps, you will find him there. Do you know the way?"

"Yes, ma'am. We've been to Provo before. Thanks."

"We were just sitting down to eat dinner in the basement dining room with the few of us still on the estate. Could you take the time to join us?"

Connal Lee looked at White Wolf, who nodded. They followed Brigham Young's wife through the entrance and down the stairs into a big staff kitchen beside a long dining hall. Half an hour later, they said their thanks and goodbyes and returned to their horses. The traffic often slowed them down, but they rode as fast as possible. Sometimes they skirted around the lumbering wagons and sprawling herds of livestock when they had an open path to the side. As they drew closer to Provo, their travel slowed down to an intermittent walk. They encountered workers returning to their family camps and guest accommodations from the fields and pastures outside the city. Wagons departed to travel back north, taking advantage of the lighter traffic during the evening and night.

The delegation stayed on State Road, riding slowly closer to the square city blocks of Provo. Around six that evening, they stopped at the Seminary Building on the west side of State Road and asked for President Young. The young men unpacking crates inside the two-story adobe brick building sent them on to the Provo Music Hall. "President Young went to see where the Church Historian's Office is setting up shop for the interim."

They crossed a crowded square where the Church stored twenty-thousand bushels of tithing flour in great crates covered with canvas from tents and wagon tops. Connal Lee spotted Brigham Young leaving the music hall. The delegation caught up to him just before he stepped into a waiting carriage. President Young appeared weary. He stared at them for a moment before he recognized them. Connal Lee hopped down off his mare and strode towards Brigham Young with his arm extended for a handshake. "Good evening, President Young. How are y'all doing this evening, suh?"

"Why, Brother Connal Lee Swinton. Whatever brings you all the way down here to Provo? I thought you were up at Fort Hall."

They shook hands. "Captain Reed received some express dispatches two days ago. He and Chief Arimo wanted you to be advised of recent activities in the Federal Capital."

Brigham Young waved his hand at the delegation still on horse-back. "Hello, White Wolf. Good evening Short Rainbow. Please secure your horses to the hitching rail and come into the music hall. We can talk there."

Short Rainbow and White Wolf tethered their trains of horses to one of the wood hitching posts in front of the small concert hall. They followed Brigham Young into the adobe building. Connal Lee noticed pipes neatly stacked against the wall. "Is that the tabernacle pipe organ Ah see over there, suh?"

"Absolutely correct, young man. They made the final delivery this morning. Now, what is this information you have for me?"

They stood around in the relative silence of the nearly aban-doned music hall. Connal Lee quickly summarized the information sent to Captain Reed and their efforts in bringing the proclamation to President Young. He reached into Captain Reed's dispatch bag and extracted a folded page of a newspaper. "Here is the Proclama-tion printed by the Daily National Intelligencer. Y'all can read it for yourself, suh."

Brigham Young held the paper at arm's length so he could read the small print. He mumbled a bit to himself as he read. "Whereas the Territory – a spirit of insubordination – acts of unlawful violence – and maturely weighing the obligation – attacked and destroyed by a portion of Mormon forces – this is rebellion – I offer now a free and full pardon – signed, James Buchanan. Why, of all the unmiti-gated gall! This document is nothing but a pack of lies wrapped up in flowery words. We were never in rebellion. We are all loyal citizens of the United States of America!"

Brigham Young threw down the newspaper, drew his lips tight in a frown of great displeasure, and stared into the distance, fuming. Connal Lee, White Wolf, and Short Rainbow waited respectfully for the leader of the Mormon Church to digest all the new information.

President Young focused back on the messengers standing be-fore him with a deep breath released in a long sigh. "I apologize for being so short-tempered. I have had a bad toothache distracting me from my duties for the past three days now. Many thanks for bring-ing me the text of this foul document. I am so enraged at the mis-characterizations of my loyal people and our defenses, I can hardly bring myself to address it." He shook his head angrily while massaging his sore jaw.

Connal Lee nodded. "Captain Reed and Chief Arimo believe Buchanan wrote the proclamation more to justify his blunder in sending the army rather than to pardon the Mormons. The press and Congress have turned against him in pursuing this war. It seems the cost is bankrupting the treasury, among other problems. However, Captain Reed said the part about a pardon is very important. The Mormons did, after all, cause damages and loss of property when they burned the commissary's wagon trains and stole their livestock. If everyone accepts the pardon, there won't be any demands to make good the losses or to prosecute criminal activities. At least that's what Captain Reed told us. He's a pretty smart man, in case y'all haven't met him, suh. He graduated from Harvard University after all."

"Yes, young man, Captain Reed is correct. Let me think about this. Hmm. Clearly, we need to work with Governor Cumming to keep the army from invading until the Peace Commissioners have time to make it to Fort Scott. I hope the Overland Trail will be clear this early so they can make good time." Brigham Young paused a moment in thought. "I believe we should share this information with Governor Cumming at the earliest possible moment. Unfortunately, I have important matters scheduled all day tomorrow. I plan to return Thursday afternoon to accompany my wives and children back here to Provo on Friday morning. Might I request your services again? Would you please take this proclamation to Governor Cumming tomorrow? Ask him if he would please reserve an hour for me late afternoon on Thursday, the day after tomorrow. We need to coordinate between the Territorial Government and the Mormon Church."

"President Young, suh, we are here at y'all's orders."

"Thank you. Our Shoshone allies have proven themselves friends of the Mormon people time and time again. I would normally offer you some hospitality, but I don't have a home set up here in Provo."

"Oh, don't y'all worry none about that, suh. We'll ride on down and visit with Captain Hanover, who led the handcart company Ah traveled with. We're real good friends. We'll leave early in the morning and see the governor before noon."

"Please leave this vile document with me. I will have the text copied so my people and I can study it in more detail. Please pick up the newspaper article at the Seminary **B**uilding on your way north in the morning. Do you know where that is?"

"Yes, suh. It's right on State Road. We stopped there looking for y'all, but they sent us on to this music hall."

"Excellent. Delivering this document to Governor Cumming tomorrow morning would be most advantageous, Brother Swinton. Safe travels to you all. I shall see you Thursday evening at the meeting with the governor, representing our Shoshone allies. Kindly send word to Beehive house as to the time and place of the meeting. Thank you once again. Good night."

The delegation rode south to Captain Hanover's homes on Hobble Creek. Captain Hanover advised them to be on the road before daylight so they could avoid the heavy daytime traffic. They enjoyed supper and conversation with Captain Hanover before collapsing exhausted into bed.

They reached the Staines mansion just before noon. Connal Lee handed White Wolf his reins. "Please wait a minute while Ah see if the governor is here before we dismount."

A young kitchen maid answered his knocks. She opened the door to an entrance hallway empty of furniture, rugs, and art. "I'm sorry, sir. His Excellency is working today in his new office in the Council House. Do you know where that is?"

"Yes, Ah know. Thanks. Good day, miss."

Five minutes later, they tied up their train of horses on Main Street in front of the entrance to the Council House. The three delegates entered the cool shade of the large building. As they strolled past the open doors of the Territorial Library, Connal Lee waved to his friend, Elder Lyon, who stood inside packing wooden crates full of books. The doors to the office suite reserved for the governor stood open. A well-dressed young man sat writing at a desk just inside the door. When he heard footsteps, he looked up. The sight of Indians walking towards him gave him a bit of a start. He stood up and demanded in a condescending tone of voice, "Yes? What can I do for you? What are you youngsters doing here in Council House?"

"Ah am Connal Lee Swinton, suh. This is White Wolf and Short Rainbow. We are a delegation sent by Captain Reed, the commander of Fort Hall, and by my adopted father, Chief Arimo of the Shoshone Nation. They sent us with critical intelligence for President Brigham Young. We delivered it to him down in Provo last night. He asked us to share this information with our friend, Governor Cumming, as soon as possible. Please let him know we are here."

The Governor's secretary stood for a moment, trying to decide if he believed these teenagers covered in the dust of the road. He pursed his lips, stepped over to the door behind him, and knocked softly three times. "Governor, there is an oddly dressed white boy accompanied by two Indian youngsters who claim that Brigham Young sent them. Will you see them, sir?"

Governor Cumming groaned when he pushed himself up by the arms of his chair. "Of course, Mister Currey. Don't keep my friends waiting. Show them right in."

"Please come this way. The Governor will see you."

"Thanks very much."

"Connal Lee, my boy! How nice to see you again. Welcome, White Wolf and Short Rainbow. Now, what mischief are you three getting up to this morning?"

"Good morning, Your Honor. It's a pleasure to see y'all again, suh." Connal Lee glanced back at the door where the officious secretary stood listening. He stepped over to pull the door shut. "May we have the door closed for privacy, suh? Ah don't believe President Young wants what we are about to share with you to be public knowledge, at least until the two of you come up with a plan."

"Of course, Mister Swinton. Of course."

The governor waved at varnished wood chairs in front of his desk and then sat down with an audible grunt behind a large desk. A fine mahogany and brass travel desk sat in the center of his messy desk, surrounded by its inkwell, pen holders, and blotter. "Please, have a seat. Now, what is going on, my friends?"

Connal Lee briefly summarized their activities over the past three days. Governor Cumming leaned forward, paying close attention. Connal Lee extracted the newspaper article from Captain Reed's dispatch case and handed it to the governor. "Please, suh. Y'all can read it for yourself."

The governor accepted the folded page of newsprint without saying a word, shook it out, and read the proclamation. When he finished, he leaned back in his chair. The chair squeaked when he shifted his heavy bulk. "I see. I see. Well, now. This puts things in a new light, doesn't it? Thank you for bringing me this good news, Master Swinton and fellow delegates."

"Yes, suh. It certainly changes things for the better, or so it would appear. President Young asked us to tell y'all he is returning tomorrow afternoon so he can move all his family to Provo Friday. He asked if y'all might spare him an hour to discuss what this Peace Commission and pardon means and what should be done. We only have four weeks until the commissioners are expected to arrive at Camp Scott. President Young asked me to leave word at Beehive House as to the time and place that he can join y'all to make plans. He invited us to attend, as well, representing Shoshone interests."

The governor sat thinking about how this Peace Commission changed everything. He straightened up and nodded his head decisively. "Please join me at five o'clock at the Staines mansion. We will have supper while we figure out the best course of action for all concerned."

"Very good, suh. It would be our pleasure to join y'all. Listen, suh, we didn't bring anything to write with. Might Ah borrow some paper and a pen so Ah can write a note for President Young?"

"Certainly, young man. Mister Currey, my new secretary, takes Pitman shorthand. You can dictate, and he can scribe it for you."

"Oh, thank you, suh, but Ah know how to write. No need to bother your secretary, suh."

"Very well. Thank you, again, for your services to the citizens of the Territory of Utah." He leaned back in his chair. "So, what are your plans between now and tomorrow afternoon, young man?"

"Well, suh, we wouldn't mind a bit of a rest, truth be told. We've covered a lot of ground over the past two and a half days. Ah think we will also want to pay a call on some of our friends, like Major Robert Harris, Elder Staines and his wives, and Elder John Lyon, here in the library. If there is anything we can do for y'all, suh, y'all need only ask. We are here at y'all's service, suh."

"Why, thank you. Now that I am settled in my new office, all I need is time to review the books and records of the territory. I'm still waiting for our new federal officers, chief justice, superintendent of Indian affairs, and other territorial appointees to arrive and take over their duties. I'm sorry to be the one to inform you, but Mister Staines, his wives, and staff have all gone south to Payson, lock, stock, and barrel. He owns acreage down there, where he is growing fruit trees from seeds. They won't return until we have peace in the territory. They left behind one of their gardeners and his family to wait on me, though. The man's wife is a pretty good cook. Better than my teamster who served as my field cook on my journey here from Camp Scott, that's for certain. The gardener's two daughters keep the house and help their mother in the kitchen. He and his son take care of the garden and orchard. They have their white top already packed and parked beside the carriage house, ready to flee for safety if the army marches into town."

"Oh. Well, it's too bad the Staines left already. They are really nice people. Ah had hoped to hear the pianoforte again while we were in the area, but Ah guess not this trip. Well, suh, we should be going then. Until tomorrow at five o'clock, suh."

Everyone stood up and shook hands. Connal Lee stopped at the secretary's desk to borrow a nib pen and paper. He leaned over the desk and wrote a simple note. The secretary clucked his tongue when he noticed a little splatter of ink on the page caused by Connal Lee's inexpert handwriting. After Connal Lee signed his name, he held the small piece of paper up and blew on it to dry the ink. "My thanks, suh. Y'all have a nice day now. Goodbye."

Connal Lee folded the paper in half as they left the office suite. They stopped briefly to greet John Lyon in the library. Elder Lyon had a team of men crating books, so they didn't linger after saying hello.

They mounted their horses and rode across the street to Beehive House. Connal Lee hopped down. "Ah won't be long. Y'all might as well wait here." Connal Lee handed the note to Sister Young. "President Young is expecting word on an important meeting tomorrow afternoon. Would y'all please see that he gets this note? Thanks very much, ma'am. Goodbye, now."

Connal Lee led his family up the hill to Major Harris' home. Ingrid told them he was at work at the Legion headquarters. "Oh. Do y'all think we might disturb him at his work? We know where the Legion offices are."

"I'm sure he would be delighted to see you again. If he's busy, he is blunt enough to tell you so. Go ahead and pay him a call."

Ten minutes later, they tied off their horses away from the busy traffic around the Tithing Office. Major Harris saw them walking through the open gate in the wall surrounding the Legion offices, barns, and corrals and rushed out to greet them. "Connal Lee! White Wolf! Short Rainbow! What are you doing back so soon? How are you? It's so good to see you, my friends."

Major Harris' big smile made them feel welcome. After shaking hands, they followed the major into one of several small buildings in the Legion's compound. Lines of men in civilian work clothes waited for assignment before they left to help secure the public buildings for evacuation. Major Harris led them to the front of the line and inside the largest building. "Please come in. I would like to introduce you to General Wells while you are here."

The Major knocked on an interior door, opened it, and stuck his head inside. He chatted quietly for a moment, then held the door open. "Come on in, everyone. General Wells, these are three members of the Shoshone delegation I told you about last week." He introduced each with a short summary of their accomplishments and relationship to Chief Arimo. "It's my great pleasure to present General Daniel H. Wells, my commanding officer. He has been with the Nauvoo Legion since back in Nauvoo before he joined the Church. He served as a city councilman and judge back in Nauvoo. He is now an Apostle serving as Brigham Young's second counselor in the First Presidency of the Church. In addition to leading men in the Territorial Militia and the Church, he is also our Superintendent of Public Works here in the territory – in his free time."

160

Connal Lee stepped forward and shook hands as he looked into large eyes in a narrow face. An abundance of curly brown hair topped the man's high forehead. Curly mutton chops grew down under his chin like a rim around his face, with his chin and upper lip shaved clean. He had narrow shoulders beneath a simple suit of clothes. He wore a floppy bow tie. He smiled warmly. His eyes seemed to peer deep into Connal Lee's soul. "It's a pleasure to meet you, young man. Major Harris told me good things about you and your Shoshone family. I am enchanted to meet you, Missus Short Rainbow. And it's very nice to meet you, Mister White Wolf. Welcome to Great Salt Lake City."

"It's nice to meet y'all, too, suh. Boy, with so many jobs and responsibilities, y'all must keep yourself real busy."

"Well, I serve where I am needed, Brother Swinton. Someone has to organize the men to defend the territory and take care of the public works our community depends upon. Of course, my service to the Lord and Brigham Young is a labor of love, so that hardly counts. Now, while I would very much enjoy a leisurely conversation, we are pressed for time here. We are busy closing up all the public buildings as part of the general evacuation orders. Naturally, when we need manpower the most, everyone is preoccupied with taking care of moving their own families. Please excuse me now. I have people waiting."

Major Harris escorted the Shoshone envoys out to the courtyard. "He's a very busy man, as you might have gathered. You see, property taxes provide money to buy supplies but the members of the Church supply the labor for our public works. Each man donates one out of every ten of his workdays to help out. A tithing, don't you see, of their time. Everyone helps. You know. Building roads, bridges, dams. Building schools and ward meeting houses. Now everyone is scrambling to preserve the doors and windows of all our important buildings and prepare the structures for burning if necessary. Listen, my friends, my little office here at the Legion doesn't have room for us to all sit down. Might I invite you to come to my home where we can relax and talk for a while? Do you have any pressing matters you need to attend to?"

"No, suh. We delivered our message to President Young yesterday evening and to Governor Cumming this morning. We have the rest of the day free. We were only going to go make camp on the Jordan River and rest up a bit before a meeting we have tomorrow at the Staines mansion."

"Well, let me saddle my horse, and I'll join you in front. Give me five minutes."

"Very good, Major Harris. We'll be waiting for y'all, suh."

Fifteen minutes later, they rode up to the major's bungalow. "Connal Lee, you might as well bring the horses back to my corral. I have a small irrigation ditch running alongside it, diverted from City Creek. Your horses can rest and have water while we talk. Come on. I'll help you unsaddle them."

They entered the major's adobe house through the back door. Smells of baking bread permeated the little cottage. They heard two young boys fussing in the kitchen. The major led them to the parlor and invited them to take a chair around the board table. "Have you had dinner, Connal Lee? Could I offer you something to eat?"

"Oh, thanks, Robert. That would be great. We only ate a hot roll in the saddle while we rode to meet with Governor Cumming as early as possible this morning."

"Wait here a moment while I see what Ingrid can whip up for us. I'll be right back."

He returned carrying a clay pitcher of creek water. While he poured everyone a drink, he smiled at White Wolf. "I received a letter a couple of days ago from Jim and Evelyn. They reported that Evelyn has enjoyed a full recovery from the food poisoning. Jim also wrote that they dug up all the poisonous false onions like you recommended. They sent their thanks, once again, for when I see you next."

"Oh, good. Ah'm glad Evelyn is better now. Huh, White Wolf? That's really great news."

Ingrid brought in a simple wood tray carrying four wooden bowls and four tin spoons. "Here's a little soup to get you started. I'll be right back with some bread fresh out of the oven."

They all said thanks. Connal Lee had never eaten meatball soup with thick noodles before, but he found it very tasty. Ingrid carried out a cutting board holding a loaf of bread, a dish of butter, and a knife. "I'll fix an early supper if you can stay the afternoon."

She looked at the Major for instructions. He nodded. "Thank you, Ingrid. Can you relax here a while, Connal Lee?"

"Yes, thanks. That would be great."

The Shoshone envoys left the Major's home early in the evening in plenty of time to pitch their tent on the Jordan River.

Chapter 8: Risk and Reward

They spent the next day leisurely attending to mundane chores. White Wolf inspected all the horses' hooves. They didn't want a stone or a bruise to bring one of their horses up lame. Short Rainbow repaired a halter strap she had noticed fraying unevenly. Connal Lee rode off hunting for something for a hot dinner. By midafternoon they took a break to bathe in the Jordan River. They delighted in leisurely washing each other, sensually massaging their weary muscles. Connal Lee leaned over and kissed Short Rainbow's wet belly where she carried their unborn child.

The strong desert sun warmed the air to a comfortable seventy degrees, so they lay on the grassy riverbank to dry. Connal Lee walked over to one of the saddlebags and retrieved a cattle horn comb and a boar bristle brush, more luxuries purchased at Mr. Mackey's trading post. They spent an hour grooming each other's hair until it glistened in the sun. Short Rainbow took her time dressing White Wolf's luxuriously long hair, adding bits of furs and feathers on beaded ribbons of leather. White Wolf returned the favor. Connal Lee thought they both looked beautiful when they finished. Short Rainbow brushed Connal Lee's short hair, parted it in the middle, and tied it down with a beaded headband. She then tied three eagle feathers to the thin leather cords dangling beneath the headband's knot. They dressed in nice clothing but not their fancy ceremonial robes.

Around four o'clock, Major Harris rode up. Connal Lee stood to go greet him. "Major Robert, suh. This is a nice surprise. How are y'all doing this afternoon?"

The major dismounted his great stallion, removed his riding gloves, and shook hands. "Hello, Connal Lee. Good afternoon Short Rainbow and White Wolf. This morning, General Wells received a note by express rider from President Young inviting him to attend a policy meeting with Governor Cumming this afternoon at five. He sent the Orderly of the Day requesting that I accompany him. However, since he might be running late due to prior commitments, he asked me to be there to start the meeting. When I read you were attending, I decided to ride out and accompany you like old times. Ha! Old times, like a whole two weeks ago."

"Well, Ah'm glad y'all are joining us, Robert." Connal Lee invited the major to join them lounging around the fire with a sweep of his hand. "We just made a pot of coffee, suh. Would y'all like to join us before we head over to the Staines mansion?"

"Yes. Thank you. Very hospitable of you."

Short Rainbow poured them each a cup, served black. The major took a sip and looked at the Shoshone envoys. "You wouldn't happen to know what this meeting is about, would you?"

Connal Lee looked at White Wolf. They nodded at each other. "Why, yes, suh. As a matter of fact, we do. We've been keeping it confidential. But since y'all were invited to the meeting, Ah think it's proper for y'all to know. A couple of weeks ago, President Buchanan wrote a proclamation. In it, he offered pardons to any Mormons who would obey federal laws and support the Constitution. He sent two Peace Commissioners to carry the proclamation to the Territory. They are expected to arrive in Fort Scott the last week of May, around a month from now."

Major Harris sat up and gazed around at his Shoshone friends in amazement. "Well, now! That changes everything for us, doesn't it? Like Shakespeare said, that's a horse of a whole different color. An offering of peace rather than the threat of invasion. Let me think."

The Major gazed into his tin coffee mug as though it were a crystal ball. He glanced around, looking each person in the eye. "Hm. While this is really great news, I'm afraid that until the Peace Commissioners actually arrive, it won't change a thing. Even when word gets out, until the Army disperses peaceably, the evacuations must continue. What if General Johnston invades before he gets news of the Peace Commissioners and the proclamation? We won't want to see any of our people at risk, put in harm's way by staying in the path of an invading army. It is good news, though, isn't it?"

They all nodded their heads. "That's what we thought. We were very happy to bring this news to President Young and Governor Cumming."

"How did you get the news so quickly? Even if it's in all the newspapers back east, word won't reach here for another couple of weeks at the earliest."

"Oh, Captain Reed at Fort Hall received an express dispatch from Fort Laramie. Major Sanderson thought everyone should know, out here on the frontier. We're lucky that Major Sanderson has friends in Army Intelligence. We're also lucky he believes in the value of keeping us informed about events that affect our lives. As soon as the major received word of the proclamation, he sent a rider with the good news. Captain Reed shared the news with Chief Arimo. They decided we should let the people down here in the Territory of Utah know as soon as possible."

Major Harris pulled his pocket watch out of his everyday uniform vest and checked the time. "Well, let's not keep the president and governor waiting. Shall we ride on?"

They took off at an easy trot which brought them to the Staines mansion about twenty minutes later. They tied up their rides to the hitching posts. Major Harris frowned. "Hm, I don't see the president's carriage or the governor's, either. We must be the first to arrive. Will you join me for a turn in the garden while we wait for everyone else?"

The garden interested White Wolf. Flowering plants and herbs lined the pathways winding between fruit trees. White Wolf walked nearly bent over, carefully studying each specimen. He pinched off a leaf or a blossom at each new plant and examined it carefully. After he smelled the plant and its sap, he asked for the English name. Robert knew many but not all of the plants' names. However, when White Wolf asked the purpose of the different plants, if they weren't for seasoning food, the Major didn't have an answer.

They ended the tour walking through the planting beds in the cold frame greenhouse. Only the white painted wood frame remained. All the valuable glass window panes, imported from San Francisco three years earlier, had been carefully packed away in straw for safekeeping in the ice house. Finally, Robert pulled out his pocket watch again. "Well, maybe we should go check at the house. Perhaps the governor left word or rescheduled, and we just don't know about it."

A teenage girl answered Major Harris' knock. "Good afternoon. I am Major Robert Harris of the Nauvoo Legion. My Shoshone friends and I were invited to join the governor for supper at five o'clock. It's coming on to six, so we wondered if you had any word for us."

"No, Major. I'm sorry. We are holding supper for them. We have been wondering where everyone is, ourselves. Would you like to come in and rest while we wait on the governor's pleasure?"

The major looked at Connal Lee. Everyone nodded their heads. The girl led them into the parlor where Elder Staines had held the formal reception two weeks ago. Connal Lee hardly recognized it as the same place. They had removed all the curtains, carpets, chandeliers, and wall sconces. The bare room held a suite of upholstered furniture, a grand piano, and nothing else. All the original furnishings, paintings, vases, and fine candelabra that had given the room such distinctive charm, had been removed for safekeeping.

The young kitchen maid invited them to have a seat. "I'll be right back with something cold to drink from the cellar. Please make yourselves right at home."

Connal Lee drifted over to the piano and ran his hands over the reddish mahogany wood of the closed keyboard lid. He glanced back at the major. "This isn't the same pianoforte I heard Sister Elizabeth play after the governor's supper. How odd."

The young maid returned with a tray holding four glasses of fresh-pressed cider. They all said thank you. Connal Lee pointed at the piano. "Tell me, miss. Why is there a different pianoforte here today?"

"Why, Sister Elizabeth took her piano down to Payson with her. This is a piano that Brother Kimball couldn't move because they have no place for it in Provo. He loaned it to the governor since he heard the governor's wife plays. I overheard Brother Kimball say that with the governor living in this house, perhaps it wouldn't be burned. If the army comes, the piano would be safer here than in the Kimball compound. He just received the piano last fall, shipped all the way from London. Can you believe it?"

The friendly little group had pretty much talked themselves out at the major's home the day before, so they didn't have a lot to say.

Time seemed to slow while they waited. Connal Lee's stomach growled. He looked up with an embarrassed smile to see if anyone had heard. Judging by the grins on their faces, they had all heard. Around six-thirty, they heard a knock at the front door. General Wells sent his Orderly of the Day with another briefly scribbled note. Robert read it aloud. "President Young delayed. Governor Cumming delayed. I'm delayed. Supper will begin at eight. Regards, Daniel H. Wells. So. Now we know."

Connal Lee stood up. "It's going to be a late evening, then. Let's go loosen the saddles and remove the bits so the horses can rest easy while we wait, shall we?"

Robert nodded. "Good idea, Connal Lee. Let me pass this note along to the cook. Hopefully, she can salvage supper."

Twenty minutes later, they gathered back in the parlor. The same young kitchen maid brought them a platter with tiny pieces of fried toast garnished with smoked fish paste and slices of olives and grilled red peppers. "We hope you like these little savories. The governor loves these little treats, so we're learning how to make them for him. He calls them hors d'oeuvres. May I bring you anything else to drink while you wait?"

Just before eight, as the sun fell below the mountains to the west, the young maid returned with wax candles in simple brass candlesticks. She lit the candles using a thin lighting taper as a match. They heard horses and carriages pull up in front of the house. The Major stood up. "They are here, at last. Let's go meet them, shall we?"

They opened the front door and watched Governor Cumming and Brigham Young shaking hands on the garden path. Porter Rockwell, the President's bodyguard, trailed behind Brigham Young. General Wells and Colonel Kane brought up the rear. After greetings, apologies, and handshakes, the governor spoke up over the hubbub. "Please follow me into supper, gentlemen and dear Miss Short Rainbow. I don't know about you, but I, for one, am positively famished!"

Governor Cumming laughed loudly at himself as he led the way to the dining room. When He opened the door to the dining room,

Connal Lee hardly recognized it. The Staines had removed the draperies, huge dining table and matching chairs, and the oriental carpet. In their place sat a plain but nicely turned oak table and simple colonial-style dining chairs on the bare wood floor. Fresh flowers graced the table. As they entered, two teenage girls dressed for the kitchen arrived to light the candles. They already had a cheerful fire burning in the fireplace. Governor Cumming pulled out a chair. "Here, President Young, please sit next to me so we can talk. Excellent. Everyone, please take a seat."

A constant stream of food and spirited conversation ensued. At first, they all complained about the galling misstatements in the proclamation. Then the discussion turned to considering the best policies for dealing with the Peace Commissioners. A good hour later, the governor had just agreed to do everything possible to delay General Johnston from entering the territory before the Peace Commissioners arrived. President Young shared his concerns should word of the proclamation and pardons become known among the Church members. "If they know peace is coming, they will be even more reluctant to leave. But they must move out of harm's way. I don't want a chance that even one person might lose his life because the army advanced ahead of the Peace Commission. I, myself, will move my family tomorrow morning as planned, setting an example to those who have waited to see if I would follow my own advice."

Governor Cumming tried to persuade Brigham Young to give up the mass exodus, but President Young remained adamant. "Every Saint must be removed to safety!"

The cook and her two daughters cleared the plates and then returned with platters of fancy little petit fours. The cook left her daughters to serve while she wheeled in a rolling cart with coffee and tea service. Conversation stopped while everyone focused their attention on dessert.

In the near silence, Connal Lee heard a grunting sound from beyond the door leading to the kitchen and pantries. He looked up. Short Rainbow heard it, too. Connal Lee raised his forefinger, which grabbed White Wolf and Short Rainbow's attention. He whispered in Shoshone, "Something isn't right."

The three stood up. Connal Lee pulled his revolver from the holster with his right hand. His knife appeared in his left hand. Stealthily, he moved towards the closed doors. Short Rainbow and White Wolf followed. Their lovely beaded moccasins made no noise on the wide varnished floorboards. Porter Rockwell noticed their attention focused outside the room. Concerned, he stood up. He took a couple of steps, but his boot heels struck the floor with sharp bangs. Connal Lee spun around and imperiously held up his hand to stop. The room grew quiet. Everyone wondered what Connal Lee and his spouses were up to.

Slowly, Connal Lee lifted the latch and opened the heavy door. He peeked through, then rushed into the hall, dodging smoothly to the right. Short Rainbow and White Wolf followed, ducking left. The door latched silently behind them. Colonel Kane began to ask what was going on, but Porter Rockwell hissed, "Listen!"

They rose to their feet. Porter Rockwell drew his large pistols. Robert unsheathed his sword. He wasn't carrying sidearms. Colonel Kane instinctively reached for his gun before he remembered it lay upstairs on top of his dresser in his guest bedroom.

A loud gunshot shattered the silence. Then another and another. A male voice screamed then abruptly cut off. Porter Rockwell and Robert rushed the door, shouting, "Get down! Take cover!"

The two men rushed through the short empty hallway and into the unoccupied kitchen where candles and cookfires burned unattended. They stopped up short, surprised at finding an empty room. They heard moaning from beyond the door leading to the herb garden behind the house. Worried about his Shoshone friends, Robert rushed to the door, pulled it open a crack, and peeked out. What he saw drew him up short. Four raggedly dressed bearded men lay on the ground. White Wolf knelt, tying the hands of one behind him. Short Rainbow held her knife to another man's throat. "No move. I kill."

Porter Rockwell rushed out. He saw the gardener, his teenage son, wife, and two daughters tied up, gagged, and dumped beside a big empty freight wagon. As he walked over to free the gardener's family, he glanced at Major Harris. "Well, sir, police actions are the province of the Legion. I believe these thieves are in your charge for the time being."

The Major nodded with a grim look as he rushed over to Connal Lee. "Are you wounded? Is everyone all right?"

Colonel Kane, the Governor, and President Young followed along, astonished at the scene before them. White Wolf stood up and brushed off his hands. He picked up Connal Lee's Bowie knife and handed it to him with a bow. "Good throw." White Wolf then helped Short Rainbow tie up the burglar with his own rope. They stood up and looked each other in the eye. In Shoshone, he asked, "You aren't hurt, are you? I was worried he might have hurt you."

"No, they were too surprised when Connal Lee came out shooting."

With lots of exclamations and shouted questions, they untied the Staines' employees and helped them to their feet. The two teenage girls burst into tears and ran to hug their mother. The gardener and his muscled son stood guard over the three robbers still alive. Connal Lee walked over to one of the smelly old men laying on the ground and kicked him over onto his back. "This one is dead."

He looked at another writhing on the ground holding a bloody hand to his shoulder, moaning loudly. Connal Lee turned to White Wolf. "Please tie him up and gag him."

White Wolf nodded. He picked up the rope he had just removed from the cook's bound wrists and made short work of securing the wounded thief.

Major Harris stepped over to the man Short Rainbow had fought to the ground. She still stood over him, holding her knife threateningly. The major picked up the man and shoved him back against the big empty freight wagon. "Now, what do you think you were doing, attacking the governor's home?"

Porter Rockwell loomed over the major's shoulder, scowling. "Speak up, man, as you value your life!" He waved his big revolvers in the thief's face. "I would as soon shoot ya as look at ya, ya low-class piece o' shite. An' what I shoot stays shot, dammit!"

President Young placed his hand on Rockwell's shoulder. "Thank you, Brother Porter, but our good Major Harris has things well under control here. Please see me home while the legion sorts this out."

The governor scowled as he glanced around. "Where are my servants, Jim and Petty? I don't see them."

The gardener answered in a loud voice, "They ate supper early and retired to the coach house, Your Honor."

Major Harris looked at the gardener. "Which building is the coach house?"

The gardener pointed. Robert shouted, "Connal Lee, come with me!"

They ran to the shed. They each grabbed one of the big rolling doors and pulled them open. The black coachmen lay sprawled beside their cots. One appeared unconscious. The other struggled against the ropes binding him. They both had gags in their mouths. The Major and Connal Lee rushed over to cut the ropes. They checked that the unconscious servant was still alive, then hurried back to the group crowding around the thieves' freight wagon.

Brigham Young shook hands with Governor Cumming. "You don't look so good, Governor. Perhaps you should go back inside and catch your breath."

Colonel Kane helped the governor lumber back into the house. General Wells nodded at Major Harris and the Shoshone envoys. "You seem to have everything well in hand here, Major. I will escort the president back to Beehive House."

They saluted each other. The cook shook herself free from her hysterical daughters. "You're all right now, my dears. Go take the governor some bourbon whiskey. He's going to need it. Hurry along, now. Wipe your tears and go tend to the governor."

She rushed to hug her husband, relieved their family had escaped with only a bad scare and rope burns on their wrists. Major Harris raised his voice. "Who are you men? What are you doing here?"

Connal Lee heard the filthy man whimper when Short Rainbow pushed her knife up against his bearded chin. "Tell the Injun squaw t' back away! This is all yer fault. Yew damn Mormons stole our freight wagons an' our mules. Ya burnt up all our freight. Cost us our jobs, yew did. Yew bankrupted us. We're hungry, an' it's all

172

because o' yew goddamned Mormons. Yew owe us, so we was only here collectin' on a just debt!"

Connal Lee had heard enough. He untied the filthy bandana around the prisoner's neck and gagged him with it. Major Harris turned to the gardener and his son. "Please secure the prisoners in the back of their wagon. Can one of you drive the wagon over to the Legion offices for me? We'll have to find a place to lock them up for the night. Tomorrow will be soon enough to sort out this mess."

The major turned to Connal Lee and held out his hand for a handshake. "Thank you, young man, for your fast thinking and quick response. You may have just saved the lives of the governor and President Young with your quick thinking. I'm glad you were so alert."

Connal Lee holstered his pistol. Robert shook his hand rather formally, then pulled him into a big bear hug. "Thank you, Connal Lee, my friend." The Major let go, then turned to Short Rainbow. "You were so brave, Short Rainbow. Thank you, my dear." He pulled her into a hug. Then he faced White Wolf. "Thank you. Thank you all." The Major stepped back and looked everyone over carefully. He reached out and straightened Connal Lee's jacket. "Are you all right? None of you suffered any wounds, did you?"

Short Rainbow brushed off the knees of her leggings with a curt shake of her head and pointed at the men being loaded in the wagon. "We not the ones hurt, Major."

"You young people are just remarkable. And so calm, too, even after all this excitement. I am so grateful the good Lord sent you to our aid this evening. If there is ever anything we can do, that I can do for you, you need only call on me."

Connal Lee hugged Short Rainbow and White Wolf. "Do y'all need us any more tonight, Major Harris? If not, Ah think we'll head on back to our camp."

"No, Connal Lee. You've done more than enough. Go get some rest. Then come see me in the morning at the Legion head-quarters, will you please? We'll need to take your statements as to what transpired tonight. Again, on behalf of Governor Cumming and President Young, you have our sincere gratitude."

Before he left to drive the prisoners to the legion compound, the gardener walked up to Connal Lee. "My name is Brother Gilmore, young man. I want to thank ya kindly fer savin' our lives tonight in our hour of need. My family and I will always be grateful to ya. I would be honored to know yer names and call ya my friends."

Connal Lee introduced Short Rainbow, White Wolf, then himself. Mr. Gilmore climbed up on the wagon seat next to his strapping son and took the reins. They slowly pulled out of the yard.

The major turned to watch the prisoners leave for legion headquarters. Connal Lee led his family through the kitchen. He had left his hat and riding gloves under his dining chair. The cook ran up to them with tears in her eyes. She had to stop and hug all three with whispered words of gratitude. "You brave young people saved our lives tonight. Thank you. Thank you. Thank you. God bless you one and all."

The governor and Colonel Kane also expressed their thanks, delaying them even more as they passed through the dining room. The kitchen maid who had served them earlier in the evening poured the governor another generous glass of bourbon. He downed nearly all of it in two big gulps.

The Shoshone family finally reached their horses. They cinched up the saddles and rode west to their camp on the river. They each felt let down after their adrenalin wore off. By the time they reached their tent, they wanted nothing more than hugs and sleep.

Connal Lee awoke before White Wolf and Short Rainbow and stretched. Light illuminated the canvas tent, although direct sunlight hadn't yet touched it. He pulled on some clothes and stepped outside to stir up the fire. He set coffee to boiling in their now blackened tin coffee pot. Ever since riding to Fort Hall with the Baines, they liked starting their day with plenty of hot coffee.

White Wolf grabbed a tin coffee mug, helped himself to the coffee then looked over at Connal Lee. "What has you scowling so early in the morning, Connal Lee? Are you feeling all right after last night's little fight?"

"Oh, yes, White Wolf. Ah feel fine. Ah'm just worried about what Screaming Eagle is going to say. He's going to be furious at missing out on even a skirmish as small as last night's. Y'all know how he lives for action."

"Don't worry about it. He'll be angry at me for convincing him to stay behind. Once he's over it, he will be very complimentary. To you, especially. You identified a problem, moved in without any hesitation, and did what needed to be done to save the gardener's family. And, by the way, very possibly saving the lives of Governor Cumming and President Young while at it."

Short Rainbow joined them for coffee before she prepared a simple breakfast. After they ate and enjoyed another cup of coffee, Connal Lee reminded them of their invitation to see Robert. They still had to give their statements about what happened. None of them thought it was a pressing priority, so they took their time dressing and straightening up the campsite before riding to the legion headquarters.

They arrived around two hours after sunrise to find the broad avenue in front of the Nauvoo Legion compound blocked. Twenty-two wagons and carriages, each pulled by two, four, or six horses or mules, stood two and three deep along the hitching rails. Teamsters struggled to hold their livestock in place as people climbed in with their personal bags, ready to depart. A chaos of people and rolling stock, loading supplies as fast as they could, crowded Main Street to the west of the Tithing Office. The Shoshone envoys ended up hitching their horses on Main Street in front of Council House. They walked back across the street to find Robert. The major had been watching for them. When he spotted them entering the gate, he strode over to welcome them. "Quite the parade, isn't it? This morning, Brigham Young is moving his family and their personal effects to Provo. The wagons will return tomorrow to remove all but the barest minimum of furniture needed to keep the house usable for the president. Well, come on in. We certainly appreciate you coming by this morning. You are quite the heroes around here. I wouldn't be surprised if The Deseret News will want to interview you for a story. Well, come on. Let's get your statements about last night's unfortunate events."

They walked into General Wells' office. His duties had called him away, leaving the large room available for their business. "Here, please have a seat. I have a shorthand court reporter waiting in my office, ready to take your sworn statements. Wait here a moment. I will bring him right over."

Connal Lee held up a hand to stop him. "Ah know how to write, Robert. Ah can write down our stories."

"Thank you, Connal Lee, but it will be easier for me to ask you questions and then have the court reporter write down what you say. There are certain formalities in cases where unnatural deaths occur. We don't have much experience here in Zion with such matters, but we do have protocols to follow according to Territorial Law."

"Whatever y'all say, Major."

They began the transcription after Connal Lee swore to tell the truth. "Where were you at nine P.M. on the evening of April the twenty-ninth?"

"Eating supper as the guests of Governor Cumming."

"Where did this supper take place?"

"At the home of Elder Staines around three blocks west of here."

Fifteen minutes later, the major asked Connal Lee, "What did you see when you rushed through the empty kitchen?"

"The first thing Ah saw was a filthy old man fighting with the cook. She was forcibly resisting him putting a gag on her. Just as Ah rushed through the door, Ah saw him strike her with his fist, nearly knocking her unconscious. Without any hesitation, Ah shot him to stop his assault. Before Ah could even advance my bullet cylinder, Ah saw one of his fellow intruders reaching for a shotgun leaning against their freight wagon. Ah heard Short Rainbow and White Wolf behind me. Ah didn't want them exposed to gunfire, so Ah shot him in his shoulder so he couldn't pick up and aim the rifle. When he dropped the shotgun, it discharged harmlessly."

"Did you kill the first attacker?"

"Yes, suh."

"The rifleman you shot, do you know if you killed him?"

"The last Ah saw him, he was loaded in the wagon, holding his shoulder but still alive. If my shot punctured his lung, he probably died during the night. If Ah missed the lung, he's probably still alive." Connal Lee glanced over at White Wolf to see if he understood correctly. White Wolf nodded.

"For the record, Connal Lee, the so-called rifleman died of his wounds shortly after being locked up in the barn's tack room here in the legion compound. Now, back to last night. What happened to the other two thieves? What did you see?"

"White Wolf leapt for the closest man. Ah saw him begin to pull a pistol from a holster on his hip, so Ah threw my Bowie knife and knocked the weapon from his hand. White Wolf wrestled him to the ground and choked him until he passed out. Short Rainbow rushed the fourth thief. Her knife flashed back and forth in her hands, confusing the man. He was so much heavier than Short Rainbow, Ah believe he underestimated her. He tried pushing her away, but she kneed him in the groin. When he collapsed, she held him still with a knife to his throat until you came to her assistance, suh."

An hour and a half later, they finished with Connal Lee's statement. Connal Lee asked if they could take a break to use the toilet. "Ah drank a lot of coffee this morning, suh."

Robert nodded knowingly. "You, too, White Wolf and Short Rainbow? Well, follow me, please." As they walked over to a latrine beside the barn, the major looked at Short Rainbow. "We don't have separate facilities for ladies, but we will guard the door, so you have your privacy. Please go first, Short Rainbow, while we keep watch."

They had nearly completed taking Short Rainbow's statement when a knock on the door interrupted them. The door opened. A young private handed Major Harris a note. He read the message, then tucked it into his jacket pocket. They finished up everything shortly after high noon. Robert leaned back in his chair. "Good. Thank you, Brother Thompson, for taking the statements. Please bring your transcripts to me here in the compound when you have them transcribed."

"Of course, sir. You shall have them in duplicate by tomorrow. Goodbye, sir. It was a pleasure meeting everyone. And may I be so bold as to extend my personal thanks to the three of you for protecting the new governor and especially our beloved President Brigham Young. May the good Lord watch over you on your travels."

Major Harris stood up and watched the Shoshone family as they stood up. Connal Lee stretched. He wasn't used to sitting on a chair for hours at a time. "Well, the formalities are all attended to. Thank you. With witnesses such as Governor Cumming and President Young, along with your sworn affidavits, I doubt you will hear anything more about the matter. Well, at least from a legal viewpoint. In the meantime, the governor sent a note inviting us to join him for a picnic luncheon at Council House. He warned that when Elder Lyon heard the story this morning, he said he wanted an interview for The Deseret News. Shall we cross the street and have a bite to eat, then?"

Before entering Council House, they checked their horses still tied up on Main Street. As soon as they entered the cool building, Connal Lee heard his friend, John Lyon. "Brother Swinton! Please come join us in the library. Hello everyone. We're eating dinner in here."

Everyone exchanged a round of handshaking and cheerful greetings. Governor Cumming sat down at one of the study tables, converted into a dining table by the two young kitchen maids from the Staines mansion. They had even brought a tablecloth and napkins. The governor chuckled as he waved them to join him. "I heard you would be busy with legalities this morning. When I arrived, I told Mister Lyon, here, about your heroic services to President Young and myself yesterday evening. He said he wanted to write up the story for The Deseret News. We figured it would probably take you all morning to take care of your written statements, so I sent my carriage back with a note asking Missus Gilmore to send over a picnic luncheon. When she read it was for you, her heroes from last night, she really outdid herself."

The kitchen maids uncovered the pans and bowls used to transport the food, revealing fried chicken, coleslaw, potatoes au gratin, a meat pie, and fresh rolls. The governor smiled in anticipation. "Dig in, everyone. Don't be shy!"

While they ate, John Lyon handed Connal Lee a small clay jam pot. "Here, Brother Swinton. Try some of Elder Staines' peach preserves with your roll. He grows six different kinds of peaches in his orchard in Bountiful. It's delicious!"

"Oh, thanks, Elder Lyon."

"I doubt you know that I write an original poem for each bi-weekly edition of The Deseret News. I don't, however, write the news. But Brother Cannon and Brother McEwan transported the presses south to Fillmore City where they are setting them up in the basement of the Utah Territorial Statehouse."

"Fillmore City? Ah've never heard of it. Where's that?"

Robert answered. "It's about a hundred and fifty miles south of us. Eighty or ninety miles south of my farm. Fillmore was origi-nally selected to be the capital of the State of Deseret because of its central location, but Congress turned down the petition for state-hood. They created the Territory of Utah instead. After completing only one wing of the Statehouse, President Fillmore lost his reelec-tion and couldn't finance the construction of the rest of the building. At the legislature's first session, they deemed Fillmore too far away from Great Salt Lake City, so they moved the capital back north to the center of population here in the valley."

John Lyon nodded and turned back to Connal Lee. "Since I am the only writer for the News still left in the City, I thought I should interview you. Would you mind, terribly? A lot of people will be very interested to read about your heroic rescue of Elder Staines' employees, not to mention saving the lives of the good governor here, and especially saving the life of our beloved Brigham Young."

"Can't y'all just publish our written statements, Elder Lyon? We've about worn out the subject, reviewing it for hours this morn-ing with Major Harris."

Elder Lyon chuckled and shook his head. He pulled out a diary of blank pages and took notes as Connal Lee answered questions during the meal. Once in a while, White Wolf or Short Rainbow answered. By the time the kitchen maids cut and served an apple pie made from the last of the apples from the fall harvest, John Lyon had his story. "Many thanks, Brother Swinton. You, too, Short Rainbow and White Wolf. Thank you for the interview, but more importantly, thank you for protecting my friend's home and preserving the lives of Governor Cumming and President Young. What are your plans now? Are you heading back to Fort Hall? Do you have room to take more books with you?"

"Ah have two empty saddlebags, so Ah could probably take a dozen or so more books." Connal Lee looked at White Wolf. "Are we ready to head back? Ah think our mission has been accomplished, don't y'all?"

"Rest tonight. Leave in morning. No rush to return."

The governor heaved himself up, wiped his lips with a cloth napkin, and placed it beside his plate. "Please extend our thanks to Captain Reed and Chief Arimo for sending you to us with a copy of the proclamation. Thank you for all your services to the territory and its fine citizens. It's an honor to have such fine people as our allies and friends. I look forward to seeing you the next time you visit Great Salt Lake City. My door is always open to you, my friends. Now, if you will excuse me, I have work waiting for me in my office next door."

The Governor shook hands with everyone. Connal Lee watched the kitchen maids as they began wrapping up the dishes to return to their mother. "Please tell Sister Gilmore everything was just delicious. And our thanks to y'all for bringing it to us."

Half an hour later, Connal Lee tucked several books into an empty saddlebag, including *The Complete Works of William Shakespeare*. They said their goodbyes and headed back to their camp on the Jordan River, glad they had fulfilled their obligation and could now return home.

Chapter 9: House Raising

Connal Lee and his family felt no pressure to hurry back to winter camp, other than missing Screaming Eagle and Bright Star. They trotted and walked on their way north, enjoying the lush green spring around them. They arrived four days later to a joyful reunion. After big hugs and bigger smiles, Screaming Eagle and Bright Star helped their spouses unpack the horses and turn them loose with the main herd.

They all walked back towards Short Rainbow's tipi, talking non-stop and laughing joyously. They stored their saddlebags, medicine bags, and sleeping furs. Bright Star invited them to sit beside the fire and rest while she cooked supper. Screaming Eagle had taken his shotgun hunting ducks earlier in the day. "Last year, it took a lucky shot to bring down a duck during their migration north. They fly so fast it's hard to hit one with an arrow. But with a shotgun, it's easy."

White Wolf told Screaming Eagle and Bright Star about their adventures. When he described the fracas at the Staines mansion, Screaming Eagle leaned over and glared at White Wolf. "I should have been there to protect you. Why did I let you talk me into staying home while you walked into danger?"

"Screaming Eagle, you would have been proud of Connal Lee. He heard a noise that didn't sound right and investigated. Quick as a wink, he subdued four big thieving teamsters. Even I was impressed. Besides, you now look rested and completely healed. How do you feel?"

Begrudgingly, Screaming Eagle nodded his head. "I feel all back to normal. I only needed a little rest. But you know how I hate to miss a good fight. It's my job to guard your safety." He paused and gazed into the fireplace while he imagined the scene of the confrontation. "Connal Lee, thank you for stepping up and protecting our family. It sounds like you did a great job of it. Well, I guess I can sit back and take it easy from here on out while you go fight all our battles. Good to know."

Connal Lee laughed and shook his finger at Screaming Eagle. "Oh no. Ah'm still learning. We will always need y'all, Screaming Eagle, our champion, our battle leader. Ah wasn't happy traveling without y'all and Bright Star. When we are together, we are complete, one big happy family. Ah'm glad we are all back together again. Ah hope we don't have to split up in our travels ever again. Don't y'all?"

Everyone nodded their agreement.

After they finished eating supper, White Wolf stood up. "Well, Connal Lee, let's go report to the Chief what we learned and saw this trip. You know how concerned he is about the Mormons down south."

Connal Lee and his family settled into their usual routine. They spent the next few days hunting, trapping, and tanning pelts, taking advantage of the warmer spring days. They no longer needed their warm leggings. Connal Lee found wearing only a loincloth a little odd at first but quickly became accustomed to the comfort of it.

Connal Lee resumed his weekly visits to Fort Hall to visit the Baines and trade furs with Mr. Mackey. When he completed his duties and business, he then passed the night with his handsome military older brother, John Reed.

The middle of May, Connal Lee led three heavily laden packhorses into the fort's courtyard. Lorna Baines saw Connal Lee enter the Fort's open gates. She pulled a shawl over her shoulders and walked across to the trading post. "Hello, son. How are you this beautiful day?"

"Mother Baines! Ah'm well. We're all doing well, enjoying the warmth of spring. Ah was going to come see you and Father Baines after Ah finished up with Mister Mackey."

"Listen, son. Would you please see if the good captain could join us for supper this evening? I don't have classes today, so I would like to prepare something special."

"That sounds really great, Mother Baines. Ah'll be sure to bring the captain along if he is free. See y'all later."

"Around seven would be good. We'll eat in the classroom."

Connal Lee sold the furs to Mr. Mackey, then visited his cavalry lover, John, in his log cabin office. After the captain completed his reports, he took Connal Lee on an inspection tour of the new barracks, barns, corrals, and workshops north of the old fort. Around seven that evening, the captain and Connal Lee knocked on the classroom door. With such a pleasantly warm day, Lorna had not set a fire in the potbelly heat stove.

Gilbert told about riding out hunting north of Fort Hall, where the Blackfoot River emptied into the Snake River, a few miles north of Zeff's clay pit. "The land around the confluence of the two rivers is lush, the soil is rich, the wildlife abundant. Lorna and I made the acquaintance of some settlers already beginning to farm the flatlands up and down the river. With so much water so close to hand, it's a simple matter to divert the water in irrigation ditches to water crops."

Lorna interrupted. "You see, son, we decided to homestead in the area even though there is no Mormon congregation nearby. It's really a lovely valley up there, nearly flat in the river basin. We're going to build a little log cabin to live in. We'll also put up a small lean-to barn to get us started. We can always expand the barn as our needs grow. We decided to raise cattle for their milk and meat and grow hay. We noticed this past winter how everyone needed hay for their livestock. I may come back to the fort in the fall to teach school again. We'll have to wait and see. First, we want to get our little plantation organized and get our crops and kitchen gardens in the ground." She reached out and squeezed Gilbert's hand.

"Why, that sounds really great, Mother Baines. When do y'all want to start?"

"We would like to leave as soon as possible. It's time to get our gardens planted."

"Well, how about if Ah ride down to the Chief's winter quarters and bring my family back with Short Rainbow's tipi. Then we'll get Zeff and Sister Woman to bring our big army tent. We'll join y'all at the Blackfoot River and help raise the new house. Zeff knows all about constructing log cabins and building cooking fireplaces. Ah'll pick y'all up the day after tomorrow, and we can travel to the Blackfoot River together."

"Oh! That's better than I ever could have hoped for. Thank you, Connal Lee."

Lorna and Gilbert beamed at each other, delighted. Captain Reed pushed his chair back from the plank wood table. "You are absolutely correct, Missus Baines. This area needs a reliable supply of hay. I'm sure the army will be glad to buy any surplus you have. It should be an excellent cash crop for you. If I may, I will come along and lend a hand at your house raising for a day or two."

"We would welcome your company, Captain." Lorna gazed around at her guests. "We need to buy some livestock for our little plantation. Please let us know when you hear of any for sale. Mister Mackey is keeping his eye open for us as well."

Lorna surprised the men around her table by serving a hot pie, its buttery crust filled with wild berries harvested from down in the Snake River basin. Connal Lee spent the night happily making love with the captain.

Two days later, Connal Lee returned to the Fort with quite a caravan of draft horses carrying huge, heavily laden travoises. He and his family brought dozens of horses with packsaddles overflowing with tanned leathers and their food stores. They had all their belongings with them. Connal Lee and White Wolf immediately took the pelts and sold them to Mr. Mackey. They harnessed the Baines' handcart to a strong horse and then helped the Baines pack up their meager possessions. A few days earlier, Gilbert had purchased a newfangled self-scouring steel plow made by John Deere and a robust young mule from the trading post. Connal Lee helped him tie the heavy plow's disassembled parts onto the mule's packsaddle for transportation.

Ned saddled up Paragon, then saddled up his own favorite young mare. The captain had decided Ned would be another useful pair of hands to have as they helped his friends establish their little plantation and cattle ranch. An hour later, they headed north to Zeff's clay pit homestead. Traveling at a walking pace, they arrived midafternoon.

The change in Zeff and Sister Woman's simple riverside home amazed Connal Lee and his family. After they unburdened their horses, Zeff proudly took them on a tour. "With the big brick contract with the army, Ah had enough money tuh buy me a freight wagon an' another mule fer the deliveries. We worked all winter long firin' bricks. Once the watermill was operational, Ah felled me some big trees an' took 'em tuh the mill tuh be cut into lumber. Ah bricked up the ol' hut so it could be our root cellar. It's now the downstairs door tuh the river basin from the house, too. The lieutenant that the army has operatin' the sawmill knows all about buildin' houses outa wood, so he advised me. Right helpful. Nice guy. Ah followed 'is instructions an' laid out a brick foundation fer our new house, jus' like I saw 'em do fer the watermill. Little by little, we framed out the house. The new house up on the plateau above the river basin has two whole bedrooms and a nice brick cookin' fireplace in the kitchen. It even has us a parlor fer sittin' in. Let me show y'all."

Zeff's success and lovely home impressed Connal Lee. "Ah ordered us some glass winders all the way from San Francisco. A big one fer the parlor an' three small ones fer the bedrooms an' kitchen. Mister Mackey thinks they'll get here sometime this fall in time tuh secure the house fer the winter."

"Wow! Glass windows! Zeff, this is really great. Whoever would've thought y'all would end up building yourself a real mansion for y'all's family."

Sister Woman proudly showed off her spacious new cooking fireplace while cooking supper for everyone. She baked loaves of brown bread in the ovens to the right of the firepit. Short Rainbow and Bright Star helped with supper. Zeff and Sister Woman didn't have any real furniture yet, so they all chipped in and carried supper down to the campfire pit beside the river to eat. They had a lively conversation catching up on all the news and planning their excursion to Lorna and Gilbert's new homestead.

Connal Lee noticed how Chester Ray had grown noticeably bigger, actively crawling around and making a nuisance of himself. Connal Lee chuckled when he saw how Sister Woman had tied the child up to a tree in the front yard. "Ah couldn't find 'im the other day. All concerned, Ah rushed about huntin' fer 'im everwheres.

Ah found 'im just afore 'e fell into the river. Scared the livin' day-lights outta me, let me tell ya. Since then, Ah don't dare let 'im outta muh sight. He jus' travels too dang fast on hands an' knees. What-ever am Ah gonna do when 'e starts walkin'? He's always explorin', pokin' 'is nose into ever little thing. Kinda reminds me of y'all, Connal Lee, when y'all was a youngun."

Connal Lee got down on his knees beside Chester Ray and tick-led him until they were both laughing. The entire crew ate a lei-surely supper, talking nonstop through the evening.

The next day, their house-raising party departed for the Black-foot River, a few slow miles further north.

Gilbert took the lead and guided his friends to the area he and Lorna had selected for their farmstead. Everyone helped pitch the big army tent for Zeff's young family, a pup tent for Ned, the Baines' two-man tent from the trail, and Short Rainbow's spacious tipi.

Connal Lee, Zeff, and John grabbed hatchets and a heavy ax and led their packhorses down to the river basin. They needed fire-wood for the cookfires and long logs for Lorna's cabin. They re-turned, dragging logs behind them on the ground. The hard physical labor of chopping down trees and cutting off the branches had ex-hausted the men. The hard work had given them quite an appetite.

After supper, when everyone stood up to go to bed, Connal Lee took hold of John's elbow and escorted him to Short Rainbow's tipi. Short Rainbow lit a second tallow candle and began pulling it up over their heads with a long Indian hemp cord. The two candles and the small hardwood fire bathed the interior of the tipi with a soft, romantic light. Connal Lee, his Shoshone family, and John un-dressed in the warm evening. They lounged casually around on top of the dark brown buffalo hide sleeping furs. It didn't take long before the men began showing their sexual excitement as four cocks slowly rose to their full stand. Connal Lee let his urges guide him. He leaned over and kissed John, then Screaming Eagle, then White Wolf. He lingered over a slow sensual kiss with Bright Star. As Connal Lee kissed Short Rainbow, he caressed her intimately. She wriggled in pleasure as their kiss drew longer. When he felt her becoming moist, he lowered her back down to the furs. Holding his torso up on his arms while still kissing, Connal Lee slowly entered her. He happily took his time, relishing every slick sensation they shared together. The other three men moved in closer to watch.

Short Rainbow began writhing in pleasure below Connal Lee as she achieved her first orgasm of the evening. Bright Star knelt up behind Screaming Eagle and hugged herself against his broad back. She boldly reached around and fondled his erection as he suckled Short Rainbow's tender breasts.

John felt left out watching the erotic scene in front of him. Connal Lee noticed and gestured for him to draw closer to their intimate grouping. John happily shuffled over on his knees with his erection pointing the way. Connal Lee reached out and caressed his hairy balls, then toyed with the head of John's erect phallus. He ran his forefinger around and around the swollen head under John's generous foreskin. John leaked lots of precum, providing plenty of lubrication. The natural slickness turned Connal Lee's caresses into an erotic adventure, focused on the covered head of John's sensitive cock. When Connal Lee soared to his climax, John pulled down on Connal Lee's dangling testicles, exposing all of his shaft to Short Rainbow's tight embrace. Connal Lee calmed his breath and then grabbed John's cock. Using it as a handle, he pulled John over and pushed him in to take the next turn with Short Rainbow.

Delighted with the warm slickness of Connal Lee's seed inside Short Rainbow, John began enthusiastically thrusting and withdrawing. The young family all leaned in to watch, their hands sensuously caressing each other wherever they could reach.

Connal Lee snuggled up close to John's side and ran his hand up and down John's solid muscled back. He lingered longer when he reached John's clenching, muscular hairy buttocks. Connal Lee had always found man hair attractive. To him, body hair signified being a grown-up, an adult, a real masculine man. His Shoshone spouses had little to no body hair. They only sported small black tufts in their armpits and sparse pubic hair above their genitals, with no beards and no hair on their legs or arms. Connal Lee relished petting the lush blond hair growing between John's beefy buttocks, firm from hours spent on horseback. He thrilled to feel those hairy muscles clench and relax as John took his time enjoying Short Rainbow's exotic lusty dance.

Connal Lee's fingers gently caressed John's hairy hole and taint when John surged over the top. Connal Lee loved feeling how John froze with his entire body rigid with ecstasy while he ejaculated. Connal Lee felt the base of John's penis pulse as he planted his seed deep inside Short Rainbow's slick entrance. When John caught his breath, he eased back and reluctantly withdrew from her warmth.

When Screaming Eagle saw Connal Lee and John's sperm leaking out of Short Rainbow, he aggressively muscled them aside. He leaned in and began slurping, licking, and kissing lustfully between her legs. But his blood ran too hot. He became impatient to begin the main event. He picked up Short Rainbow's knees, spread her legs so he could line up his swollen erection, and took possession of her in one smooth thrust.

Connal Lee and John knelt beside them with their arms over each other's shoulders. To Connal Lee's delight, neither his nor John's cocks went completely flaccid. Screaming Eagle became too stimulated to take his time and draw out the lovemaking as he usually would. He thrust and thrust more and more aggressively until he burst with a deep growl of passion.

White Wolf impatiently waited for his turn with his lovely wife. He playfully shoved Screaming Eagle away so he could find his release at last. Bright Star laughed and tucked herself under Screaming Eagle's sweaty arm. With sighs and smiles all around, White Wolf quickly reached his climax. He leaned forward and caught his weight on his extended arms without withdrawing. He lowered his face down and gently kissed and licked his beloved wife's lips. She had silently climaxed several times during their revels. She sank into a blissful listlessness, so happy with the men in her life. The men turned their combined attention to Bright Star, licking, kissing, fondling, and stroking her lithe body until she soared to her own ecstasy.

After they finished playing, the loving group cuddled up on top of the furs with their arms and legs intertwining naturally. Connal Lee lay his head down on John's muscled arm like a pillow and allowed his eyes to close. He felt so happy and secure basking in his spouse's and John's love. His heart overflowed with joy. He rolled over and hugged John's blond hairy chest with a happy sigh. He felt John's heart beating beneath the palm of his hand as he drifted off to sleep. Bright Star turned from Screaming Eagle and snuggled up to Connal Lee's exposed back.

A few days later, John made his excuses to Lorna and Gilbert. He needed to return to his command at Fort Hall. He and Ned rode south, waving their hands and shouting their goodbyes.

After a week of hard labor, Lorna strode into her new dream home, a snug little one-room log cabin close by the riverbank with a conveniently located outhouse beside it. The men had split cedar logs to make large shingles for the roof, held in place with smooth fist-sized river rocks. Zeff finished chinking the stone cooking fireplace with clay mixed with Indian grass straw. He left a hole into the chimney to vent Lorna's cookstove. The following morning, the men dammed off a small feeder creek and dug a ditch to divert the water to Gilbert's new garden and field.

The next morning, they all lounged around, preparing and eating leisurely meals. The ladies washed everyone's dirty clothing in the river and spread them over bushes to dry. Connal Lee smiled as he hugged Short Rainbow to his side. He lovingly caressed her slightly swollen belly, thinking of the baby inside. "The only thing that would make this more perfect would be if we had a hot spring close by. Don't y'all agree, Screaming Eagle?"

Screaming Eagle nodded his agreement. "I would love a hot soak for my tired muscles. Building a cabin is harder work than hunting, that's for certain."

Zeff and Sister Woman packed up the army tent in their new freight wagon. Connal Lee gave them a hand harnessing their big draft mules. They wanted to go home so Zeff could complete the last of his order for the army's waterwheel mills and water sluice. Sister Woman also wanted to expand her little kitchen garden this summer. She needed to get her seeds in the ground. She untied Chester Ray from the back of the wagon and climbed aboard.

Connal Lee and his family decided to remain by the Baines' new log cabin a bit longer. They enjoyed the lovely campsite, but more importantly, they relished the Baines' company. Connal Lee's family returned to their regular routines during the day. Four of the young family took their shotguns and hunted. Bright Star didn't enjoy shooting, so she stayed behind to take care of daily chores. She worked with Lorna to prepare special midday meals. The hunters returned to camp with their kills around noon each day and shared a communal meal. They all worked together tanning hides in the afternoon. Lorna wanted to lay in a good supply of leather to sew into hats, gloves, vests, and chaps. She had a standing order from Mr. Mackey for all she could produce.

After clearing away their supper dishes, they lingered around the fire. Connal Lee, Lorna, and Gilbert took turns reading out loud *Bleak House*, another Charles Dickens novel.

About a week after completing the house and barn raising, they finished reading *Bleak House.* The following morning, Gilbert plowed a tiny plot of land running along the Blackfoot River, breaking up the thick sod to prepare the ground for a vegetable garden. When he guided the big mule to turn around and reverse course, he noticed a large troop of riders approaching. Alarmed, he loosened the harness on the mule and left the plow right in the field. He hopped on the mule, kicked it into a gallop, and took off towards the Snake River to sound the alarm. He found Connal Lee's family on their way back to camp. At Gilbert's urging, they hurried to defend their homes.

Screaming Eagle shaded his eyes with his right hand to peer more closely at the approaching group of riders. More and more horses rode into view. "It looks like Uncle SoYo'Cant traveling with his clan. Let's go greet him."

Relieved, Gilbert returned to his work. He hooked up the plow and grabbed its two wood handles. He goaded the mule with a shake of the reins into heaving the curved iron blade along, turning over the sod in a furrow.

Connal Lee and his spouses trotted south to meet the slow-moving clan. They pulled up alongside the chief and White Dove, calling out their welcomes and happy greetings. Connal Lee invited his stepfather to stop and meet his white foster parents. The chief said the clan would continue on, but he would stop for a short visit and then catch up. All the clan, including Chief SoYo'Cant, looked forward to reaching the Salmon River for the annual fishing camp. They still had six days of travel before reaching the river. Screaming Eagle turned his great war steed around and guided Chief SoYo'Cant and White Dove back to their camp beside the Blackfoot River.

Connal Lee heard his name shouted over the noise of the procession. He turned in his saddle and spotted Captain Reed and Major Harris riding beside Teniwaaten further back in the column. With a yelp of joy, he took off riding to meet them. The Captain and Major turned their stallions out of the path of the travois train and stopped. Connal Lee raced up in a flourish of dust. Smiling, all three pulled off their riding gloves and shook hands. "Major Harris, what the heck are y'all doing all the way up north here? Captain Reed, Ah'm glad to have y'all back again. Is that Edward Ah spot behind y'all? Hi, Edward! Welcome to the Blackfoot River, everyone. Please come on in and meet my white family, Major Harris."

They all took off at a trot towards the Baines' new log cabin, dragging their packhorses behind them.

John called out loudly to be heard over the horse hooves thudding on the dry desert soil. "So you see, Connal Lee, the good Major Harris and his son arrived at the chief's camp just as they began pulling out. They came looking for you and your family. When they passed by Fort Hall, they stopped in to make a courtesy call. The major introduced himself and brought me up to date with all the news down in the Territory of Utah. I told him I knew where to find you and offered to be their guide. Do you think you can put up three lonely travelers for the night?"

"Of course we can, John. Y'all are always welcome. Come on, Robert. Come on, Edward. Ah want y'all to meet my foster parents and see the new house we just raised for them. Follow me!"

They pulled around the chief and Connal Lee's family and galloped up to the log cabin. While they tied up their horses, Connal Lee called ahead. "Mother Baines! Mother Baines! Come on out and meet my friends from Great Salt Lake City."

Lorna opened the board door of her one-room cabin, her hands covered with flour. She pushed a stray lock of hair off her forehead with the back of her hand. "Hello. Welcome, everyone. Give me a moment to clean up, and I'll be right out."

She ducked inside to wash her hands. When Gilbert saw guests ride up, he left the plow and mule in the field and trotted over to greet everybody. Bright Star heard all the commotion and ran over to say hello. After hugs and introductions, she invited everyone to sit by her fire to talk. The chief and his entourage rode up and joined them. Lorna served oatmeal raisin cookies, still warm and gooey from her oven. Short Rainbow and Bright Star handed everyone a drinking horn of fruity sweet red tea brewed from serviceberry leaves.

About an hour later, Chief SoYo'Cant stood up. He reached down his hand and helped White Dove to her feet. "Good see eveyone. Nice cabin, Missus Baines. Congratulations. Good luck with farm, Mister Baines. Nice to meet. We need rejoin clan. Connal Lee, when finish business down in Territory of Utah, come join at Salmon River. If delay, we next go to the tribe sun dance north fork Snake River. Tribe there one week. Celebrate longest day all year." The Chief switched to Shoshone. "Connal Lee, you must take special care there, as Pocatello and his warriors will also be attending. After the conclusion of the sundance ceremonies, we will head east to our summer camp in Jackson Valley in the Teton Mountains. I hope you can all come and enjoy the summer high up in the beautiful mountains where it is cool."

The Chief, White Dove, and Teniwaaten mounted up and trotted away to resume their place at the head of the clan's spread-out convoy. Connal Lee sat back down at the fireplace and watched the clan pass by them. It took another hour before the last of the travois and horses moved past the Baines plantation. "Ah'm really happy to see y'all, Major Robert, suh, and Edward. Though Ah am dying to know what brought you to leave the city during the crisis. Now, please tell me why y'all came looking for us."

John turned and walked away from the campfire, accompanying Lorna to her log cabin. He already knew why they had come. Robert and his son sat down, facing Connal Lee across the fire. White

Wolf joined their little circle. The rest of Connal Lee's family returned to their chores. Short Rainbow and Bright Star organized a feast to welcome their guests. Lorna baked a pie for supper.

Major Harris took a sip of tea from the buffalo drinking horn in his hand. "Delicious tea. So fruity and sweet. Well, my friends, there have been a number of developments in the peace process in the Territory of Utah since you departed at the end of April. Governor Cumming and Colonel Kane have made several trips around the territory, trying to convince the people to stay in their homes or return to their homes. They traveled north once, along the settled corridor, then made three trips south to Provo and beyond. I've heard the Governor bemoan many times how hard it is for him to watch women and children walking barefoot through the desert when there's no need for them to suffer so. Back around the middle of May, the governor drove to Camp Scott to fetch his wife and their belongings. Colonel Kane accompanied him to the camp before continuing on his way to Washington to make his report to President Buchanan.

"In the meantime, we only have about six-hundred of us home guard still in the city, left behind to protect it or burn it if ordered. Edward decided to stay with me and help out at the library until things settled down. Sister Ohlsson offered to stay and take care of us until we evacuate. General Wells remained in the city, supervising what limited manpower we have to defend the city and protect our public works."

Connal Lee shook his head sadly. "What a waste that will be if the army attacks."

"That's why we've all been working with the governor to keep the army away until the Peace Commissioners arrive. The Nauvoo Legionnaires spying on Camp Scott sent us an express rider who arrived Sunday afternoon. The Peace Commissioners reached Camp Scott last Saturday, the thirtieth of May. They held a conference with General Johnston and Governor Cumming the following day. The Governor sent word that he, his wife, and the Commissioners would leave Camp Scott later that week with the intention of arriving in Great Salt Lake City by Monday the seventh, just six days from now."

Connal Lee turned a smile to White Wolf. They nodded their heads. "That's really great news, isn't it? The commissioners arrived before the army left Camp Scott. What a relief!"

"I was in a meeting with the governor and General Wells when we received the news. Brigham Young happened to be in the city that day. I tracked him down and invited him to join us at the governor's office. As we discussed who should attend the negotiations and meetings with the Peace Commissioners, Governor Cumming asked if I thought the Shoshone delegates should attend as emissaries and observers for our allies. Brigham Young nodded his approval. I told them I thought it would be a good idea, especially given all the help and support you have rendered over the past few months. General Wells agreed. He told me since it didn't look like I would be needed for guard duty or fire duty, now that the Commissioners met with General Johnston, I should ride up and invite you to join us. I invited Edward to come along so he could gain experience traveling for military duties.

"We made good time to Chief Arimo's camp. We met with him yesterday evening as his clan prepared to leave their winter quarters. We invited the chief to come to Great Salt Lake City, but he said he would be content to have your family represent him and the Shoshone people. He invited us to ride with him to Fort Hall this morning, which we did."

"Well, Robert, suh, Ah'm surely glad y'all came up north to find us. We will be happy to return to Great Salt Lake City and listen in on the negotiations. It sounds like a real interesting trip. Don't y'all agree, White Wolf? Wouldn't y'all like to see the Peace Commissioners and be there when they make peace? Ah've never seen a peace treaty signed before."

White Wolf stood up. "Yes. Thank you for invite, Major Harris. I go tell Screaming Eagle we leave in morning."

Short Rainbow and Bright Star listened as they cooked. Happy to hear of another diplomatic trip, Short Rainbow suggested they travel with all their possessions except winter gear, which they could leave with Lorna Baines until they returned. White Wolf approved. They scattered and began packing. Connal Lee invited Robert and Edward to walk with him downriver to their horses. Connal Lee started to inspect the horses needed for the journey. John joined them. They examined the hooves for problems. Two hours later, they concluded all the horses could make the journey. It surprised Connal Lee to discover a young mare was pregnant. They decided she was not so far along she couldn't carry a pack and make the trip.

This time, when Connal Lee invited Robert to travel south with them, the major agreed. "Yes, my friend. I'm not in a hurry this time. It would be our pleasure to accompany you and your family."

"Oh, great! Well, we're going to need extra meat for supper tonight. How about it, Edward? Would y'all like to ride out hunting with me for a while? We don't need to travel far to find game around these parts."

"Sure! If it's all right with you, father, I would like to go hunting with Connal Lee."

"Go right ahead, son. You're a grown man, now. You don't need my permission. Good hunting, men."

The boys ran ahead and grabbed their rifles. Robert and John took their time walking beside the chuckling waters of the broad river, heading back to the Baines little plantation. With the easy patter that seems to come with military service, they chatted about their past travels and experiences, becoming better acquainted with each other. John shared his thoughts. "Since the Federal Government announced the Overland Trail to California impassable due to the Utah War, we have seen less and less traffic lately. We have completed all the construction projects at the fort. Yes, I believe I might be able to get away for a while and travel with you. I've heard a lot about the Mormons down in Great Salt Lake City, but I've never been further south than the chief's winter camp on the Portneuf River. I'm curious to visit the Great Salt Lake I've heard so much about, too."

"It would be our pleasure to have you travel with us back to Great Salt Lake City, John. By the way, you would be welcome to quarter at my place while you're in town if you would like."

"Thank you, sir. However, I'm very close friends with Connal Lee and his Shoshone family. I will most likely stay with them. But thank you for inviting me."

"Well, while everyone else is busy getting ready for the trip, I think I will pitch Edward's and my pup tent for the night."

John helped the major raise the simple tent. When they finished unpacking the saddlebags, Robert looked at the log cabin not far away. "The Baines seem to be really nice people."

"Yes, they are. They lived this past winter in the schoolhouse in Fort Hall. Lorna taught school. We came to know each other very well. They are good friends with great hearts. I can see why Connal Lee came to love them as they trekked across this great land."

Everyone spent the evening around the fireplace, eating and joking, telling about their adventures and misadventures. Connal Lee found himself in his element, surrounded by so many family, friends, and loved ones. A waning gibbous moon rose overhead, casting a gentle light on the cheery scene. Suddenly, the Major began chuckling. Connal Lee shot him a questioning glance. "What's so funny, Robert?"

"Oh, Connal Lee. I delivered a report on the Territorial Militia to Governor Cumming two, no, three weeks ago. When I arrived, a poor farmer stood in the governor's office with his wife and two children. He told the governor the Mormons wouldn't issue him a pass to leave the territory because they were not Mormons and asked for the governor's protection. They failed to tell the governor we suspected them of being spies and informants for Johnston's army. After the governor agreed to help them leave, the farmer told the governor about our subterfuge at Echo Canyon. He went on to say that we only had a hundred and fifty men stationed there, not the fifteen-hundred the governor had been led to believe. Governor Cumming angrily pushed himself out of his chair and stood up. His face started turning purple right before my eyes. I thought he was going to have a heart attack. He shook his fist in the air and cursed. How dare they lie to me. And I believed them, too. Oh, they made a right fool of me. Damn them to hell! I believed them! He carried on in this vein for some minutes. Concerned he would give himself a stroke, I stepped over to the little console below the window and poured him a couple fingers of Kentucky whiskey.

"When I handed it to him, I urged him to calm down for his health sake. He took a big swig, then lowered himself into his chair. He was madder than a stirred-up hornets' nest. In retrospect, it's funny, but I didn't find it so at the time. He was livid. When the gentile farmer saw how the Governor received his gossip, he grabbed his family and fled. I sat down and commiserated with the governor, trying to calm him down. I pointed out how the stratagem had served the purpose of preserving peace, convincing the governor to discourage General Johnston from invading through the canyons."

Connal Lee chuckled. "What do y'all suppose he would do if he found out we were all in on tricking him again at Little Emigration Canyon? He might never talk to us again!"

"Well, the cat's out of the bag, now. He finally calmed down, so I went on about my business."

Out of the corner of his eye, Robert caught Bright Star yawning. He looked at Edward, still smiling. "So, what do you say, son? Shall we retire to our bedrolls? Tomorrow's going to be a long day. Good night, everyone. Thank you, Short Rainbow and Bright Star, for your wonderful supper. Thank you, Sister Baines, for your delicious pie. Good night."

Everyone called out good night as they split up to their various beds.

Lorna greeted the new day by serving a farewell breakfast of freshly baked whole wheat bread with sweet butter. The experienced travelers waved goodbye to the Baines as they began their journey. The two military officers ended up riding side by side. Edward pulled his lively young gelding up so he could ride with Connal Lee. Screaming Eagle led the way, proudly wearing his feathered warbonnet.

For two days, they followed the Portneuf River and its many subsidiaries south to the hot springs. The whole company luxuriated in the bubbling springs. Edward had never seen girls without clothing before. He felt quite shy and intimidated. After watching his father strip off his uniform and plunge in, he followed suit. Soon everyone sat basking in the heat with big smiles as their travel-weary muscles relaxed.

After the hot springs, they struck south across the barren desert. That evening they camped beside the creek that would grow into Bear River further south. They traveled close to the meandering brook as it swelled from feeder creeks until they reached Box Elder. Connal Lee suggested they call on Jedediah and Jeff. Jedediah invited them to stay. They raised their big tent beside the Morgans' log cabin. The girls lit a cookfire. Over a pot luck supper that evening, they told the Morgans about the arrival of the Peace Commissioners. Jedediah's face lit up. He jumped to his feet. "Praise the Lord! Our families can come home, now, at last. Halleluiah. Thank you, Lord."

Major Harris raised a cautionary hand. "It's not over yet, Brother Morgan. Please be patient. You will receive word when it's safe for your loved ones to return home. In the meantime, be vigilant. We still have more than five-thousand soldiers and camp followers poised over in Camp Scott, ready to descend on our homes. Until the army withdraws, we are still under orders to stay out of harm's way."

"Of course, major. Yer right. Still, don't begrudge an old man fer being happy to see some light at the end of the tunnel."

Jedediah sat down and gave Jeff's shoulders a big one-arm hug. They looked at each other with beaming smiles of relief and joy.

That evening, Connal Lee and his family pulled John into their blankets for a rather boisterous bout of lovemaking. Robert and Edward heard from their pup tent but politely attempted to ignore the soft moaning and groaning. Edward strained to imagine what they were doing, four men with only two women. Finally, he rolled over, crushing his erection against the blankets spread over the bare ground, and fell asleep despite his arousal.

The following day, they skirted east of where the Bear River's meandering course had leveled the immediate area. An abundance of weeds, rushes, and grasses grew in the flat wetland basin. Connal Lee's sharp eyes spotted the fluttering of large yellow butterflies hovering about the thistles, milkweeds, and wild carrots. "Hey, everyone. Look over there!"

His shout disturbed the flocks of butterflies. They rose in a fluttering cloud of color, drifting north. Robert pointed at them. "Look. Monarch butterflies! How beautiful."

White Wolf pulled up beside Connal Lee. "The Monarchs fly north, following the warmth as summer arrives. Later they fly back south, escaping the cold that comes with the fall season. Every year they cross our sacred lands twice, spring and fall. It's considered a good omen to see them in flight."

Connal Lee, with his eyes wide with delight, nodded his head. "Ah can see why. What a sight for sore eyes. They are so beautiful."

While the company sat their horses watching, the butterflies began alighting on them. Soon each person, their horses, and travois were bright with fluttering gold and black wings. They all grinned at each other. Mere moments later, the butterflies took wing at some unseen, unheard signal. Connal Lee sighed. Robert broke the enchanted mood. "Let's keep moving, my friends. We still have a way to travel."

For the next few days, Screaming Eagle, Robert, and John led the train of travoises and packhorses south. As they passed each fort, they stopped and briefly shared the hopeful news of the Peace Commissioners with the home guard. They encouraged the guards to stay alert for news. "Things are coming to a head, one way or the other, in the very near future. Good luck."

Midafternoon on the sixth day of their trip, they pulled up to the usual Shoshone campsite on the west side of the Jordan River not far from the city gates of Great Salt Lake City. Robert invited John and Connal Lee to ride with him and Edward into the city for news while the rest of the Shoshone delegates pitched their tipi and made camp. "Please do join us, John. If General Wells is in his office, it would be my honor to introduce you."

"Thank you, Robert. Lead on, please, sir."

Chapter 10: Commissioners

They entered Great Salt Lake City, four lonely horsemen: Major Harris, Captain Reed, Connal Lee, and Edward. The silence of the evacuated city rang in their ears. They couldn't see any pedestrians on the streets or walkways. The broad avenues stood empty of all traffic. They passed by the Staines mansion, one of the few homes with smoke rising from a cook fire. Along their leisurely ride, Robert shared the highlights of General Wells' history with John. Connal Lee and Edward followed, gawking left and right, taking in the strange sight of the vacant city and boarded-up houses. Edward frowned. "This no longer feels like my home. It's too quiet and lonely, now."

They hitched up their horses on the empty avenue in front of the Nauvoo Legion's headquarters. Robert led them through the stone wall. A blacksmith shoeing horses in a back corner of the compound made a loud clang of hammer on iron, the only sound. A young officer, acting as clerk and Officer of the Day to General Wells, stood up with a smart salute when they entered his office. "Good afternoon, Major Harris, sir. How may I help you today?"

"Good afternoon, Private Sessions. Is the general in? May we see him, please?"

"One minute, sir. Let me check."

The slender young man knocked on the board door opposite the entrance and stuck his head in. Moments later, he pushed the door open and waved for Major Harris to show his guests through. Connal Lee recognized the office from when he made his statement regarding the attack on the Staines mansion.

Major Harris came to attention and saluted the weary-looking man sitting at a desk. "General Wells, sir, I have the honor of introducing you to my friend and colleague, Captain John Reed of Company G, Sixth Infantry. He is the commander of Fort Hall and the western Overland Trail. He is a close personal friend of Connal Lee Swinton and the others of the Shoshone delegation. He traveled here at my invitation."

Captain Reed came to attention and saluted the general.

General Wells stood up and returned the salute. Major Harris smiled. "Captain Reed, sir, it gives me great pleasure to introduce you to one of our most distinguished citizens and my personal friend, Daniel H. Wells, Lieutenant General of the Nauvoo Legion. He is also an important official in the Mormon church, in addition to serving as the county's Superintendent of Public Works. He remained behind in command of our home guard until the Saints are safe to return or we fire the city."

General Wells leaned over his desk and shook hands. "Pleased to meet you, sir. Although I have to confess, I never expected to welcome a man wearing a Federal uniform to the city until after a resolution of the Utah War, one way or the other. Nonetheless, you are welcome as an interested party and personal friend of our Shoshone allies. Since you officially answer to the federal government with whom we regrettably find ourselves at war, I must ask for your parole while visiting our territory, sir. Do you solemnly swear to take no action inimical to the Territory of Utah or to the Mormon people?"

"General Wells, sir. It is my pleasure to meet you as well. You have my parole, sir, so long as I am a guest in your territory, and I am not asked to do anything contrary to the Constitution of the United States of America, which I have sworn to support and defend."

"Thank you, sir." The General turned his attention to the others. "Nice to see you, Brother Connal Lee, was it? How are you this evening, Brother Edward? Please, everyone, have a seat." After the four guests pulled up chairs and sat down, General Wells nodded at Major Harris. "Well, Robert, I see you and young Edward made good time. Did you have a good trip?"

"Yes, sir. Thank you, sir. We brought Connal Lee and his family as emissaries and observers from the Shoshone Nation. Tell me, please, sir, have you received any update on the progress of the Peace Commissioners? We haven't missed anything while on the trail, have we?"

"Well, Robert, in point of fact, the Commissioners arrived yesterday in five great mule-drawn ambulances. They still had the entourage of fifteen heavily armed men who accompanied them from

Fort Leavenworth. The escort included six dragoons commanded by a Sergeant, five teamsters, a wagon master, and a guide. I had the honor last evening of greeting the distinguished Lazarus Powell, the former governor and current United States senator from Kentucky. He was accompanied by Ben McCulloch, a Texas Legislator and famous captain of the Texas Rangers. Mister McCulloch was the person President Buchanan first proposed to replace Brigham Young as governor. Despite being weary from weeks of forced travel, they were very impressive men. Very correct and gentlemanly in their behavior. Governor Cumming hasn't returned from Camp Scott, where he went to escort his wife back to the city, so I invited the Commissioners to go down to the Globe Restaurant and Bakery for their board. We have no hotel or open private home to offer them. They shrugged off the inconvenience, telling me they were very comfortable sleeping in their ambulances as they had since leaving Fort Leavenworth five weeks ago."

"Well, I look forward to meeting them later, then. I guess it's a good thing President Young sent Brother Candland back to reopen the Globe, isn't it? Otherwise, there would be no place for them to find fresh food."

"The Globe is also entertaining some land agents trying to sell President Young thirty million acres of the Mosquito Coast down in Central America for the relocation of the Saints. The Globe has the only barber, chef, and pastry cook left in the county. Our gentile guests complain at having to camp out along the creeks, but at least they can find boarding at the Globe. Brother Candland told me his customers protest the expensive war prices for food. He charges them up to two dollars per day for their boarding, though he gives them excellent food and beverages in return. They might complain, but they show up every morning for fresh breads and rolls, and they return every evening to buy more alcohol after enjoying a gourmet supper."

Major Harris leaned forward. "What is our schedule, then, General Wells?"

"Well, sir, the Commissioners asked me to deliver a letter inviting Brigham Young to meet with them about the unfortunate difficulties, as they called it, between the Mormons and the United States

202

government. I confess I read the letter before I dispatched it south. President Young should have received the letter early this morning. I expect to receive instructions from him later today. You might also like to know that I received a note from Governor Cumming that he arrived with his wife and can be found at the Staines mansion."

Robert looked at his guests. "We have a couple of options. We could go pay a social call on the governor and meet his wife. We could go to my house for supper. Or we could return to your camp to eat. What is your pleasure?"

A knock on the door interrupted them. Private Sessions rushed in with a letter for the general. "Excuse me, General Wells. From President Young, sir. It's marked urgent."

They watched quietly while the general broke the seal, opened, and read the letter. He placed the letter on his desk, then leaned back in his chair. Connal Lee waited anxiously, bursting to know what it said. The General sat up and squared off his narrow shoulders. "Excuse me now, if you would, please. I need to organize a work crew to reinstall the windows in the large second-floor meeting chamber in the Council House. President Young and other church officials plan to arrive Thursday evening to meet with the commissioners Friday morning. They asked me to travel to Provo, so I could escort them to Great Salt Lake City and confer with them during the drive. As soon as I have the work crew assigned, I will ride to Provo. I want to see my family before I return with the church authorities. Major Harris, I leave you in charge of the city defenses until I return."

"Yes, sir. Thank you, sir. Please excuse us now. We will leave you to your work. Have a safe journey. Until the day after tomorrow, then."

Robert escorted John, Edward, and Connal Lee out to the bright sunny day in front of the headquarters building. "So, what would you like to do now?"

"Well, suh, if the Governor just arrived at the Staines mansion today with his wife, Ah doubt they will be in the mood to entertain. They'll probably want to rest and get cleaned up first, Ah'm sure. Let's send him a note that we arrived and can be found in our camp on the Jordan River. Perhaps we can see him tomorrow once they are settled in and unpacked."

"That sounds like a good plan, Connal Lee. Since I am now on duty until the general returns, I should stay close to headquarters or in my home where I can be easily reached if something comes up."

Connal Lee looked at John and Edward. "Would y'all like to go hunting with me this afternoon and join my family for supper this evening? We have time to relax a bit before all the excitement begins."

Edward nodded. "Is that all right with you, father? Do you think you will need me this evening?"

"That's fine, son. I will send Private Sessions for you at the river if something changes. Good hunting, everyone!"

Connal Lee asked Private Sessions for a piece of notepaper and the use of a nib pen. He quickly scribbled a brief note to Governor Cumming. They dropped it off on their way to the Jordan River camp.

Robert Harris galloped into camp late the following morning. After greetings all around, he handed Connal Lee a folded note. Connal Lee read it out loud. "Dear Master Swinton, my wife and I would be honored if you and your fellow delegates would join us this afternoon for high tea at four o'clock. Please invite your Cavalry guest, as well. Sincerely yours, Governor Alfred Cumming."

Connal Lee looked around with a big smile.

"When I received this note at Legion headquarters, it came with an invitation for Edward and me to join them as well. Since the governor will formally present us to his wife, I recommend we wear our dress uniforms and ceremonial finest, once again."

Short Rainbow invited Robert to join them for a cold midday meal before they dressed to meet the governor's wife. Robert and Edward left to change their clothes as soon as they finished eating.

Screaming Eagle led his family to the Staines mansion. While tying up their horses, Robert and Edward arrived. They all walked through the gardens together, enjoying the warm summer sun and the fragrance of herbs on the gentle breeze. Connal Lee stepped up and knocked on the door. One of the cook's daughters opened it with a big smile. "Good afternoon, everyone. The governor and

Missus Cumming are waiting for you in the drawing room. Please follow me."

"Good afternoon, Sister Gilmore. Our thanks. Very kind of y'all."

They walked into the sparsely furnished parlor. Connal Lee noted how the governor had added a few small pieces of furniture to the suite of chairs and the grand piano. Two folding camp tables stood to the side, covered with a white tablecloth. The governor pushed himself up out of his upholstered armchair with a grunt. "Welcome, everyone. Please come on in and join us. It's good to see you, my friends." He held out his hand and helped an attractive woman in her forties rise and stand beside him. He picked up her left hand and placed it in the crook of his elbow, then smiled at everyone. "My dear, I am delighted to introduce our friends, saviors, and allies, Master Connal Lee Swinton and his illustrious Shoshone family."

The Governor took his time and introduced them one by one. "And this is my darling Wife, Elizabeth Wells Randall Cumming of Boston. We have been happily married these past twenty-two years. Somehow, she still manages to look as young and delightful as ever, despite the hardships of accompanying me on my various posts all these years."

As he introduced them, each person stepped up and shook Mrs. Cumming's hand. She looked surprised at hearing polite speeches from savage Indians. Their lovely clothing and polished manners intrigued her. Mrs. Cumming smiled around at everyone. "Please have a seat, won't you? It is such a relief to finally be in Great Salt Lake City. And such a beautiful city, although it breaks my heart to see it empty and abandoned." She waved for the cook's daughter to come closer. "Please pour and serve the tea, Miss Gilmore. Thank you, dear."

Captain Reed leaned forward. "My dear Missus Cumming, it is such a pleasure to meet a fellow Bostonian out here on the frontier, so far from civilization. I was also born and raised in Boston, as were my parents and their parents. My mother's father and my father's father both served with distinction in the Revolutionary War."

"How nice, indeed, Captain Reed, to meet another native Bostonian. My great grandfather was Samuel Adams, so we were also raised on family stories of patriotism, sacrifice, and honor. How wonderful to see you following in your family's tradition of service to our great nation, Captain."

"Yes, ma'am. I graduated from Harvard back in fifty-five. I tried reading law in my father's law firm. He's an important judge now, back in Boston. I wasn't happy with the thought of going into law, so I wrote my grandfather, General Reed, for advice. Even though retired, he managed to pull a few strings in the war office and secured me a commission. I have primarily served by fighting renegade Indians and safeguarding the Overland Trail."

"Why, you know? I do believe my mother wrote me about a friend of hers, a Missus Jennifer, who is the wife of a local Judge Reed. She said they are members of the same clubs and service organizations back in Boston. Isn't it a small world?"

"Why, Jennifer is my wonderful mother! Isn't it a small world, indeed? Now that her children are all grown up, mother devotes more and more of her time to charitable and civic activities. I'm afraid father doesn't quite know what to make of her campaigning for women's rights, though."

Mrs. Cumming laughed with him. Connal Lee accepted a cup of tea and took a sip. It was steaming hot, so he blew on it while listening to the conversation. He found Elizabeth Cumming quite attractive and well-spoken. She wore a full-skirted white dress edged in glistening blue silk. She had pulled her hair up behind her head with the bun covered with a blue silk bonnet. Crocheted lace and a couple of dramatic white swan feathers decorated her small cap. She wore a diamond pendant hanging from a gold chain beneath a triple row of pearl necklaces. Her delicate hands waved expressively as she chatted. Her fingers glittered with sapphire, aquamarine, and diamond rings. Connal Lee leaned in and smiled at her. "Missus Cumming, it is so nice for the Governor to have y'all here at long last. He told me he regretted that y'all had to stay behind in Camp Scott. Ah...we hope y'all are happy and comfortable, now, here in the governor's new post."

"Thank you, Master Swinton. How very kind of you to say so. My dear Alfred introduced you as the adopted white son of Chief Arimo of the Shoshone Indian tribe, didn't he? How on earth did that come about?"

Connal Lee shared a very short version of how his family saved his life, and they fell in love. "To reward me for saving Screaming Eagle's life, the great Chief SoYo'Cant, whom the Mormons call Chief Arimo, adopted me in a beautiful ceremony. Ah smoked the peace pipe with him. He welcomed me into his family, clan, and tribe."

"Well, Master Swinton, I have to say I am most favorably impressed with what I have seen so far of your Shoshone family. My, but this is a far cry from my experience attending the governor when he served as Superintendent of Indian Affairs for upper Missouri. The native tribes of Missouri were so dirt poor they had to scramble just to survive. I understand the Otoe and Missouria tribes had once been great nomadic nations. But warfare and smallpox left them so decimated they joined together just to survive." She sipped her tea and gazed around at her guests. "On my journey here from Camp Scott, I rode out on my little pony so I could see and experience the dramatic mountain terrains. I have never seen anything like them before. Everyone else rode in the carriage or the luggage wagon. Oh, it was beautiful riding in the sun, surrounded by wildflowers and green grasses at every turn. Several times some ugly Ute warriors rode up close to us. I wasn't nervous, though I felt quite taken aback when I saw they only wore fur necklaces. One grizzled old man, as naked as the day he was born, pulled up close to my pony and grunted out, governor squaw? I told him yes. He nodded and rode away, an ignorant savage."

Connal Lee nodded his head and shrugged. "Some of the desert tribes from these arid southern lands live very poor lives. They've lost much of their culture, arts, and medicine due to white man diseases and the daily struggle to feed their children. The Shoshone are lucky to live north of here. The mountains up in the Oregon Territory are full of streams teeming with trout and salmon. The forests abound with all kinds of game and birds. Buffalo roam the plains in great herds, providing most of the essentials of living. Life is easier for the Shoshone, Bannock, and Blackfoot tribes up north of Fort Hall. It's also easier for others like the Nez Perce, Iroquois, and Coeur d'Alene tribes even further away from the Shoshone tribal hunting grounds. The Shoshone are an ancient, honorable people, hardworking, brave, and intelligent. Did the Governor tell y'all that Chief Arimo is a member of the Mormon Church? He's been a personal friend and ally to Brigham Young almost since the Mormons first arrived."

"Well, I have to tell you that the Indians I've seen back east are tragically reduced and impoverished. They are a beaten people, conquered after years of fighting. Perhaps one day, I will have a chance to meet your adopted father, Chief Arimo. It might prove quite interesting."

"It is summer now, Missus Cumming. The chief took his clan to the Salmon River, where they will smoke and dry lots of fish for the winter. After that, he will lead his people to his favorite camp during the summer season, high up in the mountains the explorers named the Grand Tetons, where it's cool. He won't return south until the fall. The desert lowlands are not friendly places during the fierce summer suns. Perhaps y'all can meet him this fall."

"That would be lovely. I look forward to it, Connal Lee. I just love smoked salmon. I know the Governor does, too. We haven't had any for a few years now."

One of the kitchen maids entered with a rolling cart laden with cakes and scones. Connal Lee loved scones topped with wild strawberry jam. White Wolf turned to the governor. "You meet Peace Commissioners, Governor? They stay here with you?"

The Governor nodded, swallowed a small cake in one gulp, then took a sip of tea. "Yes, we met them back in Camp Scott when they first arrived. Even though they are truly fine southern gentlemen, I'm afraid my dear Lizzie didn't take a shining to them. So, no, we did not invite them to stay here with us."

Mrs. Cumming made a delicate little sniffle. "Huh! Those self-important gentlemen came to make peace. Only they arrived too late. My dear Alfred had already made peace with the Mormons. I told them they should just return back home and let my talented husband's diplomatic skills finish what he has so ably begun. I told them their services simply weren't needed anymore!"

Connal Lee grinned. "Somehow, Ah don't suspect they appreciated hearing that, Missus Cumming, not after traveling so far."

The governor nodded his agreement as he stuffed another cake in his mouth. Short Rainbow smiled at Mrs. Cumming. "You like eat smoke salmon, Missus Cumming?"

"Yes, dear. The fish markets in Boston often had salmon during the summer, ferried in from rivers further north. My mother used to have our cook grill them or bake them stuffed with savory bread crumbs. I preferred them smoked and served with a tarragon hollandaise sauce."

"No sauce, but we have smoke salmon. We invite you come to dinner at camp tomorrow? We serve smoke salmon dinner."

Missus Cumming sat up in surprise and looked a question over at her husband. She looked at Short Rainbow, sitting daintily on her chair with her legs crossed beneath her. "Why, what a kind invitation, Missus Short Rainbow. I hardly know what to say."

Connal Lee saw and understood her hesitation. "Short Rainbow and Bright Star are excellent cooks, Missus Cumming. So is White Wolf, as a matter of fact. They will invite y'all to sit on clean buffalo pelts on the ground around the cookfire to eat. Ah believe y'all will find the meal and experience tasty and satisfying. Please accept Short Rainbow's invitation to visit her tipi. Y'all, too, Governor Cumming. It will give us an opportunity to become better acquainted.

The governor understood Elizabeth's concern about sanitation, proper attire, and the etiquette of eating rough without tables, chairs, and fine China dishes. "Lizzie, my dear, let's take the carriage out to their camp tomorrow and have an adventure. We can have Jim and Petty set the cushions from the carriage on the ground. We will be quite comfortable. Please join me. I'm actually quite interested in trying out what the natives of this land like to eat. You know me!"

Mrs. Cumming laughed cheerfully. "Well, if you think it will be all right, dear. Missus Short Rainbow, we would be delighted to accept your kind invitation to dinner tomorrow. Now, what can I bring, dear?"

Short Rainbow smiled. She asked Connal Lee for the word she couldn't remember. "Appetite. Big appetite."

Everyone chuckled. When the cakes ran out, Mrs. Cumming stood up. "Thank you all for coming. It has been delightful meeting each and every one of you. Thank you for saving my dear Alfred's life when those horrible teamsters tried to mob and ransack the house. You are welcome in my home at any time."

They shook hands goodbye. Connal Lee waited until everyone else left. "Well, ma'am, if there is ever anything we can do to help y'all, please call upon us. We are here at the governor's service."

"Thank you, Master Swinton. Goodbye, now. Until tomorrow."

Robert and Edward walked the delegation to the horses on the street. Connal Lee leaned in close to Major Harris. "Robert, we don't have any alcohol. Do y'all think the Governor will be happy eating without something to drink?"

"Don't worry about it, Connal Lee. I'll have a discreet word with Sister Gilmore and have her send a bottle of white wine and goblets with the governor's drivers. We might as well keep the Governor happy."

"You and Edward will join us, as well, won't y'all?"

"Why, thank you. Very kind of you. I'll tell you what. I'll have Sister Ohlsson bake up some rolls. The Cummings are used to eating bread with their meals, I'm sure."

"Great. Thanks. We'll see y'all tomorrow."

Major Harris and Edward arrived early for the picnic luncheon. After hugs all around, they sat down beside Connal Lee and watched his family prepare a great feast for their guests. "I wonder if you even know what an honor it is for you to have the governor and his wife accept your invitation, Connal Lee. He's undoubtedly the richest man in the territory. The governor and his wife both come from old, old money. The governor's family owns an enormous cotton plantation outside of Atlanta, worked by hundreds of slaves. His family also owns cotton mills. Then, he has his salary as a governor. He earns two-thousand five hundred a year. Since his wife is so well educated and so well qualified, he hired her to be his confidential secretary, which pays another thousand a year. She is in his confidence, anyway, so why not benefit from it?"

Connal Lee's eyes grew large as he thought about all that money. "Well, no wonder Missus Cumming looked so grand and proud yesterday, putting on such elegant airs."

The governor rode up in his great carriage and six, promptly at high noon. Mrs. Cumming cheerfully rode her high-stepping little pony alongside the coach. She wore a plain brown riding dress. A wide-brimmed Leghorn straw hat, pinned to her hair with three long hat pins, shaded her face. She wore gold-rimmed spectacles with smoky tinted glass lenses. Connal Lee stared. He had never seen dark glasses before. A small guitar case hung behind her saddle.

The governor's black drivers removed the carriage seat cushions and placed them beside the fire. They arranged them so the Governor could lounge on the furs surrounding the firepit. Jim and Petty helped ease the corpulent governor down to sit on the ground. Elizabeth skipped lightly over to the big, smokeless hardwood fire. She shook hands all around as she cheerfully called out her greetings, addressing everyone by name. She gazed around the camp with a big smile. Fascinated with the huge tipi, she walked around its perimeter and examined the lovely symbols and geometric patterns decorating the buffalo skins. When she arrived back at the fire, Short Rainbow opened the leather doorway. "Like see, Missus Cumming? Please come in."

"Oh! Why yes, actually. I would very much love to see the inside of your home. I believe Master Swinton told us you own your tipi. Is that correct?"

"Yes. Shoshone wife own tipi. We wise people. Good customs. Please come in."

Rather than pull out the hairpins and remove her sunhat, Elizabeth merely tucked the sides down around her face so she could duck through the small oval doorway. She entered the tipi, stood up, and gazed around. "Why, this is so much bigger and nicer than the Sibley Bell tents the army has back in Camp Scott for their hospital. This is actually quite luxurious."

Since it wasn't needed for insulation, the interior curtain had been left partially open. Elizabeth bent down and examined the beautifully crafted and decorated saddlebags, woven baskets, and clay containers neatly stored in the low edges around the perimeter. Short Rainbow had rolled up the bottom of the tipi a few inches above the ground to allow sun and air to enter. Short Rainbow opened the doorway, and they stepped back out to the company sitting around the cook fire. "Thank you, my dear, for showing me your lovely home." Elizabeth complimented Short Rainbow in a lilting, cultured voice. "Such a lovely home. And to think you can pack it up and carry it with you wherever you go. It's actually very civilized, isn't it? And isn't this a delightful campsite nestled in the bend of a rushing river with majestic mountains around us on all sides? What a lovely place for a home. Tell me, my dear, does this river have a name?"

Connal Lee nodded. "Yes, ma'am. It's called the Jordan River because it empties into a salty lake, just like the Jordan River in the Bible empties into the Dead Sea." Connal Lee gestured towards his red fox fur blanket. "Here, ma'am, please have a seat while we wait for dinner to be served. We are so delighted y'all could join us."

With a smile, Elizabeth sank gracefully and sat on the fur with her legs tucked to the side. She arranged her long skirts around her. Jim, the governor's driver, handed Elizabeth the guitar case. Captain Reed sat down Indian-style next to Elizabeth. "You play the guitar, ma'am?"

"Why yes, indeed, Captain. I have enjoyed singing and playing all my life. I couldn't carry a piano with us across the Overland Trail, but a guitar is quite manageable. Wasn't it nice of that Mister Kimball to lend me his grand piano when he heard I like to play?"

"Connal Lee loves listening to all kinds of music. He just can't get enough. Perhaps you will honor us with a song or two after we eat."

"That's why I brought my guitar, Captain."

Elizabeth laughed brightly, delighted at the relaxed atmosphere around the Indian camp. She enjoyed feeling so rustic and primitive, free of the restrictions of being all prim and proper in front of all the endlessly watching and judging eyes of society. Bright Star handed around little cones of green leaves filled with roasted pine nuts. "Eat."

Elizabeth nibbled a couple of nuts. "Delicious. Thank you, Bright Star. Absolutely scrumptious!"

Jim returned from the carriage carrying a small woven hamper. He pulled out and passed around wine glasses and napkins to Elizabeth, the governor, Major Harris, and Captain Reed. He opened a dusty bottle and poured the wine before returning to the coach.

Over the next hour, Short Rainbow, Bright Star, and White Wolf served everyone small portions of fried wild turkey and grouse. Short Rainbow handed Elizabeth a small serving of liver pate. She didn't know how to eat it until she saw White Wolf scoop up a dollop with his first two fingers and pop it in his mouth. With a shrug, she followed his lead. *When in Rome, do as the Romans do.* Short Rainbow served smoked salmon with wilted wild spinach and roasted wild onions. Bright Star passed around smoked sturgeon with sautéed sego lily roots. The governor asked what they were eating. Connal Lee explained they were plants native to the area. The governor liked the sweetness and soft, potato-like texture of the sego lily roots.

After they finished eating, Captain Reed extended his hand to Elizabeth. "Would you care for a short walk to aid the digestion?"

She stood up and smoothed down her riding dress. "Why yes, Captain. Very thoughtful. What a fine gentleman."

While they strolled through the sparse woods growing along the river, Bright Star took Jim and Petty platters of food by the carriage.

The Governor poured himself another glass of wine and popped another handful of pine nuts in his mouth. When John and Elizabeth rejoined the picnic, Elizabeth carefully laid down the fistful of wild-flowers she had picked to take home and removed her guitar from its case. After taking a moment to tune it, she began playing to warm up her fingers. Connal Lee moved over and sat beside her where he could watch her hands plucking and strumming the strings. She sang for half an hour. The music enchanted Connal Lee. He told her so. When she stopped, everyone applauded. The governor struggled to sit up. "Well, dear friends, this has been a most delightful interlude. Now, I hate to be the one to bring this party to its end, but I'm afraid I have work awaiting me in my office. Duty calls." The Governor called out, "Jim! Petty! Come help me to the carriage if you please."

The entire party stood up as the black, uniformed drivers helped the governor clamber to his feet. Major Harris shook hands and kissed the girls on the cheeks. "I, too, need to return to my office and my duties. Thank you, everyone, for a delightful luncheon. Always a pleasure. Do you want to ride with me, son, or do you want to stay here?"

After many compliments and expressions of gratitude, Elizabeth mounted her little pony and led the parade back to the emptiness of Great Salt Lake City.

Connal Lee and Edward rode north towards Antelope Island to see if it really had any antelope to hunt.

Chapter 11: Non-negotiable

The evening after the Shoshone picnic for Governor and Mrs. Cumming, Thursday the tenth of June, young Private Sessions galloped into camp. Connal Lee and Edward stood up to greet him. Edward jogged up to the horse before the private dismounted. "Perry, is everything all right with my father?"

"Hello, Edward. Don't worry. Major Harris only asked me to ride out and tell you that President Young and his entourage arrived this afternoon for the peace negotiations."

"Oh. Thank you. We were wondering when they would get here."

Connal Lee walked over and held the horse's headgear while the teenage private dismounted. "Good evening, Private Sessions. We were about to have some supper. Would y'all like to come join us and tell us all the details?"

"Why, yes. Thank you. You are Brother Swinton, correct? One of the Shoshone delegation who saved the President's life at the Governor's supper a while back?"

"Yes. That's me. Connal Lee Swinton. Please come join us at the fire and meet the rest of my family."

After they took a seat around the fire, Edward pointed to their guest. "Listen, everyone. This is my friend and fellow student from the University of Deseret. When the hostilities began last July, he volunteered to serve with the Nauvoo Legion. His name is Peregrine Session after his father. But he goes by Perry to distinguish him from his other two brothers, who are also named Peregrine. He is currently serving as one of General Well's clerks. When on duty, he also has the duties of the Orderly of the Day."

Edward then introduced his Shoshone friends, one at a time. Short Rainbow and Bright Star served everyone sage tea while they chatted. After the introductions, Connal Lee leaned forward. "Nice to meet y'all, too. We saw y'all in General Wells' office, but we weren't introduced. So, Perry, please tell us the latest from Great Salt Lake City."

The young private enjoyed being in the spotlight with an attentive audience. "Well, a little after three o'clock this afternoon, I heard a great commotion of carriages and horses turning onto Brigham Street, or South Temple as it is now called. They stopped east of the Legion headquarters in front of Beehive House. Curious, I dashed out to watch. Brigham Young and his wife, Mary Ann, whom we all call Mother Young, stepped down from their big carriage. His counselors in the First Presidency, Heber Kimball and General Wells, then got out. Nine other members of the Council of Twelve Apostles climbed out of assorted other carriages, buggies, and wagons. Riders dismounted and tied up their horses. It was quite the crowd. President Young's secretary, Albert Carrington, and Church Patriarch John Smith dusted themselves off the dust of the road. I heard Brigham Young invite everyone to be his guests at Beehive House since it was one of the few homes not completely closed and boarded up. The church officials followed him into his home. General Wells posted men at guard positions around the estate and then walked over to the Legion headquarters. Your father joined the general in his office and relinquished command to the general. The door stood open, so I heard the general tell Major Harris about their trip this morning."

Connal Lee leaned forward as he sipped warm sage tea. Perry Sessions smiled at him. "It seems the whole party, with three armed legion officers as escorts, departed Provo at four o'clock this morning. They stopped around eight in American Fork for breakfast at the Stake President's homes. From there, they had a straight ride north on the empty State Road to President Young's mansion. About an hour after they arrived, Brother Carrington brought General Wells two sealed letters with President Young's request to have them delivered with all dispatch. The General sent me to deliver the first of the letters to Governor Cumming in his office in Council House. I waited while he read the letter. He thanked me and asked me to carry the general a note of his acceptance to the peace conference tomorrow morning.

"As soon as I had his letter in hand, I rode on down to the Globe Saloon to find the Peace Commissioners. Brother Candland pointed them out to me, camped over by a creek with their ambulances and military escort surrounding them. I introduced myself and handed Texas Ranger McCulloch the President's letter. He read it out loud to Governor Powell. The letter invited the Peace Commissioners to meet in the large room on the second floor of the Council House tomorrow at nine o'clock. Governor Powell objected to the wording of the invitation but sent me back with a note confirming they would be there. After I delivered their letters, the General asked me to ride out here and invite you to join them to witness the conference tomorrow. General Wells and President Young have a meeting with the Governor and Missus Cumming this evening to prepare their strategies. President Young received word a few days ago from Camp Scott that the two Peace Commissioners have taken a hard line against the Mormon Church and the Territory. So President Young is letting them fend for themselves, unlike his courtesy to Governor Cumming in finding him lodging in Elder Staines' lovely home. Ha! Serves them right, I think, for treating us as enemies."

The private gazed around anxiously to see if they liked his report.

"Thanks so much, Perry, for bringing us the invitation." Connal Lee glanced over at White Wolf. White Wolf nodded his approval. "Please let Major Harris and General Wells know that the Shoshone delegation will be delighted to be there to watch the historic event of bringing peace to the Territory of Utah."

Private Perry stood up. With smiles and thanks for supper, he shook hands goodbye. "I'm still on duty, so I should ride back to headquarters now that I have delivered my message. Thank you for a delicious supper. Perhaps I will see you tomorrow at Council House, although probably not."

Edward also stood up. "Wait a moment, please, Perry. Let me fetch my horse, and I'll ride back with you." Edward put his hand on Connal Lee's shoulder. "I probably won't be invited to attend the peace conference with my father and General Wells, but if I am, I will see you tomorrow morning. Thank you, Short Rainbow and Bright Star, for another wonderful supper. Good night, everyone."

Friday morning dawned bright and clear. The sun quickly warmed the land from a pleasant sixty to nearly eighty degrees.

Connal Lee and his spouses donned their ceremonial finery. The Shoshone wore their hair parted in the middle in two ponytails, loose at the top, bound at the bottom with ribbons of lush mink. Short Rainbow parted Connal Lee's lightly oiled blond hair and brushed it back in waves behind his ears. His beaded headband kept it neat under his big leather cowboy hat during the ride into the city.

Since they didn't know what to expect, they left early. They tied up their horses on Main Street in front of Council House, apparently some of the first to arrive. The Governor's carriage stood parked alongside the pebbled ditch a little further south of the building. They walked past the closed door to the library. Connal Lee knocked on the doorframe of the open doors to the governor's suite. The governor's prim and proper secretary stood up. "Good morning. The governor left instructions for you to go right in when you arrived."

Connal Lee led his family through to the next set of doors. "Our thanks, Mister Currey. We wish y'all a good morning, too."

Connal Lee knocked three times. He heard Governor Cumming call out, "Come." He opened the door and then led his family inside.

The governor greeted them in a jovial voice. "Ah, excellent. You arrived early. Thank you for attending us on this most momentous and auspicious day." The governor pointed to a well-dressed gentleman in his forties sitting on the other side of his desk. "My friends, I would like you to meet Mister Jacob Forney, the new Superintendent of Indian Affairs for the Territory of Utah. He traveled to Camp Scott with me last fall. Superintendent Forney, may I present my personal friends, the Shoshone delegation from up north around the Fort Hall area in the Territory of Oregon. They traveled here to witness the peace conference on behalf of Chief Arimo and the Shoshone Nation. The Shoshone have been allies of the Mormon people since they first arrived back in forty-seven. The Chief is, himself, a member of the Mormon Church."

The Governor introduced each member of Connal Lee's family. Mister Forney scowled as he realized the governor intended him to actually shake hands with native Indians as though they were civilized white men. He reluctantly rose to his feet to shake hands. He lifted his chin proudly and declined to shake hands with Short Rainbow and Bright Star when they offered their hands. He considered shaking hands with inferior races beneath his dignity and shaking hands with their squaws completely unthinkable. When Connal Lee observed his rudeness, he felt sorry for the Indians living in the Territory of Utah who would be under his mercy and control.

The Governor beckoned for his black servants to help him to his feet. "Jim. Petty. Come help me climb the stairs. I want to be upstairs before everyone arrives."

Connal Lee watched the obese gentleman from Kentucky laboriously climb the wooden stairs with his heavy arms over the shoulders of his two strong black attendants, his living crutches. They took the stairs one slow step at a time. The governor became quite short of breath by the time they ascended eighteen feet to the second floor. With the lantern cupola boarded up overhead, their only light came from the open double doors of the large meeting room where the Mormons used to conduct endowments.

The governor invited the Shoshone delegation to take seats on simple oak pews running up the center of the room. Shorter rows of pews ran along both sides, with generous isles between the three columns of benches. The stage rose on three levels behind a pulpit shaped like an altar. Each level held varnished wooden chairs for dignitaries. Between the stage and the first row of pews sat a large table with three chairs on one side and two chairs facing the audience. The table held glass tumblers and glass pitchers of water. Each seat had an inkwell, nib pen, paper, and blotter.

Connal Lee gazed around, curious. He noticed that the chamber's three large windows had been reinstalled for the conference. Strong morning sunlight streamed into the spacious room. They had left the bottoms of the windows open a few inches to let in fresh air. A two-foot-high plaster molding surrounded the top of the walls. Above the molding, the ceiling curved up gently into a slightly arched plaster ceiling. Simple geometric stencils in muted colors decorated a band surrounding the room beneath the molding.

They soon heard men talking as they climbed the stairs. One by one, the Mormon contingent entered and took their seats in the auditorium. Several prominent Mormon businessmen also attended.

Brigham Young solemnly greeted the governor and the Shoshone emissaries before he walked over and stood behind the center of three chairs at the conference table. His two counselors took position standing behind their chairs on either side of the president, their backs to the audience.

At the stroke of nine o'clock, a tall, portly well-dressed gentleman walked up and introduced himself to Brigham Young, General Wells, and Heber Kimball. "Good morning, gentlemen. I am Commissioner Lazarus W. Powell, former Governor of Kentucky and currently serving as Senator to Congress from Kentucky."

A man with a proud military bearing followed Commissioner Powell. As he shook hands with Brigham Young, he spoke with a heavy Texan accent. "Good morning Mister Young, sir. I am Major General Ben McCulloch of the Texas State Militia and Peace Commissioner appointed by President Buchanan to present his proclamation to the Mormon people and the Territory of Utah."

Brigham Young curtly invited them to take their seats. Before he sat down, Brigham Young looked the two commissioners square in the eye. "I am greatly displeased, gentlemen, that the fate of my people is in your hands rather than in the hands of Governor Cumming, whom we know and trust."

Commissioner Powell stood up. "Nonetheless, sir. This is how the President of the United States of America has ordered. To put it bluntly, sir, Commissioner McCulloch and I have been dispatched by the administration for the express purpose of seeing that law and order are reestablished in the Territory of Utah. We are here to insist that the rebellious people of the Mormon Church uphold the Constitution and faithfully obey the laws of the United States of America. We are here to see the Mormons accept and submit to the duly constituted officers of the United States. We were ordered to bring the Presidential Proclamation with a pardon for all your seditions and treasons heretofore committed. I urge you and all Mormons to accept the pardon, sir. Have you and your counselors read the President's Proclamation, sir?"

Brigham Young curtly nodded yes once.

"Do you and your entourage understand it, or do we need to have it read aloud for the edification of your representatives."

Brigham Young nodded yes, again. "We understand that the proclamation does not apply to the Saints because the charges of sedition are completely false, sir."

"Do you agree to wave the reading of the Proclamation, sir?"

Brigham Young looked at his counselors. They all nodded their agreement.

"Let the records show..."

For the next two hours, General Wells, Erastus Snow, and Gilbert Clements, among others, forcefully reminded the Commissioners of the Mormon experiences in Missouri and Illinois, where the Government had done nothing to protect their rights, property, lives, or liberty.

Commissioner Powell asked Governor Cumming if he had anything he wanted to add. The governor stood up and informed them he could swear from his own knowledge that the charges of Buchanan's administration about Mormon sedition were utterly false. Others spoke up, demanding that their rights as American citizens not be trampled underfoot. They argued that the President's Proclamation did not apply to the Saints because they had committed no offense requiring pardons. They were now and had always been loyal to the Constitution. General Wells pointed out how each community flew the American flag and had from their very first day in the territory.

Commissioner Powell called for a one-hour recess. Several men headed downstairs to the small water closets in the back of the building. Others gathered in tense groups, clearly agitated about the proceedings. Connal Lee and his family happily to stood up and walked around. They didn't understand why the Mormons insisted on sitting on such hard benches without any furs to cushion them. A concerned group of church authorities swarmed around President Young, loudly voicing their complaints and concerns.

When the conference reconvened, General McCulloch stood up and took charge. "Gentlemen of the Mormon Church, concerned citizens of the Territory of Utah, and interested bystanders. Commissioner Powell and I now realize you believe we were sent to negotiate a peace treaty with you. This is indeed not the case. The president gave us no authority to negotiate in any particular whatsoever. We have been sent to deliver the presidential pardon and see federal law established in the territory, either voluntarily or by force of arms. Period. You either accept the proclamation, or you don't – and pay the consequences. There is no need for further conversation on the matter. President Brigham Young, sir, do you and your entire congregation accept President Buchanan's pardon? Do you each and every one pledge your allegiance to the United States of America? Do you all swear to uphold the Constitution and obey Federal law?"

Men in the audience stood up, offended by McCulloch's blunt, undiplomatic form of address and rudeness towards their beloved leaders. They raised their voices, expressing their indignation. Connal Lee sat stunned as he watched. He thought they were there to witness the negotiation of a peace treaty, not to see their Mormon allies ordered to surrender unconditionally to the American government. After a quarter-hour of loud protests, Brigham Young calmly stood up. The room quieted down out of respect for him. Still fuming, the others in the audience resumed their seats, frowning.

"Commissioner Powell, sir. Commissioner McCulloch, sir. We cannot agree at this moment to accept the president's offer under these circumstances. I received word this morning that General Johnston and his entire encampment of over five thousand soldiers, teamsters, and camp followers are breaking camp even as we speak. General Johnston ordered his troops to march against Great Salt Lake City this Sunday in just two days. How can we yield our freedom and autonomy under such a dire threat?"

Governor Cumming pushed himself to his feet and bellowed out in his loud public speaking voice, "Excuse me, President Young, but you are mistaken, sir. Less than two weeks ago, on Sunday the thirtieth of May, the commissioners and I met with General Johnston in Camp Scott. He assured us he would not march until he received more supplies and men. He further agreed to wait until he received word from the commissioners and me that he was cleared to enter the territory in peace."

The Commissioners raised their voices, confirming the meeting in Camp Scott and General Johnston's statements.

"Nonetheless, Governor Cumming and honorable commissioners, we have definite word from impeccable witnesses watching the camp. Johnston received plenty of new provisions and reinforcements ahead of their anticipated arrival date, so he moved up his departure schedule. He ordered the entire camp to be on the march Sunday morning at daybreak. We will not permit the army to advance against us, gentlemen. We will not allow them to conquer anything but a desert wasteland. We will burn our settlements and Great Salt Lake City before his men arrive. Gentlemen, this meeting is concluded!"

Brigham Young pushed back his chair and stomped out of the room. Caught by surprise, his fellow Mormons hurried to follow him as quickly as they could. Stunned, Connal Lee and his family followed out the door but stood beside the dim stairwell waiting for Governor Cumming. Connal Lee had a lot of questions about what they had just witnessed. In the quiet after the crowd descended the stairs, they heard the governor and commissioners through the open doors.

The governor stood glaring at the commissioners as the room cleared out. When all the Mormons and their sympathizers had departed, the Governor lumbered over and collapsed in the chair Brigham Young had occupied. "Do I remember incorrectly, Governor Powell? Didn't you hear and understand the same thing, General McCulloch? I'm afraid I assured President Young just yesterday evening that we had Johnston's word he wouldn't advance until we authorized it. Now my credibility with the Mormon people I am here to govern is irrevocably damaged. God damn General Johnston to hell! I have expended weeks developing a mutual trust and rapport with the Mormons. I must write General Johnston immediately and demand an explanation of why he broke his word to us. But, how will I ever regain the confidence of the citizens of the territory, and more importantly, of their religious leader, Brigham Young?"

After another ten minutes of trying to figure out how they could rectify the situation and discharge their duties, the Governor offered to host a private meeting at the Staines mansion with just the top leaders of the Mormon Church and the two commissioners. They agreed to invite Brigham Young, Heber Kimball, and General Wells to a work session in the governor's parlor to iron things out.

The governor left the conference room. "Jim! Petty! Come help me down the stairs. I have work to do." He noticed the Shoshone delegation waiting beside the dark staircase. "Oh, you are still here. Well, my thanks to you all for coming and lending your support. This obviously didn't go quite how we planned it, but never you fear. We will not give up until we accomplish peace. Now, please don't wait for me. It is harder climbing down stairs than climbing up. My good servants will see to me."

Connal Lee and his family shook hands and took their leave. They untied their horses and walked them across the broad avenue to the legion headquarters, where Major Harris greeted them. "We're still waiting to find out the president's plans. You may as well return to your camp. I will send word as soon as we know what comes next."

Several times that evening, Connal Lee frowned. "Ah sure do wish Governor Cumming had invited us to their private meeting tonight. Ah'm just dying of curiosity. What are they saying? Are they working things out? Ah hate being kept in the dark!"

Before sunrise, Edward and Perry trotted up to the camp beside the Jordan River. The sun, peeking over the jagged mountains, lit them from behind. Short Rainbow already had a pot of coffee boiling beside the fire. Connal Lee heard their horses and quickly pulled on his breechcloth, moccasins, and vest. He pushed his hair back off his face and rushed out to see who had come visiting so early.

Connal Lee smiled when he saw his young Mormon friends pull up. He held their horses' reins just below the bits while Edward and Perry dismounted. "Good morning! Glad to see y'all. Come sit a spell, or do y'all have to hurry on back?"

Edward smiled as he pulled the reins out of Connal Lee's hand. "We can stay long enough to have some coffee and share the news."

"Oh, good. Come sit down. Breakfast will be ready soon."

They walked their horses over by the others down the river, then returned to the camp. By the time they sat down beside the cookfire, everyone else had gathered around, anxious to hear the news of what happened after they left the meeting. Bursting with excitement, Edward and Perry took turns telling what they had learned this morning.

Private Sessions gazed around at the attentive audience. "Last night, it seems Governor Cumming invited the two Peace Commissioners to the Staines mansion for a private conference. He also invited President Young, of course, and his two counselors in the First Presidency, Heber C. Kimball and General Daniel H. Wells. Elias Smith also attended at the invitation of President Young."

Connal Lee held up his hand. "Excuse me, Perry, Ah haven't met or heard of Elias Smith. Why was he invited along?"

"You haven't met him? He's a really important man, Connal Lee. He's a county probate judge, the postmaster, and the editor of The Deseret News. President Young wanted him there to make a record of their conversation to be reported in the newspaper."

"Oh, Ah see."

Edward Harris took over. "General Wells told my father very early this morning that it took them hours. Governor Cumming informed the group that General Johnston had clear orders to build a fort in the Territory and establish a permanent military presence. Neither the Governor nor the Commissioners had the power to change or delay those orders. President Young insisted the Mormons could overcome the army if forced to, but only at a great loss of life on both sides. He finally agreed to let the army enter as proof of our peaceful intentions and willingness to obey federal laws. Brigham Young obtained promises from the governor and the commissioners that the army would not remain in the city. They also promised the army would not build a fort within forty miles of a Mormon settlement. They swore the army would obey the governor's orders like any armed forces in any American territory. Evidently, it took quite some time. President Young kept insisting the forty-two charges in the Proclamation were false. Eventually, he agreed to accept the pardon if it saved the lives of innocent members of the Church."

Perry bubbled over with excitement about sharing the news. When Edward took a breath, he leaned forward and added, "So everyone is invited to a meeting this morning, back in Council House at nine o'clock. They have an announcement to make. Judging by the smiles on General Well's tired face this morning, I think it will be good news."

Connal Lee instinctively glanced towards the sun, judging the time before they needed to be at the meeting. He calculated they had an hour and a half to change their clothes and ride into town. "Wonderful! We appreciate y'all bringing us the news. Ah can't wait to hear what they worked out."

Perry and Edward looked at each other and nodded. Edward stood up. "Well, we've got to go get dressed for the announcement, then accompany father and General Wells to the meeting. Thanks for breakfast, Short Rainbow and Bright Star. We will see you all there."

The Shoshone delegation wanted to look their best. They took their time bathing, dressing, and arranging their hair. Connal Lee wore the hair bone breastplate, proud to represent his adopted father. Even though they arrived early, they found Main Street already crowded with people and horses. Apparently, news had spread among the home guard and the gentile visitors staying by the Globe Saloon. Everyone remaining in town who could be spared wanted to be on hand to watch the proceedings.

Since the doors to the library and the Governor's office were closed, the Shoshone delegation followed the others up the dim stairway. They found seats partway back and shuffled across to sit down in the center of the pew. They smiled and waved at the people they knew. When Major Harris came in with General Wells, followed by Edward and Private Sessions, Connal Lee jumped to his feet. "White Wolf, please save two seats for our friends. Ah'll be right back." He hurried to the front of the room and shook hands with the major and the general. With a gesture of his hand, he beckoned Edward and Perry to follow him. "We saved seats for y'all by us."

At the stroke of nine o'clock, Commissioner Powell stood up, snapped shut his gold pocket watch, and shoved it into his vest pocket. "Governor Cumming, President Young, fellow citizens of the Territory of Utah, distinguished guests, and allies. It gives me great pleasure to announce to you, indeed to all the world, that the difficulties between the Territory of Utah and the United States of America have happily been settled."

Before he could continue his prepared remarks, the audience spontaneously broke into applause. Shouts of Halleluiah, Peace at last, and Thank the Lord resounded in the chamber. Connal Lee, Edward, and Perry all stood up and shook hands, excited to hear about the peace. When the applause tapered off, the Commissioner called out. "Order, please, gentlemen. Please, everyone, take your seats." He concluded the meeting by thanking everyone who had a hand in bringing peace to the territory. "That concludes our announcement. Thank you for coming, everyone."

Commissioner Powell formally shook hands with Brigham Young and the Mormon representatives. Governor Cumming beamed as he went around congratulating everyone and thanking them for their part in bringing peace to the territory at last.

Edward and Perry accompanied Connal Lee and his family out of the building. "What a day! Chief Arimo will be relieved to hear the army will not invade and attack Great Salt Lake City. Now the Mormons won't have to burn the city." Connal Lee glanced around at his young friends. "What shall we do to celebrate?"

Perry held up his hand. "My father founded Bountiful, just north of here, the second day after the Saints first arrived in the valley. One of my favorite places in the world is east of dad's saw mill, up at the headwaters of Mill Creek. Would you like to see it? I have always found good hunting up there. We could get in some hunting and just relax. I'm off duty today. And I know Elder Lyon finished at the library, so your services aren't required today, either, Edward. What do you say, Connal Lee?"

"Sure. We would love to explore some new territory. Let's all go change our clothes. Shall we meet back at our camp?"

Half an hour later, Edward and Perry arrived. The Shoshone delegation leapt into their saddles and took off riding north in a cloud of dust. As they approached a spur of the mountains separating Great Salt Lake City from Fort Bountiful, they passed a large adobe structure with high walls on their right. Perry explained. "That's a social hall built some years back around our natural hot springs. It has an indoor pool for women and an outdoor swimming hole for the brethren. It was our first public place for dances in Great Salt Lake City. It's very popular. The Saints have loved the healing properties of the sweet hot springs since shortly after they arrived in the valley. The Ute Indians showed it to them."

Connal Lee and Screaming Eagle looked at each other with big smiles. Connal Lee winked. They both nodded their heads, thinking they would have to visit it before they returned back north.

They trotted around the mountain towards Fort Bountiful. Perry rode point to lead the way toward his family homes and properties. They rode east around the walled Fort and immediately began climbing the foothills rising above the fertile valley. Perry led them up a riverbed past his family saw mill and the Kimball grist mill. Both stood empty and boarded up. Perry told them they had buried the millstones and sawblades in case of invasion. Riding higher and higher up the steep incline, they followed the babbling creek towards Grandview Peak. They climbed up past Right Fork Creek and Elephant Rock. The mountains grew steeper, and the terrain became more rugged. Tall pine trees, logged over the years for lumber, grew up the precipitous inclines. Connal Lee craned his neck and gazed up. Even though the valley enjoyed summer weather, snow still covered the peaks ahead. A cool breeze blew in their faces, bringing the dusty smell of old snow, warm earth, and pine trees.

Perry stopped with his hand held high to attract everyone's attention. Silently, he pointed up the rise on their left at two young bucks standing in the grass beside a cluster of low scrub oaks. This early in the summer, velvet still covered their growing antlers. A proud mature buck stood further up the incline. Four mule deer fawns with big alert ears and white spots on their backs frolicked around their mothers. The deer focused on eating the grass and weeds growing up the hillside. Silently, Perry pointed at Connal Lee and Edward, indicating for them to take their shots. Minutes later, one young buck and a yearling doe fell dead on the mountainside. The rest of the herd leapt away in a panic, jumping uphill in graceful arcs to escape the loud noise.

They all dismounted and worked as a team to clean and skin the kills. Connal Lee and Edward cleaned their shotguns and loaded more lead bullets. Short Rainbow built a small fire and broiled the livers and hearts for their midday meal while the others butchered the meat. The corpses weighed too much to transport down the mountain without packhorses, so they took the best cuts bound up in the hides to carry back to camp.

As they descended down through the orchards growing on the bench of the foothills before they reached the fort walls, Perry pointed out the only two-story structure inside the adobe walls. "That's my family inn. It's also the post office. Two of dad's wives and five of their children normally live there. I have a brother, a brother-in-law who is now a widower, and two cousins – all unmarried men like me – who were assigned to stay and protect the property from looters and encroachments of animals. Those danged mule deer just love our fruit trees and vegetable gardens! The guards are all staying at the inn. I would like to stop in and see them before we return. It will only take a minute. Would you mind?"

They trotted through the unfinished doorless walls surrounding the small farming community. Connal Lee wasn't surprised when he saw the streets laid out like in Great Salt Lake City in a straight north and south grid, only on a smaller scale. Two of Perry's cousins rushed out to meet them when they rode up to the inn. "Hey, Perry! How ya doin'?"

Perry climbed down off his horse and hugged his cousins. The others dismounted as well. After introductions, they shared drinks of water and visited for a few minutes. Captain Reed walked around the boarded-up town, curious about how these pioneers lived on the frontier. Perry's cousin told them to wait a minute while he fetched some early harvest to share with them. Perry agreed to try and find a wagon to carry food down to their families relocated south to Salt Creek, about twenty miles south of Payson. They all worried about food going to waste. Some of their fresh produce, like lettuce and summer squash, couldn't be dried or preserved in cellars. Before the hunting party left, they found room to tie on flour sacks and potato bags filled with new potatoes, onions, carrots, and beets, dirt still clinging to their roots. Smiling at the windfall, Perry suggested they divvy up the food back at the Shoshone Camp to share with those still guarding the city. Connal Lee nodded his head. "Ah see what Elder Staines said about his farm here in Bountiful. Y'all sure do raise some nice food hereabouts."

They rode back to camp at a leisurely pace. After splitting up the vegetables, Edward and Perry headed east to the city. Short Rainbow prepared a venison stew brimming with fresh vegetables.

Late the following morning, they still hadn't received any word from the city. Connal Lee invited his family to ride in with him to learn the latest news. They were all busy drying and smoking the venison from yesterday's hunt before it went bad and turned down his invitation. Connal Lee asked Bright Star to wrap up a haunch of venison to share with Robert and Edward. He tied the meat to the back of his saddle and rode east across the narrow Jordan bridge. The sun rose above the craggy mountains directly ahead. He stopped at the legion headquarters. Major Harris invited Connal Lee into his small office. The window stood open, letting in a freshening breeze. "Please have a seat, Connal Lee."

"Thanks, suh. And how are y'all doing this fine day, Robert?"

"Very well, thank you. Edward told me about your hunt yesterday. The mountains above Bountiful are beautiful, aren't they? I found the dramatic view of the valley with the Great Salt Lake and Antelope Island awe-inspiring. Did you? I watched the sunrise from up there one day. I never felt closer to God than I did that morning."

"Oh, yes, suh. It sure is beautiful country up there. Ah brought some venison for Sister Ohlsson to roast up for y'all. Now, tell me please, is there any news since yesterday?"

"Why, yes, as a matter of fact, there is. President Young plans on returning to Provo tomorrow. He scheduled a speech tomorrow afternoon at a sacrament meeting in American Fork to start spreading the news of peace. He made it abundantly clear he still doesn't trust General Johnston to pass through the valley in peace, despite the promises and assurances of the commissioners and Governor Cumming. You see, our spies have informed the president how Johnston and all his encampment suffered during this past brutal winter, due in large part to the deprivations of our guerilla irregulars burning their provisions and stealing their livestock. The whole camp is seething with resentment. They have been looking forward all winter to smashing us to make us pay for dragging them across the continent and stranding them all winter, suffering in a desolate camp. President Young ordered us to stay here, alert for when the army comes down through Emigration Canyon. They begin their march tomorrow from Camp Scott. According to our best estimates, we expect them to pass through our empty city in about two weeks. You don't move thousands of men and all their wagons, heavy artillery, and provisions very fast without plenty of healthy livestock. They will probably average less than ten miles a day. Virtually all the men except the top-ranking officers will be walking, carrying the bulk of their possessions on their backs. Despite the arrival of fifteen hundred new draft animals and tons of supplies, they still lack sufficient draft animals for such a large company. I'm afraid President Young is right. By the time they get here, they will be angry and tired and looking for a fight."

Connal Lee leaned forward and rested his hands on his knees. "It sounds like they could still be a serious threat, then, Robert. What are y'all going to do?"

"Governor Cumming and the commissioners have already dispatched express riders with letters to General Johnston and his toadies. Several newspaper reporters from the big papers back east have been traveling with the General. All winter they have been sending dispatches back east, full of lies and innuendo about us Mormons and the Utah War. We only hope some arrangements to maintain peace can be reached between now and when the army arrives." The Major stopped speaking. He looked at Connal Lee's bright eyes and eager face. "Listen, Connal Lee. Edward asked if General Wells would invite you to stay for when Johnston's army arrives. He said he thought you would be interested in seeing the military parade and finding out if they will maintain the peace."

Connal Lee nodded his head yes so vigorously his hair flopped down into his eyes. He pushed it back up off his forehead with both hands. "Oh, yes, suh. Ah would very much like to be here to see that."

"This morning, I asked General Wells his thoughts about your delegation remaining on hand. He was clearly preoccupied and only shrugged. He said whatever you want to do is fine. You are free to come or go as you wish. He then ordered me to organize messengers to take word to the forts along the settled corridor north of here. He wants everyone to hear the good news. He also wants to warn them to remain vigilant against a last-minute change of plans. I first considered sending Private Sessions since Perry grew up knowing the trail north of here all his life. Edward doesn't have any work now that we shipped off the library for safe keeping. With the library closed, he can't do much studying, either. I thought about sending him to the farm. However, since he wants to pursue a career in military service, I thought he might get some valuable real-life experience if he went on the trip. If he goes, I can think of nothing better for the boys than to learn cross-country survival skills from you and Captain Reed. We have plenty of time to accomplish the mission and return before the army could arrive. What do you think?"

"Wow! Ah would really like to be here when Johnston marches through with all his troops. Ah would also enjoy a trip north with Edward and Perry. They are real nice people. We made some friends up north of here during our last few diplomatic trips, and it would be nice to drop in on them, too."

"Well, come on up to my house. We'll grab a bite of dinner. Edward told me Perry was coming to spend the day with him. Perry has a book of famous battles in military history he wanted to share with Edward."

"Ah'm ready, Major Harris, suh. Lead the way!"

Two days later, Connal Lee and his family decided to relocate their camp further north, away from possible trouble when the army passed through the valley. General Wells received word that Johnston planned to march through the city and cross the old Jordan River Bridge. He would make their first camp west and south, well away from the abandoned city. They planned to rest there a few days while Johnston decided on a site for the new fort. Eventually, they would march southwest to found a new military outpost according to their orders.

Perry offered Connal Lee and his family the use of a fenced pasture owned by his family for their new camp. "It's an ideal campsite, Connal Lee, just north of Fort Bountiful. It's watered by a small stream diverted out of the mountains. All the cattle have been driven down to Salt Creek, so the field stands empty. Your family will find plenty of game up in the mountains. Hunting is better in Bountiful than around the city."

After they pitched Short Rainbow's tipi in Bountiful, they planned their mission for General Wells. White Wolf, Short Rainbow, and Bright Star decided to stay in camp, hunting, fishing, and preparing food for their return trip up north. White Wolf reminded them they would be facing a two week journey to reach Chief SoYo'Cant's summer camp up in Yellowstone Valley. White Wolf recommended they plan to stop for a rest on the Salmon River. They could smoke salmon and preserve it for the winter before finishing the climb up the great, jagged Teton mountains.

After the three best cooks in the family announced they didn't want to go along, Connal Lee looked dejected. "It looks like us bachelors will be on our own then, men. Ah'm not looking forward to eating my own cooking. Oh well. No matter. Without the tipi and travois, it will only take us a week or so to make the round trip. Ah sure will miss my loving family at night, though. Ah'm not used to sleeping alone anymore."

Edward and Perry glanced at each other, amused. Only fifteen and sixteen and raised in righteous Mormon families, they hadn't experienced any of the joys of married life and making love. They actually felt jealous that Connal Lee could enjoy sex regularly.

Shirtless in the summer heat, Screaming Eagle walked over, put his muscled arm over Connal Lee's shoulders, and pulled him into a hug. "Connal Lee, sleep with me. No worry. You no travel alone."

That night Connal Lee reveled in sharing his love with his spouses and John. Their sexual games lasted late into the night. Nonetheless, Connal Lee, Screaming Eagle, and Captain Reed rose early the next morning, ready to head out with Edward and Perry. After long farewells and big hugs all around, the men took off at a steady trot. First stop, Fort Farmington.

Chapter 12: Invasion

Connal Lee and his company returned from their military mission to the forts along the settled corridor north of Great Salt Lake City. At first, it seemed everyone wanted to be in charge and make decisions on the trip. Captain Reed was used to commanding. Screaming Eagle always led their family excursions. Connal Lee's quick mind inevitably saw solutions and didn't hesitate to share his suggestions. Private Sessions, the only member of the Nauvoo Legion in the company, thought the others had come to help him accomplish his mission. Edward Harris just smiled and went along with the consensus once they agreed on a decision. Along the way, Edward came to appreciate the value of having a clear chain of command in a military operation.

By the time they reached Box Elder Fort, the northernmost Mormon settlement they had been ordered to visit, Captain Reed decided he would continue on north to his command at Fort Hall. That night he invited himself into Connal Lee and Screaming Eagle's blankets for a farewell spot of revelry. Edward and Perry looked at each other when they heard all the grunting and moaning. Edward shook his head and turned his back to the writhing furs on the other side of the fire. Perry turned over as well, but his imagination worked overtime while he listened to the men enjoying themselves. He had trouble falling asleep.

After they said goodbye to John, the rest of their party turned their horses south.

They arrived at Short Rainbow's tipi in Bountiful late Tuesday morning. The searing sun had heated the summer day up into the eighties. Bright Star jumped into action, hugging and kissing Connal Lee and Screaming Eagle, making everyone feel welcome. "Short Rainbow and White Wolf left early this morning to go hunting up Stone Creek. I expect them back by midday. By the time you get unpacked, I will have food prepared. I'm so glad you are back at last!"

A little later, Connal Lee saw White Wolf and Short Rainbow riding towards them, leading heavily laden packhorses. He jumped up and ran to hug them, thrilled they were all together again. After they ate a light dinner and shared the past week's news, Edward and Perry said their goodbyes. They both wanted to report to Major Harris and General Wells about their successful mission. Parry waved. "We will see you soon, I've no doubt. Thank you for accompanying me on my mission, everyone. Bye for now!"

Connal Lee enjoyed being alone with his family. However much he enjoyed company and friends, he preferred living with his spouses without sharing with outsiders. That night they spread their sleeping furs beneath the brilliant stars and enjoyed a boisterous homecoming celebration. Once sated, Connal Lee snuggled up using White Wolf's arm as a pillow. He watched the stars twinkling in the crystal clear night sky, glad to be alive.

They spent the next day hunting, preserving meats, and tanning hides, resuming a semblance of their regular routine. It felt good to be back on such solid footing.

Thursday morning, Connal Lee decided he wanted to go visit friends in Great Salt Lake City. He informed his family as they ate breakfast. "The army might arrive early, and Ah would hate to miss when they march through the streets. Ah think Ah'll go buy some fresh vegetables from Perry's cousins in Fort Bountiful and head into the city. Depending on what is happening, Ah will most likely overnight there with Major Harris. Ah want to be sure Ah'm there when General Johnston arrives. Ah bet that's going to be a sight to remember. Does anyone else want to go with me?"

His spouses looked at him with shrugs. They really weren't that interested in white man armies, so long as they didn't have to fight them.

Connal Lee cleaned his shotgun and pistol. With such a hot day, he wore an unbuttoned old cotton shirt with the sleeves rolled up above his biceps. He saddled his pretty mare and two packhorses. Bright Star gave him two empty potato sacks. He tied on the two wild turkeys he had shot, cleaned, and plucked the evening before to share with Elizabeth Cumming and Sister Ohlsson. He hugged everyone goodbye. They admonished him to avoid getting into trouble with the soldiers and to return home safe and sound.

He rode up to the Sessions Inn and Post Office. After greeting Perry's brother, he asked to buy some fresh produce to take to his friends in Great Salt Lake City. He offered to pay, but the young guard told him most of the food would just go to waste. "Take all you want, Brother Connal Lee. Any friend of Perry's is a friend of ours." Perry's brother handed him a bag of cherries he had picked that morning. "Please make sure Perry gets some. He just loves cherries."

"Why, thank y'all kindly. Very neighborly of y'all. When Ah come back, Ah'll be sure to return the favor."

Connal Lee took his time riding southerly around the low foothills separating Fort Bountiful from Fort Great Salt Lake City. Dark green scrub oaks spotted the grassy hills on his left. A couple of rock slides exposed reddish-brown soil and rocks under the dry grasses. He led the packhorses around the hot springs, making himself a mental note to visit them before they departed to return north. A few minutes later, the dramatic craggy mountains of the Wasatch Range on the city's east side came into view, blued in the distance. He spotted snow on the mountain tops, predominantly along the northern sides of the ridges.

By the time he entered the west gate of the empty city, he dripped sweat under the sweltering sun. "Now Ah understand why Chief SoYo'Cant likes to spend the summer up in the northern mountains. It's too danged hot here in the south."

He stopped at the Staines mansion and knocked on the door. He waited and waited. Finally, Elizabeth Cumming opened the door, drying her hands on a dishtowel. "Connal Lee, how nice of you to come calling. Where is the rest of your family?"

While they shook hands, Connal Lee smiled. "Sorry, ma'am. Ah'm here all by myself today. My family sent a gift for the governor's supper. Ah have a wild turkey on my packhorse, along with some fresh vegetables and fruits from Bountiful."

"Why, how thoughtful. How very generous of you to think of us. Please take your fine gifts around back to the kitchen garden to unload them. Truth be told, you found the queen in the kitchen preparing fresh strawberries from Mister Staines' garden. The king just loves strawberries with sugar and cream. His majesty is in the library smoking one of his interminable cigars." She laughed out loud. "Thank you for the food. Really. There is nothing to buy in the entire valley."

"Why were y'all in the kitchen, ma'am? Where are Sister Gilmore and her girls?"

"Even though we entreated them over and over again, they obeyed Mister Staines' order to move their family south before the army arrives. They left after breakfast this morning to set up a camp above the Globe Saloon. Mister Gilmore said that if the city burns, they will continue on to join the Staines in Payson. If the army leaves the city unmolested, they will return. In the meantime, I am once again my own chief cook and bottle washer, just like back in Camp Scott."

"Oh. That's too bad the Gilmores aren't here helping y'all. Well, Ah suppose if ya have fresh strawberries, y'all probably wouldn't care for any fresh cherries. They were picked this morning up in Bountiful, where we moved our camp. Ah ate a few on the ride here. They are real delicious."

"How delightful, Connal Lee. We both love cherries, too."

While Connal Lee delivered the food to the kitchen door in the back of the house, Elizabeth asked what he was doing in the empty city. "Why, ma'am, Major Harris invited me to watch the military parade on Saturday or whenever they actually arrive. Ah've never seen an army on the move. It should be quite the sight!"

"Yes. The Governor planned on reviewing the troops from the windows of his office in the Council House. However, General Wells told him he had to vacate so they could load it up with straw in case they have to burn it. We are going to watch the men march by from our front porch. You are welcome to join us if you don't have a better vantage point."

"Why, thanks very much, ma'am. That's very nice of y'all. Ah just might take y'all up on it. Ah understand there's going to be marching bands and everything. Ah can't wait!"

Fifteen minutes later, Connal Lee rode off to the legion headquarters. He knocked on the door to General Well's office. Private

Perry Sessions answered. "Hello, Connal Lee. Come on in. How're ya doing today?"

"Ah'm doing great, Perry. Here. Have some cherries. Y'all's family back at Fort Bountiful picked them just this morning."

Perry's eyes opened wide. He accepted the little bag jury-rigged from a cut-up floor sack. He opened the bag and held it out to Connal Lee. Connal Lee smiled and picked up a couple of cherries by their stems. Perry pulled a cherry off its stem with his teeth and ate it with a look of ecstasy on his face. "Delicious. Thank you, Connal Lee. Mm. This is really great."

Perry discreetly spit the pit into his hand to discard when he finished. Connal Lee finished off his cherries. "It's good to see y'all, my friend. Is Major Harris in his office?"

"I believe so."

"Well, Ah think Ah'll be moseying on over to his office. Ah brought some cherries for him, too. Ah will probably be hanging around until after the army leaves, so Ah'm sure we'll see each other later."

"Oh? Where will you be staying? You didn't move your camp back to the valley, did you?"

"No. Ah suspect Robert – er, uh, Major Harris and Edward will invite me to stay at their place. They said Ah'm always welcome."

"Great! I'm staying with Edward for the time being, too. Sister Ohlsson is sure a great cook, isn't she? I'm glad they invited me to stay with them. Otherwise, I would have to ride up to Bountiful and stay in the inn. That's a long ride twice a day when I'm on duty."

"Maybe Ah will see y'all tonight at supper then. Please give my respects to General Wells when y'all see him."

When he knocked on the Major's door, Robert welcomed him with an energetic handshake. "Connal Lee. I wondered when you would arrive for the parade. You are just in time. I was about to leave for dinner at my house. Please join me."

While they rode the short distance up the hill to the Harris home, Robert asked about the trip with his son. "We had a good trip, suh. Ah had a nice visit with my friends, the Morgans, up in Box Elder Fort. Since we were already so far north, Captain Reed continued on up to Fort Hall. We had no adventures to speak of, which means no misadventures, either. My family sends their best. They didn't want to see the army. Screaming Eagle said if he doesn't have to fight them, he doesn't care what they do."

They chuckled companionably.

The Major led Connal Lee back to his corral behind his adobe home. Edward came out to help them. It took a couple of trips, but the three men carried all the food into the kitchen. Sister Ohlsson was thrilled. If it didn't grow in the Major's garden and Edward didn't hunt, they wouldn't have anything to eat. She complained they didn't have anywhere they could buy anything in the now totally empty city.

The evening remained hot, so Connal Lee recommended the boys sleep under the stars. He spread a buffalo blanket on the wild grasses in the front yard overlooking the dark city. Edward brought out a soft, worn quilt to cover the hide. Edward and Perry stripped down to their rough, handwoven undergarments. With the women folk away for so long, their underpants looked quite grungy, not that anyone cared. Connal Lee slipped on his loincloth. The three boys chatted away as they watched a full moon rise over the Wasatch mountains. A chorus of crickets serenaded them to sleep.

The boys had plenty to do after they finished breakfast. Despite Edward's strenuous objections the night before, he had agreed to drive Sister Ohlsson and her two children down south of the Globe Saloon. The Major ordered them to make a camp at the point of the mountain where they could escape south to Provo if the city ended up in flames. "If the city burns, I don't want you trapped in our home here on the north side of South Temple, with the army and possible fighting between you and safety with the Saints down south."

Edward assured Connal Lee he would return as soon as they received word that the army had departed in peace. "Dang, but I'm going to miss the whole exciting thing. You've got to watch carefully so you can tell me all about it. I'm really jealous, Connal Lee. I expect we will be back Saturday night, having missed everything for nothing. But, like father said, better safe than sorry."

The three boys quickly worked up a sweat in the hot sun. They removed their shirts while they finished loading the small canvas topped wagon. Connal Lee helped them hitch up two long-eared mules. Edward said goodbye to his father and then helped Sister Ohlsson climb up to the board seat on the front of the wagon box. He leapt up and took the reins. Connal Lee lifted the boys into the back of the wagon. They both began crying. The youngsters didn't want to leave their home. With a snap of the reins, they pulled off down the hill to turn south onto the deserted State Road.

Major Harris and Private Sessions went into the quiet house to clean up and dress for the day. They both had duty that morning. General Wells needed their help securing the city for the imminent arrival of General Johnston, his troops, and all the camp's auxiliaries and hangers-on. Connal Lee didn't have anything else to do, so he washed up and accompanied them. As they rode down to the legion headquarters, Connal Lee volunteered his services. "If y'all need help with anything, Ah'm happy to lend a hand, Robert."

"Thank you, Connal Lee. I'm sure there will be plenty to do."

Later that morning, General Wells asked Connal Lee to begin at the east end of South Temple and work his way to the west end, lowering all the flags in view along the line of travel of the army. "Rather than remove them and fold them up, what I would like you to do is tie them around the base of the flagpoles so they can be raised quickly once the army has passed peaceably by. That will be our signal to the Saints watching from the point of the mountain down at the Jordan Narrows. When the flags fly again, it will let them know that Johnston kept his word and left the city unmolested. They will take word to Brigham Young within hours. Everyone anxiously awaits the news down in Provo."

"Very good, suh. Ah would be happy to take care of it."

"While we can't order the Governor to lower his flag, ask him nicely if he would please permit it. We want the entire territory free of American flags to protest their invasion. Oh, and don't forget the flag in front of the gristmill in the Kimball Compound. It's visible from the route the army will be taking along South Temple. Over the past few days, we have already lowered and removed the American flags from the rest of the valley. Please report to Major Harris when you have finished."

"Very good, suh. And may Ah extend the hopes from all my family and the Shoshone Nation that this beautiful city will not have to be put to the torch tomorrow?"

"Thank you, young man. That is the hope and prayer of all of us. Now, on your way."

Connal Lee walked his high-stepping mare towards the looming mountains, riding between the tall rock walls surrounding the different properties and compounds lining South Temple. He noticed how all the doors to the walls and the buildings stood open in the silence. One by one, he lowered the flags. The day grew hotter. Soon the headband of his leather cowboy hat grew dark with sweat. His shirt stuck to his skin. Perspiration ran down his back and chest in deep Vs and left dark rings under his arms. He wished he had kept on his loincloth when he pulled on his work trousers that morning. He wanted to remove his long pants in the heat. He lowered the flags in front of Beehive House and Lion House but left the flag flying over the Legion headquarters. He figured he would lower it last when he returned to report the completion of his assignment. He rode further west and lowered the flag on top of Council House, then beside the tabernacle on Temple Square.

It took several hours zigzagging across the wide empty avenue to lower all the flags in sight. Governor Cumming hemmed and hawed but finally permitted Connal Lee to lower the flag in front of the Staines home. Governor Cumming sat watching from the porch, puffing away on a great cigar, scowling. While Connal Lee worked the thin rope holding the extra-large flag overhead, the governor told him that Johnston had sent him orders to meet the army east of the city and ride in with them. "The General wants a show of unity and support with the federal government and the military." The governor explained he had decided not to obey. He wanted to show the citizenry he was there for the entire territory. He also wanted to show the general his displeasure at commanding the army to march before he received authorization from the Peace Commissioners and himself.

A couple of hours later, Connal Lee took a deep drink of tepid water from his canvas water bag. With plenty of fresh water available in the city to replenish his reserves, he splashed water over his head to cool off. He rode back to the legion headquarters, lowered the flag, then reported to Major Harris' office. "Ah have lowered all the flags, suh. What else can Ah do for y'all?"

"Even the flag at the Staines mansion?"

"Yes, suh. The governor wasn't too happy about it but finally gave in."

"I'm nearly done here, Connal Lee. Take a break for a few minutes, and we can go home for a bite of supper."

That evening Connal Lee and Perry built a campfire in front of the major's home. He helped Perry prepare a primitive supper like when they were carrying news to the northern forts. A glorious moon rose overhead, softly illuminating the landscape. As the evening drew late, Robert brought his quilts out and joined the boys on the buffalo hide. In the sultry heat, he removed his undershirt. Not a breath of air stirred. Connal Lee stared at the luxurious black hair covering the major's chest and running down the middle of his stomach to disappear beneath his drawers. Connal Lee's fingers yearned to reach out and stroke all the luscious hair, but he wasn't sure how the major would take it. He knew the Harrises weren't physically affectionate like his family. When the major folded his hands behind his head, Connal Lee stared at his moist armpits, fascinated with all the lush black hair.

As conversation tapered off, Connal Lee told the Major he had noticed the American flag for the first time that afternoon. "Ah never realized it before, but the flag has thirteen red and white stripes and thirty-one stars. Ah had ample time to count them. All the flags are exactly the same. What does it mean, suh?"

"The flag has one stripe for each of the original thirteen colonies that became our first states and one star for each of our current thirty-one states. Before the war interrupted communications, we received news that Minnesota would soon become our thirty-second state. When that happens, we will have to retire all the flags and make new ones with thirty-two stars. Our country is growing larger right before our eyes. I only hope Utah will be granted statehood soon. Congress turned down our petition for the State of Deseret and made us the Territory of Utah instead. But statehood is coming. And soon, I hope."

At the crack of dawn, Connal Lee felt a gentle nudge on his bare shoulder. He opened his eyes and looked up into the face of Major Harris. "Good morning, Connal Lee. Time for coffee. Today is the day of reckoning. Wake up, Private Perry. We need to report to headquarters early. Time to rise and shine."

They ate a simple breakfast of day-old rolls and cold ham with plenty of hot coffee. The Major studied Connal Lee over the brim of his mug. "I've been thinking, Connal Lee. I would like you to promise to keep yourself and your horses north of the line of march down South Temple. If disturbances break out, you are not to participate. You are not to join in any firefight that might put you at risk. This is our fight, not that of our Shoshone allies. If you are on the north side of the army, you can take off for Bountiful and rejoin your family. If it looks bad, I recommend you break camp and hightail it away from our Mormon settlements as fast as you can. Perry's family in Bountiful will burn the town if that happens. You need to be gone from the area if things go bad. Will you promise me?"

Connal Lee nodded his head, a frown on his face. "Yes, suh, Robert. Ah promise. Anyway, Missus Cumming invited me to watch the parade from their front porch, where the governor said he will review the troops as they pass by. It should be quite interesting. Ah'm so excited Ah can't wait!"

"Yes. I'm sure it will be interesting. Just do me a favor and leave your horses saddled and provisioned behind the house in case you must make an escape. You needn't worry about the safety of the governor and Missus Cumming. They are known to the soldiers from wintering with them at Camp Scott. They will be safe no matter what happens."

"Very good, suh. Ah understand."

Connal Lee dropped off Robert and Perry at the legion compound and rode on down the empty street towards the Staines mansion. He called back as he rode away, "Ah sure hope ah see y'all tonight at supper, Major. Good luck saving the city!"

When Connal Lee arrived at the Staines mansion, he waved at Jim and Petty, carrying comfortable chairs from the parlor to the front porch overlooking South Temple. They also set up two folding camp tables behind the chairs. Connal Lee took his horses around back to the kitchen garden and tied them up beside the carriage house. A small ditch of water ran beside the carriage house from the vegetable garden, so the horses had water to drink during the day. He loosened their cinches and removed the bits from their mouths. He strolled over and knocked briskly on the kitchen door. When no one answered, he walked around to the front of the house, enjoying the perfumes of herbs warmed in the hot sun.

As he walked up the stairs to the front door, Elizabeth Cumming waved him over to join her on the shaded porch. She stood directing their servants in setting out a variety of beverages and foods left by Mrs. Gilmore for the occasion.

Connal Lee watched for a moment until his curiosity and excitement overcame him. He excused himself and jogged over through the gate in the wrought iron fence to look up the broad avenue towards Emigration Canyon. He shaded his eyes with his big leather hat. Unseen by Connal Lee, the army had taken advantage of the full moon to line up in marching order starting at four o'clock that morning. Their march had finally brought them to the valley's edge. The soldiers caught their first glimpses of an orderly city spread out in front of them. Around nine-thirty, Connal Lee spotted the glint of sunlight reflected off shiny bayonets moving up in the foothills. Then it happened again and again. The army began marching down the bench of the mountains. With a surge of adrenaline, Connal Lee ran back to the porch. "They're coming, Governor! Ah saw them."

Connal Lee's excitement would not let him sit still. He walked back to the road and stood in the shade of one of the young maple trees lining South Temple. The day had dawned bright, the air clean. He enjoyed a clear view of the line of march descending towards the city. Soon the white tops of the first wagons drove into view, glaring far away in the bright sun. It took nearly two hours before the men and flags drew close enough to make out clearly, but Connal Lee didn't care. He lost track of time. Faintly he heard brass horns and drums beating time as they marched in good order, all in step. Clouds of dust rose in the air above the line of march. With no breeze to clear it away, dust enveloped the sweating uniformed men.

While Connal Lee watched the road coming down from the canyon, he saw several men in civilian clothes ride up to the intersection of State Road and South Temple. They congregated beneath the young poplar trees in front of the now barricaded Beehive House and across the street alongside the Council House. Connal Lee figured they must be the non-Mormons boarding down at the Globe Saloon, interested in watching the army enter the territory.

The governor's secretary pulled up in a light one-horse buggy to watch the festivities with the governor. Connal Lee waved. "Good morning, Mister Currey. Warm day, isn't it?"

"Good morning, Mister Swinton. It's going to be a scorcher. I'm sure glad I'm not marching in the sun today. Excuse me while I park my rig out back by the coach house."

About the time the leaders of the march approached Beehive House, Connal Lee scurried up to the porch and helped himself to two large glasses of cool creek water.

Governor Cumming's young secretary removed his jacket and rolled up his shirt sleeves. The governor told Elizabeth, "In the last letter I received from Johnston, he wrote that he had issued orders commanding the strictest discipline while passing through the city. He informed me he had ordered the arrest of anyone who left the column, no matter what the reason or pretense. They were not to trespass or have altercations with any men. He knew many of his men held resentments against the Mormons for the bitter winter spent waiting to attack them because he was one of them. Oh, look! Here they come."

Elizabeth sat demurely in the shade. A hoop of embroidery kept her occupied while she waited. She looked up. "Listen! I hear singing. Isn't that nice! I can't quite make out the words. Do you gentlemen recognize it?"

They listened attentively for a few moments. Suddenly the governor's secretary frowned. "I'm afraid I do, Missus Cumming. It's nothing more than a coarse barracks ditty usually sung after too many drinks late in the evening. I beg your pardon, Missus Cumming. They shouldn't subject a lady like you to such vulgarity. They must mean it as an insult to the Mormons – only no one is around to hear them."

As the troops grew nearer, Connal Lee heard them belting out the chorus, *"Giddy eye ay, giddy eye ay, giddy eye ay for the one eyed Reilly..."*

Jim and Petty stood against the wall behind the governor's chair. When they saw the governor struggling to stand up, they stepped up and helped him to his feet. They walked him over to stand at the sturdy railing between the elegant porch columns. Smartly uniformed riders approached at a slow horse's walk. As they pulled up to the fenced enclosure around the mansion's gardens, a proud middle-aged man wearing a fancy plumed hat raised his hand. Sergeants shouted out orders. Everyone stopped. Silence rang out. The governor leaned over the railing and called out in his loud public speaking voice, "Good morning, Brevet Brigadier General Albert Sidney Johnston, sir. On behalf of the Territory of Utah, it gives me great pleasure to welcome you and your entire staff in peace on this momentous day."

While the governor delivered his rehearsed welcome speech, the company of cavalry and a section of artillery fell into parade formation behind the general and his staff. A color guard ranged behind the general, carrying an American flag, a unit flag, and a departmental flag high overhead. The six select young officers all wore dress uniforms, including brightly polished sabers to defend the colors they carried. The peace commissioners proudly accompanied the general's staff in plain view. The army band marched briskly forward and formed up on the general's right. Dust covered everyone and their horses. The drum major dramatically flourished his five-foot-long baton. The band played a loud trumpet fanfare introduction. The drum major then led the men in singing a selection of patriotic songs to honor the governor and celebrate the event of occupying the territory. The governor and Elizabeth glanced at each other. The men sang in an obvious lackluster and desultory manner, even though the brass instruments rang out loud and clear. Connal Lee heard the governor murmur to Elizabeth at his side, "The men think I'm sympathetic to the Mormons rather than to the army. They resent that I didn't ride into the city with them as victorious conquerors."

Elizabeth patted the chubby hand gripping the white porch rail. "Don't worry about it, dear. Put on your best face and smile. Maybe a little wave to the men would be in order."

"Yes, dear."

The general gave orders. Three of his smartly dressed color guard walked over to the flagpole in front of the Staines mansion. A sergeant behind the general yelled out, "Atten-SHUN!" The entire body of men snapped upright, standing erect and still. The sergeant ordered, "Present HARMS!" All the soldiers held their rifles vertically in front of them, saluting the flag. The flag detail came to attention, stepped up to the flagpole, and untied the flag from the base of the pole. The drum major lifted his baton high and led the buglers and trumpeters in playing *To the Colors*. While the trumpets played the familiar staccato tune, the flag detail raised the large flag as briskly as they could manage. The senior officer carefully held up the flag to keep it from touching the ground. The sergeant screamed out, "Order HARMS!"

General Johnston and his mounted officers removed their hats and held them over their left shoulders with their hands covering their hearts. The entire army saluted the flag and repeated the pledge of allegiance in loud voices. Connal Lee followed the governor and Mrs. Cumming's example and placed his hand over his heart. He hadn't heard the pledge of allegiance before, so he only listened.

With the ceremony of officially occupying the territory concluded, General Johnston saluted the governor and gave orders to move out. Officers and sergeants yelled their orders up and down the length of the parade. The band struck up the popular marching song from the Revolutionary War, *Yankee Doodle Dandy*. The rows of men moved into marching order and stepped out in unison, belting out the familiar lyrics. Colonel Smithes' battalion followed the general and his senior staff. A section of artillery with several mule-drawn cannons completed the vanguard. Two companies of infantry then marched by on foot. After this first wave came the vanguard's trains of about fifty wagons pulled by a variety of draft animals, six to a heavy wagon. Dust wafted around the porch. Elizabeth snapped open a silk and ivory fan and fanned her face vigorously. The governor collapsed into his chair to watch. "Jim, bring me a whiskey and creek water. Public speaking is dry work."

"Right away, suh."

Slowly the vast army marched past the governor. The Tenth Infantry column marched by, followed by their trains of supply wagons. Each man carried heavy packs and weapons. Connal Lee observed sweat dripping down their dusty faces. Division after division, the military parade went on for hours, followed by their supply wagons drawn by six mules.

Connal Lee became bored after so much of the same thing repeating endlessly. He wished Edward and Perry were keeping him company so he could share his observations and thoughts. Elizabeth urged everyone to help themselves to the buffet of cold meats, breads, cheeses, and little cakes. Governor Cumming told his small audience that General Johnston had publicly proclaimed he would give his Texas plantation for the privilege of bombarding the city for just fifteen minutes to pay the Mormons back for stranding his army in frozen hell all winter long. Connal Lee didn't like hearing that. He frowned and shook his head.

Captain Phelps' Light Battery B stamped by in thunderous unison with cannons, one after another, each pulled by six great draft horses. Each artillery company's three officers rode the left side row of horses. Each cannon's crew marched smartly behind their officers and their enormous brass weapon. Supply wagons carrying cannon balls followed the soldiers. Yet another infantry division came with their commissary wagons.

Colonel Loring's battalion of mounted rifles with their supply train followed next, looking very dapper in their cavalry uniforms. Then Lieutenant Colonel Bee led his volunteers, labor force, and their small train through the clouds of dust. Interspersed among the orderly rows of uniformed men came herdsmen with flocks of hundreds of cattle and sheep. Blacksmiths, laundresses, tailors, and numerous other support personnel and hangers-on strode along casually, gawking at the lovely deserted gardens lining the broad avenue.

Governor Cumming recognized his friend from Camp Scott, Lieutenant Colonel Philip St. George Cooke. The governor stood up and waved to catch his eye. Colonel Cooke nodded and waved back with his hat. The governor explained that the colonel rode with his hat held over his heart to show respect for the soldiers he had commanded on the long march of the Mormon Battalion. He had told the governor back in Camp Scott how he did not look forward to making war on men he had come to respect and befriend a decade earlier.

So far as the governor and his party could see, the army marched through the city without touching anything but the dirt of the road, leaving the city completely unmolested. The Second Dragoons under Colonel Cooke made up the rear guard. Swords swung from their belts as they marched through. Connal Lee figured the army must have stretched out over ten miles from beginning to end. He glanced at the angle of the sun and estimated it to be around six o'clock. After the last dust-covered men plodded wearily by, Connal Lee jumped up. "Excuse me!" He rushed out to the center of the broad avenue and looked at the diminishing rows of men walking away. The line of men, wagons, and cattle stretched all the way down to the narrow one-lane wooden bridge built in 1849, where North Temple turned southernly and then crossed the Jordan River to the Church pastures. Despite a bottleneck on both sides of the narrow bridge, Connal Lee could see that they had already erected straight rows of white tents on the far side. If General Wells hadn't recommended they relocate their camp, they would have been surrounded by men who had been harassed all winter by thieving Ute Indians.

When Connal Lee turned around, he could see flags rising over the Council House and in the legion compound. With a cheer, he ran up to the porch. "They raised the flags over at the Nauvoo Legion headquarters, suh. Does that mean we are finished with the war and safe at last?"

"Yes, young man. The general kept his word and marched through without trespassing on any private property or confronting any civilians."

The Governor had imbibed several drinks in the heat during the dusty parade and needed help standing up. The Governor and Elizabeth moved off the porch to the cooler interior of the mansion.

Connal Lee thanked Elizabeth for letting him share their reviewing stand, then took off for the legion headquarters, anxious to
celebrate with Major Harris and Private Sessions. In the silence after the monotonous noise of tramping feet, marching music, and the
rattle of freight wagons, he heard only the water of City Creek gur-
gling in the ditches lining the streets. On his way to the legion headquarters, he kept thinking, *What a day! What a day!*

He pulled up by the gate in the wall surrounding the legion
headquarters compound and tied off his three horses. He opened the
door to Perry's office and peered in. Men, in and out of uniform,
crowded the small anteroom, all talking at the same time. Private
Sessions glanced over, saw Connal Lee, and flashed him a big grin.
Connal Lee smiled back. Waving, he closed the door behind him.
He walked over and knocked on the door to Major Harris' little of-
fice. He waited. No response. He opened the door and peeked in.
No one. Disappointed he didn't have anyone to celebrate with, he
returned to the street. He looked left and right, hoping to spot the
Major on his lively stallion. He wondered how long it would take
Edward to receive the all-clear and drive Sister Ohlsson back.

He didn't feel like returning to his family in Bountiful. He
wanted to stay in the center of the action, so he rode slowly north to
the major's home. After he arrived, Connal Lee turned his horses
loose in the little corral. He could not find the major's white stallion
in the corral or lean-to barn. With a shrug, he carried his saddlebags
and sleeping furs in the back door of the adobe cottage. He called
out, but only silence answered him. After depositing his equipment
in the front yard, he searched Edward's small bedroom for something to read. He carried a history book out to the front porch while
waiting for the others to return and read about General George
Washington during the American Revolutionary War. A couple of
hours later, the light began fading. He decided he better put together
some sort of supper. Everyone would be starving by the time they
returned. He scurried down the steps of the small root cellar between the house and the barn. With only the light of the open door,
he found a smoked cured ham and onions. In Sister Ohlsson's neat
kitchen, he found a bag of beans and bunches of dried chili peppers
hanging overhead. A small clay jar held dark molasses sugar. He

borrowed an iron pot and carried everything out front rather than cooking on Mrs. Ohlsson's stove. He wanted to watch the road while he cooked. He rekindled the flame from the embers of the cookfire and added logs to build up a good fire.

An hour later, darkness descended on the deserted city. He smelled his simmering pot of ham and chili beans. His stomach growled, but he held off eating. He waited for company to share supper since he wasn't used to eating alone. He walked down to the quiet road in front of the house and gazed out over the vast dark valley. He spotted pinpoints of twinkling lights of campfires miles to the south. He figured they must be the gentiles boarding at the Globe four miles away. He looked right and felt momentarily taken aback when he saw a vast sea of campfires spreading out west of the Jordan River in orderly rows. A huge tent city glowed yellow in the light of cook fires. He nodded to himself. *Johnston's army. Ah didn't realize they were so close by. And such a big camp!*

Before much longer, he heard the footsteps of an approaching horse. Major Harris guided his stallion up the path to the barn. Connal Lee stood up. "Good evening, Robert. Glad to see y'all finally made it home."

"Connal Lee. I wasn't sure if anyone would be here. How are you this evening?"

Connal Lee helped the Major unsaddle his stallion in the corral. "Are y'all hungry, Robert? Ah made some chili beans since Ah didn't know how many we might be. There's plenty."

"Oh, thank you. Very helpful. Let me stop in the privy, and I'll join you out front."

The Major exited the front door a few minutes later, carrying quilts from his bed. He spread them over Connal Lee's buffalo hide, then sank down and sat Indian-style next to Connal Lee. He sighed wearily. Connal Lee dished up two wood bowls of chili and handed one to the major with a tin spoon. "Here, Robert. This might help y'all feel better. Was it a tiring day?"

"Yes, as a matter of fact. I think I'm tired from the strain of being on edge, waiting for the soldiers to get out of line and begin making mischief. That and the heat. I spent most of the day perched in the sun on the widow's walk atop Council House. I wanted to keep an eagle eye and close aim on the soldiers. After the rearguard marched past, I waited until they reached the west gate. When the army passed completely outside the city walls, I raised the flag, signaling the all-clear to our guards waiting in hiding. What a relief that we didn't have to torch our homes or fight the invaders."

"Yep. Ah was mighty relieved too. Governor Cumming told me to spread the word that General Johnston kept his written promise not to molest the citizens or private property and for everyone to return home. When do y'all think Edward will be back?"

"Since it's a good six-hour trip by wagon from the point of the mountain, I don't expect they will return until tomorrow afternoon."

"Oh. Too bad. Ah wanted to tell him about watching the soldiers and the marching bands and all the cannons. Will Private Sessions come back for the night?"

"No. When the excitement died down at headquarters, he obtained permission from General Wells to ride to his family in Bountiful and share the news. He will be back on duty early in the morning. I'm pretty sure he will spend the night with his family. Nope. It's just the two of us tonight, I'm afraid."

Connal Lee removed the pot of beans from over the fire. "Well, that's all right. Ah can keep y'all company tonight, Robert. Here, let me take the bowl. Y'all just relax."

"Thank you, Connal Lee. When you come back, would you please bring two glasses and the jug of Valley Tan from the parlor?"

Connal Lee recalled how the Major liked to add creek water to the whiskey, so he grabbed his canvas water bag. He rinsed off the bowls in the ditch behind the house and filled the water bag with fresh snowmelt water.

By the time he returned to the fire, the major had stripped down to his underpants. He lounged on his side, head propped up on his elbow, staring blankly at the dark city lit only by moonlight. Connal Lee poured them both small drinks topped off with cool water. The major sat up on the quilts. "Thank you. Here's to your health, Connal Lee. Thanks for all your help today."

"Cheers, Major. Here's to everyone returning home safe and sound."

Major Harris clicked his glass against Connal Lee's. They sat side by side, watching the fire and sipping their drinks. By the time they finished, Connal Lee felt a slight tingle of heat in his stomach. He changed into his comfortable loincloth and walked back to the quilts beside the fire. Robert handed him the glass. "Another one, while you are up, please."

Connal Lee fixed another light drink for the Major and filled his own glass with water. He wasn't used to drinking liquor. The campfire died down. They stretched out side by side in the warm sultry breeze and watched the bright moon rise overhead. In his simple, affectionate way, Connal Lee rolled over and placed his hand over the older man's hairy chest. He snuggled up. Using the major's strong arm as a pillow, he closed his eyes, reveling in feeling Robert's silky black hair beneath his fingers. He fell asleep with a smile on his face.

He woke up the following morning with Robert curled up around him, hugging his back. Connal Lee loved feeling the major's strong hairy body against his. He wriggled a bit, hoping to get a rise out of the older man. But instead, his movement woke up the major. Robert rolled over onto his back and stretched. He sat up and stretched again with a big yawn. Connal Lee sat up, too, hoping his erection didn't appear too obvious in his soft suede loincloth. He glanced over towards the craggy mountains looming over the city in the east. Only a hint of light showed above the mountaintops. "Coffee, suh?"

"Yes, please, Connal Lee. Much obliged."

Both men walked through the house. Connal Lee grabbed the coffee pot from the kitchen and went out back to fill it at the creek. Fifteen minutes later, he had the fire stirred up, and the smell of coffee brewing wafted around them. The Major scrounged around in the kitchen until he found day-old bread in the tin bread box and a clay pot of raw honey. Before the sun rose, they walked back to the creek and washed up. The Major shaved, using a small scrap of mirror propped on a tree branch to see himself. Connal Lee watched, fascinated, fearing he would see blood. He had never seen a man shave with a straight-edge razor before. *Ned shaves Captain*

Reed like this every morning? It sure is a lot of work to be clean-shaven.

The major splashed his face to wash off the remaining soap. Connal Lee asked, "So when do y'all think everyone will start coming back to the city, Robert?"

"Well, not for quite a while yet, Connal Lee."

"Why not? The governor said it's safe now that Johnston has passed through."

"Really? It's safe? We evacuated out of harm's way when the army camped a hundred and twenty miles east of us. Now the army camps only a couple of miles away, well within striking distance. We aren't safe yet. When the army leaves the valley all together, we can start to consider it. Until then, everyone stays where they are, safe and sound."

Connal Lee thought about it. "Oh. Well. Ah confess Ah'm disappointed, truth be told. Ah thought we were all safe after yesterday."

"Not yet, my friend. General Wells told me yesterday that General Johnston ordered his men to rest for a couple of days. He will be sending out scouts today to survey a couple of potential locations for the new fort he was ordered to establish in the territory. He's going to remain a threat poised at our throats for several more days now, perhaps even weeks."

"Oh."

"All right. Let's get a move on. I have to go report for duty. Are you going to wait around for Edward or go back to Bountiful?"

"Maybe Ah should ride up City Creek and hunt us something fresh for the pot. When Edward and Sister Ohlsson get back, I suspect they're going to be hungry. Ah don't think leftover beans will be enough."

"Good hunting, Connal Lee. I'll see you at supper if not before."

As Connal Lee saddled his horses, he decided to ride north to Bountiful and see his family. He had a lot to tell them. He arrived at Short Rainbow's tipi around seven-thirty, happy to find them together eating breakfast. After hugs, he poured himself a cup of coffee and sat down. He launched into enthusiastically telling them about the military parade and visiting with the Governor. When he finished, he invited everyone to return to the city with him. "The nights are so clear and warm, we don't need to take the tipi or the tent, either one. We can just spread our furs around the campfire and sleep outdoors. Let's load up plenty of food for Missus Cumming and for Sister Ohlsson to cook for Robert and Edward. We can make tonight's supper a big celebration of peace returning to our Mormon allies. What do y'all say?"

Connal Lee's family dressed for the heat. Short Rainbow and Bright Star wore short sleeveless vests, long beautifully beaded loincloths, and headbands. The men only wore loincloths, armbands, and necklaces. Even though Connal Lee had developed a suntan, he habitually wore his hat to protect his nose from burning.

They loaded up packhorses with two small does, a dozen sage grouse, and half a dozen cottontail rabbits. While they tied on the second small doe, Connal Lee told his family he wanted to give it to Perry's family at the Sessions Inn, to thank them for their generosity a couple of days earlier.

They stopped at the inn, delivered the already cleaned and skinned deer, and loaded up more freshly harvested foods. Perry's cousins pressed them to take all they could carry. A teenager handed Connal Lee a bag of apricots. "These are the first of the crop. We were going to dry them, but please take and share them with Perry and his friends. Oh, and don't forget some peas. I picked them just yesterday evening, myself."

"Why, thanks so much. This is great! We'll see y'all soon."

"No, thank you for the meat. We're too busy watering and harvesting to get in any hunting. Say hello to Perry for us. Happy trails."

They rode up to the Staines mansion around high noon. Connal Lee led the way around back. While his family unloaded foodstuffs for Elizabeth Cumming, Connal Lee knocked on the kitchen door. Mrs. Gilmore opened the door. When she saw Connal Lee, she smiled a big welcome. "Good morning, Brother Swinton. How nice to see you again. Won't you please come in? I'll let Missus Cumming and the Governor know you are here."

255

"Oh, thanks, Sister Gilmore, but we're here only long enough to drop off some fresh meat and vegetables for the governor and Missus Cumming. Please tell her the apricots are particularly for her. Give them our regards, please. Now, where should we leave all these groceries? Do y'all have a root cellar?"

"Right here beside the door is perfect. My girls and I will sort it from here. This is most generous of you, my friend. I'm sure the governor will be most appreciative. You know how he likes to eat well!"

They rode directly to Major Harris' house, sweating in the intense noonday sun. "Let's get in the shade before we melt!"

Even the horses had begun perspiring. They pulled up to the corral behind the house. Edward rushed out and hugged everyone, delighted to have company. He then gave them a hand unloading and unsaddling their horses. Sister Ohlsson was thrilled to see her root cellar filling up with fresh vegetables. When Connal Lee mentioned apricots, she grabbed the cloth bag from his hands. "Really? I just adore apricot crumble. I'll go bake us up a big cobbler pie for dessert tonight."

Short Rainbow offered to cook venison steaks over the fire so they could eat supper outside. Mrs. Ohlsson sent her sons out to the woodpile as soon as she went into the kitchen. She needed plenty of wood to re-light her cookstove and stoke up a hot fire for baking. She already had bread dough rising under a dishtowel.

Connal Lee and Edward spent the hot afternoon lounging beside the tiny creek behind the house. They leaned against the trunk of a cottonwood tree, enjoying the shade. Connal Lee told Edward about the army's march through town the day before. When he couldn't think of anything to add, he recommended they read more of the history of the Revolutionary War. Edward had studied the war in class at the university and shared a lot of information not found in the textbook. Connal Lee's family occupied themselves butchering the doe and tanning its hide. They smoked the meat into jerky so it wouldn't go bad in the heat.

Major Harris and Private Sessions pulled up to the house just before the sun touched the mountains to the west of the broad valley. There hadn't been a cloud in the sky all day. Robert and Perry greeted everyone and then rode to the corral to tend to their mounts. They bathed in the cold creek when they finished, delighted to feel cool and clean again after sweating all day.

They noticed the boys sitting around shirtless, so they slid on their pants and joined the group around the fireside, glad to go barefoot for the evening. Mrs. Ohlsson's boys, wearing only their underpants, ran out and joined the group. They both jumped onto Robert's lap to welcome him home.

Major Harris told everyone he had ridden out to General Johnston's command tent around midafternoon. "They were all just boiling up out there in the shadeless desert. The men and livestock stirred up so much dust it's a nuisance to all living things. The general said he would soon order his men to move further south and west to the foot of the mountains, to the area called Bingham Canyon. He had reports of plenty of grass for the livestock and wood up the canyon for cookfires. He told me Peace Commissioner McCulloch, the former Texas Ranger, had departed with a group of civilian and military advisors to check out potential sites for the new fort south and west of any Mormon settlements. He said he should know where he would build the camp by the end of the week. The men and livestock had stirred up the waters in the Jordon River to where it was no longer fit to drink. I, for one, will be mighty glad to see them move even further away from our fine city."

Soon Short Rainbow and Bright Star announced supper was ready. Sister Ohlsson came out and joined them. Her little boys ran over and knelt beside her, ready to eat.

The major finished his plate of venison steak served with chili. He sopped up the gravy with a crust of newly baked bread. He stretched his legs out in front of him with a sigh and leaned back on his elbows. He gazed around at his family and friends. "You boys might be interested to know. When I returned to headquarters, General Wells handed me a letter from President Brigham Young addressed to Governor Cumming. He asked me to deliver it and wait to see if the governor would reply. It seems President Young invited the governor to ride down to Provo to meet in person to work on various matters. Among other things, President Young wrote he was prepared to return the twelve-hundred head of horses, mules, oxen, and cattle raided from government supply trains last fall. He said he would only turn them over to the governor. He doesn't want to negotiate with the general. The governor decided he would make the trip early tomorrow morning rather than send a message. He asked if he might request a modest guard from the militia since he would only be taking his two drivers for such a short visit."

Connal Lee and Edward sat up attentively. Private Perry smiled. "With the kind permission of General Wells, he agreed I could bring Private Sessions, Connal Lee, and Edward as an honor guard. He also said that if any others of the Shoshone Delegation wanted to go to Provo, they would be welcome to join the party. So, what do you think, boys? Would you like to go with the governor and me to Provo? I suspect we will return Wednesday sometime, the day after tomorrow."

Connal Lee leaned forward, nodding his head vigorously. Edward smiled. "Thank you, father. I would very much like to go with you."

Connal Lee gazed around at his family. "Would y'all like to go back to Provo?"

White Wolf leaned over and put his hand on Connal Lee's bare shoulder. "We don't really have anything to contribute. On the other hand, now that peace is restored, we may as well be on our way up north. Besides, the heat is getting too strong down here. Last summer, we were already up in Jackson Valley this time of the year, harvesting berries and medicinal herbs in the great forests. I think we should pack up our food supplies and prepare to leave."

Screaming Eagle nodded his agreement. Short Rainbow shrugged. She liked to travel on new adventures, but the cool mountains sounded awfully attractive to her. "You go ahead, Connal Lee. When you return, we will pack up the tipi and head north."

Connal Lee turned back to Major Harris. "Thanks so much, Robert. My family wants to get ready to travel to the Teton Mountains and join Chief Arimo for the summer. But Ah will be happy to go along. The governor and President Young are my friends. Ah'm always happy to be of service to them."

"Well, boys. We need to be at the Staines mansion by four o'clock. The Governor wants to get as much of the trip behind him as he can before the heat of the day sets in. Let's turn in. Sister Ohlsson, would you kindly prepare a pot of coffee and leave it on the back burner so we have something hot to start the day? Thanks."

The Major brought out quilts from his bed and joined everyone around the campfire.

All too early, someone shook Connal Lee's shoulder. "Good morning. Grab some coffee and get saddled up. Pack minimal travel gear. Let's hit the road, son."

Everyone stumbled around in the dim light of the moon. Somehow, they all managed to get dressed and packed. Connal Lee said goodbye to his spouses. White Wolf told Connal Lee he could find them in Bountiful when he returned. The major led the boys down to the Staines mansion. When they rode up to the carriage house, torches burning on both sides of the kitchen door lit the yard. Jim and Petty helped a sleepy governor stumble out to the waiting coach. Mrs. Gilmore brought out a tray with warm cinnamon rolls for everyone. Jim climbed up to the driver seat, picked up the reins, and called out, "Giddup! Giddup!"

Major Harris and Connal Lee pulled ahead to lead the way. Perry and Edward followed behind.

Four hours later, the governor knocked on the roof of the carriage. Jim pulled off the dusty road. Everyone wanted to stop a moment and stretch their legs. The major spotted the point of the mountain not far ahead. "Well, boys. We're about a third of the way there. It's going to start getting hot now. Hopefully, in another four hours, we'll be close to American Fork."

They all drank plenty of water. The governor hesitated just before climbing back into his carriage. "I'm done napping. Now I would enjoy some conversation. Please come join me, Master Swinton."

"My pleasure, suh. Let me tie my ride onto the back of the carriage, and Ah'll join y'all."

When Connal Lee tied his pretty brown mare's reins to the back of the carriage, he noticed several fancy travel trunks lashed on, including a large woven basket on top. He hopped into the carriage. They took off riding south. Over the next few hours, as the sun rose higher and hotter, they passed the Jordan Narrows as it bent around the point of the mountain. The Jordan River grew noticeably broader the closer they rode toward its headwaters in Utah Lake. When they drove into Lehi, they stopped at a small inn on Main Street. While the drivers watered the horses behind the inn, the others went inside for a bite to eat. Connal Lee found eating in a public room rather strange, not at all like eating by the campfire or as a guest in someone's home. They all found the food tasted bland.

The governor, in particular, departed less than satisfied. Nonetheless, when the proprietor presented a startling large bill to feed four men and two servants, he paid up with a shrug. "I'm going to nap now. I only hope I don't expire in the heat of the day. If any of you want to ride inside in the shade, you are welcome."

Connal Lee joined the others on horseback. An hour later, they stopped beneath a stand of cottonwood trees lining the American Fork River. Jim and Petty unlashed the picnic basket from the back of the carriage. They served fried chicken, sliced ham, and fresh fruits until everyone ate their fill – including the governor. Jim served the governor a couple of stiff drinks of Kentucky Whiskey with his second dinner. He offered drinks to the others, but everyone declined.

The governor announced he wanted to relax in the shade. "I have traveled this route several times with Colonel Kane and then with the Peace Commissioners. I'm afraid we still have a hard four-hour drive to reach Provo. Let's take a siesta until the sun starts lowering. No need to push on in the hottest part of the day. Jim, wake me midafternoon if I'm not already awake."

Connal Lee spread his sleeping buffalo hide on the grassy ground in the shade. Jim and Petty brought over cushions from the carriage and helped ease the governor down to recline against them. The governor plopped his hat over his face. Robert and the three boys took off their shoes and waded in the small river, delighted to cool their feet.

By four o'clock, they climbed back into the saddle. Around eight that evening, they pulled up to the Seminary building. Brigham Young came out and greeted everyone. He told the governor he had a guest bed set up for him in one of his homes. "Your servants and honor guard are welcome to sleep under the stars. I will return back to Great Salt Lake City tomorrow, Governor. I'm taking all my family and reopening Beehive House and Lion House. We decided to travel during the night to avoid the heat and dust. Everyone should get plenty of rest tonight and tomorrow during the day. We'll leave around this time tomorrow evening."

Connal Lee spoke quietly to Major Harris, then invited everyone to ride on down to Captain Hanover's for the night. "We will come back here and join up with y'all tomorrow evening if that's all right, Governor Cumming, suh."

"Thank you, everyone, for attending me on this trip. Have a pleasant evening. I'll see you tomorrow around this same time."

Everyone shook hands goodbye. The governor followed Brigham Young into the shade of the warehouse-sized two-story adobe building. Robert and the boys mounted up for the brief ride down to Hobble Creek, only a couple miles south. They arrived as dusk settled over the land. Captain Hanover came out to greet them when he heard horses riding up.

After they shook hands and attended to their horses, the captain invited them into his parlor. His third wife, who Connal Lee knew from the handcart trip, asked if they had already eaten supper. When Major Harris said they had not, she invited them to have a seat in the kitchen. She warmed up a pot of stew by dim candlelight. The captain's first wife had been baking whole wheat rolls all day to help feed the refugees camped along the creek. They ate their fill. Captain Hanover joined them, anxious to hear the details of Johnston's march through Great Salt Lake City.

When Connal Lee woke up sprawled on top of his red fox fur blanket, he wondered if he had time to ride down to Payson and pay a call on the Staines. While they ate breakfast, he discussed it with Major Harris. "I would like to go see my boys and their wives, too, Connal Lee. But I'm afraid it would be cutting the timing very short and leave us tired at the start of the return trip. We'll have a long night tonight, riding straight through to the city. I think it will be best if we just rest up a bit."

Edward and Perry knew a friend from the University of Deseret who lived in Hobble Creek, the tiny farming community only a mile or two away from Captain Hanover's farm and ranch. They invited

Connal Lee to ride over to find him, but Connal Lee decided he would rather spend the day with Captain Hanover. He knew once they left for Jackson Valley, he wouldn't have a chance to see the captain for many months.

Captain Hanover's three wives prepared quite the feast to send them off to travel with Brigham Young back to the city.

By eight that evening, they rode up to the new Seminary Building. Carriages, buggies, wagons, and men on horseback organized themselves in a row along State Road. When they saw Governor Cumming walk out to his carriage, they trotted up and took guard positions before and after the carriage. Everyone lit torches. The long train pulled out half an hour later. They stopped every two hours for a fifteen-minute break. Twelve hours later, the weary, dusty caravan pulled up in front of the Beehive House and Lion House. Connal Lee and his fellow guards escorted Governor Cuming back to the Staines mansion before riding on to nap the day away at Major Harris' home.

After a good night's sleep, Connal Lee said his goodbyes to Edward and Sister Ohlsson. He saddled up his ride and two packhorses and accompanied Major Harris to General Well's office. Perry was already on duty at his desk in the general's anteroom. Connal Lee asked if he might have a word with General Wells. Perry gave him a quizzical look, stood up, and knocked on the door. A moment later, he held the door open for Connal Lee to go in.

"Good morning, Brother Connal Lee. Did everything go according to plan with the governor's visit to Provo?"

"Oh, yes, suh. Everything went according to plan. But y'all see, suh, while Ah was riding with the governor, we talked about the changes the new peace will bring to the area. Governor Cumming told me that Missus Cumming was worried about where they would live when the Staines returned. She was hoping Elder Staines would lease them the house, but now that peace has been declared, she doesn't believe that will happen. The governor asked me who might know of a house they could rent for the next three years of his term as Territorial Governor. He said they could buy a house if they found one for sale, but they would rather rent. He said they will probably return back to Atlanta when he completes his term. Ah took the liberty of suggesting that y'all knew pretty much all of the people and properties in the city. The governor asked me to make inquiries and see if y'all knew of a house that might suit them."

"Hm. I see. Well, now. Let me think a minute. Of course, there's nothing as nice as the Staines residence, but we have a few adequate homes. Yes. Now that I think of it, there is a house over on State Road not far from the Social Hall, half a block south of Beehive House. The Fredericksons offered it to me to use for interim housing for evacuees during the exodus south. They decided to relocate down to their horse ranch in Fillmore now that both his wives' children were growing up. They decided they wanted to build up their operation to service the southern Mormon route to California. I'm sure they would agree to a fair rental price. Wait just a moment while I write the governor a note. If they want to see inside, please let Private Sessions know, and we'll have the boards over the empty windows removed. We could have it ready within a week for the Governor to move in if they decide to take it."

When Connal Lee left, he said goodbye to Perry. "Ah don't know when we will be back, but Ah'll be sure to look y'all up when we do. We'll be wintering up on the Portneuf River if y'all ever get up Fort Hall way. Good luck, my friend."

"Safe trails. Farewell. Until we meet again."

Connal Lee rode to the Staines home. One of the young Gilmore girls answered his knock. He found the Governor and Elizabeth eating breakfast in the dining room. They invited him to join them. "Oh, thanks, but Ah've already eaten breakfast. Don't let me stop, y'all, though. Ah just dropped by to give y'all a note from General Wells. He thinks he has a house that might suit y'all. He warned it's nothing grand like Elder Staines' home, but it has a carriage house in the back with servants' quarters above. It's just down State Road from the Beehive House, so it will be easy for your honor to get to the office in Council House. Here's the letter, suh. Well, Ah'll say goodbye for now. My family and Ah will be leaving now that peace is here at last. We're going to travel up to the Tetons in Yellowstone Valley, where Chief Arimo makes his summer camp. Ah can't wait. They tell me it's nice and cool up there. Good luck to y'all. Ah hope we see each other again, someday."

When Connal Lee rode past the hot springs, he wondered if he could interest his family in stopping there before they headed north.

That afternoon Connal Lee helped dismantle and pack up the tipi. Everyone rose early to take advantage of the cool morning. They hitched up the horses to the travoises, loaded up their pack-horses, hopped into their saddles, and rode north, happy to be on their way home.

Following is a preview of the continuation
of Connal Lee's adventures in

PIONEER SPIRIT
Book Four: An Uneasy Peace

Available now in paperback and on Kindle

Chapter 1: Salmon River

Each day as Connal Lee and his family led their travoises and packhorses northward, the days grew hotter, topping ninety degrees by one o'clock. They approached Fort Buenaventura the second day. White Wolf recommended they find shade for their noonday meal. "Let's take a siesta until midafternoon when the temperature begins to fall. We'll ride later into the evening before making camp. It's too hot!"

Two days later, they stopped to visit with the Morgans in Box Elder Fort. Connal Lee hadn't hunted for the past two days, so he and Jeff spent the afternoon ranging around the deserted countryside hunting pheasants, sage grouse, and rabbits. One of the packhorses had developed a slight limp, so Screaming Eagle and White Wolf checked over all the horses. They removed pebbles and thorns, preparing the horses for departure early the next morning. When they finished, they inspected the saddles, bridles, and reins for wear and tear. Nothing needed repairing.

After another couple of hot days, they pulled up to the hot springs. They spent a day there relaxing, bathing, and washing clothes. That evening they all frolicked in the bubbling water. Afterward, they fell into a pile and made passionate love. Connal Lee, totally sated and happy, gazed at the milky way shining behind bright twinkling stars in the moonless sky until he fell asleep.

They pushed a little harder and pulled up beside the Snake River west of the gate to Fort Hall and made camp in the dusk. While Short Rainbow and Bright Star lit their cookfire, Connal Lee walked to the fort to find his handsome foster older brother, John Reed. He found Captain Reed lounging naked on his bed with the windows open, hoping for a bit of breeze to cool him down. When Connal Lee yelled up from the courtyard, John leaned out the window and waved. "Hey, Connal Lee! Come on up, Little Brother!"

Ned slept in the office below John's bedroom. He poked his head out the door to see who had come calling on the captain so late in the evening. Connal Lee smiled and nodded. "Howdy, Ned. See y'all later."

He took the stairs two at a time. The captain opened the door. They crushed each other in a big bear hug until Connal Lee laughed and pulled away. "Come on, John. Pull on some pants and join us. We're camped down by the river. Ah need a swim to cool off before supper."

John frolicked with the Shoshone family, enjoying the cool river water and Short Rainbow's delicious fried pheasant. They passed the evening making love, reveling in the cool of the night and their clean bodies. The following day, Captain Reed accepted Connal Lee's invitation to ride with them to see Zeff and Sister Woman, then ride on to spend a day at the Baines plantation on the Blackfoot River.

They pulled up to Zeff's new home. After hugs and kisses, Connal Lee invited them to go with him to visit his foster parents. "Come on. We'll tell you all about the excitement down in Great Salt Lake City."

Zeff and Sister Woman loaded up their wagon with food and bedding. Sister Woman grabbed Chester Ray and climbed up on the wagon's seat. They followed the Shoshone family north along the Snake River.

That evening and the next day, Connal Lee's family and friends listened with rapt attention to the stories of the empty cities, the governor, the Peace Commissioners, and the march of Johnston's army through Great Salt Lake City. Lorna and Gilbert Baines felt relieved to learn the Saints could finally return to their homes. Lorna prepared creamed new potatoes with freshly hulled peas to accompany Short Rainbow's fried grouse and fresh trout.

Connal Lee and his family said goodbye to the Baines and Captain Reed before leaving early on the third day. They rode slowly northwesterly between two low mountain ranges and stopped several days later when they drew near Fort Lemhi. Connal Lee sat on his pretty brown mare and gazed around at the abandoned log cabin homes, barns, sheds, and the meeting hall. He remembered visiting back in February with Captain Reed. He looked at the gardens and fields, now abandoned, not planted for the summer growing season. Weeds and grasses had already overrun them, returning them to their natural state. With a sad shake of his head, he led his family past the deserted fort.

Traveling more northerly, the slow caravan took another two days before they arrived at the chief's favorite fishing camp. While Short Rainbow and Bright Star erected the tipi, Screaming Eagle walked around the woods searching for long hardwood branches or young tree saplings he could carve into harpoons. White Wolf made a fishing net from strong cords he had made from the fibrous stalks of dogbane plants and Indian hemp during their journey. He wove the lines together around a bent willow branch and soon had a strong net for dipping in the river. Screaming Eagle quickly whittled the ends of his spears into sharp points.

In no time at all, Screaming Eagle and White Wolf stripped off their clothing and began fishing from the shallow sides of the raging river. Connal Lee walked over to watch, amazed at the size of the salmon they pulled out of the whitecapped waters. He looked closely into the green river water and noticed how the salmon all swam upstream against the current, clearly visible against the stony river bottom.

After Screaming Eagle speared a fish, White Wolf lifted the salmon with his net and tossed it up on the riverbank. Connal Lee picked one up to examine it. "Ah've never seen a fish so big, have y'all? It's nearly three feet long! Ah swear it must weight close to fifty pounds." He carried it over and placed it on the grass beside the tipi's cookfire. He touched its scaled skin. "Look what a pretty red color. Ah've never eaten salmon before."

The fishermen walked up to the cookfire, carrying two cleaned salmon by the gills. "Don't worry, Connal Lee. Short Rainbow knows just how to broil them. I think you'll really enjoy the tender pink flesh. Come with me down to the river. I'll show you how to clean salmon."

"White Wolf, Ah know how to clean fish. I've just never cleaned one this big before. Ah have fished before with Zeff's fishing pole."

It turned out White Wolf was correct. Connal Lee relished the salmon steak Short Rainbow served him that night. He asked for another fillet.

After a good night's rest, they went to work in earnest. The boys fished. The girls cleaned the salmon and carved them into thin slices. They draped them over miniature willow branch wigwams to smoke over the fires. They carefully placed the rest of the fragile flesh out to dry in the sun. They wanted to have enough preserved salmon to last them well into winter.

After supper, White Wolf invited his family to go for a swim in the side eddies of the raging waters. Even though the snowmelt water warmed up to sixty degrees, they felt a cold shock when they first jumped in from the mild eighty-degree air. They soon adjusted to the cold water and frolicked, playing with each other and washing each other clean. All four Shoshone pulled their braids loose and washed their hair. Refreshed, they raced back to their tipi.

That evening, young Arimo arrived with Kimana and Koko. They traveled in the company of several other families from another Shoshone clan, friends for many years who enjoyed traveling together. Over supper, Kimana announced they had invited Koko to join their tipi. The three newlyweds beamed. Connal Lee gave them each a hug as he expressed his congratulations and happiness for them. The joyful sound of children playing intruded on the peace and quiet of the dense forest camps beside the raging river.

Connal Lee woke up earlier than his spouses, who lay sprawled on top of their sleeping furs, legs intertwined, blissfully asleep. Connal Lee smelled the pine trees surrounding their tipi. He relished the trees' clean perfume. When he sat up, he admired everyone's long black hair fanned out around their heads. He hardly ever saw them without neat braids or fancy hairdos. He gazed at them fondly, thinking their loose, messed-up hair gave them a soft, gentle look entirely at odds with their fierce warrior status.

He pulled on moccasins and tucked his loincloth into his knife belt. He dressed in a sleeveless vest and picked up his leather hat. He decided he wanted to try harpoon fishing. He picked up a hatchet and walked through the woodlands along the river until he found an eight-foot-tall sapling of a skinny lodgepole pine tree.

By the time Short Rainbow and Bright Star roused themselves to prepare breakfast, Connal Lee already sat beside the fire, whittling a sharp point on the narrow end of the rod. It gave him a sense of satisfaction making it by himself without help from his spouses.

After breakfast, while his family neatly braided each other's long, black hair, he removed his vest and moccasins and headed to the river. He spent the morning gleefully spearing huge salmon and hefting them up onto the shoreline. The fish flopped around, trying to return to the water so they could breathe. Connal Lee took a break from fishing and cleaned them beside the river. He threw their innards into the river and watched as the swimming school of salmon attacked the offal and ate it all in a feeding frenzy, gone in an instant.

He picked up two of his catch by their gills and lugged them over to the tipi. He made four more trips to deliver his entire catch. That afternoon he helped Short Rainbow and Bright Star slice them thin and start the pink flesh to drying, smoking, and roasting.

After another supper of salmon, Short Rainbow complained she wanted fresh meat tomorrow. "I'm getting tired of eating salmon three times a day, as much as I like it."

Connal Lee offered to ride out hunting. He found hefting heavy fish up onto the river bank hard work. Muscles in his arms and back ached from the unaccustomed labor. Besides, he liked to ride out and hunt as he had on the trail. He woke up and saddled his brown mare and big packhorse. He grabbed his shotgun and ammunition and rode further north into the increasingly rugged foothills along the river.

Away from the river, his ride took him back into untamed desert. Small, low sagebrush and browning summer grasses covered the rocky ground. He spotted a large herd of hundreds of antelope feeding off the tall grass. They all had light brown backs with white bellies and rumps. The males sported tall black horns. From a distance, their large dark upright ears also looked like horns. He loaded lead slugs and rode slowly closer. Suddenly he saw a stir around the middle of the herd. The antelope all looked up from eating, alert but not alarmed. Out of nowhere, he heard children's laughter. Then he saw several preteen children of Arimo's friends playing with the antelopes, chasing them, trying to leap up on their backs and ride them. He decided he better not shoot into the pack for fear of hitting a child by mistake.

An easy hour's ride later, he spotted another small cluster of antelope on the side of a grassy hill. With two shots, he bagged fresh meat for Short Rainbow. The rest of the antelope scattered, turning their white rumps towards the noise. Connal Lee made short work of field dressing them and tying them onto his packhorse. *This is just like old times, back in the saddle, hunting for food by myself.*

Connal Lee dropped off the carcasses beside a large cottonwood tree near the cookfire, then tied up his horses. He wrapped leather ropes around the antelope's rear hoofs and hoisted them up to hang head down. He helped Short Rainbow and Bright Star skin and butcher them. Short Rainbow put aside steaks and chunks of meat to stew. She planned on drying the rest of it for their winter stores of jerky. When they finished, Connal Lee heaved the bare skeletons on his packhorse and disposed of them away from camp. After he returned and unsaddled his horses, he walked down to the river and washed up in the cold running water.

A couple of days later, they caught a white sturgeon nearly six feet long. It required both Screaming Eagle and White Wolf to carry it out of the water. Short Rainbow loved having some of her personal favorite fish to smoke. They all worked diligently at fishing, hunting, and preserving meats for the winter.

A week later, White Wolf announced they had enough salmon stored up. He suggested they depart at dawn to join Chief SoYo'Cant in the Teton Mountains.

The convoy traveled southeast nearly to Fort Lemhi, then veered east along a winding canyon through the mountains. Dry desert landscape baking in the summer sun stretched out around them on all sides. They followed a few small creeks and unnamed rivers until they reached the Snake River at Henry's Fork a few days later. They stopped for a day in the cool green of the trees, rushes, and grasses overlooking where the stream merged into the broad Snake River.

White Wolf told Connal Lee over supper about a white man named Andrew Henry and sixty other men of the Missouri Fur Company. They had built a fort here in 1810, the first white man fort west of the continental divide. They had abandoned it the following year. He went on and explained how the broad plain surrounding the juncture of the rivers hosted the Shoshone Tribe's traditional locale for their annual Sun Dance. Not many places in the Tribe's territory could accommodate six-thousand people with all their horses and dogs at the same time.

"The entire tribe comes together to celebrate the longest day of the year. Every clan joins in with feasting. We build a huge open-air lodge around a special center pole with a Sun Dance doll or a buffalo head fastened on top. Once the drums begin, they play day and night continually for four days. Everyone dances themselves to exhaustion. Oh, the opening ceremonies are beautiful. Everyone dresses up in their finest and fanciest clothing and jewelry. Our Clan's famous shamans, Firewalker and Burning Fire, purify the lodge and the dancers and sanctify the dance to the gods. The young men dance to impress the young girls. A lot of marriages and babies begin every year during the festival. The young dancers prepare themselves by fasting and practicing the dance steps in advance. Each dancer paints their body with white clay from their loincloth up. They all wear whistles made of eagles' hollow upper wing bones on a string around their necks. They dance barefoot in honor of the sacred, dedicated ground of the lodge."

Screaming Eagle shuffled over closer to listen, dancing to a drum heard only in his memory. With a smile, he sat down beside Connal Lee. "I wish we had been here this year. I wanted to dance again. I danced last year until I collapsed in a blissful joyful trance. I felt much stronger spiritually afterward."

White Wolf patted him on his bare shoulder. "Maybe next year we can make it. Anyway, Connal Lee, we place any who are seriously ill inside the holy lodge so they can be healed during the sacred ceremonies. The singers gather around a large drum in the southwest corner of the lodge. Everyone helps sing while waving fronds of sagebrush up and down in rhythm with the drums and the rattles made from buffalo testicles. The young men jog up and down in place, blasting their whistles. Some dance during the night, while others sleep and return. Everyone but the dedicated, fasting dancers eat and rest in between dancing. Chief SoYo'Cant watches over everyone throughout the entire dance ceremony.

"Outside the lodge, our people spend their time gossiping, flirting, racing, and gambling. Lots and lots of gambling. Lots of wrestling and mock fighting. We have great fun, Connal Lee. The children play war games and practice their skills with weapons. At night the old men tell of their glory days, counting coups against the tribe's enemies. Girls go out and pick berries during the day. Boys go out to find firewood. Every night we enjoy a feast where people move from fire to fire, sharing their bounty. Everyone has a great time. Then it's all over after four days of non-stop dancing. It's a magical time, Connal Lee. I hope you get to see it next year."

Three long dusty, hot days later, they departed the desert lowlands and began the climb up into the Grand Teton mountains. They traveled more slowly as the terrain grew steeper. Their path wound through steep valleys. Rugged mountains rose higher around them. The days grew cooler the higher they climbed.

Chapter 2: Summer Camp

Connal Lee and his family arrived at the chief's summer camp along the shores of a big lake in what white trappers called Jackson Valley. The trappers named the valley after David Jackson, the first mountain man who spent a winter on the lake trapping beavers. Great craggy stone mountains rose as a backdrop to the lake, their tops still white with snow. The vast lake had clear unmuddied water with a rocky bottom visible through the water. Boulders and rocks of all sizes lined its shores. Great cottonwood trees, tall pine trees, and clusters of quaking aspens surrounded the lake and covered the foothills rising above the valley floor. The growth created a haven for a vast variety of wildlife. Even though they had trapped the beavers nearly to extinction, the valley still teemed with abundant wildlife.

Connal Lee and his spouses enjoyed a joyous reunion with Chief SoYo'Cant. After unpacking their horses and travoises, they pitched Short Rainbow's tipi. That evening they spoke late into the night, telling Chief SoYo'Cant and Teniwaaten all about their adventures in the Utah War. The chief thanked them for representing the Shoshone Nation to their allies.

The young family fell into a bucolic routine of hunting, picking berries, cooking, preserving the meats and berries, then relaxing. Many evenings over the next few days, Chief SoYo'Cant invited them to join him around a roaring fire while people took turns telling stories. Connal Lee heard about famous chiefs of times gone by, of great battles, of different clans' favorite hunting grounds, and of visits to exotic faraway places.

One day, White Wolf suggested they build a raft and pole themselves across the lake. Working as a team, they felled trees and lashed the logs together. They cut down tall narrow lodgepole pine trees and made poles to push the clumsy raft. Shortly after dawn, Connal Lee and Screaming Eagle manned the poles and pushed them away from the shoreline. Connal Lee pushed down and back on his long staff to propel them forward. The bottom of the lake fell away at that point, and his pole didn't touch the lake bottom. His momentum tumbled him forward. He lost his balance and fell into the icy water. He didn't know how to swim. He had never before been in water over his head. He panicked and lost his grip on the pole. He felt himself sinking and began splashing his arms, struggling to climb out of the water. He couldn't catch a breath to scream. He became frightened he would drown. Screaming Eagle struck Connal Lee's shoulder with his long pole. Connal Lee instinctively grabbed hold. His spouses worked in concert and pulled him out of the water. He lay sprawled on the gently rocking raft, coughing out water and struggling to catch his breath. He felt like he would never stop shivering. His head rested on Bright Star's lap as she patted his cheeks to comfort him. They had nothing to use to cover him. White Wolf managed to snatch his leather cowboy hat before it floated out of reach.

With only one pole left on the raft, it took them until nearly dark to return to the shore beside their camp. Exhausted, wet, and chilled through, they rushed shivering into their tipi. They stripped off their sodden clothes and rubbed each other down with soft chamois skins used as towels. Everyone hastily pulled on dry clothes. Short Rainbow scurried out and stirred the coals of the fire, building up a roaring blaze to warm them. While they sat around the fire, Connal Lee watched Screaming Eagle carefully dry and polish his silver armbands. Connal Lee coughed and coughed. He complained his throat hurt. He shook his head and gazed around at his family. "Y'all can go rafting again, but Ah'm never going to go floating over water ever again in my whole entire life. It's just too dangerous. Ah nearly drowned out there!"

The lush forest surrounding the camp offered White Wolf a variety of herbs for his medicine pouches. When he identified medicinal plants, he took Short Rainbow and Connal Lee with him to harvest them. They collected wild rye, cattails, wintergreen, strawberries, water lilies, white willow, lupines, wild roses, and the fleshy roots of irises. White Wolf celebrated finding abundant witch hazel bushes. As he processed the various herbal harvests, he taught Short Rainbow and Connal Lee about what ailments they treated and how to prepare and use them. "Witch hazel is effective in reducing swelling and soothing sore muscles. It's very helpful in treating scrapes and open sores. It cleans them, so they heal properly. Massaged on the back, it can ease back pain. Always keep an eye out for witch hazel."

Connal Lee happily learned about all the local remedies available just for the picking. Screaming Eagle hunted and fished. White Wolf harvested and prepared medicines. Bright Star found contentment remaining quietly at the tipi. As a very traditional young woman, the domestic arts of tanning, sewing, cooking meals, and preserving foods brought her pleasure. She didn't feel the least bit adventurous or interested in hunting and warfare like Short Rainbow and the men in the family. For Bright Star, just marrying into her warrior family provided her enough adventure to satisfy her for the rest of her life. While male and female roles were somewhat fluid in the Plains Indian tribes, most men preferred to be warriors and hunters, while the majority of the women chose to tend the hearth fires, prepare food, and rear the young.

One day a Shoshone warrior rode in, shouting a warning that they had spotted a Crow war party heading their way. His shouts disturbed the peace of the camp. Everyone erupted into action with cries of alarm. The women and girls screamed as they anxiously sought their children and grandchildren. The women and children retreated to the rushes and willows along the shores of the lake, cowering in fear, trying to hide the young. The warriors saddled up their horses and armed themselves. Within moments they assembled in a milling herd around the chief's tent and council lodge. Screaming Eagle spotted Chief SoYo'Cant's elderly friend, the tribe's War Chief, and headed in his direction, anxious to join the fight. White Wolf, Short Rainbow, and Connal Lee followed hard on his heels. Bright Star strung her bow and bravely remained behind, determined to defend their home if necessary from marauders.

The War Chief stood up in his saddle and raised a war spear over his head. Everyone saw all the scalps decorating the spear, proclaiming him an accomplished fighter. When the warriors quieted down to receive their orders, Connal Lee heard the War Chief command Screaming Eagle to stay behind with his band to protect their chief and guard all the women and children. "I will lead my band to go confront the Crow warriors immediately."

Screaming Eagle felt a terrible disappointment with his blood raging as adrenaline surged through his body. He wanted to be in the middle of the fight, not defending the women and children back in the safety of their camp.

The War Chief's band thundered away. Chief SoYo'Cant rode up and stopped beside Screaming Eagle. He clasped Screaming Eagle's bare muscled arm and pulled him in closer so they could talk over the noise of the excited men. "I know you want to be in the fight, apprentice War Chief, but someone has to stay and protect the camp. When you become our War Chief, you can lead your warriors into glorious battle at your own decision and command. For now, set your guards so we don't suffer any surprises."

Though disappointed, Screaming Eagle turned his attention to giving his men their orders. White Wolf, Connal Lee, and Short Rainbow rode up close behind to assist him. The camp slowly quieted down. The women and children standing in the cold lake water began taking a chill. They gradually came out of the water in small family groups but didn't stray far from their hiding places. The older women comforted the crying children and babies. A strained quiet settled over the disturbed camp. Screaming Eagle led his family around the camp perimeter, making sure everyone had taken what precautions they could.

A young warrior rode in about four hours later, waving his tomahawk over his head. "Our great War Chief sent me ahead to let you know the alarm was all a mistake. There is no Crow war party headed our way. Our brave warriors should arrive back within the hour." He rode up to the Chief's council lodge and made his report. "One of our scouts saw a herd of elk off in the distance. He thought they were horses carrying a war party. Rather than waiting until he knew what he saw, he rushed off and raised the alarm in error."

When her warrior spouses returned to Short Rainbow's tipi, Bright Star ran out and tearfully hugged each one. "I was so frightened for you out there facing our enemies. I'm so glad none of you were hurt."

That night Connal Lee and his family joyfully celebrated their relief at not having to fight and place any of their family in jeopardy.

Connal Lee heaved a sigh of relief he hadn't needed to shoot at men that day. When their passionate lovemaking ended, they all cuddled up in the sleeping robes for warmth.

The nights dipped down nearly to freezing temperatures by late August due to their high elevation. When the sun shone during the day, the air felt comfortable. White Wolf knew the Chief would want to leave his camp in the Tetons before it became too cold for little children to sleep in the open. He discussed with Short Rainbow how they needed to prepare more travoises and packsaddles to transport their new food supplies back to winter camp south of Fort Hall. They calculated they would need six new big travoises for the heavy food in addition to the seven travoises they had brought with them. And they would need at least a dozen more packsaddles to carry their tanned hides. Connal Lee offered to chop down trees. Short Rainbow shook her head. "Thank you, but we can use my tipi's poles rather than carry them on the travois like we normally do."

White Wolf nodded his head approvingly. "Good thinking Short Rainbow. That will save us a lot of time and trouble. Well, let's dig out some big buffalo hides for the travois and get to work making packsaddles. I suspect the chief will order us back on the trail before we know it."

They worked together and made two dozen crosstrees with split branch bases for the new packsaddles. Short Rainbow soaked raw-hide strips in water, then tied the pieces together. As the rawhide dried, it shrank, firmly securing the parts into one strong saddle.

That evening, White Wolf thought out loud. "With this many travoises and packhorses, we'll need a lot more lead ropes. We better get busy braiding some up tomorrow. It's going to take time to make enough."

After breakfast, Short Rainbow fetched an untanned buckskin and began cutting narrow rawhide bands. As fast as she cut them, White Wolf and Bright Star braided them together. Connal Lee watched for a while. Without a word, he took the next batch of strips and began braiding. His ropes weren't as tight and neat as White Wolf's, but they would serve just as well. While they made lead ropes, Screaming Eagle hunted and fished for their meals. He didn't share their talents for crafts like weaving ropes or making packsaddles.

On the morning of their departure, it took two hours of hard work to load their travoises and packhorses. White Wolf scowled. "We prepared too much food this summer. How will we manage this every morning and evening for the next several weeks?"

Short Rainbow patted White Wolf on the back. "We can never have enough food preserved for winter. Remember last spring? We ran out of almost everything."

"Of course. You are right. But still, this is hard work!"

Short Rainbow's pregnancy had begun showing more and more during the summer mountain interlude. After they finished loading the last of their tanned hides, she placed her hands on her lower back and stretched backward. "I can't wait to sit down in the saddle and rest my poor aching back. Carrying this big boy child in front of me all the time puts a strain on my lower back."

White Wolf walked over to her. "Put your hands on your knees, Short Rainbow."

After she leaned over, White Wolf began massaging her back with his thumbs. He ran his thumbs up and down her spine, then concentrated just above the swell of her athletic buttocks. "Ooh. Aah. That helps, White Wolf. Thank you, husband."

By the time they organized the packsaddles and travoises, they ended up trailing most of the others of the clan. Connal Lee mounted up, leaned over, and rubbed his lower back. "Ah'm not pregnant, but my back's aching, too, from all the lifting. What a lot of work."

Screaming Eagle chuckled. "Well, you better get used to it. We have to load and unload the packhorses every morning and evening until we reach the Tobitapa River. At least we don't have to unload the travoises, too, only lift them down off the horses while still loaded with our gear. With all five of us working as a team, the weight of the loaded travoises will not be too big a strain for us to handle."

Before they reached Fort Hall around the middle of September, Connal Lee regretfully changed his open vest for a long sleeve tunic and vest. They all strapped on their leggings. Within a week, the temperature never rose above sixty during the day. It dropped nearly to freezing before dawn. They all snuggled up together in their sleeping furs.

Short Rainbow's swollen belly occasionally hindered their lovemaking, but they improvised and made do without complaint. Most Shoshone women withdrew from their men when they discovered they were pregnant. They typically refrained from further sexual intercourse while swollen with child. But Short Rainbow didn't care how other wives handled their pregnancies. She only wanted to be with her men as much as possible and help keep them contented. Bright Star happily assumed a more active role in satisfying her lusty husbands' needs. One evening after making love, Short Rainbow complained she was past the time to give birth to their boy child. "He's getting too big for me to carry. Come, feel him kicking."

Connal Lee reached over, thrilled to feel the life in her belly. "White Wolf! Screaming Eagle! Ah never knew one could feel a baby while still in its mother. Isn't it amazing? It's a miracle of life!"

Screaming Eagle and White Wolf joined their hands with Connal Lee's. They all beamed at each other, delighted with the new life joining them. White Wolf solemnly pronounced, "You will give birth very soon now, Short Rainbow. Do you have everything ready?"

Five long weeks after they departed Jackson Lake, they reached the Blackfoot River. Connal Lee's family said their goodbyes to Chief SoYo'Cant. Connal Lee thanked him for taking his family with the rest of his clan to the Teton Peaks. "We will stay here and visit with my white families for a while, then stop at Fort Hall and do some trading. We will join you at your winter quarters in a week or two. Farewell, Father SoYo'Cant."

When they pulled up at the Baines little plantation and cattle ranch, Short Rainbow had trouble dismounting her great horse. Screaming Eagle rushed to help her. Later, when they raised the tipi, Short Rainbow had difficulty working with the heavy poles and hides. She could hardly bend over, much less lift. She ended up directing Bright Star and her husbands while she watched from the sidelines, holding her swollen belly protectively in her hands.

That evening Short Rainbow began going into labor. When her water broke some hours later, Connal Lee's rushed to fetch Mother Baines to help her. Bright Star gently undressed Short Rainbow and bathed her face with fresh, cold river water.

With Lorna's experienced and loving assistance, Short Rainbow gave birth that night, the first day of October of 1858, to a chubby, pale-skinned boy with a fringe of black hair. White Wolf helped. Bright Star danced attendance during the entire ordeal. Bright Star affectionally cuddled Short Rainbow's head on her lap. When Lorna placed the baby on Short Rainbow's breasts and cut the umbilical cord, Short Rainbow gazed around at her men, kneeling or sitting cross-legged around her in the warm tipi. "You see? I had a true vision. Connal Lee sired this child when we made love on the road back from Great Salt Lake City. Isn't he wonderful?"

Connal Lee's joy left him speechless.

Made in the USA
Middletown, DE
23 April 2023